MASON

LEILA JAMES

Copyright © 2023 by LEILA JAMES

All rights reserved.

No part of this book may be reproduced in any form or by any electronic or mechanical means, including information storage and retrieval systems, without written permission from the author, except for the use of brief quotations in a book review.

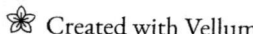 Created with Vellum

CREDITS

Editing: Krista Dapkey
www.kdproofreading.com

Photography: Michelle Lancaster
@lanefotograf

Cover Design: Lori Jackson
www.lorijacksondesign.com

Interior Formatting: Shauna Mairéad
@shaunamairead_author

Model: Thomas James
@revolutionary_badboy23

PLAYLIST

"Fire Up the Night" New Medicine
"RUNRUNRUN" Dutch Melrose
"In the Air Tonight" Natalie Taylor
"Talk Dirty" Daniel D'Angelo
"Bastards" Kesha
"Wicked" Miki Ratsula
"Kryptonite" Jeris Johnson
"Someone Else" Loveless & Kellin Quinn
"Toxic" 2WEI
"Fuck You" Silent Child
"Where Are You?" (slowed) Elvis Drew & Avivian
"My Bad" Shaker & Cobra
"Breakfast" Dove Cameron
"Middle of the Night" Dom Lives

PLAYLIST

"Medicine" Syd
"Get Out Alive" Andrea Russett
"Meet You in Hell" Jade LeMac
"Pieces" Muscadine Bloodline & Lainey Wilson

A NOTE FROM THE AUTHOR

Mason is the first book in the Bastards of Bainbridge Hall trilogy, centering around three men and one woman. It's MFMM for now.

WARNING: This trilogy contains dark elements, graphic content, and situations that some readers may be particularly sensitive to. If you have triggers or are remotely unsure, please check out the Content Warnings on my website, available through the link below.

https://www.leilajames.biz/content-warning

ONE

LENNON

THE VICE-LIKE HOLD Tristan Valentine has on the back of my neck leaves no room for argument. His fingers dig into my skin, but there's no escape in sight from the hell he's about to force me into. My eyes flick up toward the enormous two-story Georgian-style home before us. I'll give him this much—it's stunningly beautiful. From what I've been told, it was built during the years my stepfather attended Kingston University, but somehow, they've given it a certain Southern charm that makes it seem like it's been standing here for ages, though it's no more than thirty years old, tops. All the frats on campus are housed in buildings that are almost a century old.

The alumni of Bainbridge Hall are a tight-knit

bunch of bastards—and so are the current members of the brotherhood, which include my stepbrother, Duke.

And Duke? He hates me. There's no way in fuck I'm living here. I don't even want to be at KU in the first place. I want a college education, but this is the last place I'd pick because he's here. I can make something of myself on my own. That's what I've been working so damn hard for, and I'm determined to see myself succeed whether out of sheer desperation or my keen instinct for survival. But then, as is inevitable when I ponder my future, doubt creeps in, delving deep into my fear that I'm more like my mother than I let myself believe. I hate to admit it to myself, but I'm concerned—no, *terrified*—that I'll fail and end up marrying some prune-cocked old man like my mother, Nikki Bell, did.

I shudder at the thought, but then adrenaline surges through me as Tristan shuffles me roughly toward the back end of his Escalade and manages to keep a tight hold on me as he wrangles my suitcase from the back.

As if I'm going to take off like a shot and run down the expansive driveway and somehow get away? Where the hell would I go? My stepfather is one of the most powerful men in this town, and I've come to learn over the last few years, he's not someone I want to anger. I'm stuck. There's no way out from under his thumb because his reach is far and wide. This could be a way to distance myself, but will living here be worse? Maybe if I bide my time, I can find a way out.

My stepfather steers me toward the flight of stairs and ushers me up them. My legs are long, but his are longer, and it feels like he's dragging me by my neck. "That hurts," I hiss through gritted teeth.

He chuckles low, in a way that makes another shudder of distaste run down my spine. It gets worse the longer his hand is clamped down on me. Something prickles along my nerves in a way that is wholly uncomfortable. My mother's husband is one of those men who manages to intimidate without saying a damn word.

But then we reach the front door, and he pulls me to a stop, turning me to look at him, his blue eyes assessing. "Keep your mouth shut until you're asked to speak. Got it, Lennon?"

I suck in a breath and practically choke. The late August humidity is cruel, the heat oppressive. The sun beats down on us as we stand there, and sweat trickles down my back, sticking my tank top to my skin. It won't help to argue. This man sees the worst in me, and honestly, I don't give a fuck. He might make my mother happy, but he's hardly given me the time of day—not that I want or need his attention—so I don't know what's crawled up his ass now. Doesn't really matter. I give him a curt nod, tucking away my true feelings on the matter. "Yes, *Tristan.*" He hates that I won't call him Dad. But ... why *would* I? Shaking my head, my jaw locks, waiting for his next move because no way am I going to be the one to let a bunch of college frat boys know I'm about to blow up their lives by moving in.

Without knocking, he reaches forward and twists the doorknob, opening the door. I have an odd feeling that if the place were locked, he'd probably have a key, anyway. I can't imagine the founding brothers don't have access to the house. Ha. House. Mansion? Shit, maybe it's technically an estate. This place is freaking huge, judging from the outside. I can't guess the exact dimensions, it's so unlike anything I'm used to. It's even bigger than Tristan's home with my mother.

He finally releases me from his grasp, placing a hand on my upper back instead, and guides me into the entryway, which boasts amazing twelve-plus foot ceilings with a sparkling chandelier that is meant to draw the eye upward.

It's breathtaking.

And I'm so far out of my element, it's not funny.

Tristan takes a moment to punch a code into a fancy security panel beside the door. Maybe in a home like this it makes sense to have an alarm set all the time. With a shrug of my shoulders, I go back to looking around while my stepfather sets my luggage beside the door.

I hate that my eyes are wide and wondering when I spot Duke coming toward us down the marble-floored hallway. I don't know where he came from, as I was too busy gawking. Him catching me with my mouth hanging open is just what I need. He and I—we're like oil and water, not that we've spent all that much time together but when we do, he's always coming after me. Inwardly, I cringe. We've spent just enough awkward family holidays together to know he thinks my mother is a money-grubbing whore. His words.

"Stella Bella," he mocks, running a hand through his blond hair, "what the fuck are you doing here?" My stepbrother's fierce blue eyes train on me for a heavy, curiosity-laden moment before they flick to his father. "What's she doing here?"

Oh, fuck. I study Tristan out of the corner of my eye, but he shows no sign of discomfort at all. Not even a hint of remorse that he's putting me through this—because now I get it. He didn't ask Duke if I could stay here. He's going to demand it of him.

And I'll be the one to deal with the blowback.

It's because of this I let my mouth run away from me. I can't even help myself when I get pissed off. I cock one saucy hip to the side, giving him a sweet smile that belies the words I'm about to spew. "I have a name, asshole, and it's not fucking Stella." His lip curls, but before he can fire back, I toss him an amused smirk. "And wait, didn't Daddy tell you? We're gonna be roomies. So much fun, right?"

I only get to enjoy the way Duke's face is reddening with anger—or maybe embarrassment—for a split second because Tristan grabs my upper arm, practically encircling it with his meaty hand and yanking me face-to-face. His fingers bite into my flesh, his hot breath fanning over me as he grits out, "You disrespectful little cunt. I told you to keep your mouth shut. You will *not* disrespect me or the head of this house. If you want to get the college education you so desperately seek—" He stops to smirk at the way my brows jump high on my forehead. "Oh yes, I'm well aware of your desire to claw your way out of the circumstances you were born into. And for that reason, you'll do exactly what my son tells you to do while you're living here. He says jump, you nod your pretty little head and reply 'How high?'" He squeezes my arm viciously. "Got it?"

Finding it hard to hide the wince tugging at my lips, I wrench my arm free and glare at him as I rub the injury with my hand.

He runs one hand over his bearded cheek as he shrewdly studies me. "Lennon, let's not play any more of your little games. How many times do I have to tell you

—when I ask you a question, I expect the courtesy of an answer."

I exhale slowly, my eyes taking in both of them as they watch me—one irritated and the other adept at hiding all emotion. I can't read him. Bastard. "Yes. I understand." I wait a beat before narrowing my eyes on Tristan and adding a flippant, *"Sir."*

I'm not surprised in the slightest when he doesn't react to my attitude, but instead focuses on his son. "Duke. I'll speak to you in the office."

Letting out an exasperated groan, he heads in that direction. Before Tristan follows, he points a finger at one of two enormous stairways curving upward along both sides of the entry. "Sit. Right there on the steps, and don't you dare move an inch."

I wait until they're both ensconced in the aforementioned room before I trudge over to have a seat. The marble step is cold even through my jean shorts, but it's a relief after the sweltering heat outside. Propping my elbows on my thighs and my chin in my hands, I release an uncertain breath. This isn't what I was expecting. Really, though, I never thought Tristan would stare at me like I had two heads when I said I'd saved enough money working at Stella's Diner to attend the local community college.

I'm fucking proud of what I was able to plan and

save for on my own. But apparently, it's not good enough for the Valentine name, and as his stepdaughter, he's made damn sure I understand that it's not permitted for me to be an embarrassment to him.

But here's the thing—I'm not a Valentine, not by a long shot. I'm a Bell, and I'm definitely not good at taking handouts. It irritates the shit out of me that the idea of getting an education at KU is the tiniest bit enticing. I never would have asked, but hell, if he's going to force me into this ... maybe I should shut up and go with it. I let out a sigh because I'm still uncertain if my mother married for love or money. We aren't super close. I can't believe that her choices have landed me here.

And fuck this, they're talking about me in there. Hearing the volume of the voices in the other room slowly beginning to rise, I kick off my flip-flops and shoot from the step. On quiet bare feet, I creep toward the room they disappeared into. Cautiously, I lean in, barely able to make out their distinct voices through the door.

"You'll take responsibility for her. Watch her. I'm not asking. This is the way it's going to be if you want to maintain your position in this house," growls Tristan.

"She's not staying here." Duke's voice is a low rumble. "No fucking way. I have my hands full with the incoming freshmen this year. They're due any fucking minute."

"You will. And you'll see to it that she goes to classes and does well. Keep her in line. She's been sneaking out of the house, and I don't know where she's been or what she's been up to. But I think dangling the carrot of a solid education in front of her, well, it'll be what we need to keep her here."

"Awesome. So, you're saddling me with her for the entire year? Fuck this!"

Tristan's voice is calmer. Deadly calm. "Like I said, you'll do as I say. It's necessary."

My brows pinch, confusion weighing heavy on my mind. Then there's the sound of what I think is a hand slamming down on something, but I have no way of knowing who did it or what they hit. A desk, maybe? My heart thunders in my chest. I don't understand …

Several seconds go by with no noise at all, and I'm torn between returning to the step and staying where I am. Before I can decide, Duke mumbles, "This is going to be a goddamn disaster."

Whatever Tristan's talking about, he doesn't say it loudly enough for me to hear. I strain closer, gripping either side of the doorframe and placing my ear directly on the door. "Go ahead, require anything of her that you'd put the grunts through."

My eyes go wide, and my heart rate ratchets higher. *Shit. Grunts?* What on earth?

"What are you doing?"

The smooth voice behind me makes me simultaneously yelp and jump in place, almost forcing me out of my skin. I whirl around, breath heaving from me as my gaze connects with a pair of chocolate-brown eyes. I sigh in relief, but there's an odd light to them that sets me off-kilter. It's distinctly possible I'd be better off in the office with the other two.

I go to back up but find I'm trapped between this guy and the solid hardwood door behind me. I lose all track of the conversation I'd been listening to. He leans in, the longish hair on the top of his head sweeping over his dark brow while his forearm plants above my head. I blink hard, unsure what to do. I don't know who he is but can only assume he lives here. He's got about half a foot of height on my five-foot-seven, and as I peer up at him, his tongue peeks out to slide slowly along his perfectly full lower lip as he assesses me.

It's mesmerizing. I stutter out a breath, finally dragging my eyes up to meet his, and as I do, he shifts, bending at the hip to bring our noses—he wears a small silver hoop there that I find totally sexy—within an inch of each other. His breath feathers over my lips, smelling of mint and something I can't quite place.

"I asked you a question," he says softly. His tone shouldn't scare me, but it kinda does. My stomach drops as his free hand lands on my black tank, just below the valley between my breasts. Steadily, it moves upward.

I should scream. I should tell him to stop. But all words are caught in my throat, and I'm powerless to set them free. Entranced, I stare into his eyes as his hand moves slowly, my chest rising and falling with shallow breaths. "I—"

When I don't finish, his jaw twitches, his lip curling ever so slightly. "Were you sent here to punish me?" His fingers crest the top of my tank top, then skim over my collarbone before he grasps the front of my neck. "Answer me," he rasps as his grip tightens. "Fucking answer me."

TWO

LENNON

This guy is *not* playing around. We're so close, he focuses first on one of my eyes, then the other as I struggle to pull air into my lungs. My heart picks up speed, pounding so hard, I wonder if he can hear it. I don't know what he sees when his gaze roves over me with those sinfully decadent brown eyes, but whatever it is isn't good. His strong fingers clench reflexively for another moment before he reluctantly releases me and backs away, leaving me to find support for my trembling body against the door.

Now that I can finally breathe since the asshole no longer has my oxygen cut off, I gulp in a breath and am ready to fire back at him when all at once the door behind me is forcefully yanked open, and I'm freefalling into nothing. An undignified noise escapes me as I land in strong arms and am scooped up before I can hit the unforgiving hardwood floor. Blinking up at my savior, I realize with dismay that it's Duke. *Fuck.* I groan internally, but quickly admit to myself that his dad coming to my rescue wouldn't have been one iota better.

"She was listening at the door," the jackass offers with an uncaring smirk and a shrug. "I told her it was a bad idea, but she didn't seem to want to listen." His body language is very much *I don't give a fuck,* even with my stepfather glowering.

"Deal with her," Tristan grunts, shaking his head as he steps around us and walks out the door.

Rude asshole. And he's leaving me here with these two. I hardly know Duke and already have a ton of misgivings about his friend.

Duke dumps me unceremoniously from his hold, his lips pursing in displeasure as his brows pitch sharply at his father's command. With every step that carries his father away from us, his jaw hardens. From the foyer, the sound of the door slamming shut makes me jump.

What the fuck kind of craziness have I been dropped into? This dynamic between them that I've just witnessed is far different from anything I've seen from them on the few occasions our blended family has been together. Whenever Duke came home from KU for holidays or breaks, each interaction between father and son had seemed oddly ... polite. So this? It's caught me off guard, almost as if they'd been putting on a show for my mother and me.

Several seconds later, Duke's gaze flicks to the dark-haired guy—haven't forgotten for a second what he'd uttered right before I fell through the doorway—and gives him a cold glare. "Don't say it, Mason."

"What? That you're busy jerking your daddy's—"

"Better than what you deal with, I'd wager. But how about we set that aside for the moment, huh?" The tension spikes between them as Duke's blue eyes glitter with ice-cold hatred. Those same eyes then dart toward me, and I swear he's trying to signal Mason to shut up, no matter that they seem to not like each other very much.

I don't claim to understand the relationship between these two, but it doesn't matter. There's no way this is going to be my life for the next year. I don't need or want a babysitter. Tristan can pay for my college degree if he really wants to, as I'm sure it's the image he wants to present to the rest of the world, but I sure as fuck don't have to put up with Duke, this guy Mason, or anyone else who materializes inside this beautiful hellhole. I cock my head to the side and let my lips twist, drawing his attention to them. "Don't worry. No way in fuck I'm staying here with you clowns. I'll find a spot in a dorm." I can't resist reaching out to pat Duke's smooth cheek and watch with satisfaction as his eyes widen from the surprise of it, especially when I let my hand linger.

Duke huffs out a sharp laugh, but in the same breath grasps my wrist and wrenches it away from his face. "Honey, believe me when I say you don't want to know how much it costs to live on KU's campus. This?" He looks around as a wicked smile finds its way to his lips to match the one I'd shot at him. "It's free to you. But let's face it, we know how you and your mother are willing to whore it out for a little money, so if it'd make you feel more comfortable paying for your rent in the only way you know how—"

"You're full of shit and you know it." Color hits my cheeks and my face burns like someone smacked me.

"Oh, really? Then what's this on your neck?" He reaches out, sliding the pads of his fingers over the spot Mason had squeezed the hell out of.

I try to avoid flinching as my heart hammers an erratic beat in my chest. What Mason did couldn't have left a mark. Not only do I not bruise that easily, I can't imagine even if I did that it would appear on my skin so quickly.

He withdraws his hand with a cruel smirk. "Already hard at work, Stella?" His eyes flick to Mason's as he turns to fully face him, one brow lifted in question. "Bad night, brother?"

And when I shift to catch Mason's response, holy shit. What the hell? His expression has lost all hint of that smirking attitude and gone right back to the peculiar gloom he'd shown me at our first meeting. "Fuck off," he growls low enough to make my insides quake.

"What the hell is going on? I heard the door and—" The new guy who's entered the fray is tall, dark, and muscular, a god in human form, his body technically perfect. I don't have to see him without clothes to be aware of the well-honed form I'd find underneath. His hair is still damp from a recent shower, curling slightly, and I spend several seconds too many drinking him in. *Holy shit.* I blink, and his eyes are on me.

"The fuck?" he breathes out, jerking to a stop and I can tell from the confused nature of his expression that he's struggling to understand the situation before him. Mason continues to glare daggers at Duke, but Duke is now giving Mason a chilly blast of indifference.

And I'm caught right in the middle of their standoff. Self-conscious, I let my hand creep up to cover whatever Duke was seeing on my neck and send this big guy a look of desperation. *Save me.*

A ghost of a smile curves his full lips, then he lifts his arms, latching a hand on the opposite wrist and resting them on top of his head. My eyes are immediately drawn to the bold lion tattoo covering the back of his bicep. A Kingston lion? His eyes casually bounce back and forth between Duke and Mason, though I don't miss the way they skirt over me, like he's trying not to look too hard. "Who's the chick?"

When neither of his buddies bothers to answer him, I let out an exasperated sigh and offer him my hand. "Lennon."

The deep chuckle that erupts from his lips takes me by surprise, and while I'm still gathering my wits about me, he takes my hand in his much larger one, squeezing gently. His palm is a bit rough—not in a bad way—maybe like he does something with his hands, works outside, plays a sport, or lifts weights a lot. "Bear," he rumbles, eyeing me curiously.

Did he just say Bear? He does look kinda bear-like, big all over with scruff lining his jaw. The nickname fits, no matter how strange I find it.

"Well, *Lennon*"—his gaze drifts down over my body, then journeys up to meet my eyes with his warm hazel ones—"you're dead sexy, but we've got a couple cars pulling up, so you'd best be on your way." He nods as he plants his hands on hips encased in dark denim. Addressing Duke and Mason, he grunts out, "Fresh meat. Whatever your beef is with each other, drop it and get your fuckin' heads screwed on straight. Time to scare the piss out of some freshmen."

Almost as if it's taking everything in him to admit it, Duke tips his chin in my direction. With a beleaguered sigh, he groans, "She's not going anywhere, man. I'll fill you in later."

I look at him like he has three heads. I'd been sure when I gave him the out, when I said I could live elsewhere that he'd let me go. That he'd been blowing smoke by telling me it was too expensive elsewhere. I don't have a clue as to why he'd want me to stay, but I haven't forgotten for a damn second that he implied that my mother and I use our bodies as currency. Normally, I'd wait, see how things play out, strategize—but my brain short circuits, the urgency to be away from here overwhelming me. "You're fucking crazy if you think this is happening. I'm leaving." I dart from among the three of them and hurry toward the heavy wooden door of the office, yanking it open and hauling ass out of the room.

My eyes shoot only for a split second to my flip-flops at the base of the stairs and I decide on the fly to abandon them. Racing for the front door, my feet slap against the marble tiles. Like some sort of miracle, the door opens as I get to it. "Excuse me! Coming through!" The guys who were about to enter step to the side, laughing, like I'm a bit of comic relief planned for their enjoyment. Without stopping to count, I'd say there are no less than seven dudes watching me flee barefoot down the driveway.

I hear footsteps pounding behind me and a bunch of shouting, though my ears are buzzing so harshly from the rush of adrenaline spiking through my system that I can't tell what they're saying. But it's clear, they're not going to let me go.

My lungs scream as I keep running, but two powerful arms loop around my middle, shift me around, and then I'm flying through the air like I weigh no more than a sack of potatoes. There's no mistaking the fact that it's Bear; the magnitude of his strength shouldn't be so shocking, yet it is. I'm in awe as I land on his shoulder and let out a strangled noise full of agonized frustration.

"Come on now, little gazelle. You're going to have to learn to play nice with Duke."

"No, no I don't." I struggle, knowing I sound like a petulant child, but he holds me in place—one of those big, rough hands gripping my left thigh while the other is spread over my right ass cheek. Embarrassment washes over my skin, and I have the distinct feeling that I'm pink with it from head to toe.

The upside-down position I'm in puts my nose up close and personal with the broad expanse of his back, the clean scent of the soap from a recent shower invading my nose with every inhale.

Hoots and hollers greet my ears as Bear marches up the drive toward the house, and I'm fully aware that my backside is on full display for the entire Bainbridge brotherhood, new pledges and full-fledged brothers alike. I strain to look upward, pressing my hands on Bear's lower back, and wish I hadn't because as I angle my head, I can see plainly that their eyes are alight with the hilarity of the situation, like I'm their new favorite streaming comedy show on Netflix.

I take a deep breath and bellow, "Put me the fuck down!"

At the front entrance, Mason begins to disperse the crowd, who seem to think my outburst is funny, sending them inside with a I-mean-business glare and a point of his finger.

Setting me on my feet at the bottom of the steps, Bear shakes his head, exhaling harshly. "The fuck, woman."

But before I can say a word to defend myself, Duke steps in and grasps me by the back of my neck and yanks me close. So close that I put my hands up, pressing them against his chest to put distance between us—but it's mostly ineffective. With Bear and Mason now immediately behind him, he hisses in my face, "Stella, let's get a few things straight. Whether or not you live here isn't up for discussion. It's not something you get to *choose*. You're living in my world now, and it's my motherfucking *mission* to watch over you, little sister."

My eyes flick to Bear's, and I watch his mouth slowly drop open as the full truth of who I am hits him. Mason smirks, "Yeah, dude. She's his fucking sister. Stella. Lennon. Same girl."

Duke's face turns an impressive shade of red. "Stepsister," he grinds out, his perturbed gaze narrowing on Mason before returning his attention to me. "You'll do whatever we fucking say. Whatever we want you to do. No matter what. And if you don't, I will make you regret it every fucking second of your greedy, whorish existence." Duke pauses, his breath hot as it gusts past my cheek. I'm stunned by the wickedness of his words, all the sassy comebacks I would normally make caught up in my throat. He tightens his hold when I don't answer, and viciously forces my head back so he can look me directly in the eye. His cold blue eyes narrow on me until it feels like they're piercing my very soul, then his voice lowers, and I see the awful truth. He's going to make this hurt. "Are we in agreement, or do we have a huge fucking problem, Stella?"

My mind races as I come to grips with what he's saying. He's going to make me pay for being here, in one manner or another. Tristan had even demanded that Duke treat me like a grunt. I didn't understand what that meant at the time, but it's clicked in my head now. I'm about to have the shit hazed out of me in this house along with the rest of the incoming freshmen. A fresh wave of unease skitters down my spine and my stomach roils. I've never been afraid of Duke Valentine before—but I am now.

THREE

DUKE

I reach up, tugging at my hair as I watch Mason usher Lennon into the house, his charcoal-coated fingertips brush the back of her upper arm, leaving dark smudges on her skin. Unaware that he's marked her again, she walks with a haughty step, those wide, luscious hips of hers swinging, head held high.

Fuck. Her body was made for destruction ... as in, she's going to wreak havoc on this house. Destroy us. *Me.* I can see it coming a million miles away.

But my father's word is law, so there's not a goddamn thing I can do about it but suck it up and watch her like I've been tasked to do. But damn, I fuckin' hate that my old man comes around and makes me feel like a surly teenager all over again. As one of the founding brothers, there's no going over his head. Tristan Valentine, Derek Pierce, and Murdock Mikaelson rule a good portion of this town—the dirty side—and definitely those of us here at Bainbridge Hall.

"Holy shit. *That's* your fucking stepsister?" Bear's deep, growling voice shakes me free of the unending loop of *what the fuck* I'd been circling in my head.

I glance at him, working my jaw back and forth. The look on his face is priceless. I give a stiff nod, my lips pressed together as I try to formulate the right words to express the torment in my head. "He fucking *knows* how I feel about her and her mother," I grit out. Nikki had come sauntering into my father's life—some supposed rich bitch he met at a bar one night. At a full twenty years my father's junior, it's obvious why he'd missed the fact that her clothing must have been purchased from some upscale secondhand store—the old man was too busy thinking with his quickly shriveling dick to recognize that she was a siren in disguise. A beautiful young thing willing to suck it for him because she knew what it would get her.

"So you've said." Bear's shrewd eyes focus on me while waiting for me to continue instead of commenting. He has this habit of letting me talk shit out.

"It's the fuckin' truth. Nikki's nothing but a gold digger." I throw out my arms from my sides, agitated.

"She mesmerized him with her penis trap without telling him about the fact that she had a kid until it was too late for it to matter."

Bear's brows raise, and he lets out a low whistle. "And that kid is now all kinds of grown. Fuck, man. It's a good thing you were already here when they got married and she moved in. I'd have—" He stops himself, biting down on his lip and groaning as he slams one fist into his palm.

I get his drift. Yes. Lennon's fuck-hot. But she's also my goddamn stepsister. "Don't be fooled, man. She's using us to further herself. She's money hungry. In fact, her mouthing off and running like she did is all a ploy. She's clever and manipulative, just like her mother. Whip-smart, sassy-mouthed *bitch.*"

Bear clears his throat, eyeing me with his arms crossed over his broad chest. "Did your dad give you any specifics about why he punted her to your watch? Fill me in on what I've missed."

"As far as I know, it's about the Valentine image. He doesn't want his stepdaughter attending some community college like she'd planned. It'd look bad, and it'd be fairly difficult to conceal. So, he's bought her way into KU and has threatened me within an inch of my life if I don't keep an eye on her." I heave out a breath. "I need you with me, man. I'm fucking stuck with her, so we're gonna put her through the paces just like we would any other new pledge coming in. Grind subservience into her until it's fully ingrained. She's a nuisance that's been dropped at our doorstep, but we're going to have so much fun putting her in her place ..."

Bear barks out a laugh. "That's if she doesn't fuck you up with that bangin' body of hers." At the annoyed look I shoot him, he holds his hands up. "Just sayin'." He chuckles again before his firm hand clamps down on my shoulder. With a sigh, his tone shifts to a more serious one. "Of course. Whatever you need. The new generation has to stick together." He holds out his fist to me. "Friends to the end?"

I smack his fist solidly with mine. "Friends to the end. Mason's going to be a fucking pain in the ass about her, isn't he?"

He bobs his head, smirking a bit. "Yep."

I blow out a breath, leading the way into the house. Bear and I walk through the entry, past the staircases that curve up either side of the room and take a right. Our feet carry us quickly to the den where Mason's got the entire brotherhood, as well as the two new pledges and Lennon, ready and waiting.

It's a fairly large room, full of cushy leather couches and other assorted seating, perfect for times when we have to call the entire brotherhood together. There's still some light streaming in through the windows, but not much as the harsh summer sun sets. I flip on overhead lighting and fans as I walk to the front of the room with Bear. Mason joins us, a cloud of gloom surrounding him as he studies Lennon, his misery-filled eyes glued to her. He's been strangely vacillating—one minute finding amusement in taunting me and messing with Lennon and the next wallowing under whatever depressing thoughts he's having today. Dude has fuckin' issues galore.

Mason and I have had complications stemming from a blowup freshman year, but we've agreed to at least *present* ourselves as a united force this year. It's the only way to gain the respect of the initiating brothers and maintain it with the remainder of the brotherhood. Every year, the heads of house lead with an iron fist—but we're going to have to double down on that. We're the sons of the founding fathers, and I'm aware there are at least a couple members of the brotherhood who would love to see us fail. They know we didn't ever have to worry about our admission to the Bainbridge Hall brotherhood. Unlike the rest of them who paid up and then clawed their way through initiation, we're sons of the OG Bainbridge Bastards. They think our lives are easy. But we're the ones with an inkling of what belonging to this house means. And I do mean belong to. The alumni own us and will forever.

My eyes land on Lennon the moment I turn around to face everyone. How could they not? As the sole female in attendance, she sticks out like a sore thumb with waves of blonde hair and long legs hanging out of frayed and holey jean shorts. Her lush breasts push the limits of her strappy black tank top. And those fucking lips. *Jesus.*

I blow out a breath, tearing my eyes away and observing for a moment how the others are reacting to her. Tucker's a year behind us, on the football team with Bear, and he's pretty obvious about his interest in her. Too busy on his phone to care about the feminine presence in our house, the other junior, Warren, sits with his head bent, reading his text messages. Pierre, Brendan, and Kai—the sophomores—appear to be leery of getting their hands slapped, having just come out of their probationary period last year themselves, so their glances her way are few and far between. And the grunts, I don't even have their fuckin' names straight yet. The one with white-blond hair notices me studying him and quickly looks away. My gaze moves to the second one who, much like Tucker, can't seem to unglue his dark eyes from Lennon, though he's doing it kind of shiftily, since she's sitting right next to him.

And then, there's my stepsister. I haven't fully

processed this, so having her sitting in the middle of our den is jarring. Wrenching my gaze from her, I give myself a shake. The aberration of our plans, the mere idea of Stella being here day in and day out has me all twisted up. I don't trust that she won't delight in causing ripples throughout the brotherhood. It wouldn't surprise me in the least if she started hooking up with half of them. Like mother, like daughter. She'll go until she finds one who gives her what she wants, just like her mother did with my father. Probably has a magic muff, too.

I groan internally, irritation rising within me that she's already got my attention diverted to places it shouldn't be. But one thing's for certain—Stella Bella had better listen up once we get started, because I will treat her just like any of these other grunts. She'll do everything they will, exactly like my father said, because from experience, we know it's the best way to keep newbs in line.

I clear my throat, getting everyone's attention, ready to get this over with. "Okay, here's the deal. I'm going to keep this short and sweet. Welcome, Arik and Quincy. Congrats on making the cut." I pause, my eyes shifting to Lennon as I run my hand back through my hair, pushing it from my face.

Before I can explain her presence to the group, Brendan mumbles, "Who's the bitch?"

The deafening silence in the room serves to let him know that he's taken a misstep, but then Mason finishes the job. He takes a half step forward, cocking his head to the side and staring at Brendan. "Don't you think we're getting to that, dumbass?"

Brendan's mouth snaps shut, his face coloring. The swift intakes of air around the room don't surprise me, these guys no doubt are now nervous to open their own mouths for fear of saying something stupid.

I tip my chin at Mason, acknowledging that his bold move was fairly effective, then glance to my side toward Bear, who I can tell is inwardly laughing again. With a roll of my eyes, I wet my lips. "Boys, meet *the inconvenience*. This is Lennon Bell, and she'll be living here this year."

Her pretty face screws up into a scowl, clearly pissed off by her introduction. "Well, believe me, I don't want to be here either. It's not by choice."

Her biting words trigger a rumbling from the brotherhood. It starts quietly, then builds to a dull roar until I slice my hand through the air. "Nope. We're not here to discuss Lennon's situation. What we are here to do right this moment"—I look pointedly at the grunts, and even include Lennon in my stare—"is give you a rundown on the rules we have here, and how this entire process works."

MASON

Like we'd planned, Mason steps in. "Your daddies paid a metric fuck ton of money for you to be here, to have the advantages we, as part of this brotherhood, have. Advantages that extend beyond graduation that you'll have for the rest of your would-otherwise-be-pathetic lives. However ..." He pauses for effect—fuckin' Mason is nothing if not dramatic. "That doesn't necessarily mean you've automatically earned the right to call yourself one of the Bastards of Bainbridge Hall just yet. As you may or may not be aware, you'll go through what we call a probationary period where you'll be tested at every turn." He nods to Bear, who steps up. It's comical to watch all three sets of eyes drift up another four inches, taking in Bear's height. If I didn't know him better, I might be intimidated, too.

His low voice comes out full of gravel. "Obedience. Loyalty. And the ability to keep your mouth shut about anything that goes down here. That's what we're demanding of you. If you're told to do something, you fuckin' do it. No questions. You will level up, earning various privileges throughout this period. A few examples are access to the code for the alarm system so you can come and go as you please"—he catches Lennon's gaze and gives a little shake of his head—"eating with the brotherhood, attendance at events, etcetera, as we go through this probationary period. Prove to us you're worth our while and you'll be golden. Should you demonstrate that you're capable, then you'll one day make it to full-fledged brotherhood status."

The kid with the white-blond hair has been listening intently, but I can see questions pushing their way to the surface.

I point at him. "Go ahead. I can tell you're curious about something."

"Um, so what kinds of things are we talking about?" He huffs a little. "I'm not saying I won't do it but knowing what to expect would help."

Mason snorts, staring stonily at the kid. Slowly, he enunciates the answer, dumbing it down for the guy. "Any. Fucking. Thing." One dark brow arches on his forehead. "Got it?"

When he's met by wide, nervous eyes, Mason shakes his head. "You're never going to hack it being a scared little pussy." Glancing at Bear and me, Mason's lips curve into an awful grin. "How about we give them an introduction to what's coming?" Both of us nod in agreement, so he juts his chin toward the door. "Go get me a beer from the fridge, kid."

The guy blinks, and I step forward and clap my hands right in front of his face. "Dude. Did you hear Mason? He wants a fuckin' beer. *Fetch.*"

As if I've bodily shaken him awake, he inhales sharply then jumps up and hurries out of the room.

Bear's gaze swings toward the other new guy. "What's your name?"

"Arik."

Taking longer than necessary to look him over, Bear finally grunts his approval. "Good. Come here, Arik."

This one isn't messing around. He stands right away and crosses the space between us, then waits for instruction. Arik might have what it takes. He's got guts. He hasn't looked away from the intense stare down at all. Bear folds his arms, sizing him up, then briefly nods at the spot beside him on the floor. "Down and gimme twenty. And make 'em good."

Fortunately, this newb looks like he might be able to handle twenty push-ups, even when Bear puts his foot on his back and applies a good amount of pressure. Arik groans, but only pauses for a moment before he gets to it.

Pulling my focus from the push-up party, I meet Lennon's defiant eyes. My lips curve into a goading grin, and I crook my finger at her. She blows out a hard breath, but gets up from her spot on the couch, then lifts a brow in question as she calmly folds her arms over her chest. I point toward a table at the side of the room which has several decanters of alcohol. "Go pour a shot of the Patron over there. It's on the far right."

Her brow furrows, and she gives me a perturbed smile before she saunters over there. "Yes, sir," she throws over her shoulder.

A roll of laughter moves through the room ... but she won't be laughing in a sec. Not if I have anything to say about it.

Just then, the kid who must be Quincy jets into the room with Mason's requested bottle of beer, handing it off to him before he reclaims his seat. Mason shoots me a wink, then tips the bottle to his lips, downing half the beer in one go. "I fuckin' love grunts."

Meanwhile, Arik completes his push-up challenge and waits in plank position until Bear eases his foot off his back. The kid stands and after checking with Bear—nothing like starting off with a little ass kissing—he returns to his seat as well, in time to watch Lennon cross the room to me with the shot. She holds it out, but I slowly shake my head.

Her brows draw together, and I watch as it dawns on her that it's not me she's poured the shot for.

"Drink up, Stella Bella."

"But I don't like tequila." Her face blanches.

Mason leans close. "Had a bad experience?"

She shrugs, chewing on her lip as she eyes the liquid in the shot glass and wrinkles her nose. "Maybe."

I take a few seconds to consider, but it's best she learns this lesson right now. "Unlike the others, you aren't allowed to leave the house, walk away. We won't ever kick you out because for whatever reason, it's been deemed you stay." I pause, rubbing my hand over my clean-shaven jaw. "So, if you want me to make this worse for you, I will."

Lennon looks like she's going to vomit without ever drinking the tequila.

A hush falls over the room. Leave it to Tucker, though, to give the rest of the brotherhood a confused look before he smirks and throws out, "If she doesn't want to drink it, do a body shot off her—" He interrupts himself with a quick snort. "Unless you think she'd like it too much. But hell, you could make her take off her shirt in front of us to do it. Maybe that'd—"

"Shut your fucking mouth, Tucker. You have zero say in it." My stern face has him holding up his hands in front of him, the *forget I said anything* clear on his stupid fucking face. I take a step closer to my stepsister, glaring at her, ready to take action if she doesn't comply. "Do as you're fuckin' told."

Lennon draws in one unsteady breath, then another before meeting my eyes with boldness in hers. She lifts the glass to her lips and throws the shot back. I can visibly see how it hits her as it slides down her throat. Her entire body shudders, revolted by the taste, but to her credit, she did as I requested. Spinning toward the rest of the brotherhood, she gives them an eye roll. "I'd much rather drink it myself than let my stepbrother suck liquor from my belly button or tits. Thanks, though." With that, she stalks back to the couch and plops down between the other two pledges, amid more hushed whispering. She looks straight ahead, her eyes burning twin holes into me.

My jaw twitches as I watch her with interest. "That's it, everyone. Head upstairs—rooms are assigned, just look for yours, your names are on Post-it Notes on the doors. The three of you have two hours to unpack and settle in. Everyone else is free to go for the time being. Meet on the pool patio at eight sharp." I roll my lips into my mouth for a moment, knowing I've got a bit more to do before I can relax for a while. "Lennon, hold here for a moment, we need to discuss which room to put you in, along with a few other points of business."

Slowly, everyone files out of the room, leaving Bear, Mason, and me with her as she stubbornly waits on the couch for us to speak, not giving up her true thoughts on what transpired.

I walk up to her and bend at the waist, grabbing her

chin. My lips twist as I murmur softly, "I hope you'll decide to take that lesson and learn it now, because every time I need to reteach you, the consequence you reap will be worse. Whenever you leave this house, one of us will be with you. You won't leave our sight unless you're in class." We engage in a stare off so intense, I'm surprised to find I'm unsure who the winner will be.

"You should probably head upstairs and decompress." Bear gestures in the general direction of the entryway. "Take the stairs up to the landing, go left and all the way down the hall. The last bedroom on the right is yours."

I figured Bear would come to the same conclusion I already had about which room should be hers, but Mason jerks beside me, frowning. His eyes implore me to put her somewhere different, and I think I get why and wish there were another option, but we only have so many open rooms. She'll stay near us so we can watch her the way we need to.

Lennon's eyes flick from Mason to Bear, and finally to me before she pushes to her feet. "Just so you know, you may be willing to blindly obey Daddy Valentine, but blind obedience isn't something that sits well with me. I'll play nice for now, but you'd better fucking believe I've been through enough shit that you will *never* break me."

She spins on her heel, and we watch as she stalks from the room.

"She's a fuckin' spitfire." Mason gives me a wicked grin. "I think I like it."

Bear shakes his head. "No, she's going to be a fuckin' handful."

Ignoring Mason's asshole response, I hiss out a long breath. "No shit."

FOUR

LENNON

I'd love to know what they said after I walked out, but something tells me it'd just piss me off. I grab my suitcase from beside the door where Tristan had left it upon our arrival, which seems like days ago. Putting in the time dealing with these guys is doing weird things to my head.

At the foot of the stairs, I scoop up my abandoned flip-flops, then heft my suitcase along with me as I ascend to the second floor. These guys don't know me, and I don't have any idea what Tristan has told Duke, but fuck. I'm no whore. And I'm not after their fucking money. I don't deserve to have every single thing I do compared with my mother's actions. How would I have been privy to most of it as a younger teen? In truth, I still have no idea what she did that was so wrong.

A bit of commotion reaches my ears as I get to the top of the staircase, but it's all coming from the opposite end of the hall. It seems like the other two new guys have rooms in the far wing of the house. I suppose you'd call it a wing, since they live in such fancy digs. I turn and head in the opposite direction. There are several doors leading off the main hallway, but the big guy had told me to go all the way down, and I'm the last room on the right.

I don't know what to make of him. Bear is huge and seems kinda nice, but I could totally be reading that wrong. It's way too early in whatever game we're about to play to determine anything. He's definitely strong, though. Burly. Maybe a football or rugby player? He seems the type that would delight in tackling someone. I wonder if I'll have a bruise on my lower abdomen from the ride I took on his shoulder back up to the house.

Mason? Honestly, he seems like a straight-up psycho. Who the hell grabs someone by the throat the first time they meet them? But even so, there's something about him that intrigues me. I need to keep a lid on that spark of interest because he seems like the type capable of pure havoc.

And Duke is just fucking Duke. We've never gotten along since our parents were married. I find it irritating that he gets under my skin the way he does. I don't claim to understand him because I don't know the first thing about him, except that he's been attending school here and any time he was home on break he'd spent it sniping at me. It's almost as if he doesn't remember me from before.

But now that I'm stuck under his thumb, it's going to shift the power dynamic between us even farther in his direction. I hope I'm wrong, but I'm nervous that I'm right, and Duke is about to take a serious bite out of me.

I pass by quite a few doors on my way to my room. There's one directly in front of me, but now I can't quite remember if they said I'm right at the very end of the hall or if I'm at the very end on the right. I feel like it was the latter, but I pull open the one on the end just to take a quick peek.

A huge flight of stairs leads upward, so I seriously doubt this is my room. Probably just attic storage. I pull the door shut and, pivoting to my right, give a cursory glance at the enormous door and let myself in. My jaw drops. It takes me a few seconds, but I huff out a laugh at the way my mouth is still hanging open. I should have known that the room would boast insanely high ceilings from the size of the door but jeez. It looks like eighteen feet, easy. Slowly, I close myself in, then wander the gorgeous room I've been appointed. There's a big bed dead center on the back wall with nightstands on either side and one of those padded headboards. I can imagine piling my pillows against it and reading in bed for hours.

I'm delighted to find both a window seat on the left side of the bed and a glass-paned door that leads to a balcony on the right. Wandering over, I glance outside, noting that I have a great view of the pool patio where we're supposed to gather later, and it looks like the building on the far side might be a pool house. I crane my neck, noticing the balcony extends pretty far to the right, so I'm likely sharing it with the occupant of the room beside mine. I go to reach for the doorknob, but then remember something one of the guys—Bear, I think it was—had said earlier about leveling up and one of the things to be earned was an alarm code. So ... I wonder if it'll go off when I open this door, or if it's simply the downstairs exits that remain armed all the time.

Rather than doing something dumb and risking inciting the wrath of the brotherhood, I tuck the question away for later and turn to my left, scanning the far side of the room. I have a small couch and a TV mounted to the wall. *And, oh shit, is that what I think it is?* Wandering over, I throw open the door to find a gorgeous bathroom of my own, all sleek lines and shiny fixtures. There's even a closet tucked inside. I'm a little in awe of the entire setup.

I don't have a clue what Mason's issue was about me staying in this room—it'd been obvious from the shutters going down behind his eyes that he wasn't pleased—but I'm unsure if I care because this is a really nice place to be forced to live for the foreseeable future. Maybe he's my neighbor and doesn't want to share his balcony.

As I'm looking around, I catch my reflection in the mirror over the sink and stop in my tracks. *What the hell?* Duke wasn't messing with me. There really are marks on my neck. Mason. He put his hand on my neck and squeezed, but this is ... black. With my hand shaking, I stare as my finger traces over the discoloration on my throat. *Wait, what?* I lean in, realizing whatever is there is smudging all over. My brows pinch, and I glance down at my finger, rubbing it with the pad of my thumb. It's some sort of chalk—no, maybe pencil lead? Or charcoal? My brain does a bit of a short circuit, thrown back into those few seconds when he had me pressed up against the door. Really, what the fuck was all that about? Am I here to punish him? I don't even *know* him. I glance down at my tank top because it's belatedly occurring to me that he had his hand squarely between my breasts before he slid it up to my throat. If my tank hadn't been black, Duke would have seen a whole lot more than the prints on my neck. No wonder he asked if I was "already hard at work." *Fuck.*

I exhale harshly, then carefully sweep my hair back, making a loose knot at the nape of my neck. There's soap in a dispenser at the side of the sink, so I run water over my fingertips, then quickly scrub the residue off my skin.

The last thing I need is for these dudes to think I'm their plaything, here to do whatever they please.

Two hours later, I've unpacked and changed into a simple white T-shirt and a fresh pair of shorts. I check my phone and see it's five until eight. Slipping on my flip-flops, I pull the door open, only to suck in my breath. Mason stands on the other side, hands on his jean-clad hips. He looks up at me from under hooded eyes, his lashes inky dark like his charcoal-coated fingertips. His gaze zeroes in on my neck, and I swear his lips quirk the smallest bit with silent amusement.

"I washed up. Thanks for touching me with your filthy fingers."

He smirks and lifts his hands, showing me they're clean before he silently reaches for me and guides my face to the side, elongating my neck. The way he's studying me, assessing me—it's completely unnerving. I swallow hard, and his knowing eyes watch my throat work, a ghost of a smile twitching to his full lips. He has really great cheekbones and is devastatingly, dangerously good-looking.

I watch him just as carefully as he's observing me. I can't understand this strange feeling I get when I'm near him. Feeling like he's practically hypnotized me, I can't find it in me to look away when he pulls the side of his bottom lip into his mouth for a few seconds, briefly sucking on it before setting it free again. *Fuck.* Can't get enough of that. I'm so overwhelmed by him that I openly stare for another few seconds before jerking out of his hold. I grit out, "What do you think you're doing?"

He wets his lips, ignoring my question completely. "You ready?"

My brows snap together, finally getting a grip on reality. "That's debatable, but we don't have time for a discussion, nor would you be the one I'd talk to." I take off down the hall, not waiting for him, which I only realize is a mistake when I discover he's perfectly content to follow behind me.

"Damn. Baby sis is lookin' good from this angle. I don't know why Duke is so bent out of shape. Or you for that matter, getting to stay in a place like this. Duke told us where you came from. You know, before your mama married into all that money. I wonder what she had to do to convince Tristan fucking Valentine that she was worth his while."

I flip him off and keep going. I don't have time to deal with what's clearly a bid at flustering me when I've got somewhere to be. I reach the stairs and flee down them with no real idea where I'm going, though I do know I'm headed in the general direction of the pool at the back of the house.

Mason's not far behind me, but it still makes my heart thud when he speaks up. "They're waiting outside."

Lights flicker through the windows up ahead, and I pick up my pace. At the door, Mason catches up to me, and before I can pull it open, he slaps a hand on it above my head, coming in close. I feel him behind me, his heat seeping into my body. It should make me panic to have him get so close, but for some reason, I allow it. My hands grip the door handle as I question him and hope my voice doesn't betray any anxiousness. "What are you doing?"

Then I feel his hand on the back of my upper arm. My heart rate ratchets higher, and I try to jerk away from him.

He gives a rough chuckle at my attempt. He's got me fully trapped between the door and his body. He whispers, his voice silky smooth, "I thought maybe you wouldn't want them to see my fingerprints on you."

I blink. "What?"

He leans in close, his body curved indecently around mine as he slides the pads of his fingers over my skin. "Or maybe you left them there on purpose?"

I can feel the beginnings of an erection pressed up against my ass, and I forcefully wrench air from my lungs, struggling to exhale the breath I've been holding. Then inhale. Exhale. *Breathe, Lennon.* "I didn't know there was more on me." I hesitate, unsure what the right move is. "A nice guy would help a girl out."

"No one *ever* said I was nice," he grits out. "In fact, I'm probably your worst nightmare." He slides his hand over my arm a few times, making my entire body shiver, then rumbles low near my ear, "There. It's gone. For now. But don't let this one act of kindness fool you. I'm no hero."

I hear his words, but I'm caught up in the way our bodies are curled together. It makes my mouth go completely dry. I know I should push him the fuck away. Run. But for whatever reason, I'm frozen in place.

Mason doesn't seem to catch onto the confusion in my head. "Step aside, baby sis. I've got shit to do." He maneuvers around me, opens the door, and walks out onto the patio without a backward glance.

Following behind, I grimace at the nickname he seems to have given me. I'm no one's baby sister, that's for damn sure. Mason, though, he's an enigma, one that I probably can't afford to figure out. I note with interest how easily he flips from moody darkness to asshole frat boy. It's a bizarre thing to watch. I wonder if his friends notice ... or if he really has any. Duke and Mason seem at odds, that's for damn sure.

I take a deep breath, joining the small crowd gathered around the pool. The night air is warm, and most everyone has grabbed drinks and is lounging around either on patio furniture or at the edge of the pool with feet dangling in the water. I do notice that Quincy and Arik sit apart from the rest at a table where some sort of citronella candle burns. Bugs. Georgia's got 'em.

I give the heads of the house a glance, but they aren't currently paying attention to the grunts. Mason leans down and whispers something that I'm too far away to hear, but I know they're talking about me because all at once all three pairs of eyes settle on me—piercing blue, glittering gold, and sinful chocolate.

"Any clue what they've got on tap for us tonight?"

I turn my head toward the guy with the curly brown

hair. Arik. I shake my head at his inquisitive expression. "I don't have any idea."

He gives the other guy a look that is unmistakable. He doesn't believe me.

"Think what you want. I'm probably more clueless about how this place runs than any of you. At least you were prepared to be here."

Quincy slowly shakes his head, and Arik gives me a lazy shrug. "Whatever you say."

Great. What the hell did I do to get on the bad side of the other pledges? Fuck them if they want to act like that.

While I'd been focused on these two, somehow I missed the rest of the brotherhood circling around us. Duke claps his hands together, getting our attention. "Line up at the side of the pool."

As I stand, Bear grasps me by the back of the neck and pulls me close to whisper, "Come on. Over here." He guides me directly where he wants me, but stays at my side for several more seconds, his warm hand gently massaging my skin like he's seeking to calm me. Duke's gaze sweeps the group before he continues. "We want to make sure you're capable of running all sorts of errands for us. But tonight? We just want you to *run*. Each pledge runs ten laps around the house before you're allowed to stop."

I side-eye Arik and Quincy, who are too busy groaning to realize what else is about to happen.

Bear rather reluctantly leaves my side as he and Mason each select a pledge. Duke smirks, meeting my eyes as he steps up to me. "But to make things more interesting, in you go."

I draw in a deep breath just as Duke's hands connect with my shoulder blades, and he shoves me into the pool.

Shit.

I saw it coming, but it's still a shock to hit the water. I allow myself to sink down until my feet hit the bottom. The laughter from the brotherhood is distorted, coming to me faintly as I push off the tiles and swim upward. I break through the surface, gasping for air and treading water. Arik and Quincy pop up seconds later, sputtering and gagging like they swallowed half the pool when they went under. Duke, Bear, and Mason stand right at the edge, the younger brothers directly behind them. Their amusement is obvious.

Dipping backward, I smooth my mane of wet hair from my face before taking inventory of what I'll be running my ten laps in. My flip-flops float about six feet from me, not that I'd wear them anyway. And fuck me, I changed out of the black tank for a white T-shirt. It's one of those thin, slub-material ones. Practically transparent when wet. Beneath that, I hadn't even put on a proper bra, just a lacy bralette.

The other two guys head for the side of the pool while I continue to tread water in the middle. It's critical that I don't show any hint of embarrassment or fear.

"What's the matter, Stella? Got an issue?"

I steel my nerves and swim to the edge where Duke shoots me a wicked smile before bending down to hold out a hand to help me up. *Fuck you, fucker.*

I reach up, grasping Duke's hand, and yank as hard as I can, sending him over my head where he splashes into the water behind me. I try not to laugh at the coughing as he comes up with a mouthful of pool water. Quickly, I plant my hands on the edge of the pool and push myself up, nimbly climbing out on my own.

I'm so pleased with myself I almost forget that everyone has a fairly decent view of my tits through my sopping-wet shirt.

Mason's brows shoot up when his eyes land on my chest.

"Oh, fuck." Bear runs a hand over his jaw.

I turn my back on them, staring down at Duke as he swims to the edge.

"Nice tits. Your nipples are hard. What is it that's got you all worked up, Stella?" He gives me a sly grin.

I can either race back into the house, covering my all-but-exposed breasts with my arms, or— I put one hand on my hip, cocking it to the side as I look down at him in amusement. "Look all you want, but you can't touch, big brother." Without further ado, I peel the offending shirt off, whipping it at him. It smacks into the water right under his chin, but I swear he doesn't notice as his eyes are stuck to my chest like they're glued there.

I give him my back. He doesn't deserve to look at my body. On full display to the rest of the brothers, I shrug. "When you're done drooling like animals, maybe close those mouths you've left hanging open. I'll be running my laps." I take off like a shot, determined to finish quickly so I can be alone in my room. I don't hear the other two behind me, and I don't give a shit.

A minute later, as I round the corner of the house, completing the first lap, I create quite a stir. There are a fair number of catcalls and whistles, and a whole lot of clapping as I race by, well aware that my tits are bouncing like crazy in this ineffective excuse for a bra. I'm beyond caring. I am, however, very pleased with my stepbrother's reaction.

Duke's face is absolutely rigid, a fun shade of cherry red high on his cheeks, yet he can't pry his gaze from me. Good. Asshole.

"Dear fucking god," Bear groans out. "This might be more torture for us than for her. She's fucking fast, too."

He gives me an appreciative look and a simple nod of his head.

Mason subtly readjusts himself before shouting, "Go, baby sis!" Then he snorts with laughter as Duke cocks his arm back and punches his bicep.

I smirk as I pass them, blowing a kiss as I continue on to my second lap.

FIVE

MASON

My eyes blink open, and I lie in my bed for several seconds before it dawns on me that I must have heard something that pulled me out of a deep sleep. I hesitate, doing my best to steady my breathing, listening to the thudding of my heart and the quiet of the night.

Wait. Am I awake? I close my eyes again—or I think I do—and attempt to get my brain to focus on something else. But I never have peaceful dreams, whether I'm asleep or awake. Never. Rolling over, I reach out for my phone, which I left charging on my bedside table, and pry my eyes open again to see it's 4:15 a.m. I haven't had a good night's sleep since about the age of eight, but lately, man, it's really bad.

Feeling groggy, I roll to my back again, peering up at my phone as I hold it in the air over my face. I should put it down because it never fucking helps to stare at the bright screen in the dark when I should be trying to sleep, even if it does pass the time. Frustrated and out of it—no doubt from the Tylenol PM I took a few hours ago—I toss the phone down on the mattress and groan, covering my eyes with my forearm. Maybe I should head up to the attic and get some work done since it's clear all I'll ever do is go from one nightmare to the next.

God, I'm fuckin' dramatic when I'm awake in the middle of the night.

But then I hear the noise again, throwing me into high alert. It's a door opening. Or maybe closing. And not far away either. My brow furrows, my mind racing. Slowly, I pull my arm away from my face and open my tired eyes. I swear the sounds are coming from the direction of the balcony. My heart lodges somewhere in my throat, and I turn my head on my pillow, blinking through the dark of the room to the equally pitch-black night. There's a violent lurching in my chest, my lungs have trouble deciding in what manner to function. A cold sweat breaks out all over my body, clammy and unsettling. I shove the light sheet covering me to the side and slip from the bed.

My face crumples at what I see through the glass panes of the door. The ache I feel is so fucking intense, I wish I could tear out my goddamn heart. *No. Why are you out there? No.* Sick rises up in my throat, preventing me from screaming at her, and I swallow it back down, unwilling to let her do this to me again.

An unexpected surge of anger hacks its way into my chest, replacing the sadness, and I bolt across the room to throw open the balcony door. With my entire body heaving, I stare at the wildness of her hair as a balmy breeze blows gently over us, her long, blonde locks floating out behind her. As I watch her standing there, she grips the railing, and her toes curl a bit, as if the stone of the terrace is cold, which it might be because it's the middle of the fucking night.

What the fuck am I thinking? *She's not here.* She can't be here. My heart alternately hammers and clenches behind my rib cage. I stalk over to her—this fake, this imposter. This can't be her. She's a riveting, *awful* dream. My unending nightmare. I reach out, grip her shoulders, and tear her away from the railing.

She turns in my arms, unbalanced, her eyes unfocused. My jaw tightens as I grasp her by the upper arms and shove her back against the railing, putting my face right in hers. "You're not real," I growl, my voice scratchy from sleep. Swallowing roughly at the faraway look in her eyes, I repeat myself, punctuating every word with an angry huff of breath. "You're. Not. Real." Rage coursing its way through me, I shake her violently. "You're not fuckin' real! You're not! You can't be!" My jaw clenches as my mind turns over and over on itself until I don't know which end is up. I don't know what's real and what's not.

Her eyes finally focus on me as my hands slip up to curl around her throat. Blood pounds through my head in a frantic rhythm. I know I'm losing it. I'm on the verge. But I can't see past the raw anger boiling inside me. Can't hear a fucking thing but her breath rasping in and out.

"Why do you do this to me?" I whisper raggedly, each word scraping from my throat as misery rolls through my body in great waves. "Why do you punish me?" Tears leak from the corners of her eyes, and her hands grapple at my wrists, pulling weakly. I blink, taking in the horror in her eyes as I bend her farther over the rail. There's something about the way she's looking at me that twists in my brain.

I throw my head back, anguish flowing freely now. I shove her away from me, and she lands in a heap on the floor of the balcony. In a fit of fury, I snatch up a metal table from behind me and heave it over the balcony's rail. It soars through the air, splashing into the pool a moment later.

"What the fucking hell is going on here?" Bear crashes through the open doorway and skids to a stop.

Our eyes meet as my arms jerk erratically. I reach up and grab at my hair just to have something to hold onto. And I pull. Hard. *Wake up.* This is all just a really bad fucking dream.

"Make it stop. Make her go away," I moan as I clamp my eyes shut.

"Calm the *fuck* down, Mason." His big paw of a hand slaps my cheek.

Stunned by the sting, my eyes flick open in time to see his gaze shift to *her*. His eyes widen as his gaze swings back to me. "What the fuck is wrong with you? What did you do?" he growls.

He lets go of me to go to her. Out of the corner of my eye, I watch him kneel down beside her. He's whispering something, but the blood is crashing through my head, whooshing so hard I can't hear. My chest heaves in great jerking movements, and I clutch at the back of my neck with both hands, pacing the length of the balcony. I glance at her, at *them* where Bear's trying to calm her. I might not be hearing well over the roaring in my head, but I can see she's gagging and coughing and crying.

Fuck, the way she torments me. My hands fist reflexively, fingernails cutting half-moons into my palms. I drop to my knees, leaning forward and supporting myself with my hands. I pant. How is this possible? That slap was real. So fucking real my cheek still burns with it.

But he's over there with her, lifting her panty- and bralette-clad body off the floor and into his arms. My gaze follows as he exits the balcony via the other door.

The door to the room where I didn't want Lennon staying.

Lennon. I shake my head, trying to understand what the fuck I just did—and hating myself for the answers I'm coming up with.

"WHAT THE EVER-LOVING FUCK WAS THAT?" Bear storms into my room a while later, hands on his hips, rage seething from him. He's an imposing figure with the extra height, but he doesn't fucking scare me. Goddamn teddy bear if you ask me, but then again, I don't face him in the places where he truly lets loose. He's ruthless, both on the football field and elsewhere. Get in his way and regret it. Willing to do some sketchy shit when pushed.

I don't have a clue how much time has passed because I've been so lost in trying to figure out what's happening to me. I glance up from the YouTube video I'd been mindlessly watching and shrug.

"No. You don't get to brush this off like it's nothing. You've got a real fucking problem, man. You're fucked-up. Can't even admit it to yourself."

"Fuck off," I mumble, infusing my words with a coldness I generally only reserve for Duke because I know it pisses him off. He's wrong. I'm well aware that I'm fucked in the head. I'm a nightmare of my own making.

Bear shakes his head, seeing right through my BS, and I can feel the impatience simmering within him. "Don't tell me to fuck off. You could have seriously hurt her. I'm trying to look out for you, but you're making it really goddamn difficult right now."

I return my gaze to my phone and grit out, "So don't fucking look out for me. I can take care of myself."

From under my hooded glare, I can see Bear staring daggers at me. "That's not the goddamn point, and you know it. You need therapy or something." He hesitates, his lips twisting. "That's not her, man. It's not. She's got long blonde hair and is built the same. But that's where the similarity ends. The problem is you're hovering somewhere between reality and your nightmares."

"You can leave now." I run a hand through my hair, finally lifting my head to meet his eyes.

"You and I both fucking know you weren't in control of what you were doing. But I'm gonna ask

Duke in the morning about how we program that fucking alarm to go off when those doors open."

"Don't," I heave out, fear climbing into my throat like it's going to rob me of my breath.

"Why not?"

My voice cracks as I whisper tortured words. "Because I don't want to forget her."

SIX

BEAR

A FINE SHEEN of sweat covers my body as I work my quads. Coach doesn't like to train us too hard before the first game of the season, so he'd called for a rest weekend, then we'll be back at it on Monday to prepare for the big game Saturday night. At KU, football is life. The Lions win. It's what we do. Our reputation attracts the best of the best players. Hell, Duke probably should be playing, too, but there's never been any convincing him once he made up his mind that he was done forever. He'd refused to play our senior year of high school, and he was one of the best wide receivers our school had ever seen. He was too messed up in the head over Juliette. His dad, the unfeeling prick, couldn't understand his decision and even tried to get me to badger him into playing college ball. I guess he could have bought Duke's way onto the team with a few well-greased palms, but Duke would have refused the offer if it came like that, anyway.

Tristan Valentine—the fucking arrogant asshole—doesn't know his son, nor does he understand why he's no longer playing. Doesn't give two shits about it either.

It's not the first or last time Duke, Mason, or I have seen poor behavior from our predecessors. It sure as fuck won't be the last. They have their fingers in way too many dirty pots. Even Mason's dad, who is still serving time in prison, manages to run things from behind bars. That's power right there. I've always wondered how he inspired such loyalty, but I don't want to get close enough to find out. My own old man is more than enough to deal with, and I'm caught up in all his shit with no way to escape.

All the family drama aside, I'm down here this morning because I don't fucking know how to rest. I'm always moving, always seeking to physically improve myself because it's all I have. That's all I know. I need football to work out for me. Go pro or go home. Period. It's the one thing my old man and I agree on, but I really hope that when I'm playing at that level that he'll leave me the fuck alone. Gripping the handles, I shake myself of my mind's wanderings and concentrate on my breathing and my form as I straighten my knees, pressing upward with all my might. Just a few more reps.

When I'm satisfied I've pushed myself hard enough, it's up and to the next piece of equipment. I hit the seat with disinfectant spray and a towel, then head to the rack of weights at the center of the room. I pick up a pair of twenty-five-pound dumbbells, then step up onto a raised platform. Pushing off the ground, I bring myself up to stand on the platform. Up, up. Down, down. Repeat.

It's as I'm doing this I realize there are eyes on me. I'm not alone, like I almost always am at this hour while the rest of the brotherhood sleeps.

Lennon stands in the doorway. From her expression, I doubt she thought she'd encounter anyone else up at this hour. Not a bad time to take a little tour, actually.

There's a certain exchange here, a curiosity as we study each other. My eyes roam, and I wonder how Duke never once mentioned that his stepsister is a total smokeshow. Considering it's like six in the morning, she looks damn good, especially after what transpired less than two hours ago. Her face is free of makeup, long hair swept on top of her head and secured with a pen. My brow furrows for a moment at the odd hair accessory, but then my eyes continue on their downward path, taking in the well-worn T-shirt that reads *Girls rule, boys drool* in bold lettering across her chest—kinda funny considering how she confronted the brotherhood last night—and joggers that hit mid-calf. She's barefoot again, and maybe I've been too distracted by other details, but her toes are painted a mint-green color, like the mint chocolate chip ice cream I keep in the freezer.

My brain does a hard left, and images from last night flash through my mind, how she'd had the guts to yank Duke into the pool. And then she'd taken things up a notch, tearing off her sopping-wet shirt and jogging around and around and around the house in nothing but her shorts and a lacy scrap of material that just barely held her tits. I'd watched the entire time. All ten laps. Fuckin' sue me.

But still, I haven't forgotten for a goddamn second how I found her and Mason out on the balcony or how she'd felt shaking and confused in my arms. I don't have the full picture of what happened out there, and it's possible neither of them were coherent enough to explain it either.

I blink a few times, unsure how long I've been standing here with these weights in my hands, not doing a single rep. Only staring. At her.

"Sorry. I didn't mean to break your concentration." She offers me a tight smile, tilting her chin toward me and the weights I hold with a death grip.

I shrug, grunting a bit as I restart my reps. "No big deal."

She wets her lips. "Um. Do you mind if I sit in here

while you work out?" She gestures to one of the weight benches nearby.

My eyes flick to hers. "Your call."

She watches me execute a few more flawless reps, then switch and use the other leg as the starting leg. "You're talkative this morning."

I lift one brow, eyeing her, and can come up with nothing but the truth. "I don't know you." And I'm working out. I can't say I've ever willingly had a conversation with anyone while I'm trying to concentrate on my form.

"I introduced myself yesterday." She wrinkles her nose. "I'm Lennon."

And there's something about the playful quality of her voice that breaks through my steel-like composure. But still, I can't help but put her in her place, trying really fucking hard to remember my promise to Duke to help him with her. Huffing out a dry laugh, I shake my head. "So you said, Little Gazelle."

It's a not-so-subtle reminder that she can run, but I'll catch her. Every. Fucking. Time. She presses her lips together and rolls her eyes. "Okay. Look, you can be standoffish and grumpy this morning. It's whatever. But since I found you, I figured I'd say thank you for calming me down on the balcony."

Shit. She's right, I'm being ... well, a bear.

"It's fine. I'll go."

Frustration burns through me in equal measure with the worry about how to maintain Mason's trust yet talk to Lennon about what happened between them. I still have plenty of questions, but he's my friend and I don't want to fuck this up. It seems significant. "Wait," I grit out, lobbing the request at her back as she gets to the doorway.

She stops, turning on her heel. Her brows lift when her eyes meet my exasperated ones across the gym.

"Sit back down. You can stay. I'm just ... I wouldn't feel right discussing anything before I've had a chance to speak to Mason this morning."

"Bro code." She rolls her eyes again.

"Don't fucking roll your eyes at me." I blow out a hard breath. "But you're welcome. And yeah. Bro code is a real thing."

She pauses to think about what I've said for a moment, then comes back in to reclaim her seat. "Okay, I guess I can handle that." She gestures toward me with one hand as I begin calf raises. "Lemme guess." She taps a finger to her lips, eyeing me carefully. "I think either football or rugby, but I'll go with football."

"Yep." I breathe steadily as I lift up onto my toes then lower my heels just below the edge of the step, feeling the burn throughout my lower legs. She's quiet for several minutes, but it's not an uncomfortable silence. She watches me, and I go about my business. I do wonder what happened last night. I want to ask. But I really can't without expecting her to fire questions right back at me.

Reps completed, I set the weights back on the rack, then go down onto all fours on one of the mats. Extending one leg straight back, I slowly and methodically lift it straight up toward the ceiling, clenching my glute hard at the top of the motion.

"What position do you play?"

I turn my head, grimacing through the exercise. "Tight end."

There's no response at first, but when I glance up, she's covered her mouth with a hand, trying to hide her laugh.

A brief smile splits my face as I pause in working out my *tight end* to shake my head at her. "Bad girl," I grit out. "Bad fuckin' girl."

She lifts her hands with a shrug. "Not me. I can't help it if I happened to ask the tight end what position he plays just as he's working on his tight end."

I groan. "You know the name of the position has nothing to do with the development of the muscles in a player's ass, right?"

She laughs. "I don't even care. It was too good not to point out."

Behind us, a throat clears. "Well, well, well … what's going on here? You two besties now?" Duke's question catches us both unaware, as neither of us had been facing the door. The grin stretching his cheeks is not a good sign. I know him well enough to know that means trouble. It means he's pissed off and putting on a front.

I push upright but remain kneeling on the mat as I wait for whatever he's about to unleash. I swipe my forearm over the sweat collected on my brow. "Duke, man. Come on. She was just learning the lay of the land and happened to find me down here. We were talking football."

His gaze shifts to Lennon. "Is that so, Stella? Already got him fucking fooled, working those feminine wiles. Maybe you think if you open your legs to enough of us things won't go as badly for you."

"I already told you once. You won't break me. Not with cruel words or push-ups or alcohol or dunks in the pool. So, rather than deign to acknowledge your disgusting comments, I'm going to take this opportunity to walk away." Her words are pretty convincing, but the way her back has gone rigid and her cheeks have flushed pink tell another story. But to her credit, Lennon stands up from the bench and walks toward the door.

"Stella," Duke murmurs, the command evident in his tone.

She stops, cocking her hip to the side, and crosses her arms over her chest. She waits but doesn't turn around.

His voice takes on a dangerous quality that's downright menacing as he clarifies the situation for her. "I'm allowing you to walk away from me because there's nowhere you can go to escape. Nowhere to hide. Eventually you'll have to face me. You *will* have to own up to your ambitions."

She gives a swift nod, then keeps going.

Duke watches until she's out of sight to round on me. "The fuck, dude. Down here laughing and cracking jokes with her. I thought we were on the same page."

"We are. But there's some shit that went down in your absence. While you were out doing who knows what, because apparently you don't trust me enough to tell me, our boy Mason had one of his nightmarish episodes and attacked Lennon."

He grimaces, scrubbing his hands through his hair. "Did you ever think for a second that maybe she deserved it?"

Uncertainty seeps through me, but I shake my head. "Either way, a conversation with Mason is in order, whether that pisses you off or not. We agreed to have each other's backs this year. To present as a single force leading this house."

Duke's gaze pierces me. "For brotherhood stuff. Whatever the fuck Mason gets off on during his own time has nothing to do with me."

I'VE TRIED REALLY HARD NOT to let what Duke said bother me, but hell. What I witnessed on the balcony early this morning has had me shook all damn day, and the fact that Duke doesn't want to hear any of it leaves it to me to figure out. Saturdays are meant to be relaxing, but how can I do that when every time I look at her, I see the girl I scooped up off the balcony floor. The one who huddled against me until she could stop the quaking of her body. Ugh. Finally, I can't stand it any longer. I glance at Lennon who's on the couch, scrolling through her phone, lean over the couch and murmur, "Can I ask you one question?"

Almost as if she senses the direction of my thoughts, she nods, a slightly panicked expression crossing her pretty features. "I guess so."

I draw in a deep breath and let the words out. "What were you doing out on the balcony?"

Slowly, she shakes her head. "I don't remember."

She means it ... and it's so far from the answer I was expecting, it makes my head spin.

SEVEN

LENNON

Steering clear of ten other people in a house this size shouldn't be so damn difficult, yet, that's what today had been. An unending loop of me finding a spot to hang out, only to have others join me—and seeing as how I'm not trying to join their damn brotherhood, I don't feel the need to participate in all the bonding and togetherness unless I'm directly asked to participate. It's bad enough that if I don't comply with their demands, they could make things really shitty for me. My current plan is to keep my head down and try not to get too tangled up in what they tell me to do. I'll let it all roll off my back.

That is, until I wake up on the balcony with no recollection as to how I got there, with Mason's hands wrapped around my neck again. Because if that was the first half of a double feature, I do not want to stick around for the second showing.

I wonder if what happened on the balcony has something to do with what he'd said to me earlier that day. It'd almost felt like he'd been warning me away from him when we talked before going down to join the others out at the pool last night.

And I haven't seen a sign of him today, not on the balcony or anywhere else in the house. Could he be as thrown by what happened between us as I was? I'm not mad. I *am* a little freaked out, though. I see something inside him that's so clearly and deeply wounded, I couldn't possibly anticipate what else he might do. One minute he seems perfectly normal, if a little asshole-ish. But the next? *Shit.*

As I walk down the stairs to find something to eat, my fingers probe the skin of my neck. I can't see anything yet beyond some redness, but I have a horrible feeling from the ache I feel from the slightest touch that I might end up with some visible bruising by tomorrow. I'll have to think about what I want to do should it be obvious.

Ducking into the kitchen, I find Arik and Quincy seated at the small table there, already finishing up their meal. Like a trio of toddlers, we're banished to the kitchen for meals until we've earned the right to eat with the brothers in the dining room. It doesn't bother me as much as it does these two. I give them a little wave, but they hardly respond. It's cool if they don't deem me worthy enough to join their conversation, but they're so busy grumbling about the way they've been separated from the brotherhood that they don't realize their sullen voices are plenty loud enough for me to hear them—and possibly the brothers, too.

I skip getting food in favor of seeing if Mason is in the dining room. I don't owe him a damn thing, but I've been so curious, especially once Bear refused to say anything.

It's probably fucking stupid of me, but if there's a chance he has something to say, well, I might allow it, if only to get another peek into his psyche. I've never met anyone like him. I find him both intriguing and terrifying. And ridiculously attractive.

I'm probably setting myself up for disaster. It's kinda odd that I'd open myself up to something like that, but I can't help the pull I feel toward him. He's so agonizingly tempting, despite the darkness that seems to seep from his pores.

I let out a disappointed breath when I peek into the dining room and he's not present. And apparently, my exhale was too noisy because all at once, I'm the center of the entire table's rapt attention.

"Did you need something, Lennon?" Bear looks up from the mashed potatoes he'd been scooping onto his fork. "There's food on the stovetop if you're hungry."

I nod. "Thank you. Um, I was wondering if you know where Mason is?"

Duke's brow hikes up on his forehead, but he doesn't say a word. A hush has fallen over the table, too. I couldn't say if I stuck my foot in my mouth or not.

Bear shakes his head. "Sorry. Haven't seen him."

"Okay, no big deal. Thank you."

"Listen to her kissing their asses now after showing off her titties to them yesterday."

What the hell? I'm about to spin around and give whichever asshat said that a piece of my mind, but before I can, Bear snaps, "Whoever the fuck just said that, get in here."

My eyes widen at the growl in Bear's voice, and I turn tail, heading into the kitchen. I'm not really hiding; however, I have the distinct feeling that things are about to get awkward, and I don't need to witness this guy's humiliation. I busy myself studying the offered food while keeping my ears open. Out of the corner of my eye, I watch Quincy slide from his chair and slink into the room.

There's dead silence for several moments, and I can only imagine that Quincy has got to be ready to shit his pants while Bear sizes him up. I quickly pile food onto my plate. Mashed potatoes from the huge pot on the stovetop, then a few pieces of sliced chicken, and a serving of green beans. Someone around here likes to cook.

I don't have time to wonder who it is because I catch the lethal tone of Bear's voice. "Quincy? You want to listen in on conversations and make judgments about how we handle things in this house? Go scrub my toilet. It'd better sparkle when you're done or next time, I'll make you clean it with your toothbrush."

"But—"

I cringe, experiencing some very real secondhand embarrassment for this idiot. The other brothers have similar responses as there's a bit of muffled gasping, along with one amused "Oh, shit" muttered under someone's breath, followed by some chuckling. I think it had to be Tucker, one of the older guys.

"But. What?" comes Duke's voice, less amused than Bear's at the audacity of this kid.

Even *I* was paying enough attention last night to know what the expectations in this house are. They were very clear about it. Obedience, loyalty, and the ability to keep our mouths shut. That's literally all they're looking for. Oh, and a shit ton of money, but that's on the parents to pay up and already taken care of. I don't have to agree with what they are demanding of the grunts to have properly heard the instructions and be smart enough to not rock the boat on day two.

"She's in there, listening in on every word you say. She should have to clean a toilet, too."

"Not your call, grunt." Duke chuckles darkly. "But if you want all things equal like that, when I tell her to suck my dick, you'd better be prepared to blow me, too."

My eyes bug out. I can't believe he said that. And the fucked-up thing is that while he'd still been a dick about it, in a roundabout way, he was defending me. Or maybe I'm imagining it, and he simply really likes messing with Quincy and Arik. I pick up a green bean and stick it in my mouth.

"Stella?"

I almost choke. Clearing my throat, I squeak out a quick, "Yes?" For a second time, my eyes go wide like saucers, and I stare at the cabinets in front of me. I quickly chew and swallow, then dart over to the doorway between the rooms.

Duke's piercing blue eyes roam over me. "There's a party tonight. You should be dressed and ready to leave at quarter to eleven."

In my peripheral vision, I see Quincy's mouth drop open and his arms lift in exasperation.

Duke grits out, "Not a fuckin' word. Go clean the motherfucking shitter like you were told."

"I'll be ready." Turning, I hurry back into the kitchen, only to find Arik's dark eyes on me. Giving him a little shrug, I collect my dinner and hurry all the way up to my room, where I eat alone on my couch in front of the TV. I never switch it on, but rather sit in silence and absorb the nuances of what went on down there. One thing's for sure, if I'm to survive this place, I'd better open my eyes and pay attention to every single one of these bastards.

AROUND TEN, I begin rooting through my limited clothing options, and after trying on a couple of outfits, I finally come up with a multi-layered, gauzy chiffon skirt that hits above the knee that I think will work okay. It's my favorite color, a seafoam green, and I pair it with a lacy bralette in the same color and a sheer black shirt that closes with three ties in the front. It's kinda sexy, allowing for a tantalizing bit of skin to be exposed from between my breasts all the way down to my stomach.

I lay out the clothing on the bed, then try to

remember if I brought any decent jewelry with me. I sure as hell somehow missed grabbing hair bands out of the bathroom, hence the pen I'd used to secure my hair on top of my head this morning.

A shopping trip is in order, but I'm not allowed to leave the house without one of the guys. And the money I'd saved up, I get the feeling I should hoard it—in case of an emergency. There's no doubt that KU is a distinguished university, but while Tristan doesn't want me to be an embarrassment, I also feel like I'm somehow being bought, like he thinks if he gives me this, it'll shut me up. About what, though?

With a sigh, I undo the button of my cutoff shorts and unzip before I glance at my phone for a time check, then shimmy out of them, letting them drop to the hardwood floor. Just as I peel my crop top over my head, I make eye contact with Mason.

The breath punches from my lungs as I pull the shirt in front of my breasts, staring at him through the glass-paned door. This guy, he doesn't have any fucks to give. He's leaning back against the rail of the balcony, jerking off ... while watching me undress.

His jeans are unzipped and pulled low enough on his slim hips to set his cock free. He's shirtless, and his dick, oh god, it's long and thick. I'm finding it hard to think, and even harder to look away, so far into a daze I can't do anything but watch the firm, lazy strokes of his hand. My eyeballs ping everywhere, and it's not until his eyes drift downward, and his tongue slips out to slick over his full lip that I'm shocked back into awareness. I stand no more than six feet from him, and I'm in the skimpiest underwear and bra set that I own. It consists of mere scraps of nude lace. It'd been a birthday gift to myself when I turned eighteen, purchased with my own hard-earned money. I'm well aware of what he's seeing because I'd blushed hard the first time I put the set on and looked in the mirror. It's as if I'm wearing nothing at all. I hadn't bought the set for a boyfriend or anything like that. But now, for all intents and purposes, Mason is seeing me naked.

My hands reflexively clench the fabric of my shirt, fingers twisting it into a little ball. I've rendered it useless at hiding any part of me. This shouldn't be turning me on, but it is. My nipples become stiff peaks, and I have no doubt that he knows he's affecting me. His eyes pin me in place, the intense gaze scorching my skin.

Catching my lip between my teeth, I slowly stride closer, because, dammit, if he's been watching me, then I'll watch him, too. Swallowing hard, I take the final step, putting one palm on the glass, leaning forward. God, he's hot. Should he be outside my bedroom on the balcony we share with his dick out? No. Probably not.

But fuck, the way he slides his hand up and down his erection, twisting ever so slightly when he reaches the crown, the way the veins in his forearm bulge, and the way he swipes his thumb over the slit, collecting pre-cum and smearing it on his dick before continuing ... It's all so heady. He's a gorgeous specimen of a man.

My chest heaves as I struggle to control my body's reaction, because I so badly want to rock my hips toward him. And I do. Once, twice, ever so slowly.

The bastard winks at me, his head falling back a bit, lips parting, and his movements come faster now, fist shuttling over his cock. His tongue slicks along his lower lip in a way I can only describe as obscene. It's fire. He eyes me with filthy intent as he reaches down and cups his balls.

My breath catches in my throat when he begins to tug on them. His face as he approaches orgasm is one of rapture. Of need. Of insanity.

I could go on watching him forever, but only a moment later, a grunt of satisfaction spills from his lips as cum erupts over his hand. He slowly strokes himself through his release, his hips rocking. Anyone who is outside definitely heard that. He doesn't care, that's for damn sure.

After another few seconds, he tips his chin in my direction, shows me two fingers, then points them directly at my panty-covered crotch, moving them in a way that suggests what I should do. One of his brows arches in question— No that's not it ... he's fucking *daring* me. *Fuck! Why can't I rip my stupid freaking eyeballs away?*

I can't escape, he's got me under some sort of seductive spell. Taking a deep breath, I slam my eyes shut.

And when I finally get up the nerve to meet his sinful eyes again, he's gone.

EIGHT

LENNON

As we're heading out the door to go to the party, Mason bumps into me on the steps, and I swear, he does it on purpose. Teetering in my heeled sandals, he grasps my elbow as if he's trying to steady me, but I understand his true intention when he whispers, "You made the right choice. The skirt is a way better option than the shorts." His eyes dip to my chest. "And I like the top. A lot."

It's a not-so-subtle reminder that he observed my race around my room as I attempted to find an outfit that would be good enough to go out in. He watched me strip out of my clothes. More than once. I probably bent over and showed him my ass in this thong too many times to count.

I'm dying to know which came first—my unintentional striptease or his jerk-off session. It doesn't even fucking matter, though the idea that he saw me and couldn't help but whip out his dick and play a little five-on-one is a tiny bit gratifying.

And how the hell do I set aside that the dude freaked the fuck out on me early this morning? How? I don't know, but his odd shifts in behavior have me genuinely perplexed.

We gather along the sides of two black SUVs that they've pulled up to the front of the house. From the looks of it, not everyone is going out tonight, just the upperclassmen. And me. That's not nerve-racking at all. Tucker and Warren climb into the front vehicle and take off. I'd overheard Warren say they're stopping to pick up his girlfriend, Maria, on the way to wherever we're going. No one has given me any details, so I'm flying blind.

Duke pops open the door to the front passenger seat and gets in, oblivious to the anxiety swiftly rising in me, clawing at my chest. I'm good with people. I really am. It's fear of the unknown that gets me every time. I'll be fine. I simply have to keep telling myself that. And then we'll be in the moment, and I'll have forgotten whatever made me anxious in the first place.

Bear stops beside me, tucking his knuckle beneath my chin and lifting my face to his after he quickly glances at Mason. "If I drive, are you okay to sit in the back?"

The remainder of his question is loud and clear. *With him?*

From the way he's studying me, I bet he thinks the look of mild panic on my face has more to do with Mason and less to do with the party. With multiple encounters in the last day, it makes sense that I'd be wary—and no one knows about that last one. I'm unwilling to share that I witnessed Mason treating his dick like his favorite play toy. Or have to explain how the hot, hot looks he'd given me had made me feel. The molten desire in his hooded eyes, the tightening of his jaw, the thrust of his hips ...

Shit.

Mason gives Bear a dirty look and flips him off. "I'll fuckin' behave."

Bear stops, and I can totally tell his teeth are grinding by the way the muscles work at the back of his jaw. "Don't be an ass."

"Stop trying to be my dad."

Bear heaves out a breath, running a hand through his hair. "For fuck's sake."

"He'd be a better dad than the one who's in prison," Duke grits from inside the SUV.

This conversation has taken an odd turn, and it only reminds me how well these guys know each other—and also how they're too willing to use it against each other.

On information overload, my brows shoot up, and I hold up my hands in surrender, taking a step away from both of them. "I'm fine wherever. Just tell me where you want me."

There's an odd nonverbal exchange between Mason and Bear before the big guy finally exhales hard and gestures to the door beside me. "Behind Duke is good." Without another glance at Mason, Bear circles the vehicle to the driver's seat.

Before I can climb in, Mason grasps my hip, tugging me close, and tucks his head close to mine. His warm breath tickles the skin under my ear. "It's okay to want me after what you saw ... but you should probably wipe up the drool from your chin before we get to the party."

I glare up at him, not willing to give him an inch. "You mean I'm supposed to want the guy who practically choked me to death this morning? Mm. Lemme guess, is choking your kink?"

The only hint I have that I've gotten to him is the twitch of his jaw. His eyes bore into mine, and not bothering to respond, he forges on. "One more question. If you answer, I promise I'll stop fucking with you."

I suck in a breath, and inadvertently take a hit of the mint on his breath again, along with whatever woodsy-scented cologne he must have put on. The twist of his lips tells me this is a bad idea, but he's like the flame I can't resist. I put my hand in it and revel in the burn. "Fine."

He murmurs low, "Were you so worked up that you had to play with your pretty pussy after I went back to my room?"

Oh my god, this guy. I try valiantly to steady my breathing, to calm the frantic beating of my heart, but it's no good. I feel the heat hit my cheeks. It's no good to lie because the truth is all over my quickly reddening face. "Yeah. I had an image of Duke in my head, so I flicked my bean to thoughts of him going down on me. You know. It's a little taboo, the whole stepsibling thing. It made me come really hard." I shrug, pulling the SUV door open on my own, then toss over my shoulder, "He really knows how to use that wicked tongue of his." Shooting Mason a smug look, I climb into my seat. "You can shut the door now. Or is there a reason you're still standing there?"

Music already blares from the speakers, and maybe that's why neither Duke, nor Bear seems to have caught our exchange. Duke bellows from the front seat, "What the fuck is the hold up, you two?" He pulls down the visor and flips open the mirror to look at me, his blue eyes searching mine.

"Nothing. Not a single thing. Let's party."

MASON

Wow. This place is something. I scan the impressive old buildings where all the on-campus fraternities are housed. *Okay. I can do this.* It's just a party. People. Drinks. Dancing. "So, this is Greek Row?"

Bear bobs his head as he deftly pulls the large SUV into a parking space. "Yep. Most frats are located here, all the ones ..." He pauses to think.

"The ones with less financial backing," Mason huffs from the seat across the aisle from me, where he's been eyeing me the entire drive. "KU is full of money, old and new, but you'll discover there are many degrees of wealth. The guys who rush these fraternities don't have to pay anything to get in like at Bainbridge Hall or have family connections like those fuckers all do at Hawthorne Hall."

"We aren't even part of the"—Duke throws up air quotes—"Greek system. To the school, we're simply the brotherhood residing at Bainbridge Hall."

"The bastards you mean." Mason shoots me a wink, and I barely resist agreeing with him out loud.

"But you three actually do have connections, right?"

I've been trying to catch on, tidbits of conversation here and there, piecing everything together.

"Yeah. It's been a long time coming, but the sons of the founders are finally the ones in charge of things." Bear draws in a deep breath, then exhales in a steady stream. It almost seems as if he's not as excited as he should be about it.

I'm interested in learning more because I'm generally clueless about what goes on here at this university, not to mention each individual fraternity. Shit, or even about classes and professors and majors. I don't know where to eat lunch on Monday. Or what my schedule is. *Shit.* That's a panic attack for another day. I drum my fingertips on my thighs and make a stab at keeping the conversation going. "Well, however old Kingston University is, it seems like they have plenty of money to deal with the upkeep. The buildings are striking, and the landscaping is just beautiful. It's a pretty place to be. I like it." I catch Bear's eye in the rearview. "Are the educational buildings on campus similar?"

Duke interrupts, laughing. "Oh, god, you haven't seen the campus yet?"

I'm not amused. I squint my eyes at him as he turns around in his seat. "When would I have been on campus? Your father gave me an hour to pack a bag, didn't provide the slightest idea where I was going, then he pulls up to Bainbridge Hall and announces I'm now living with people I've never met and attending KU. When *exactly* was I supposed to have seen the campus?"

Duke heaves out a breath and throws his door open. "Touché, Stella. Point taken. Come on. Time for a lesson in what a frat party is like."

As I get out, he comes in close, studying my face in a way that makes me wholly uncomfortable. He growls, the rumble coming from deep in his chest. "Fuck," he bites out, "You're too fuckin' pretty." He presses his lips together, looking behind me toward our intended destination before returning his gaze to me, his irritation showing. "Stella, don't do anything stupid." He walks off, hands in his pockets, shaking his head.

Bear and Mason join me, and we follow Duke up to the house, where there's a long-ass line of people waiting to get in. Just when I think we're going to get into said line, Duke pivots and beckons me forward to walk in with him, his jaw tight. Who the hell knows what he's thinking. He puts his hand on my lower back—surprising the hell out of me—and guides me up a short flight of stone stairs to the porch with Mason and Bear following. I don't even have time to look backward at the people watching us skip the line. He lifts his hand in greeting to the guy at the door, who immediately ushers us inside.

Huh. Well, as much as it makes me feel bad for cutting ahead of all those people, I'm glad to be inside the air-conditioned building instead of standing in the line outside for an undetermined length of time. Though I'll likely be thrust among a sauna of sweaty, drunk bodies in no time flat.

My gaze moves swiftly around the house, trying to take in as many details as possible. This is no Bainbridge Hall, but it is a pretty nice setup. And it certainly looks nothing like the frat houses I've seen in movies. It's beautifully decorated. I cringe, thinking about how likely it is that it'll be trashed by morning. *Oh, who am I kidding?* The university probably sends cleaning and repair crews in to make sure these buildings are kept in tip-top condition even after the debauchery of a party.

Forgetting for a moment that Duke and I don't particularly like each other, I glance up at him before my eyes wander the expansive first floor for a second look. "How many brothers live here?"

He shrugs, distracted by something—someone?—across the room, but Mason appears on my other side. "Probably twenty or so?"

My brows dart up. "And you have about half that ... and a house four times as big."

Bear leans in from behind me with a deep, dark chuckle. "Something like that."

A guy approaches us with a few shots in his hands. "How about a drink?" He holds the small shot glass in front of my nose, and the smell of the tequila hits me hard. I jerk back.

Before I can say a word, though, Mason swiftly removes the shot from the guy's hand and downs it himself before handing the glass back with a tight smile and walking away.

I frown, unsure what to think, but then the guy tries to offer me another, and Duke holds his hand up. "She doesn't do well with tequila."

We continue deeper into the party, Bear now stepping in on my other side. My eyes are big as I take in every last detail of this party, the house itself, the bodies wedged together on the dance floor, and definitely the booze. I've never been to a party like this before where alcohol is freely flowing and no one appears to care about adhering to legal drinking ages.

"Here." Mason rejoins us, yanking me from my thoughts when he puts a hard cider in my hand. "This is probably more your speed."

My brow furrows. "Um. Thanks?" It comes out sounding like a question because Mason's wild mood swings confuse the shit out of me. Unexpected kindness one minute, ice-cold like this bottle the next. And to think it's only been a little more than a full day of it.

Duke grits his teeth. "Just do all of us a favor and don't get into trouble."

I feel the snarl rising up from my chest, but instead, I slowly fold my arms over my chest before I calmly respond with a hint of snark. "You brought me here. If you thought I was going to do something crazy or stupid, maybe you should have brought Arik or Quincy instead." My brows raise, and I chew on the inside of my cheek while waiting for him to respond.

Before he can say anything to me, a girl races over to us, dodging one body after another in her bid to get to him as quickly as possible. "Duke! Hey! How's it going?" The redhead is smiling big and quite obviously tipsy as she grips his hand with both of hers and presses her chest to his arm. "We were beginning to think you weren't coming."

He spares her a glance before he grunts out, "I'm here. Just had shit to do."

"Good, well, we're all dancing if you want to join us." She points toward a group of no less than five other girls who writhe to the sensual rhythm of the music before giving him what I'm certain is supposed to be a seductive smile, but in her inebriated state, it seems desperate.

Not my business if that's what he likes. I tip the cider to my lips and chug half of it before I give my stepbrother a smile full of challenge. "Yeah, *big brother,* run along. Your posse of girlfriends dutifully awaits."

Mason snorts beside me. "Goddamn, she has your number." He shakes his head, glancing at my half-empty bottle. "I'd better go grab you another, baby sis."

I nod my acceptance, ignoring the *baby sis* jab that was meant for Duke, not me, and note that a storm has begun to brew in his eyes. "You're not fuckin' cute, Stella." And to the desperate girl next to him, he grits out, "Give me five minutes, Darcy." He runs his hand over his jaw, once again gazing off across the room, his eyes following someone.

I swallow down the rest of the hard cider, finding it refreshing. I'm beginning to think I was right—it's warmer in this house with all these bodies than it was outside. I'm parched.

Bear corrals both of us into a corner, Mason joining us again with another cider for me a moment later. "I'm going to go see what trouble I can find," he mutters.

My eyes flick to his. "You *are* the trouble."

He touches his forehead to mine, our eyes connecting, electricity zapping between us. He breathes out, "You know it, baby." An amused huff of laughter passes his lips, then he takes off across the room, out of sight, swallowed by the crowd in mere seconds.

"What the fuck is going on?" Bear's thick brow lifts as he studies Duke for a clue.

My attention pulls back to them, and I look around. Duke's definitely been distracted since the moment we entered the house. I sip at my cider with the idea in my head that it's not really my business, but I have no fucking problem watching the stepbrother show.

Duke stiffens beside me, and he gets Bear's attention over my head, nodding in the direction of a hallway off the living area. "Are you seeing this?"

"What?" Bear's gaze follows Duke's stare as his brow furrows.

"Hawthorne and his entourage. He just threw people out of that bathroom and took some dark-haired girl in there. Then his boys, Cannon and Archer, followed them inside."

Bear shrugs. "Your point? Since when do you care about shenanigans at a fuckin' party?"

The guy I've come to know through our limited time together is carefully in control of his emotions and, therefore, hard to read. But right now? He's very clearly agitated, not hiding a bit of his feelings.

Just then, the bathroom door flies open and the girl stomps out, moving as fast as she can. She looks *pissed.*

"Is Kingston with her? Who is she?" Duke's stance is rigid, his hands balled into fists at his sides as we watch the pretty brunette haul ass to the front door. A musclebound dude follows her very determinedly with the other two trailing behind. One of those two guys is very familiar to me, though I'm having some trouble placing him, and he's definitely the one Duke's staring daggers at.

"Judging by the raging hard-on in his pants, I'd say yes, he at least likes her. Why do you care, is the question." Bear wets his lips, then closes his eyes for a moment, almost as if he's praying for patience.

Duke bristles beside me, and his jaw is twitching like mad.

Bear focuses on him, almost as if I'm not standing right here, and gives each word in his question special emphasis. "Seriously. Why. Do. You. Care? Juliette is gone. She's gone, man."

The mention of Juliette reaches out and grabs me by the heart. I haven't forgotten her. And I also haven't forgotten that it was through Juliette that I'd first met Duke, well before our parents were married. Back then, he was nothing more than Juliette's boyfriend, a guy who waited outside the diner to take her home. I don't remember him ever setting foot inside. She'd claimed it was because he didn't like her working there.

From the distraught look on Duke's face, it's obvious that he still feels some heartache or holds a grudge—and whatever blame he's placing is squarely on this Kingston guy's shoulders. *Oh, hell.* "Wait," I whisper, "is that Juliette's ... brother?" That's why I'd thought he seemed familiar, I'm almost sure of it without anyone's affirmation. They could easily have been twins. Same hair color, same sun-kissed skin, same good looks, only Kingston is way more masculine. Obviously.

Duke takes a couple of deep breaths, then grabs the back of his neck with one hand, his features going stony. "I— I need to ..." From the way he's having trouble expressing himself, it must hurt like hell to see someone who looks so like the girl he once loved.

"Will you be okay on your own for a bit?" Bear is speaking to me but studying Duke. And he doesn't look too happy about whatever is going on in his friend's head, which I presume he understands a hell of a lot better than I possibly could.

"Yeah, I'm cool. I'll just be dancing."

Bear gives me a swift nod, then motions to Duke to follow him.

Left to my own devices, I finish my second cider, and find the cooler where there are more. Taking my third drink with me, I hit the makeshift dance floor at the center of the expansive living room. Whatever high-quality speaker system they have, I swear it feels like the bass of the music is pounding through my blood. It's not that I don't like it. I'm just completely out of my element with all these rich, well-dressed college students, and it's a bit distracting. I blink hard. But ... I'm now one of those college students. I simply have no real money to my name, so while I sort of fit in, I still don't.

I go further and further into the fray, finally losing myself in the music and the people and the drink in my hand. I rock my hips side to side and raise both arms over my head when a sexy-as-hell song comes on. I haven't had much of a chance to go out and have any fun lately because it gets in the way of working the best shifts at the diner. Of course, I guess I don't have to worry about that anymore. I hadn't even gotten to say goodbye to anyone. Tristan just up and yanked me from everything I knew.

Determined to enjoy myself, I close my eyes and just let go, inhaling this new experience and exhaling all the ridiculous bullshit. The music moves me, and I'm perfectly happy dancing on my own in the middle of the crowd. At some point, Mason trades out my empty cider for a bottle of water, dark eyes watching me carefully. He's drinking and holding up a wall while talking to some girl who seems way more interested in him than he is in her.

I don't know whether I'm drunk or simply annoyed, but I'm quickly overheating and certainly don't need a babysitter. Whirling around, I weave my way through the crowded dance floor, and burst through one of the double doors that leads to the backyard, in search of some much-needed fresh air.

Only ... that's not what I find.

NINE

DUKE

Goddamn, this girl gives superior blow jobs. I heave out a breath, watching my dick slide between glossy pink lips. So, why is it that I can't freaking come? Darcy's head bobs and bobs on my dick, but no dice. It's not that I'm not enjoying it. Her mouth is warm and wet, and she sucks like this is her full-time job.

Right after I finished hashing things out with Bear, I'd let her coax me outside to the stone wall that runs behind all the frat houses for the length of Greek Row. It's not private by any means, but why the fuck not? I lean against the low wall with my vodka, she gets on her knees. This girl is always after my dick.

It must be that my mind is fuckin' elsewhere. Kingston. It's hard not to remain pissed off at the guy who was responsible for your girlfriend's death. If he'd been paying fucking attention instead of being so self-absorbed, things could have turned out so differently.

I grunt, threading my fingers through the sorority chick's pretty red tresses and guide her to move a little faster, thrusting my hips and driving my cock to the back of her mouth on each stroke. She makes a garbled noise, and I slide my hand to her throat, where I can totally feel her gagging. *That's more like it.* "If you're not gagging, you're doing it wrong, honey, so be proud."

A twig snaps to the left of the door where everything has been thrown into shadow. My brows raise as first Lennon comes into view, followed by Mason.

Darcy pauses in her efforts, and I give her a cursory glance. "No one told you to stop," I rumble low as I lift my gaze, eyes glued to the approaching pair even when Darcy takes my dick to the back of her throat.

Mason has a hold of Lennon's upper arms, walking her forward until we're only about eight feet apart. He gives me a shit-eating grin. "Look who I caught watching you."

I never quite know whether Mason and I are more friends or enemies, but we know each other so well that it's incredibly easy to pick out exactly what will piss the other off. And yeah. He's figured out that my dick and my brain do not agree when it comes to my stepsister. Asshole seems like he's going to use that to have a little fun tonight. I lift my chin to him in challenge, giving him a very defiant *Come at me, bro.*

I run my hand through Darcy's hair again, fisting a section of it at the back of her head. Rocking forward into her waiting mouth, I bite out a curse. But it has nothing to do with her and *everything* to do with the way Lennon's lips have parted as she watches us.

Lennon sucks in a breath, her chest rising with it, eyes pinned on me as if they're being held hostage. The shade of rosy pink that her cheeks have taken on almost has me nutting immediately because I can imagine the color on her face is a pretty good indication of her state of arousal. She was getting off on watching me from over there in the shadows. It sure will be fun to taunt her with that bit of information at a later date. But right now, I'm far more interested in whatever is in Mason's head because I imagine it's all kinds of twisted and fucked-up.

My gaze flicks to him, and his expression is an even split between pure mischief and unadulterated lust. His hands slide up to Lennon's shoulders, then dip down the front of her body, skimming her collarbones. She shivers involuntarily, her eyes crashing shut for a moment, as if she's overwhelmed. But with what? Desire or the need to run?

She's wearing this fuckhot bra under a gauzy top; the

bra is sorta like the one she'd shown every fucking brother in the house last night. There's a certain term for it, but I can't recall what it is, plus I don't really care. It's lacy and sexy and definitely nothing my mother or grandmother would ever wear.

My brain does a quick jog of my memory from last night, picking right up from the moment she'd torn her T-shirt over her head and flung it at me. That bold move had left her in nothing but the lace contraption that hardly held her tits. Yep, I don't give a fuck if I'm her stepbrother. She shows off a rack like that, I'm looking. The sheer top she's wearing has three ties holding it together, and that's all that's stopping my prying eyes from seeing everything underneath. I grit my teeth, watching Mason's hand drift between her breasts to one of the ties.

He gives a little tug to loosen it ... and my dick jumps as the bow comes undone. She gasps aloud at the same time. The odd thing is that she's still more covered than she was last night, but there's something mesmerizing about Mason undressing Lennon in front of me while another girl is choking on my dick.

It also fills me with this odd, lust-filled rage. He's touching her. Not me.

Gah! Fuck! He's totally aware of the thoughts in my head, his amused expression definitely reading *You can look, but you can't ever touch, big bro.* He smirks at the agonized confusion on my face, whispering again in her ear, his lips brushing the shell and making her shiver.

I'm dying to know what he's saying to her. Her face flushes a deeper color of pink, and she leans back into his chest, almost as if she's grounding herself, waiting with hooded eyes to see what happens next. She can flash those doe eyes at me all she wants, but I know better. I fuckin' do. She's letting him do this on purpose. Goddammit, right now I don't give a fuck.

"More? Should I keep going?" Mason's voice hits me square in the chest, almost as if he's reading my mind. His fingers trail downward, toying with the strings of the middle tie. He knows damn well I won't answer, but I swallow convulsively at the sight of her shirt falling farther open. My dick is harder than a rock, and it has nothing at all to do with the girl sucking it and everything to do with the one eight feet from me, burning me alive with the hungry look in her eyes—they're wild and completely focused on me.

Mason gives the last string a pull, and Lennon's shirt falls wide open, the bra top that was peeking out naughtily just moments before now on full, brazen display. She makes no move to cover herself, like she's trapped in the moment, thunderstruck by what she's allowing to happen. But it's giving her a rush. I see it written in the needy expression on her face and in the way her chest is rising and falling with each labored, wanton breath.

I'm totally not expecting what Mason does next. With a twinkle in his eye, he draws the fabric at the sides of her shirt back, trapping her arms behind her, and if I'm not mistaken, he's made a knot of them.

I have the most tantalizing view of her breasts jutting from her chest as her back bows.

"What are you doing?" she finally heaves out, a moment of panic crossing her face.

With her arms trapped between them, Mason's hands drift up, cupping her full tits, tweaking her nipples through the lacy fabric. "She's got perfect handfuls, man. Big enough to fuck." She whimpers at his words, and it causes a chain reaction all the way over here. I don't look down or give Darcy the slightest warning. The orgasm rips down my spine in a flash, and I pump cum down her throat like it's spurting from a fire hose. It's fucking glorious. After a few deep breaths, I remove myself from her mouth and tuck myself back in my pants.

Darcy's stunned or something, but she's nothing if not pliable, willing to do anything I ask of her. I bend at the waist and grasp her chin before whispering, "Good girl. Now, go on back inside."

She wets her lips, a grin stretching her pink cheeks.

"Thanks, Duke." She stands, albeit on shaky legs, and begins to turn her head, obviously looking around for the other parties involved, but Mason has walked Lennon over toward the firepit, her body blocked from view by his. I'm surprised that he's concerned about our fourth wheel at all, but I'd prefer Darcy doesn't get the chance to ask questions.

"Take off, Darcy. That way." I point and nudge her toward the house.

"See ya!" She waves, weaving a bit as she gets to the patio door.

I wait until she's reentered the party to head over to join Mason and Lennon. Now that the extra player in this little bit of debauchery has left us, I have a few questions of my own. I stride purposefully over to them, rounding the pair and coming to a stop directly in front of Lennon.

Her eyes widen when she sees me, arms straining against her makeshift bonds. "Okay, that was kinda hot, but I'm done now."

I cock my head to the side. "I dunno, Mason. Do you think we're done?"

He shakes his head. "Nah. Not necessarily."

I wet my lips. "Did you like watching me, Lennon?"

"No," she hisses, looking back toward the house for the first time since this started.

Mason dips his head down beside hers and whispers something in her ear.

She cringes. "I-I don't know."

"Sure you do. Answer the question, baby sis, and we're done, just like earlier." As he makes his demand, her body visibly shivers in his hold.

My curiosity is piqued. "What'd you just ask her?"

Mason slides his palms up and down her arms, then gives them a squeeze. "I asked why she was lying because she obviously did like watching. In fact, I bet her panties are soaked." His lips twitch into a smirk. "Then again, she's only wearing a tiny scrap of lace today, so it wouldn't take much."

"Mason." She huffs out his name like she wants to spin around and punch him, but unfortunately for her, he's still got her arms caught behind her back. "Let me go. Right now." She presses her full lips together, staring stonily at me.

He thinks about it for a moment, then murmurs. "Okay, but only because I want to. You're not in charge here. Not by a fuckin' long shot." While he's busy releasing her, I can't help but wonder how he's aware of what underwear she has on today. But even more, I want to dip my fingers inside them and find out if she's wet for me. Though it may have been him touching her, the connection she had was with me.

But I can't do what I want. I have to rein myself all the fucking way back in now, because I'd be risking way too much if she ever knew I'm dying to fuck her. I can't let her play me the way her mother does my father.

"There's an easy answer to your question, Mason." My lip curls as I look at her, going for what I know hurts her. "She lied because she's a lying little whore. It's what she does. Just like her mama."

TEN

LENNON

Shoving away from both Mason and Duke, my face flames with embarrassment. How fucking dare they? *Fuck this.* I run blindly, tearing back into the house while clutching my shirt closed. I don't know where to go, but I need to cool down, both literally and figuratively. I dash into the kitchen where there are far fewer people and stand in front of the sink.

I've had a few too many, and I know it. It's fucking hot in this frat house, and the dancing made me thirsty, so I drank. And then I needed fresh air, and that's how I got myself into the awkward position with Duke and Mason in the first place. My head is definitely still swimming, though I can't tell how much of what I'm feeling is undiluted *shame*.

I have no idea how long I stood like a complete

creeper in the shadows, watching my stepbrother get his knob polished by that sorority girl. And the next thing I knew, Mason was at my back, quietly asking whether I thought Duke would ever come because he looked bored out of his mind. I remember the silky, seductive words he'd whispered in my ear that'd been like an unexpected flame licking between my legs. "Maybe we should help him out." And then ... yeah, things went haywire from there, and I don't even know when it went from *this is wrong* to *Oh god, yes*. Because between Duke's desire-filled eyes on me and Mason's hands slowly undressing me, along with more dirty whispered words, things had gotten confusing real fast.

I'd like to splash water on my face, but the last thing I need is to walk out of here with mascara running down my cheeks, like they upset me so much that I cried. Not happening. This morning had definitely been an anomaly, and I'd been so embarrassed to let Bear see my tears. At least it'd felt warranted. But this? I've been through too much for something like this to bring me to tears.

Ignoring the other people moving around me, I sweep my hair up and pull it off my neck. With no hair tie handy, I knot the long length carefully at the back of my head. After that, I run my hands under some cold water, chilling them, and then hold them to the exposed skin where Mason had touched me with his rough fingers and where Duke's hot eyes had blazed a path. I repeat the process a few times in an attempt to cool myself off but seeing as how it's not working like I'd hoped, I doubt the real problem is the Georgia heat or the alcohol buzzing through my system.

Humiliation. That's all this is. I'm burning with it. *That's it, girl. Keep talking in circles around the real issue at hand. You're mad because you wanted what they were doing to you, and they made you look like a fool.*

"Are you okay?"

I nearly jump out of my skin at the quiet words. *Um. Oh, fuck I don't want to talk about this.* I turn my head toward the owner of the voice. It's a brown-haired guy of average height and equally average looks. But he seems concerned, so I throw out a casual, "Oh, hey. Sorry. I got a little overheated." And I'm pissed at Mason and Duke, but there's no need to explain all that to this perfectly nice guy.

He fidgets for a moment, then jerks a thumb over his shoulder. "I have bottled water. In my room. If you want some, I mean. I think people have already gone through what we bought for the party." He clears his throat as he discreetly attempts to look me up and down. "I'm Chris, by the way."

Uh-oh. Okay, maybe I was mistaken about him being a nice guy because he sure doesn't disguise what he's after so well. Too bad for him, but I've already had a night of it, and I don't need his shit piled on top. But maybe I can extract myself from this situation without leveling more damage on myself tonight. "Oh, that's okay. I should get going." I wrinkle my nose and shrug apologetically, though if I'm reading this dickwad right, I definitely don't owe him a damn thing.

He shoots me a placating smile like I'm some dumb little lamb who's going to follow him to his bedroom. "Oh, come on, honey. Come hang out with me. I promise it'll be a good time."

I shake my head, bristling at his tone, but give him a firmer answer. "No, thank you."

He frowns, his forehead creasing. Finally, he leans a hip against the counter, then points at the various liquor bottles scattered about. "I'm a mean bartender. Would you prefer another drink, instead?"

"No. In fact, I think I'm done here. To be clear, *we're* done here." I move to step around him, but he shifts at the same time. My eyes flick up to his and register a glint there. "That was a total dick move." Not liking the way his eyeballs are all over me, my jaw sets, and I try yet again to maneuver around him.

When he blocks me a second time and grabs my forearm, I see red. He pulls me in close, putting his other hand on my waist. Adrenaline shoots through me. This is a fight-or-flight occasion ... and his steel grip on my arm has taken away my ability to flee.

Fight it is, fucker.

"I don't fucking think so, you asshole." I stomp down on his foot with my heeled sandal, wrench my arm free as he howls and loosens his grip, then rear back and drive my fist into his cheek.

I've never hit anyone like that before. *Fuck.* It hurt. But I shake it off, my eyes widening at the dangerous fury coating his features.

"What the fuck!" He's garnering way too much attention for my liking, so I push past him to get the fuck out of Dodge. My eyes dart left and right, only I can't escape the kitchen area because people are pushing closer to see what all the noise is about. "That bitch stepped on my foot and punched me!"

I glance back over my shoulder to see him pointing at me while holding his cheek. He's fuming mad, but then again, so am I. Taking a menacing step toward him, my jaw clenches hard. "I didn't do anything you didn't deserve."

"You little bitch, you think you can waltz in here like it's your right. I know your type. Think you're better than everyone else, coming in here with the Bainbridge boys. Wake up, you're their *whore*. You're less than *nothing*."

MASON

My next intake of air gets caught in my throat because that's exactly what Duke called me. It makes me wonder if they've been talking to people about me, and I'm just this huge fucking joke to them. Who *is* this asshole? I'm a half second from lunging at the guy to claw his horrible eyes out when I'm grasped around the middle from behind. I gasp and begin to struggle, unable to see who it is that has me subdued.

Next to my ear, whoever it is rasps, "Stop fighting. We're outta here, Little Gazelle." I practically sag with relief, allowing Bear to drag me backward out of the kitchen. My eyes widen as Duke and Mason shove people out of the way in a frenzy. Their eyes both lock on me, and, strangely enough, there's concern oozing from them, which is totally fucking confusing to me.

I must be mistaken. Bear doesn't give me a chance to figure it out, though, bodily hauling me toward the exit. I catch a glimpse of Mason with that guy's shirt clenched in his fist, pulling him close to the two of them, so they can deliver … a warning? A threat? Fuck, could it be a *thank you for putting her in her place?*

Assholes. For all I know, that guy is their friend. But then something a little wild happens. Duke's raised voice reaches all the way to the front hall where Bear is ready to tear open the door and take me outside. "What the actual *fuck* did you just say to my *stepsister?*"

Bear pauses, possibly as surprised as I am. Mason's gravelly anger-filled voice follows directly after Duke's. "Bad move, you fucking douche."

The sick sounds of flesh meeting flesh and bone crunching makes me cringe. Bear doesn't hesitate any longer than that. We exit the house, and to my mortification, he refuses to put me down, carrying me all the way past the line of people still waiting to get into the party. I struggle.

"Stop kicking, or I'll throw you over my shoulder again."

"Put me down, dammit," I growl. "There's nothing wrong with my legs. I can walk."

He halts, dropping me to my feet. The impact is jarring, and frankly, I'm a little in shock that he actually did as I requested. Irritation marring his rather handsome face, he reaches out, swiftly tugging the fabric of my shirt into place, and makes quick work of tying the strings into bows down my abdomen, covering me up. When he's done, his tongue flicks out, skimming his lower lip. I can tell he's trying to decide what to say to me. A moment later, he grips my chin in his hand, forcing my gaze to his. "Lennon, you should probably not snap at the only person who has been halfway decent to you since you arrived at KU."

I blink a few times, trying to process. He's pissed.

And I suppose he has reason to be, but dammit, I'm upset, so I don't know how he expected me to react.

While I'm busy ruminating on my misstep with him, he grasps my forearm, and I try to yank it back, but he doesn't let go. He's way too strong. "Lennon, let me have a look, you've clearly injured it." I actually hadn't realized I'd been cradling my arm against me. Now that he's pointed it out, pain radiates from my hand all the way up my forearm. The adrenaline high of the moment must be wearing off. But still, I don't want him to look. I manage shit like this on my own all the time. Bigger things. I tug my arm toward me.

He spears me with a gaze that leaves no room for argument. He wants my cooperation, and he wants it right fucking now. "Would you stop fuckin' fighting me for a sec?" His deep voice rumbles out and rams me square in the solar plexus. "Oh, shit, you really did hit him." Running his thumb over my swelling knuckles, he lets out a heavy sigh.

I stare up into his gold-flecked eyes, unsure if his comment is a question or not. Nervous that he's going to yell at me, I gnaw hard on the inside of my cheek. My heart rate escalates until I feel like my chest is going to explode.

It's possible he senses my distress because a low grunt erupts from him, a muscle at the back of his scruffy jaw twitching. "I'll look more closely when we get home. Someday, when I think you won't use it against me, I'll teach you how to properly hit someone, so you don't hurt yourself like this again."

From behind me, the sound of footsteps and a verbal sparring match meets my ears. Duke grumbles, "As if she could have done him that much damage. She's like one-twenty, soaking wet."

"He was being a pussy," Mason bites out. "And it worked against him. If he'd kept his mouth shut, I wouldn't have felt the need to pound on him. And as for what he was up to—as if Lennon would fall for that shit. She's too ... I dunno ... worldly for that."

My lungs seize, and I hold my breath for several seconds. I don't know quite how to take what he said, but I suppose he's not wrong. I've seen some shit. Made some really bad mistakes. I glance down, scuffing the toe of my sandal on the ground.

Bear gestures that I should turn around, and when I do, he places a hand on my shoulder, squeezing ... even though mere minutes ago, he seemed irritated with me.

"I see you got dressed." Duke shoots me a teasing wink that I don't know how to respond to, especially since his fists are covered in blood. My gaze slides to Mason, who is even worse off, blood covering his hands and splattered over his shirt. He even has speckles on his neck and under his chin.

Except. *Shit.* I don't think any of the blood is theirs.

"Her hand is pretty banged up. Can we save the asshole act for later?"

Duke glowers at Bear, which is unnerving, considering I thought they were sorta close, but he steps closer, eyeing my hand. "Yeah. Looks like we could all use a little ice."

Mason snorts, "Kinda funny that the only one who didn't get into it tonight is our brawler." He's still chuckling as he walks over to the SUV and opens the door. "Let's go, Mighty Mouse." He makes a grand, swooping gesture in the direction of the open SUV door, and damn if the playful look on his face isn't disturbing, considering he's got blood splatter all over him.

My brow furrows, brain clicking back to what he said about Bear a moment ago. I glance at each of the trio as I climb into the waiting seat, but no one says another word about it. Maybe Bear used to get in trouble for fighting in high school or something. These guys all had to have gone to Kingston Academy. They'd have been a year ahead of Juliette. Two years ahead of me, but, of course, it was public schooling for me, I didn't have a chance in hell of attending an exclusive school like that.

Luckily no one says jack shit on the way home,

because I simply can't have one more curveball thrown my way. If this is how my life is going to be living with these guys, I'm in serious trouble because the twists and turns on top of mood swings and other assorted craziness are close to doing me in already. I can't anticipate a damn thing they're going to do.

The scary part is—I think they like it that way. And even scarier, I might like it, too.

ELEVEN

MASON

Dark, black water sluices from my hands and down my bathroom sink's drain. Sometimes, it's really damn hard to remove the stain of it from my hands after a full night of getting out my demons. I use black charcoal almost exclusively for my artwork, and it can get messy.

Fuck color. Why use it when the black expresses so clearly what's in my heart and in my mind?

When I'm as clean as I'm going to get, I lean down and splash some water over my face, then run my hands through the longer hair on top of my head. Righting myself, I rub them through the dark strands as I stare at my reflection in the mirror. After seeing Lennon practically naked yesterday, there'd been no doubt in my mind that I want to touch her. To fuck her. And now that I've felt the weight of her tits in my hands and how perfectly her nipples respond, the desire has amplified to a fever pitch. Her quick intake of breath with every dirty word and idea I'd whispered in her ear had nearly sent me over the edge.

See, baby sis? Big bro totally wants to put that massive dick of his into your wet little cunt. It's drenched just thinking about him, isn't it? Or maybe ... maybe we should make him watch us. Pretend like we aren't aware he's there. I'd breathed hot and heavy near her ear before I'd finally rasped out, "Before long, I'm going to know every fucking filthy thing that turns you on."

So, yeah, I want her, no denying it. But I'm not the only fucker who wants her either, and I do think the other two simply refuse to accept the truth.

Duke wants to bang his stepsister so bad, it's not funny. I don't know if it's obvious to everyone, but fuck. The longing in his eyes gives him away. If it ever happens, I will fucking cheer him on because way to flout society's conventions. It's really too bad for him that there's not a chance in hell she'd go there after he called her a whore last night to her face.

And Bear. Fuck, when we got back to the house, it'd been so fucking obvious that somehow she has this big dude wrapped around her finger. Or hell, maybe it's merely that he's had his hands on her multiple times since she can't seem to stay the fuck put and keep herself out of trouble. I don't know whether he'd have been pissed off at us for the stunt we pulled with her at the party or if he'd have joined in. Hard to tell with Bear, sometimes.

Last night after we got back and everyone was settled, I'd lost track of time, one image after another flowing from the charcoal and onto the paper. When I looked up, it'd been almost noon, sunlight shining through the circular window, and the temperature rising in the small space. As usual, I'd had no fucking control over what I drew, and it certainly came as no surprise that most of the subjects were Lennon. At least I think they were—because the part that freaks me out is how close in nature they are to some of my other work. That'd sent me running for the john really fucking fast and vomiting up the vodka I'd been drinking.

I need to find a way to keep what Bear told me at the forefront of my mind: Lennon is *not* her, no matter how my head twists it. Fucking aggravating that her presence makes me feel like more of a crazy person than I already am. And it's equally irritating that I don't seem to care. I want my hands on her again, fuck all the consequences and ramifications. She's the most infuriating, sass-mouthed bitch sometimes, and I admit it—I fucking love seeing her stand up to us. She challenges me like no one else ever has.

I wander from my room down the stairs and directly to the kitchen, running a hand over my chest as I attempt to squelch the confusion in my head. Lennon glances up from the kitchen island where she's assembling some sort of—what the fuck are they called?—wrap. Like a sandwich but rolled up in a tortilla. "How's the hand?" I don't have a goddamn clue where I stand with this girl after yesterday, so I'm going to choose to skirt the things I did that I know have upset her.

"Bruised. But I can obviously use it. I'm fine. Thanks for your concern." Her tone is clipped and unfriendly. But then, she glances at me, and it doesn't take more than thirty seconds of my eyes on her to see the flush rising from her chest, up her neck, all the damn way to her cheeks.

I raise a brow, waiting for her to meet my gaze again.

She deftly rolls the tortilla, then picks up the serrated knife and cuts the wrap into three pieces. Without looking up, she murmurs, "Did you need something?"

"Don't know. But every time I turn around, it seems like you do."

Her eyes flick to mine, and she wets her lips, eyeing me carefully. "You know, I'm beginning to understand you. I thought about you last night. A lot. Even considered trying to talk to you, but you weren't in your room." She shrugs. "But in the light of day, I realize what a dumb thing it would be for me to try to get inside someone's head who is as fucked-up as I think you are. And that's based on one single day's worth of interactions. Whether you prove me right or wrong, I'm going to find it intriguing either way."

"And Duke? Were you thinking about him, too?"

She doesn't even flinch at the mention of him, even though I'm aware how it turned her on to watch him get his cock sucked last night. She glances up at me after she moves her wrap to a plate. "My stepbrother has a whole slew of issues of his own. Some have to do with me. Others, not so much. I'm seeing that now." She shrugs, opening a bag of potato chips and puts some on her plate before closing the bag with a clip.

I silently watch as she moves around the kitchen, putting away everything she'd been using to assemble her lunch. Then she picks up the plate and a napkin from the counter, tucks her bottle of water at her elbow, and walks away.

Well, fuck. I find her intriguing, too. And she can study me all she wants but there's no figuring out what's in my head.

A moment later, Duke's voice carries to me. "Did you need something?"

Lennon clears her throat. "Yes, I wanted to ask—"

But before Lennon can finish, Duke laughs. "Wait,

wait, wait. What's that on your neck, Stella? Hickeys? When did *that* happen?"

My brow darts up. *Shit.* In a few quick strides, I join Bear and Duke at the table, pulling out a chair and sitting down. Fortunately, the rest of the brotherhood must already be out of the house. Bear catches my eye and tilts his head to the side. He thinks I should say something. I give a slight jerk of my head, narrowing my eyes. I want to see what she does. Calmly, I cross my arms. I don't have a fucking clue how this will play out, but there you have it.

Lennon draws in a breath, reaching up to touch the marks I'd left on her skin—not the ones in charcoal, but the ones I'd inflicted in a furious fit of rage with the pressure of my fingers alone. Her gaze slides to mine, ever so briefly.

"It's nothing. I wanted to as—"

"Not so fast." Duke's eyes glint as they focus hard on her. "You see, I asked you a question. And we ask very little of grunts—or stepsisters we're forced to babysit. Obedience, loyalty, and keeping your mouth shut. That's it. Now, did you misunderstand the third demand? Because it definitely doesn't mean keep your mouth shut when you've been told to give an answer." He lets out a beleaguered breath when she chooses to stand stiffly, staring off somewhere over his head. "Lennon, tell me who put these marks on you."

She draws in a breath but presses her lips together. Ah, hell. She's going to refuse to say a fucking word, which is only going to piss him off even worse. My brows knit together. Interesting that she'd do that.

Duke jumps out of his seat across the table from us. His chair skids backward, teeters, and falls over with a crash. "Come here." He points to the space on the floor directly in front of him.

My jaw twitches. She'll say something. I know she will. Surely, she will.

Bear shoots me a wary glance, then grips the back of his neck with both hands. "Lennon. Just tell him."

She walks around the table, coming to a stop in front of Duke. "No." He's formidable—lean, but muscular in all the right places, even years after he quit playing football following Juliette's suicide. He could have just let himself get soft, but he definitely hasn't.

Duke steps closer to her, but surprisingly, Lennon doesn't flinch, even when the way he's crowding her body has her arching her back just to be able to look him in the eye. He tilts his head to the side, like a snake ready to strike. "I'm sorry, what?"

She shrugs. "Go ahead. Do whatever it is you think you need to do, Duke. I don't care."

He grasps the braid at the back of her neck, using it to elongate her neck for a better look. Getting close, he studies the delicate skin, marred by scattered bruises. Definitely not hickeys. *Why won't she just say so? Why doesn't she lay the blame at my feet? It's what I'm expecting. It's probably what I deserve.*

My eyes crash shut. I don't open them when I confess, "I did it." A heavy breath gusts from between my lips, but for a moment no one moves a single millimeter. The tension among the four of us is palpable.

"What happened, Mason?" Duke hasn't taken his eyes from her neck, but I know damn well he's waiting for an answer. I can see from here—and I'm positive he sees it, too—the marks don't look like any simple hickeys.

My jaw works itself to the side and several breaths wrench themselves painfully from my chest before I can even think about spitting it out. "Yesterday morning. Early. I wasn't—" The words stick in my throat. "I wasn't in my right mind." Shame fills me, making my face hot. Now that the lighting is right, I see it. I've left marks all over her. And she wasn't going to say a fucking word, even when questioned about it.

Duke turns toward me. "Is that right?"

I stare stonily ahead of me, and the silence is so fucking awkward, Bear finally steps in with a sigh. Like he always does. "It's the truth. I told you he attacked her. This is what I was talking about." He stands up. "You should let go of her. This isn't her fault. She was in the wrong place at the wrong time. Period." He pauses, and when there's no action taken from any party in the room, he grunts out, *"Duke.* Let her go."

I see it the moment Bear gets through to him. His hand loosens, and he takes a step back, his jaw tight.

But Lennon ... she looks almost angry. *At me? At Duke? At the world?* Who the fuck knows with her. My eyes flick to hers, and she stares boldly at me. I dampen my lips before murmuring, "Spit it out, baby sis."

"I. Don't. Understand." Her jaw clenches hard as her eyes scan over each of us in turn. "I'm missing a set of rules or something because I've never been so fucking confused in my entire life. One minute you attack me, the next you taunt me, and then you defend me." She clenches and flexes her swollen hand involuntarily. "You already think the worst of me. But you don't fucking *know* me at all." Her brow pinches. "How am I supposed to deal with any of you? I just—" Her voice catches, then exasperation spills from her. "Fuck off. I don't need this. All I wanted was something to eat and to know what the hell I'm supposed to do to get ready for the first day of classes tomorrow. Everything else you've subjected me to, the way you treat me, the false accusations, the snide assumptions, the sly teasing—it's all bullshit. But I won't let it faze me. Do your worst, boys." She snatches her plate of food off the table and darts away, and not one of us tries to stop her.

I wait, making sure she's far enough from the dining room that she won't overhear me. I jab my finger on the table, emphasizing my words. "I didn't want her in that room, and you both know it. You saw the look on my face when you told her where she'd be staying. You fuckin' know why it's no good. Day one with her, I can't tell if I'm awake or dreaming or in the middle of a goddamn nightmare—and I see her out there. And bam. Fuckin' bam, I let loose. I lose myself." Agitated, I scrub my hands through my hair, then tug at the strands as my chest heaves. "Not my fuckin' fault. It's not." I grit my teeth and hiss, "But it is." Pain slashes at my heavy, wounded heart. "What the fuck is wrong with me?"

Bear bristles, shuffling on his feet. "Look, I've gotta get ready for tonight, but here are the straight facts. You didn't mean to do it, but you did physically harm her, and it could have been a shit ton worse. The entire thing was fuckin' traumatic, and I only saw the tail end of it. She's been really fucking cool about it, if you ask me. She could have told everyone and their mother that you fucking freaked out and tried to choke her to death. Can you imagine what would happen if that got out?"

Duke shakes his head. "It'd be a shit show, that's for sure."

Yeah. What it would be is an open invitation for my asshole older brother to show up and remind me of all the ways I'm damaged.

As if the reminders aren't seared into my very being. Punched into my soul.

TWELVE

BEAR

My knuckles hurt like a motherfucker, but that's always the way of it. I grip the steering wheel hard, feeling the sting of a couple split knuckles. I'm bone-weary and exhausted when I pull up at the house. It's late—one in the damn morning—and we've got our first day of classes tomorrow. Do you think my father gives a shit? *No.* Everything continues right on schedule, as usual. Doesn't matter if I'm sick or in the middle of finals or even if Coach Cambridge told us to rest. If my father sets it up, I'm expected to be there. And I'm expected—no, wait, more like it's demanded of me—to fuckin' win.

At least when I checked over our class schedules earlier—even Lennon's—I discovered no one had a class until nine, so at least we can take our time getting out the door. I feel bad that she's so lost and has no idea what's happening with her first day, but she holed up in her room after telling us exactly what she thought about this entire situation during lunch, and I felt it was best to give her the time to herself.

As I pull up the driveway, I note that all lights are off. I told Mason and Duke to stay back tonight, which is an anomaly because they always come to watch me—they're my support system—but I'd been concerned about leaving Lennon alone, even if she didn't want to come out of her room. I doubt any of them spoke to each other the entire time I was out of the house.

I exhale heavily. This is going to be one long-ass year if we have to deal with these two motherfuckers and their inability to communicate effectively or see reason, especially when their issues mix with Lennon's. Stir that shit up, and this brotherhood is set to be obliterated by all of it.

I'm not innocent in this mess, either. I might not be half off my rocker or angry to be saddled with my stepsister, but I have my own problems, and they'll exacerbate *everything*.

I should walk away. No one ever thinks the jock is the smart guy. And if I were wiser, maybe I would, but I can't. Not now. Not anymore.

The idea of leaving Lennon alone to fend for herself

tonight while I was out had been worrisome. Mason and Duke are my friends, sure, but Lennon—that sassy hellcat brings another layer of difficulty and strain into our already delicate friendship balance.

I wish I knew what'd happened among the three of them while I was talking to a few of my football teammates at the party. It'd gotten glossed over when that dickhead Chris tried to put his hands on Lennon and all hell had broken loose. I can't get a good read on any of them, but the vibe in the house has definitely changed.

I let out a hard breath and, slipping from the SUV, I grab my duffel out of the back and sling it over my shoulder, then jog up the steps and let myself in, carefully punching the code into the alarm panel to the side of the door to reset it. Ambling to the kitchen for a bottle of water, I take notice of every sore muscle in my body. If it's this bad now, I'm really going to be feeling it by tomorrow. The overhead light flickers on as I flip the switch.

Movement to my right has me jerking in place. "Jesus."

It takes me a second while my heart is up in my throat to recognize that it's just Warren, probably one of the only decent souls in this place. He's got a tumbler of amber-colored liquid in front of him and a glassy-eyed look that tells me he's three sheets to the wind. He lifts a hand. "Hey."

"What the hell are you doing down here? It's late."

"I know." He groans, and it's a miserable sound. "Maria and I had a, um, a disagreement."

I nod. The girlfriend. *Again.* "That sucks." He and Maria have an argument just about every other week like clockwork. He gets clingy, she gets bored, they fight. She realizes no one else will put up with her shit, he takes her back, clinging to her again. Wash, rinse, repeat. I feel for the guy, but he really should find someone who appreciates him and doesn't get bored with him wanting to spend every waking moment with her. My advice would be to cut ties with her. He can do better, but I'm afraid he won't listen or take it well. "You got an early class tomorrow?"

Warren takes another sip of his drink, moaning with a nod. "Yeah. An eight o'clock. The only thing saving me from banging my head against this counter is that it's actually a class I'll enjoy." He frowns through the haze of alcohol. "What'd you do to your hands?"

I glance down at them. They are a mess. "Happened at practice. No big deal. You should get some sleep. Come on. I'm heading up in a sec, too."

He tips the glass to his lips and roughly swallows the

rest. "Yeah. You're right." Slipping off the stool he'd been sitting on, he wanders back down the hall.

I shake my head. If it's not one thing around here, it's another. Definitely don't need him getting too curious about what I'm up to on a Sunday night. It obviously wasn't football practice, but he's too drunk to care, which is fine with me. I pull a bottle of water from the fridge and follow him. At the top of the stairs, he turns left. His room is the first on the left, sharing a wall with Duke's. Mine's on the other side of Duke's at the very end, across from Lennon's.

I can't fucking wait to fall into bed, though I'll probably read for a bit before my eyes get tired, and I give myself over to sleep.

The quiet padding of bare feet going down the opposite stairwell has my head snapping up. *What the?* I pause on the steps, squinting across the darkened entryway. It's Lennon. I lift my hand in greeting, but she continues down the stairs in some sort of short-and-camisole pajama set. Fuckin' weird that she'd be wandering around at this hour. Maybe she needs something to eat. I don't claim to know her that well yet, but I have the distinct feeling she wouldn't have left her room for dinner with everyone around. Not after this afternoon. She'd been really pissed off. I reach the landing and glance back down to see her stumble a bit, but then keep right on going.

I don't like it.

I jog down the hall to my room, drop my bag and the bottle of water on the bed, and hurriedly strip out of my T-shirt, swiping it over my body and face to remove most of the sweat, grime, and blood from this evening's activities. I drop it on the floor in my haste and hurry back out, heading downstairs. I take them two at a time, then dash down the hall to the kitchen. This time, when I flip on the light, I fully expect to find Lennon here, but instead find it empty. I frown, my concern ratcheting higher with each passing second and each room I duck into.

I feel it in my gut. Something's not right. *Click.* That's the sound made by the latch on the heavy front door disengaging. It has me freezing in place. Everyone knows not to open the door unless they have the code, and she definitely doesn't have the code. Maybe it's someone else coming in that I wasn't aware was out.

Beep. Beep. Beep. The warning tones that our alarm system makes just before it triggers begin to sound. *Beep. Beep. Beep.* My breath hitches in my throat as I run toward the entry, catching sight of Lennon in her sleep shorts and top through the wide-open door as she begins her descent down the stairs from the house. *The fuck!*

She knows damn well she's not supposed to leave the house. Tell me I'm not going to have to chase her ass down again. I suck in a breath and shout, "Lennon! Stop!"

But she doesn't, and the alarm blares before I can get to the panel to disarm it, sending off several blasts of noise into the night. Skidding to a stop, I jab at the numbers with one impatient finger. A large commotion from upstairs tells me the brotherhood has stirred and are in the process of exiting their rooms to find out what the hell is going on.

But watching Lennon, a chill races down my spine. It's as if she doesn't hear a damn thing. The way she's walking without flinching across the asphalt driveway where there are assorted rocks and debris gives me pause. What the hell? That's gotta hurt her bare feet.

Mason and Duke are with Warren, hurtling down the left staircase. Duke grits his teeth and points at the grunts, growling at Warren to make them stay put on the landing. The three sophomores, Kai, Brendan, and Pierre cautiously come partway down the other staircase located closer to their wing and stay there to watch the action. Tucker is the only one missing, and he sleeps like the dead, so I don't expect that motherfucker to make an appearance at all. One time he slept through the mandatory fire drill the university requires us to perform every year.

MASON

I watch all this happen in a flurry, then turn my attention back to Lennon. I follow her, striding quickly across the driveway to the gigantic front lawn.

Mason and Duke burst out the door and fly down the stairs to join me and before I can say a word, there's a hoot of laughter from inside, followed by a "Nice pajamas, sweetheart!" Fairly certain that was Kai, and I'm going to have to kick his ass in the morning. Irritation knits my brow, but I don't have time to worry about it as Lennon continues cutting a path across the lawn.

Duke, clearly not in the best mood after being roused out of a dead sleep, grinds out, "What the hell are you doing? Get her ass back inside." He only pauses briefly before he raises his voice toward Lennon's retreating form and growls, "Lennon, we told you we'd catch you if you fuckin' ran. Whatever stunt you're trying to pull is bullshit."

She's completely unresponsive, showing no outward understanding that any of us are out here with her. *Holy fuck.* That's when it hits me. It's not a stunt at all. She's totally been asleep this entire time. Lennon Bell *sleepwalks.*

I grip Duke's shoulders, pushing him back several steps while frowning hard at him. "Would you chill for a second?" I heave out a breath while digging around in my head for any scrap of information I know about sleepwalkers.

"The hell, man," Duke spits, voice raised with agitation.

I shake my head and hold a finger to my lips, my gaze sliding back to check on the wanderer. I kinda want to see where she's going, but I doubt she has any clue or destination in mind. She's simply walking wherever her feet take her.

Mason eyes me warily. "Ah, fuck. Tell me she isn't—"

I nod, well aware that he's connecting a few dots. I have concerns with how he'll handle knowing this likely isn't the first time she's done this while she's been here, but we can't focus on that right now. "Sleepwalking. She came all the way downstairs. I dumped my stuff off in my room and followed, but I thought she'd gone to the kitchen, so I went there first. She wasn't there, though. The office or the sitting room, maybe? I looked all over." Quietly, I murmur, "The next thing I knew I heard the click of the door opening, followed by those annoying you-forgot-to-punch-in-the-code warning beeps the alarm makes right before it goes off."

"How do you know she's not fucking faking it to get out of here?" Mason's eyes shift between me and Lennon as we walk. I highly doubt he thinks this is the case, and the agitation rolling off him in waves tells me I'm right. More likely he's trying to convince himself that he didn't lay his hands on her when she wasn't conscious. There's a certain horror in his eyes that we don't have time to deal with right now.

"Where the fuck would she be going if she were faking it?" I growl, easily dismissing his question. I know he doesn't need the answer, because he doesn't believe for a second that she's faking—because he's already experienced this with her once before.

Duke tips his chin toward her where she strides slowly in the direction of the wooded area separating our property from the road, completely unaware of the uproar she's caused. "Are you goddamn kidding me? You know the alarm company will contact your fucking dad and mine, both."

A surge of anger hits me, and my forehead creases. "How about we quit worrying about ourselves for two damn seconds and think about what we do if this happens when no one's paying attention? She could hurt herself. We'd be screwed." I scrub a hand through my hair in frustration. "Shit, we're not supposed to wake her up, are we?"

Mason rolls his eyes, pulling his phone from his joggers as we continue to follow her. "Time to Google that shit." Looking down, he quickly taps the question into a search engine. He shakes his head. "It says in most cases, the easiest thing is to guide them back to bed. Quiet voices"—he glances at Duke with the shake of his head—"light touches. No restraining, blocking, grabbing, or awakening them."

I eye them, knowing this is on me, gritting my teeth. "Well, that puts it on me to bring her back in. I'm afraid she'll react poorly to either of you talking to her."

Duke gives me a harsh look. "Why do you even care? Have you appointed yourself her guardian or something?"

My head rears back, surprised by his reaction, but maybe I shouldn't be. The way he looks at her screams of a desire he won't ever let himself give into. He's salty about it, too. "Look, the two of you need to own up to the fact that you've both had less than stellar interactions with her thus far. You know I'm right." I wet my lips. "Get the rest of these jokers back to their rooms so I can bring her in." I don't leave any room for arguing. I turn my back on them and stride across the front lawn to corral my Little Gazelle.

I approach quietly, calming my breathing now that we know what's going on. Part of it, anyway. We have to assume that she sleepwalked onto the balcony the first night. I may have to find a way to stop her from exiting through the front door. The stairs are bad enough. But a goddamn balcony in her room? *Shit.*

"Lennon, let's get you back to bed." I steer her with the lightest touch to make a U-turn. She doesn't seem to notice the change in direction and is quiet the entire walk back up to the house, staring straight ahead of her. Slowly, but surely, I guide her up the stairs with the barest word here and there. It's really fucking weird how her body—her mind?—seems to know exactly where she is at all times, and where she's headed. Not only that, but she seems to have a built-in GPS, avoiding obstacles, like walls and railings. Several times, I peek past the curtain of long blonde hair to find her eyes eerily open, but it's almost as if there's no one there. She doesn't see me, doesn't recognize me. It's weird.

At the landing, she turns left. Mason's and Duke's brows raise almost in unison from their positions against their doorframes. They're like twin sentinels as I lead her past them to her room. She goes right in, climbing into the bed as if this wasn't the strangest occurrence ever. I study her for several moments, unsure if I should leave her or stay to make sure she doesn't get up again. The errant thought that her feet are probably dirty crosses my mind, but we can always wash the sheets in the morning.

She curls up on her side, and I can't help myself. I squat down beside her and reach out with a steady hand to tuck a few strands of hair back from her cheek. She blinks. Once at first, then rapidly. Her breath comes faster as she watches me. Like *really* watches me. I skim my fingertips from her shoulder to elbow over and over again, until she calms. Softly, I whisper, "Lennon, are you awake?"

To my surprise, she murmurs, "Y-yes."

I wince at the stuttered uncertainty. "Are you okay? Do you want me to go?"

She takes one deep breath, then another. "What happened?"

I close my eyes for a moment, glancing down.

"Tell me."

I hesitate but decide there's no way around telling the truth. "You went outside while you were sleeping."

She sucks in a breath. "I opened the door and everything?"

"Yeah, I assume you flipped the lock and walked out. I'd just come in and set the alarm a few minutes before it happened. I saw you on the stairs while I was coming up on the opposite side, and it seemed odd to me, so I went back to check on you."

Her tongue peeks out to dampen her lips. "You came looking for me?"

"Yeah. But I didn't find you before you set off the alarm. You ended up all the way across the lawn."

"Did anyone else see?" Her teeth are clenched together, and even in the dark, the tightness in her features is hard to miss. It makes me want to lie to her. Tell her it was just me and not to worry.

"It was most everyone. Tucker slept through it, but that's not unusual for him. I'm sure someone will fill him in by tomorrow morning, though."

She moans, her hand shaking as her fingertips touch her lips. "Oh my god, I'm so embarrassed."

I grimace, knowing there was quite a bit of laughter and probably more than just the comment I happened to hear about her pajamas. Tomorrow might suck for her in terms of people bringing it up, but I don't know how we get around that. "It's okay. You should try to sleep now, though." I glance at her phone standing in her charger. "We'll leave around eight thirty. Your schedule and books are downstairs."

"Really?"

"Yeah. Dropped off yesterday afternoon. There's some stuff for you to sign from the registrar's office, but you're definitely expected in class tomorrow."

She gives me a relieved smile, but that's immediately knocked from her face by a whole lot of worry, and even a hint of panic. "Will you stay with me?"

I hesitate. "You mean like right now? You sure you want me to?"

"I know I'm being a pain in the ass."

"You're not." I give a sharp jerk of my head. "I just wanted to make sure—"

"Just until I fall asleep. Then you can go." Anxiety flows swiftly through her in a way that makes me incapable of denying her request.

"Yeah, okay." I stand from my crouched position, circle around to the far side of her bed, lift the sheet, and slide in behind her, tucking a pillow under my head. "I'm right here. Sleep, Lennon. Big day tomorrow."

FUCK, it's so good. I inhale the sweet smell of some sort of fruit. Mango, maybe. And coconut. My dick's harder than hell and my balls are heavy with the need to come. Sensation swamps me. I thrust slowly into Lennon's warm, wet pussy, my brain cells scattering to the far ends of the universe. I'm unable to focus on anything but her scent invading my nose, the heat of her body in my arms, and her sinful curves. Everything about this girl makes me want to hold on tight, touch her in all the ways that make her scream and moan. A strangled sound escapes me as I rock into her. Fuck, it's so good.

MASON

But I need to hang on a little longer. I want to hear her call out my name as she finds her release, the walls of her cunt milking my cock with every ripple of her orgasm. My pelvis undulates as I hold her close, groaning out my pleasure with each stroke of my dick into this girl who is damn close to rattling my composure.

THIRTEEN

LENNON

I'm surrounded by heat and warm breath gusting past my cheek. I blink hard, my head a hazy, sleepy mess. Something long and hard nudges between my legs. A set of iron arms encircles me, holding me tightly in place.

Oh, god. It's Bear. A split second after I realize what's happening, his chest heaves at my back, an animalistic groan ripping free from deep inside his body. And that thing that's tucked between my thighs is his very erect cock. He grunts a bit, pulling me close as his body shudders with the force of his orgasm.

"The fuck!" With my heart hammering, I struggle free, almost getting hung up on the sheets, which are a tangled, sorry mess. Catching myself before I fall, I twist free and whirl around, coming face to face with Mason on the other side of my balcony door. The amused glint in his gaze tells me he's more than interested in what he's just witnessed.

One dark, devious brow goes up as Mason mouths, "Next time, tell him to take the joggers off." He catches the corner of his full lower lip between his teeth, pretending to grab someone from behind and thrust his pelvis in an obscene manner. His eyes twinkle with mirth and mischief.

Fuck. For all I know, he assumes Bear and I had sex last night, even if it's obvious we're both fully clothed now. My breath comes out in jerks and starts, then hearing the man with the hard-to-miss morning wood shifting on the bed behind me, I spin around and blurt, "What the fuck?" My arms fling out from my sides in exasperation.

It's possibly the wrong move when I'm wearing a sleep cami that provides zero support because his golden eyes are pinned on my chest where my breasts bounce and my nipples are hard buds behind the lightweight fabric. And while he's staring at me, dammit, I can't seem to stop myself from allowing my eyes to travel swiftly over all his glorious, rippling muscles. He's sculpted from granite, so beautifully made, I have the errant thought that I'd like to run my tongue over all the defined dips and ridges. Follow that trail of hair downward into his pants.

Because, his dick, my god. It's pushing the limits of the gray joggers he'd worn to bed, somehow still hard, even after what'd seemed like a sizable explosion. Because I wasn't imagining things. There's a huge wet patch at the crotch of his pants. He came with his dick wedged between my thighs.

My throat goes dry as the first tingles of arousal make themselves known deep in my core. A glance over my shoulder shows me Mason hasn't stopped his naughty show. Bear quietly watches me—but maybe that's because all the blood in his body has flowed down to his monster cock.

And the hell of it is I don't know whether the inflamed state my body is in has more to do with the sexy tease out on my balcony or the hard dick in my bed. Maybe both. Probably both.

My brain is ready to riot. It's way too early in the morning for this kind of confusion.

Heat floods my cheeks as my heart hammers out of control. "Bear," I huff out, "What the fuck was that?" So freaking weird that I was fine at the party with Mason touching me, but here, with Bear, my heart is tripping all over itself. Maybe it was just the alcohol that loosened me up because I definitely know I'm far safer with Bear than with Mason ... or Duke for that matter. But ... god. Come to think of it, it might be more that at the party I was consciously aware of what was happening. For this, I wasn't. Unable to participate or even give consent. And it scared me.

Agonized, muttered curses tear from his lips, but Bear doesn't answer my question. It could also be that he doesn't know what the fuck that was either.

I glance back out the windows of the balcony door and wish I hadn't. *Duke.* He joins Mason on the balcony, giving him a weird look. "What the fuck are you doing out here?" His question is barely audible through the door, but I hear him nonetheless.

"Just watching our girl in action." Mason juts his chin my direction, and I don't know why I haven't felt the need before, but I cross my arms over my chest, swallowing hard.

My face burns, flames licking at it as Duke's eyes find me. They widen, and his jaw tightens. In two steps he's at the door and throwing it open. "What the fucking fuck, you motherfucker!"

Bear holds his hand out, growling, "I see you're pissed, but can we talk about this some other time when my dick isn't still hard?"

Mason stifles a laugh behind his hand, his expression gleeful. Of course, he would think this is funny. Meanwhile, testosterone is being flung around like confetti, and these two are about to have a pissing match right here in my bedroom.

"Why the hell are you here?" Duke's jaw twitches like mad, his glare focused on Bear.

Bear grits his teeth, sitting up in the bed. "First, did you have a reason for being here, or are you simply in asshole mode today? She doesn't need your crap. We all had a long night."

Eyeing the surly grimace on Duke's face, I hold up a hand. "You don't have to defend me, Bear. If Duke wants to be a dick, he can, but it'll be his funeral because I won't put up with it."

Duke's flinty blue gaze meets mine as he grits out, "What's he doing in your room, Lennon?"

I frown at his audacity, tilting my head to the side and squinting at him because I can't for a second figure out why he thinks this is any of his business at all. *Fucker.* He's got a helluva lot of nerve. "And who are you to say who I allow in my bed? You were told to make sure I went to class and behaved. I must have missed the special clause about you getting to watch me fuck." The blood in my veins heats quickly to the boiling point. My eyes flick to Bear's, catching his surprised expression, but I rush on before any of them can say a word. "I must have missed the memo where *any* of you get to come into my room uninvited. You"—

I jab a finger first at Duke, then at Mason—"and you. Get. Out."

Mason holds his hands up in front of him. "No problem. I'll let you two get back to it. But, Bear, next round? Try to get your dick inside her pussy *before* you come." He gives Bear an obnoxious wink, laughing to himself as he backs out through the open balcony door and disappears from view.

Duke shakes his head, his lips twisting. "I'm hitting the treadmill." He strides quickly to the door, then pauses to toss back, "The incident last night? We're going to need to talk about that, eventually. It put the entire house in an uproar."

Before I can formulate a response, he's down the hall and back in his room, the door slamming behind him like punctuation to his statement.

I turn toward Bear, a tight smile on my face.

Bear's head tilts to the side, studying me, his warm hazel eyes taking in every nuance of my expression. "Lennon—"

I can't handle questions right now, and I know he has some, but also that he's probably going to try to make me feel better about what transpired over the last few minutes ... or maybe make himself feel better about it. I don't know. Either way, I can't go there right now, don't want his kindness because if there is something that *will* break me it's that. So fucking stupid. I shake my head, closing my eyes for a brief second. "Please. It's okay. I'm fine. You and I both know nothing crazy was going on in here. I just, um, I'm going to grab a shower and get dressed. You said to be ready to leave the house at eight thirty?"

He lets out a sigh. "Just so you know, I think you should expect some comments this morning. About last night. Prepare yourself." He climbs from the bed, the hint of a boner still tenting his joggers.

I scoot downstairs at eight. The house is alive and crawling with brothers, which is exactly what I was hoping to avoid. But hell, the problem isn't really who's present now, it's who was present last night—which is pretty much every single person. They're mostly gathered in the kitchen and dining room, and of course, speaking so loudly that it'd be hard to miss a damn word they said. And I'm definitely beginning to learn their voices. It's a good thing, too, because they're talking shit about *me*. I guess Bear knew what he was talking about when he warned me.

"It was freaky." That was that sophomore, Brendan.

His buddy Pierre snickers, "Yeah, but did ya see her outfit?"

"She was asleep, dumbass." That'd be Warren, I think. "Did you expect her to get dressed before she wandered the house and then outside, all while unconscious?" Definitely Warren. I think I like that guy.

There's a cackle, followed by a rude, "I don't fucking care. I was watching from my bedroom once they got her turned back toward the house. And damn, those tits were swinging freely." There's a muffled noise followed by a yelp. "What the fuck. What was that for?" That little asshole Arik is the worst, I swear.

"You know what? If you can't figure it out, maybe we can find some toilets for you to clean. And unlike Duke, who would make you use your own toothbrush, I'll make you use your tongue, motherfucker."

My eyes widen. *Mason.* Defending me? I'd rather not let any of them talk smack behind my back, so I walk in, head held high. "I feel like I'm late to the conversation. Anyone want to give me a recap?" I look around expectantly.

Mason looks pointedly at each of the douchebags who'd had something mouthy to say. "Don't worry about it. They won't be saying another word, will you?"

There's suddenly a whole lot of head shaking, even

from the guys who hadn't said a damn word. I guess no one wants to lick a toilet, and that says a whole lot about what they think about Mason—in particular, what they think he's capable of.

Duke comes into the room behind me. "What's going on?" He scans the group, pointing to Warren. "You. Tell me."

Warren works his jaw back and forth, stalling, but then he finally sighs. "At the risk of sounding like a fuckin' tattle, I'll just say some of these guys had rude things to say about Lennon's sleepwalking incident." He meets my eyes. "Sorry. I hope you're feeling okay today."

I nod. "I'm fine. Thanks."

From somewhere over my shoulder, Duke grits out, "I need for every single one of you to understand something. Lennon is living here at the request of the OG Bastards. So, unless you somehow think you know better than them, I'm going to say maybe you should kindly shut the fuck up and eat your breakfast. It's the first day of class. Be sure you present yourself in a manner that you'd feel comfortable with me, Bear, or Mason finding out about. That's it. Fuckers."

FOURTEEN

DUKE

My phone ringing at this hour can only mean one thing. Frustrated, I hurry from the kitchen down the hall and into the office, closing the door behind me before I tap the screen to accept the call. With no preamble, I mutter, "You have terrible timing. We're heading out the door for our nine o'clock classes."

On the other end of the phone, my father chuckles, the sound of his amusement grating on my nerves. "I don't care what time it is. You should know better than that."

I roll my eyes. I'm well aware that the man couldn't care less about inconveniencing anyone else. But make him wait for you or do something he's not expecting, and all hell breaks loose. "Is this about the alarm? Because—"

"You know it is, son. I've been on the phone with Derek already this morning, and we agreed it was best if I call you."

I'd imagine Bear's father didn't take kindly to being awakened by the alarm company in the middle of the night. Bear might hear about it later ... but possibly not if Derek foisted the whole thing off on my father. "I'd like to know how exactly this is my fault. You know, you could have warned me that Lennon sleepwalks. What else haven't you told me? Can she levitate? Move things with her mind?"

"Very funny. How did she manage to get out of the house?"

"Well, I was asleep when it happened, seeing as how it was the middle of the night, Dad, so ..."

"Don't get smart with me."

I groan inwardly. "Just stating facts." I press my thumb and forefinger each to a closed eye, rubbing. I don't have the time for the interrogation this morning. "I imagine she unlocked the door and walked out. But you know what? I'm guessing you knew that already because I'm sure you've checked the footage from the camera at the front door. Tell me why you're really calling."

There's an odd pause, at the end of which, my father sighs. "Look. This needs to be kept quiet. But if she says or does anything remotely strange, I need to know about it. Immediately."

I grit my teeth, not liking the tone of his voice, but also mildly curious. "What am I looking for?"

"Anything at all. Anything that sounds off the wall or like nonsense. More sleepwalking, talking in her sleep, nightmares ... Her mother is concerned. Lennon has been increasingly difficult since I married Nikki. We were considering having her psychologically evaluated."

I run a hand through my hair, trying to think if there's been a sign that anything seems off with her, but I come up with nothing beyond the obvious trip out of the house last night. "Why the hell didn't you tell me this before?"

"Never mind that. I just need to be kept in the know. We thought a change of scenery would help. But—"

"Yeah. Well, thanks for dumping her in our laps." I clear my throat just as there's a rap on the door. "Sorry, Dad, gotta go. I've gotta take the head case to her first class now." Irritation screams through my veins as I quickly end the call. I can't believe he didn't fucking tell me what's really going on. I'm pissed—no, more like enraged. He could have fucking clued me in. I rake my hand through my hair as another series of raps sounds on the door. "Yeah. Coming." I pull it open to find Bear, Mason, and Lennon waiting for me.

"It's just us. Everyone else left on foot about fifteen minutes ago."

I stoop to pick up a black backpack and hold it out to Lennon, my jaw still twitching with annoyance. "This is yours—your class schedule should be in the front pouch, all your textbooks are in there, an iPad for note-taking, and a paper notebook and pen in case you need it."

Her eyes widen, but then her jaw clenches, and what I believe to be a show of pride crosses her face. She holds the bag to her chest as we exit the house. On the way down the steps, she asks, "How much do I owe you?"

Before I can answer her, Mason huffs out a laugh, shaking his head. "Nothing, I'd imagine. Daddy Valentine is hard at work again, showing everyone how powerful he is."

Already irritated from my conversation with him, I mutter, "Yeah, well, he can do shit like this for his stepdaughter since he's not in prison like your dad."

Bear grumbles, "All right, cut it out."

Lennon clears her throat as we approach the SUV. "Seriously. I want to pay for it." There's a proud tilt to her chin.

I grit my teeth. "He won't let you, so drop it. Consider it a gift. Or hell, an apology for dragging your ass to KU."

She slowly exhales, a scowl on her face mars her forehead with a crease right down the middle. "Whatever. I guess I'll talk to him myself." She turns to Bear—and that fucker gets a smile from her. "Is it far to campus?"

"Nah," Bear says, "we just don't have time this morning to walk it. Not to mention, you'd arrive on campus hot and sticky."

Her nose wrinkles a bit, but those luscious lips of hers stretch into another grin for him, and it makes my stomach twist inside. She let him into her bed. He's had his hands on her. Whether or not they had sex last night, I don't know, but even the idea that he had his dick anywhere near her pussy makes my chest tight. An unfamiliar feeling creeps over my cheeks, leaving a hot, pink stain. Jealousy. I'm fuckin' jealous that both Mason and Bear have touched her. Fresh memories of Mason cupping her breasts and whispering dirty things in her ear and wild imaginings of whatever happened in her bed with Bear—they gut me.

And they fuckin' shouldn't. I shove all of it down and get in the back of the SUV with her.

We haven't gone far when I notice she's focused on something in the front seat, eyes narrowing. I angle my head so I can see what she's looking at. Ah. Yep. Shit. I didn't even ask Bear how things went last night, but I'd wager just like always, he came out on top.

While I'm distracted by my own thoughts, she leans forward, catching his eye in the rearview. "Your knuckles are so swollen. What happened?"

Bear hesitates, but, to his credit, he doesn't flinch and has an answer at the ready. "It's nothing. Just did too many rounds with the punching bag yesterday."

What he's failing to reveal is that his punching bag was a human. I laugh internally as the image of some dude strung from the ceiling being pummeled by Bear's ferocious fists floats into my mind. My eyes flick back over to Lennon as she shifts in her seat, tugging on the mini skirt she's wearing in a way I wish I hadn't noticed. Her thighs on display are fucking distracting. I wrench my eyes away. Fucking hell.

Her brow furrows, but after a few moments, she seems to have accepted him at his word. "Don't forget you promised to show me how to hit someone."

Mason twists in his seat to look back at her. "Funny how you put that."

I side-eye her as her forehead creases with confusion. "What?"

"Most people would just say they want to learn how to throw a punch. Not specifically that they're going to fuckin' hit someone."

"Yeah, well—"

I interrupt with a gruff noise. "I can't say I blame her

MASON

after the Chris incident." I cross my arms and look out the window, away from the three of them. "I approve."

She snorts with derision in a way that seems to say she was *not* looking for my approval, and we ride the rest of the way to campus in silence, each of us lost in our own thoughts.

That is, until I notice Lennon's gaze is glued to the scenery as we enter Kingston University's campus. She's said over and over that she doesn't want to be at KU, that she had other plans. But now—there's a nervous excitement on her face that I don't know quite what to make of because it seems very much in opposition to everything she's said. I clear my throat, then gesture out the window on her side. "That's the football stadium where you'll see Bear play later this week."

She nods. "And that?"

"The gymnasium. It's huge. Lots of gym space, ball courts, weight rooms, locker rooms. Anything the many sports teams of KU might need."

From the front seat, Bear chuckles. "It's my second home."

Mason points up ahead. "You've got a class in that building tomorrow. Cabot Hall. It's whatever history class you have."

"Um. You guys have all seen my schedule? Is there a map or something in here?" Clearly flustered, Lennon begins to scramble for the schedule I'd told her was in her bag.

I reach over to touch her arm, but then quickly withdraw it when her eyes snap to mine. The attitude on her, I swear. If that's the way she wants to play this, fine. "I meant it when I said you won't go anywhere without us. We've reviewed your schedule so we know which of us will take you from each class. You've got three fifty-minute classes today. One of us will meet you after each until you're done. Got it?"

She sucks in an irritated breath. "Yeah. Obey. I've fuckin' got it. I'm not stupid like your grunts." Her eyes meet mine, and even though she's a little thrown this morning by all this, I still see the challenge in her eyes. I might even respect it a little. "You do know I was enrolled in community college, right? I planned to start next week, so I understand how this works. Being *here* at this particular school may have been thrust on me, but I deserve to fucking get my education, no matter what you think and no matter how Tristan bends me to his will."

By the time we park and exit the vehicle, she won't look at me, but the four of us move together along the path to Lennon's first class. Maybe it's better that she's mad at me. At least it's quieted that fuckin' sasshole of hers.

Entering Merriman Hall, we take her all the way to

the door of her lecture hall for the Psych 101 class that she's enrolled in.

She turns, facing the three of us as students mill about the hallway around us, quite a few giving us curious stares. She fidgets with the straps of her backpack. "I guess I should go in."

Mason catches her attention. "You wait for me after class. Right here. No matter what."

"Yes, sir," Lennon barks out with a flippant laugh.

I catch her firmly by the back of the neck, guiding her face to mine. The bold, brazen expression holds steady as she looks into my angry eyes. There's a dare somewhere there, a provocation. But I'll be damned if she's going to cause me to lose it right here in the middle of the hallway. Low and lethal, I grind out, "Don't fuck with me, Lennon."

Her lips twist, a brow arching. "What? Scared Daddy will come lay into you?"

I bristle. "No, but really fuckin' weirded out that you just called my father *Daddy*."

She pauses to consider. "Ugh. Okay, you've got me there." She wrenches free of my hold and backs a step away from us, eyeing me warily.

Frustration leaching from him, Bear grits out, "Jesus. Enough. Class. Now."

Lennon presses her lips together, looking him up

and down. "Watch it, or I'll start calling you Daddy instead." She pivots and saunters into class, leaving us to watch her go, her ass a fucking temptation in that skirt.

Mason subtly readjusts himself before shrugging. "She's like riding a roller coaster without being belted in. Terrifying in an exhilarating fuckin' way."

I grit my teeth, refusing to respond as I inhale sharply through my nose. *Rein. It. In.*

"Fucking hell. You all have her covered today, right?" Bear groans as he rubs a hand over his face.

I nod. Fuck, that messed with my head. "Yeah. Mason's got her after this class, I'll get her after the next two and take her home."

"Thank fuck." Bear shakes his head and storms off.

Mason eyes me, then snorts with laughter. "He totally wants her to call him Daddy, and it's making him crazy." He throws his head back, laughing, and walks off, leaving me to wonder if he's right, but also why it makes me feel unhinged.

PUSHING ASIDE THOUGHTS OF LENNON, I part ways with Mason at the front of the humanities building and head for my own class in the math department building, Harrington Hall. I'm gonna be late, but I don't give a fuck. Professors know better than to say a damn word. They don't want to cross me and definitely not my father.

Sure enough, Professor Kimble is already droning on about the syllabus for the semester when I enter my stats course a while later. I slip into a seat beside a guy I'm fairly certain I recognize as one of the Hawthorne Hall brothers and give him a brisk nod as I pull my iPad out and locate the stylus pen so I can take notes if I need to.

I draw in a breath about twenty minutes in, realizing this guy is literally just reading the syllabus to us. No notes need to be taken, no attention needs to be paid. A waste of a class period in my book, but what do I know?

May as well make it worth my while. I edge closer to this guy, hoping like hell he's not one of Kingston's lapdogs who'll rat me out. Keeping my voice low, I whisper, "Hey. Didn't I see you at the Zeta party Saturday night?"

He nods, and his head of dark curly hair moves with the motion. "Yeah. I was there for a bit. Why?"

I twist my lips, trying to decide the best way to approach this. "I went to high school with Kingston. I thought I saw him with some girl. Totally hot. Know anything about her?"

"Yeah." His beady eyes flick toward me. "She's at Hawthorne Hall."

"Uh." I tilt my head, trying to hide my curiosity. "Do you mean she's living there? Like a girlfriend?"

"No way, man." He leans a little closer to me. "Get this. She's initiating."

"You're shitting me." This dude has loose lips. Fortunately for me, it's helpful. Too bad for Kingston, though, that he has this creep living under his roof to deal with.

"Nope. There was some sort of fuckup." This guy seems oddly excited by this, almost like he's giddy that Kingston fucked up. That means he could totally be useful to me, leading up to the auction event. The trick will be getting him to feed me information when I need it, without him realizing what I'm doing.

"Sounds like it. I can't imagine having to deal with that. Kingston must be furious."

"Eh." He shrugs. "I imagine he'll have her sucking his cock in no time flat if it hasn't happened already. Hell, she'd probably do all three of them. She stripped half-naked for us and danced, night one. It was an epic start to the semester."

My brows raise. Or maybe it won't be so difficult at all to get the info I need because this guy has a serious case of verbal diarrhea. He's making it obvious that

Kingston's boys need a firm lesson on how to keep their fucking mouths shut. But that's not my problem. For my intents and purposes, this guy could be a font of useful information, a way to figure out how to continue to make Kingston pay for what he let happen to my girlfriend.

"What's your name again?"

"Alec." He says with an obnoxious wink.

"Well, thanks for the intel, Alec." And before I'm forced to share my name, Professor Kimble does me a solid and actually starts teaching.

FIFTEEN

LENNON

I'm dead tired after two full days of classes. Living in this house is tricky as hell, too. I'm slowly learning the ins and outs of the place—and more importantly, its occupants. I glance into the kitchen as I walk around looking for a good spot to sit down and get a little work done. Arik and Quincy have settled in together at the small table where we eat our meals, shooting the shit. Those grunts are the ones I have the most contact with, and they are an unfortunate pair. My gaze wanders over them, noting their polar-opposite looks—Quincy, light, and Arik, dark—and realize their personalities duel as well. I don't know whether I prefer the ass kisser or the mouthy ass*hole*. Neither has quite picked up on how things work around here, and they seem to piss off Duke, Bear, and Mason on the regular.

I let my gaze scan over to the living room where all three of the sophomores are causing a ruckus playing some video game on the gigantic TV. That noise is definitely not going to be conducive to the calculus I'll be struggling through in a few minutes. Kai flips his hair out of his eyes. He sticks out like a sore thumb in this house, very skater boy. He's now officially worn the same shirt three days in a row. Seeing as how it's the beginning of the semester, I have to assume he simply prefers to wear things over and over for the sake of comfort since we haven't been here long enough to have to do laundry.

I huff out a laugh, eyeing Pierre as he jumps up, arms in a V for victory. Yesterday, I learned a hard lesson when I went out to the pool patio to look over my notes from the first day of classes and found him there. If that dude's in the pool, I'm turning around and leaving because he'd popped out of there naked as the day he was born. And the thing is, he's got a tiny dick, so I don't know why he was so eager to run around and show it off.

Brendan tosses his controller onto the couch, clearly irritated at having lost. He leans back on the couch, a Twizzler hanging from his mouth. I overheard him tell Arik and Quincy that no one is allowed to eat from the huge candy container in the cabinet. There's a Post-it stuck on it with *Property of Brendan* scrawled across it as a warning to everyone. Little does Brendan know I'm a sugar fiend; it's my only real vice. His Twizzlers aren't my absolute favorite, but they aren't safe from me by a long shot. I ate three just to spite him, and then watched him shout because someone had been into them.

I choose my seat carefully, plunking my backpack down at the far end of the dining room table where I won't bother anyone, then dig around in my bag until I find one of the lollipops I'd thrown in there, unwrap it, and pop it into my mouth. The sweet flavor of cinnamon hits my tongue, and it makes me sigh with pleasure. My favorites are from the Original Gourmet Food Company, but give me a Ring Pop, Tootsie Pop, or even a Dum-Dum, and I'm a fairly happy girl. A wide smile stretches my lips. Heaven help Brendan if he puts lollipops into his stash.

"Motherfucker, this guy gives the most homework out of any fucking prof I've ever had. How the fuck am I supposed to get all this shit done?" Tucker's foul mouth shoots off from the other end of the table, and I wonder if he's doing it to somehow impress his flavor of the day. A cute brunette sits next to him. I bet she's unaware that she's the third girl he's invited over in a very short amount of time, though he seems pretty proud of that fact. To each his own. Are these girls simply so desperate for the attention of a Bainbridge guy that they don't care?

I frown, looking around for Warren, but see him nowhere. He has a girlfriend that he spends ninety-nine percent of his time with, but it's mostly at her place. It's really too bad he's not around more often, because out of all the guys here that I have to deal with, I like him best. He doesn't treat me like I shouldn't be here—and if the rest of them paid attention, they'd know it's Tristan who has demanded that I live in this house while attending KU. Because apparently, I need a babysitter? What the fuck ever.

I let out a sigh. Even though they're nowhere to be found either, I let my brain wander to Duke, Mason, and Bear, who are in a completely different league than the rest of these guys. Living here with them has thrown me for a loop. Every interaction pulls me deeper into their world, makes me more curious as to who they really are beyond Bainbridge royalty, sons of the founding brothers.

I slip a pair of cheap earbuds in my ears, then plug them into my phone, and pull up an instrumental playlist. I definitely need something to drown out the surrounding chaos, but I can't concentrate if the music has actual lyrics—mostly because I'll start singing, and then it's all over because when I sing, I want to dance, too. Definitely don't need to be doing that in front of all these dudes.

I have a bunch of reading to do for my English lit, psychology, biology, and history classes, then some complicated calculus, which I know is going to give me issues. It's supposed to be a review, but seeing as how I didn't do so hot in precalculus in high school, *and* I've had a year's gap between then and being ready to attend college, it's definitely going to be a pain in my ass.

I'm midway through the third of eight heinous math problems when I spy Duke at the kitchen counter out of the corner of my eye. His hip is propped against the granite and his elbow rests on top of a huge box that he must have brought in there with him. I make a snap decision to ignore him, holding the lollipop stick in one hand and a pencil in the other as I try to focus on whatever the hell I'm supposed to be solving for. I tap the sticky piece of candy against my lips as I think, then once I'm fairly certain I know what the logical progression of steps should be, I pop it fully into my mouth, sucking on it as I begin to work through the problem. Limits. Vectors. Bunch of BS if you ask me, but whatever. Gotta knock out these liberal studies credits so I can move onto whatever I decide I'd actually like to focus on. And right now, I'm kinda clueless.

After a few moments, I feel eyes on me, and when I look up, I realize it's still Duke. And he hasn't moved an inch.

"Stella Bella, I have a little something for you." He's got an odd look on his face, which I'd swear was nerves if I didn't know better. He brings the box with him to the table and sets it down in front of me. "I thought you could use these."

Movement from the doorway to the kitchen snags my attention. Arik and Quincy are definitely paying attention, as is Tucker at the other end of the table. And from the lift of their brows, they're definitely interested in what's going on between Duke and me.

With a sigh, I look up into his bold blue eyes, trying to discern what the fuck he's referring to that he thinks I need. I'm already annoyed that he forced me to accept a freaking iPad and all my textbooks from his dad. I remove the lollipop from my mouth, squinting at him. "What are you talking about?"

"Clothes. You only came with one suitcase, so I rounded up a bunch of stuff for you." His eyes appraise every inch of my body, and his tongue slicks over his lip. "I think I guessed the sizes correctly."

My gaze bounces from his careful expression—that I can't make heads or tails of—to the large cardboard box sitting in front of me. Blood rushes to my cheeks. "Duke," I heave out, "no matter what you think, I'm not your fucking charity case. I don't want clothes that your girlfriends have accidentally left behind." My eyes flash with fire. "I've been pretty clear—I don't need *or want* a goddamn thing from you."

From the other end of the table, fucking Tucker's laugh is stifled but audible.

Duke's mouth drops open. "It's not—"

"You can fuckin' save it. I don't want to hear another word." Flustered, I stand up and begin to grab my stuff so that I can extract myself from this humiliation, when he puts his hand directly on top of my notebook and calculus textbook. "Duke, stop it." I try to swat his hand away, but he's unmoving—a heaving, angry animal with flashing eyes.

"Why, so you can leave without listening to what I'm trying to tell you?"

"Get it through your thick skull. I don't want donations from your *whores.*" I push back from the table, getting up from the chair and stepping away from him. "But you know what? Fine. This is ridiculous. I'm going upstairs. Be an asshole if that's what helps you sleep at night." I rush through the kitchen past Arik and Quincy before Duke launches his parting shot.

"Too bad we can't get *you* to stay in your bed and sleep at night."

I feel the sting of his verbal slap and keep right on going.

MASON

Ten minutes later, there's a rap on my door. My face is still hot from the way Duke embarrassed me. I know at least three of the guys were paying avid attention, but it's possible the jerks on the couch were also listening in. "I'm not here. Go away."

There's a deep chuckle from the other side of the door, then a gruff, "I've got your books and things." It's Bear.

I'm partially relieved simply because it's not Duke here to get in my face again, but I'm unsure if I want to invite Bear in. My eyes flick to my bed—the place where he held me and made me feel safe ... but also where we had some questionable accidental relations. We agreed that it meant nothing—or maybe that was me who made that proclamation. Either way, I'm not naive enough to believe thoughts weren't in his head just from the circumstances alone.

I let out a sound, part groan, part sigh, finally relenting. "Okay, fine. Come in."

A moment later, the door swings open and the big guy appears. For a moment, I'm caught up in the way his warm hazel eyes travel up and down my body, which is funny because I'd thrown on a pair of cotton shorts and a slouchy T-shirt that has seen better days when I got up here. I look less than stellar, but the way he's looking at me warms me to my toes.

I drag in a breath. "Sorry, I didn't think I'd see anyone else today. I was kinda just done."

He clears his throat, hiking up the box of clothing Duke tried to pawn off on me. "Yeah, I caught the tail end of the explosion as I was coming in from practice."

"You can put my backpack on the bed. I don't want that other shit." My eyes narrow on the offending slut wardrobe in his arms. The effect it's having on me is unreal. I'm all tensed up, ready for another fight.

"Duke is pretty frustrated. He thought he was doing something nice for you. Kinda taking care of you, in a way? From what he told me, I guess he feels like he was hard on you and was trying to find a way to apologize."

I roll my eyes. "You're kidding, right? We've never been on good terms. *Ever.*"

He turns and drops the box next to my dresser. "Maybe sometime, when you're not quite so worked up about it, you could take a look."

"I really don't see the point." I glare at the box with disgust like bugs are going to come crawling out of it and cross my arms firmly over my chest.

He gives me a tight smile, rubbing his hand over the

scruff coming in on his cheek. "Well, it's not my job to play go-between, so that's the last time I'll ask you about it." He hesitates. "Can I sit with you for a sec? I wanted to ask you about something."

I eye him warily. "Yeah. I guess so." I gesture to the couch on the far side of the room.

He sprawls over one cushion and half the middle one. I carefully sit on the arm, facing him with my feet up on the seat.

"Have you felt okay since the sleepwalking incident?"

I chew on the inside of my cheek for a moment. "Yeah. I'm fine."

"Are you, though?" He clears his throat. "Because I wanted to ask—" His teeth clench together before his eyes connect with mine, concern lacing his gaze. "Is this something that happens often?"

My stomach roils. "I've been stressed out. I think that's all it is." Maybe. I don't know. "It's been happening for several years, but only every once in a while. Nightmares, too." I draw in an unsteady breath. "Lately, it's all been more frequent. I don't know why. It's frustrating."

"Does it make you nervous to sleep?"

"A little. I've never hurt myself or anything."

"But you can see where you could, right?"

For the second time today, my face flushes deeply. "Of course. I'm not stupid." My voice hitches. "I mean, where the fuck was I going Sunday night? I have no idea!" I cover my face with shaking hands and my eyes crash shut, squeezing tightly closed. I'm not going to cry, I'm just really fucking frustrated.

"Hey."

I'm far enough in my own little world that I don't notice him move. But then, Bear's arms are around me, scooping me up against his chest. He sits back down with me sideways on his lap and locks his arms around my middle. He doesn't speak, but instead waits until I'm ready. I appreciate the fuck out of that because so many times people try to talk me down or "help" before I'm truly ready for it. I don't get upset that often, but I'm on overload with everything today.

I draw in an unsteady breath, then release it, wetting my lips before I speak, my face half-buried in his chest. "Sometimes I worry about it before I go to bed and it kind of overtakes my mind. And it's on those nights that it's the worst because when I finally do sleep, it's kinda like a self-fulfilling prophecy."

Bear inhales deeply, then lets it out in one big gust. "I'm here. Seriously. Anytime you're feeling like this, if it helps to not be alone, you can come find me." He shifts both of us and pulls his phone from his pocket. I can't see what he's doing, but I have an odd feeling that I know. "What's your phone number?" he murmurs.

I twist, taking his phone from him, and find I was correct. He's opened a new text thread. Quickly, I input my digits and shoot myself a message that simply reads, "Bear," before I had it back to him.

"Good. Now, I don't claim to know what's in your head, or what you need, so if it helps"—he pauses while he fiddles with the phone again—"and it's not me you need, I've just sent you contact info for Mason and Duke. You probably should have them in case of an emergency on campus, anyway." He runs his huge hand over my back, and I can't deny that his warmth has a calming effect on me. "Do you need anything else from me right now?"

I chew discreetly on the inside of my cheek. What I really want to do is stay curled up in his lap all evening, but instead, I remove myself from that place of comfort and sit on the couch beside him. I don't need him to know that he's chipping away at the carefully structured walls I've built around myself with his kindness. I don't want to appear needy. There's something inside me that's crying out for more of this. Of him. I swallow hard past the growing lump that's caught in my throat. "No. I'm good."

He tilts his head, studying me for a moment, then

nods. "Okay. I'll be down in the gym if you need anything." He unfolds his big body and gets to his feet.

I rise from the couch, and for a few moments, the two of us stand there, unmoving. My eyes roam his strong jawline, then his full lips before returning to his hazel eyes. I bite down hard on my lip, because I don't want to be the pain in the ass who's constantly asking for help ...

He tips my head up with a gentle touch of his fingers to the underside of my chin. "What's going on?"

"I was thinking about what you said. About teaching me to throw a punch. Defend myself. Not today, but I really would like to work with you sometime. You know, if you have time. I know you're probably busy with all your football practices and stuff. But you know, I—"

"Lennon," Bear chuckles low, a hint of a smile curving his lips, "stop rambling. I said I'll help you out. I meant it." He reaches out, grasping the back of my neck, his thumb sliding over my skin at the hinge of my jaw. His brow furrows. "I've got you." After a moment, he rather reluctantly lets go, turns on his heel, and walks out.

I definitely don't have a firm enough grasp on the inner workings of his mind yet, but I'm fairly certain

Bear didn't want to leave any more than I wanted him to. And he might be as confused by our talk as I am.

While I ponder that, I slowly cross the room to the stupid Duke box he brought up for me and left next to my dresser. Shaking my head and grumbling a bit, I kneel in front of it and pry the cardboard flaps open. My eyes widen in both amazement and confusion. Because the box? It didn't contain a bunch of cast-offs like I'd previously suspected. It'd simply been a vessel hiding a whole lot of shopping bags and boxes from high-end stores, most of which I'd never dare set foot in. Fendi, Louis Vuitton, Gucci, Prada, YSL, Dolce & Gabbana. And that's just what my eyes take in at the first glance. My stomach flips as I spy something from La Perla.

Tell me my stepbrother didn't buy me lingerie.

SIXTEEN

BEAR

"Were you with Lennon just now?" His posture rigid, Duke's eyes are an ice-blue blaze, and they're pinned on me as he steps onto the landing. He's pissed off, lost, and confused all in one fun package. His usually well-groomed blond hair stands on end like he's been putting his hands through it.

He is frustration personified.

"Yeah, I was. Dropped off your box of clothes with her. She said she didn't want them, by the way, but I left them there anyway, in case she changes her mind."

He stops as I reach him, and I could continue on past, but there's something in his eyes that makes me pause. With a shrug, and a glance back over my shoulder to make sure no one is listening, I gesture that he should speak.

"You know I didn't mean to imply that she was a charity case. I say a lot of shit sometimes that I don't mean, just to get under her skin. But that's truly not what I was getting at today." He inhales sharply, planting his hands on his hips before continuing. "We all saw how little she showed up with, and I thought it would be like …"

I snort, my brows lifting because I can't believe he's being serious right now. "Like a brotherly thing to do?" I see right through him. He's attempting—in vain—to convince himself that he can think of Lennon as his stepsister. I slowly shake my head, semi-amused at his supposed intentions. I'd point out the flaw in the logic he's spun inside his mind, but it's not my job to make him see that he'll never look at her that way.

"Fuck. I don't know." His jaw clenches. "Maybe?"

I heave out a sigh. "She didn't want to open the box. That's all I can tell you. Maybe she'll do it in the privacy of her room where there aren't—I don't know—nearly a dozen eyeballs on her. Did you stop to think of how she'd feel with you dropping that in her lap in front of everyone?"

To his credit his face goes a little pale. He nods, scrubbing his hands over his face. "Yeah. Okay. I guess I fucked it up."

I scrape my teeth over my bottom lip. "Yeah, you

did." I push past him, descending the stairs at a quick pace.

He follows behind me. "What else did you talk about?"

"I asked her a little bit about the sleepwalking stuff. That's all. Figured it might be useful to know what we're dealing with. She mentioned she has nightmares, too."

At the bottom of the stairs, Duke grabs my arm, roughly yanking me to a stop. "That's it?"

I know damn well he'd like to know what else happened in there, maybe assumes that we were doing *other* things, but— "Duke, you can't ask me to help you keep an eye out for her, and then argue when I do exactly that."

"And if that lands you in her bed, that's cool, right?" One blond, pissed-off brow arches high on his forehead.

I smirk, unable to resist messing with him just a bit. "You know what? Green is not your color. If you go clothes shopping again anytime soon, forget anything in that particular hue, because it does not look good on you." I huff out a laugh at the surprised look on his face.

He grinds out under his breath. "I'm not fuckin' jealous."

"Whatever man. You're ridiculously fucked in the head about this entire situation. I'm heading down to the gym. Why don't you come with me? If it'll make you feel any better, you can throw some fucking punches. But my opinion won't change."

He heaves out a breath, eyeing me. "Noted."

A minute later, I push the door to the home gym open and walk through it, then wait as he follows, firmly shutting the door behind us. I wet my lips, toeing out of my shoes, then reaching back with one hand to pull off my shirt in one swift movement.

His eyes bore into mine, his irritation with me growing by the second as the muscle in his jaw twitches out of control. Every agitated movement makes me even more aware of his state of mind—he briskly pops the button through the hole on his jeans and rips down the zipper. He divests himself of most everything else in no time flat. In mere seconds, he stands in his boxer briefs, hands clenching into fists, ready to fight.

I jerk my head over toward the small ring we have for sparring and sit down on one of the benches at the side. We both carefully wrap our hands, then I pluck a pair of gloves out of my bag, while Duke crosses to the side of the room to grab a pair for himself from the selection we keep down here. We tug them on, and after a few minutes of jogging around and limbering up, it's on. Duke comes at me full force, like he's trying to take out every bit of pent-up frustration on me.

He can bring it all he wants. I'm willing to stand in

as his punching bag because I *am* his friend, whether he's mad at me right now or not.

He goes all out, his fist flying toward my face, and I weave and bob, tightening my ab muscles to help me maneuver out of the way. We circle each other, throwing a punch here and there, but the aggression really comes out when we get close enough to grapple. We go around and around, each of us attempting to gain the upper hand. Sweat pours from my body as we steadily taunt each other without words.

In a bold move, his hand latches onto the back of my neck, but at the same time, I grab his, and soon we're locked in a sick dance. His gaze drills into mine, eyes fiercer than I've seen in a very long time. Usually, our sparring is fun, but there's a hint of something else here. Something chaotic and filled with anger and frustration. It's a certain aggression I've never seen in him before. It's absolutely chilling.

We finally push away from each other, and I swing, catching him on the chin. But what I'm not expecting is for him to cock back and immediately swing. It's not a direct hit, but it glances off the side of my head, and hurts just the same. *Fuck*.

But, as is the norm when we fight, I definitely have the advantage, being a full four inches taller, with a bigger wingspan, and a solid forty to fifty pounds on him. Hell, I'm not trying to hurt him, just help him work out some of his bitterness. His intent, though, is way less clear. He darts in, trying to hook my leg with his, and take me down, but it's not happening. I ram my knee up and catch him right in the gut. Wheezing, he doubles over, so I take him down to the ground, where we roll, each of us getting in a few punches and jabs now that we're at close range. But then it becomes a game of submission, and this is where I fuckin' excel.

It's not long before I put him in a rear naked choke, and he's forced to tap out. I let go and he pulls away, collapsing on the mat next to me. "Mother*fucker*," he heaves out from the flat of his back. He covers his eyes with his hands as breath whooshes in and out of him. Finally, he drops his hands and comes to a sitting position. He draws his legs up, circling his knees with his arms, and grinds out, "I need to fill you in on something. There's more to this fucking mess with Lennon than we realized."

"This doesn't sound good." I get up and grab two bottles of water from the mini fridge and a couple of towels before returning to sit with him. He grunts his thanks as I toss both water and a towel in his direction. Uncapping my water, I down half of it, then arch my brow. Waiting.

Wetting his lips with a careful swipe of his tongue, he

murmurs, voice low, "So, I'm going to run through what I know. First, my fucking father drops this girl on our doorstep. She's my stepsister, so even though I don't like it and know it's going to cause problems, I go with it. Out of family obligation, I agree to look after her. He's made aware that she tripped the alarm. Then, the asshole calls me to warn me that they had been seeing a worsening trend of odd behavior with Lennon. And I'm supposed to tell him if we notice even a hint of anything fucked-up about her or not, right? I don't even know what sorts of things he might be referring to. It's like we're sleepwalking right along with her. We're in the goddamn dark."

I rub the towel over my head first, then dab at the sweat cascading down my chest. Exhausted from our brawl, I sigh, balling up the sweat-soaked towel and pitch it toward the laundry basket. "I still don't get why he'd send her here in the first place."

Duke blows out a hard breath. "Something about a change of scenery. But if you're fuckin' crazy to start with, I don't know what that helps. According to him, she's a full-blown basket case." He slams his hand down on the mat beside him. "The fuck!"

A noise from the doorway catches my attention, and my head turns in time to catch a glimpse of gray cotton shorts and an oversize white T-shirt before the wearer—Lennon—darts away.

"Goddammit," Duke mutters, but he's already on his feet and charging toward the door to go after her.

Holy fuck. How much of that did she hear?

SEVENTEEN

LENNON

"Lennon!" The sound of Duke's breath heaving and his bare feet slapping against the floor as he gives chase grows closer and closer. If I can make it to the staircase, maybe I can outrun him, maybe he'll slow or stop following me entirely if we're in front of other people.

No such luck.

He catches me by the shoulder first, spinning me around and backing me toward the wall. "Stop, Stella," he gasps out, his head ducking down to put his face right in mine.

I strike out at him, hitting him several times in the abdomen and chest but it's ineffective considering he's dripping sweat from whatever he and Bear were doing in the gym, and my blows simply glance off his slick skin.

"No, let me go." I squirm, trying to get free from his hold. "Let the *basket case* go, Duke," I choke out as I shoot daggers into his blue eyes.

"Stella. Let me explain." Duke grasps both of my wrists in his wrapped hands and forces them over my head, pinning them in place against the wall. The muscle at the back of his jaw twitches, clenching hard.

Fury streaks through me as I shout "No!" right in his face, trying to twist my body so I can ram my knee into his crotch. I blink, my brows furrowing as I finally notice he's all but naked. He must have stripped down in the gym. My eyes ping frantically over his well-muscled chest and shoulders and down to the good-sized bulge in his boxer briefs, but my brain screams at me to ignore all that and get away from him.

He steps closer to block another attempt at nailing his junk with my knee and his body flattens against mine, fingers clenching reflexively over my wrists. With every breath we take, my breasts rub right against the hard planes of his pecs.

I die a little inside with every resulting tingle that shoots through my body. "Let me go. Right fucking now, Du—"

His mouth comes down hard on mine, swallowing my words. He keeps up the bruising intensity of our lip-lock for several agonizing, breathless seconds. The smell of fresh citrus infiltrates my nose, and the part of my brain responsible for logical thinking has been shoved into a far corner where I can't hear them over the thundering of my heart.

Groaning, he wrenches his mouth from mine and stares at me for several measured beats before releasing my wrists. His jaw locks tight, and he shakes his head. "That's one way to make you shut up." His brows lift in challenge, and before I can say a damn word, he stalks off, taking the stairs two at a time. By the time I'm able to suck in a breath to scream at him how fucked-up that was, he's gone. My cheeks flame with the shock of what just happened. Duke *kissed* me.

Pulling my phone out of my pocket, I open up a new message thread between the two of us.

> Thanks for the clothes, asshole.
> Especially the panties.
> But don't ever put your lips on mine again.
> Fuck you very much,
> YOUR SISTER, Lennon

It's within seconds that a reply shoots back from him.

NOT MY FUCKIN SISTER

I touch my lips, still fuming, but remembering every second of his brutal kiss. My brain riots and confusion fills me. That fucker has thrown me so far off balance I can't think straight.

A throat clearing from the doorway to the gym startles me. I turn around, all pink-faced and disheveled, my breath coming out in ragged bursts. Bear tilts his head to the side, his eyes narrowed on me as they move down my body, and back up to meet my eyes. I'm so caught off guard that anything I could have said flees my mind in the blink of an eye. Swallowing hard, I drop my hand from my lips.

"You okay, Little Gazelle?"

I can't handle his kindness right now. I clamp down on my lip to stop the tremble, and I nod slowly before I turn and head up the stairs. I need the solace and safety of my room and I need it now. I reach the main floor and make my way through the house, ignoring the blatant stares from the brothers there to witness my escape from the basement. Who the hell knows what they're thinking after Duke barged through in his underwear, and now I've followed? Fuck, they're not even wrong, except they don't have any understanding of what set everything into motion. I huff out a laugh as I let myself into my room. *Hell, neither do I. Probably because I'm fucking crazy.*

Even though it's way too early, I brush my teeth, unhook and remove my bra, and slip out of my shorts. I slide between the sheets, hoping like hell that when I wake up tomorrow it will be a better day.

MY HEART SLAMS around in my chest. *Thud, thud, thud.* I'm hot and sticky. There are voices but I don't recognize any of them, and even if I did, they are nothing more than a faint whisper, so quiet that I doubt I'd understand what's being said. I have a sick feeling in my gut that there's something so inherently wicked about what I *can't* hear them saying, it puts me into full panic mode. I've got to get away. But I can't move.

I. Can't. Move.

Something is holding me down. Someone? Shallow and harsh to my ears, each of my breaths scrape past my vocal cords like they're abrading my throat, leaving it feeling raw. Terror streaks through me, stealing every logical thought in my head. I open my mouth to cry for help, but nothing comes out. Only silence.

MASON

I startle awake to the sound of my own scream and the sweat slicking my skin.

A dull thud on the balcony door has my head whipping in that direction. My chest squeezes, lungs seizing, and I can't freaking draw a full breath.

Mason stares at me through the door, untamed fear in his eyes. He shoves it open, but it smacks into the stool I'd put in front of it earlier in a sad attempt at barricading myself into the room. He shoves on the door, and the stool shifts out of the way, skidding with a slight screech across the hardwood floor. He's in the room a split second later, shutting the door behind him.

The moonlight coming in through the windows glances off him, highlighting every last bit of him. Oh fuck—he's completely naked, all lean-muscle and smooth skin. He strides quickly toward me, and I force my gaze upward from the rather large appendage swinging between his legs. My breath catches at the urgency in his eyes. He's in a desperate state, and it's all because of me.

He hurries to the bed, kneeling down beside it and stares at me, with a look of uncertainty on his face. He gives himself a hard shake, his hand unsteady as he brings it to my cheek. "I— Is it you—?" He clears his throat, eyes crashing shut.

I let out a shuddering breath, blinking rapidly. It

feels like my heart is threatening to leap out of my chest. I peek at him, my forehead pinching. Who does he think I am? His eyes reopen and are wild in the same way as the night on the balcony. My mind zips back, remembering the feel of his hands wrapped around my throat.

It's unnerving to know that, in this moment, before I clue him in, he might not be sure who he's looking at. I stutter out, "It's ... Lennon." Then, turning my head toward the pillow, I bring my hand up to cover the rest of my face, mortified that I was screaming at least loudly enough for him to hear me through the connected wall of our room. I want to burrow into this mattress and never show myself again.

A moment later, the sheet that was covering me is pulled back and the bed shifts, dipping with Mason's weight as he sits down on the edge. "Lennon." He exhales hard, and nods, as if reassuring himself before slipping into the bed with me. My body gives a violent lurch when he tugs my hand from my face, but what I see in Mason's eyes makes me sigh with relief, even if I hate it for him. Empathy. He understands what I'm going through right now—the racing heart that won't calm, the sick feeling in the stomach, the all-consuming fear of something I don't quite understand.

His eyes lock on mine, but his hand roams to my chest, pressing against the rapid beating at the top of my breast. "Breathe for me, Lennon. Nice and slow. In and out."

I clutch at his hand on my chest, greedy for anything that will take me away from my nightmares and back to real life, no matter how fucked-up that world may be at the moment. Mason's touch grounds me. I search his eyes, and without a clue as to what he's thinking, I nod and inhale steadily. Then exhale, just like he said. Nice and slow. I can do this.

After several minutes of us breathing together, he murmurs, "That's it. Now, let me free you from all the mad thoughts in your head." In one ridiculously smooth move, he gathers me to him and rolls me to my back. He stretches over me, his eyebrow arched high on his forehead. "Last chance to say no."

I have no words, perhaps because I don't want to say no, but also because I don't know how to deal with the repercussions if I say yes. Do I willingly allow this guy who has done nothing but taunt me to help me? The beguiling twist of his lips is what finally makes me crack. I give him the barest of nods, and it's only a moment later when his lips connect with my neck. They graze over my skin, trailing soft kisses and teasing nips. His tongue darts out for a taste, and he groans out my name. "Lennon. I know what you need."

My body heats at his words, unsure of what we're

doing or of how far he'll take this. But if there's one thing that's certain, it's that I don't want to stop. He's right, he does know what I need. I'm desperate to get out of my head, otherwise that nightmare will linger with me until morning. With every brush of his lips over my skin, he's drawing me back from the ledge, away from the awful things I'm forced to encounter when I'm asleep.

With my head thrown back on the pillow, granting him better access to my neck, I strain toward him, an ache building inside me. Need makes me wanton. I whisper, "Make me forget, Mason." Our eyes connect in the dark, and my lip trembles, unsure if I'm making the right move.

"I'll do more than that. I'm gonna make you come so hard you won't remember your fuckin' name."

Desire surges through my body, and a deep throb vibrates in my core. He shifts so he can pull my sleep shirt up, exposing my breasts, and before I can even peel it over my head, his mouth is hot and wet on me, sucking my nipple deep.

I feel the rush of arousal, the tingling spark of anticipation as his fingertips blaze a path downward. They skim from my navel to the hem of my panties, and my breath hitches as he slips them under the fabric. He wastes no time, fingers diving between my legs to explore. My pelvis rocks upward, seeking his touch. Seeking salvation.

His mouth pops off my nipple, and he groans out, *"Fuck,* you're wet." I almost cry in protest of the loss of his mouth on my sensitive skin, but the first brush of his rough fingers over my clit nearly has me coming undone and forgetting everything else. My back bows on the bed, and a throaty gasp of pleasure fills the room that can only have come from my lips. It should embarrass the hell out of me, but all Mason does is shoot me one of his signature smirking grins. "That's it. Take what you need, like a good fuckin' girl."

My pelvis chases his hand, and I do exactly that. I grind my clit on those wet fingers, losing more and more control as I surrender this part of myself to Mason. The orgasm rips through me, and I'm helpless to do anything but let it consume me. His eyes devour the sight of my body undulating, responding so easily to what he's coaxing from me. I shatter, thoughts of what came before this moment, just a dark, dark memory.

When my breathing finally regulates, I turn my head to look at him, my eyes drifting over his nakedness. He's ... beautiful.

Before I can say anything, he sits up, then kneels beside me, his hands going to either side of my underwear. His brow arches and his chin tips up a fraction.

And somehow, my body responds involuntarily, my pelvis lifting from the bed so that he can slip the panties off my ass and down my legs. While I lie there with my mouth open in surprise and my pussy exposed to his view, he climbs from the bed, my panties in hand. With a dastardly wink, he strides back to the balcony door, tossing a "You're welcome" at me as he leaves.

EIGHTEEN

MASON

My eyes crack open Wednesday evening, bleary as hell. It could be that between my own demons and Lennon's, I really hadn't slept more than two hours last night. But it's also just as likely that it's this long-ass nap I'm waking up from that's fucking with me. These late afternoon ones always leave me feeling groggy and out of it—even more so than usual. I can't make myself move yet, so I lie spread-eagle on the bed and think about how I'd handled things with Lennon last night.

For a split second as I'd burst into her room, my mind played tricks on me. It'd been terrifying. I'd been up for hours drawing in the attic and had finally decided to try to sleep. I swear my eyes hadn't been shut for more than five minutes when I heard her screaming. With my damaged heart lodged in my throat, I'd leaped from my bed and made a snap decision to try her balcony door first, figuring it was more likely to be unlocked than her bedroom door.

The screams. They'd reminded me of nights when I was a little boy and had heard stuff that would jar me awake. Lennon's cries had made my mind get all twisted up and disoriented. Bent.

Until she was able to tell me her name, I'd been stuck in a state of confusion. Long blonde hair. Wide, scared eyes. I draw in a breath. Bear is right. That's where the similarities end. But try telling that to my head when I've woken up in a sleep-induced nightmarish fog.

Thank god the moment the switch flips in my brain, and I know I'm dealing with reality, I don't associate Lennon with my mother ... because that'd be fuckin' awkward.

This girl, she's gorgeous, with just the right amount of bite. But she's only been here a handful of days, and I know better than to get too close too fast. Hell, I've never let anyone in at all. I don't date. I fuck. That way no one gets hurt.

Honestly, I don't want to take a closer look as to why Lennon has me thinking about her more often than I have any right to. And she saw the darkness that haunts me last night. She saw inside my twisted head, and I fucking hate that I let her. She saw that her nightmare threw me almost as hard as it did her.

Being around her at all is probably a huge fucking mistake, though I *am* having fun using Duke's apparent obsession with his sassy-mouthed stepsister to fuck with him. It's genius.

I throw on clothes and make my way downstairs for food. I didn't bother eating lunch on campus between classes, and I slept so long that now I'm to the point where if I have to cook something, I might keel over.

Before I can go in search of anything, my phone buzzes in my pocket. I retrieve it, glancing at the screen before I decline the call. My stomach rumbles angrily at me, getting my attention again, and I throw open the pantry, quickly rummaging around for anything that looks halfway edible.

"Was that your stomach?"

Lennon hadn't been anywhere in sight ten seconds ago. I duck my head out of the pantry, eyeing her. She's wearing the same shorts and tank that she wore to class this morning. The only difference is that her hair is swept onto the top of her head in some sort of artful mess. I tilt my head to the side. It's secured with a pencil. "Yeah. It's hangry." From the looks of it, maybe Duke should have included some hair ties in the box of shit he'd bought her. That's the second time I've seen her walking around with a writing implement stabbed into her hair to hold it in place.

She leans on the counter, bracing her forearms in front of her. "What are you going to eat?"

I come out of the pantry with a box of crackers, holding them up instead of answering, then head to the fridge, dig around in the drawer, and come up with a block of cheese. In the fruit drawer, I find a bag of grapes and grab those, too.

"Get me a plate, would you?" I stoop down and pull a cutting board out of the cabinet.

When she doesn't move, I arch a brow at her. "What?"

"I wasn't sure if you were giving me an order as a grunt or because you might be willing to share if I help out ...?" She gives me a hopeful grin. "I don't cook much, but crackers and cheese sound good."

"Yeah, me neither. That's why I take advantage when Bear cooks." Before I can finish my train of thought, my phone buzzes in my pocket again. This time, I pull it out and slap it on the counter, jabbing at the button to send the call to voice mail. I pivot, getting a knife out of the block, and begin slicing the cheese—only, I practically hack at it because the constant phone calls are pissing me off.

A moment later, the damn phone vibrates on the

counter, and I have to hold myself back. What I really want to do is pick it up and throw it against the fucking wall. But the last time I did that, I ended up with one of my father's lackeys here in no time flat. Gotta hand it to him, that man has a small army of men at his beck and call, even from behind bars, helping my brother to run his shit so that when he gets out of prison—if he ever gets out—they'll have kept things running smoothly. Tristan Valentine and Derek Pierce also have their eyeballs all over things, seeing as how their businesses are all interconnected, and they co-own a bunch of shit.

"Fuck," I bite out, setting the knife down with a clatter on the granite. If I don't answer on the fourth ring, that's it. I dig my heels in when my father calls because I fucking can and I know it pisses him off, *not* because it'll do any fucking good. In the end, he knows I'll answer eventually, unless I want to get another visit.

Lennon's hand lands on top of mine, and she steps in close. "Here's the plate you asked for. I was joking—sort of. You don't have to share with me, but it looks like you could use a hand." She gestures to the knife. "Let me help you."

"You can't help me. No one can help me," I grit out. It's not what she meant by helping, but it's what I feel. My chest constricts as I look down at her. Lennon has a softer side—one I could so easily crush. She shouldn't be any-fucking-where near me.

Surprisingly, she doesn't argue, but nods, wetting her lips as she continues to study me. I shouldn't have gone to her last night. I shouldn't have touched her. I should have just let her scream.

The screams. My eyes crash shut, and I blow out a hard breath, remembering how she'd trusted me to be there with her. Lennon finds comfort inside my chaos. But she shouldn't. Nope. She never should have.

The phone rings a fourth time, and my fingers clench briefly around the knife before I come to my senses and release it. Pulling my hand from under Lennon's, I snatch up the phone from the counter and haul ass out of the kitchen without a backward glance. I head for the front of the house, slipping outside to answer the call. I drop wearily onto the top step, resting my elbows on bent knees with the phone to my ear. "Yeah."

My father's deep voice in my ear gives me the same sense of dread it always has. "Nice greeting, son. I hear you're as big of a pain in the ass as ever."

I shrug, even though he can't see me. "Depends on who you're talking to, I suppose." I honestly don't know what the hell he's talking about, but I also don't give a fuck.

"I have my sources. As always. Eyes everywhere, Mason. Eyes every-fucking-where."

"What do you want?" I growl, letting my attitude out, in direct response to his.

"I'll be brief, as that's all I have time for."

"I'll believe that when you stop barking in my ear." I roll my eyes, wishing he were right in front of me so he could see the show of defiance.

"Listen up, you little prick. I'm sending Hunter to check on things over there. He'll show up sometime in the next two weeks."

All the air gusts from my lungs. If there was anyone else who could come—anyone—that would be preferable. But I can't say that. "Is that really necessary? Tristan is already up Duke's ass with Lennon staying with us. Derek is in contact with Bear when he needs to be, so I can't imagine he wouldn't have an inkling as to how things are going around here. We're fuckin' fine. Why send anyone else? Don't you trust your buddies?" Sweat trickles down my back and my gut twists. *Don't send Hunter. I don't fucking want him here. Don't need to deal with the shitstorm it'll create.*

He grunts. "Mm. The hot little blonde, right? Nikki's daughter."

It doesn't surprise me that he's skipped right over my fucking question about his so-called friends and focused on Lennon, instead. My skin prickles at his salacious tone. "Yeah." Thank fuck he's in prison.

"You know I like for my people to be in the know as well—monitor the boys we've brought into the house. Make sure everyone's keeping their noses clean and can handle keeping their mouths shut. It's time to test them, son."

Test them. Great. I don't even want to know what he means by that, and it makes me wonder if they've been testing the brotherhood here at Bainbridge Hall all along, or if it's just this year while their sons are in charge. I would have thought there would be less supervision this year, not more. Then again ... there's really no love lost among us and our fathers. I may have seen the worst of it, but I sure as fuck don't think Bear has had it easy with the way his father controls him. And Duke? Fuck, I wouldn't want to be Tristan's son. He's a dirty bastard. I let myself feel for Duke for a split second before I realize my father has been talking and I've missed whatever he's said ... but it sounds like he's reaffirming that I understand that I'm caught squarely under his thumb and am expected to do whatever he says. Like fuckin' usual. "Got it."

"Say hi to Hunter for me when you see him."

A sick feeling steals over me, quickly followed by rage. I punch the End Call icon, then jam the phone in my pocket, my chest heaving as I stand. While I was sitting here talking to that asshole, the sun had set, robbing me of daylight. And now, night has fallen and with it, my grip on reality is in the balance. After that phone call, I'm definitely not fucking closing my eyes any time soon. I drop my head back onto my shoulders, stare up at the sky, and roar into the dark.

NINETEEN

LENNON

A shriek escapes me, and my heart wedges in my throat. I've never heard a door slam so hard in my entire life. The sound ricochets around the house, like a crack of gunfire. I hurry out into the hallway and peek around the corner just in time to see Mason taking the stairs.

I chew on my lip. I have no clue what to do. Do I follow? No. Despite the orgasm he'd wrenched so skillfully from me last night, I wouldn't call us friends. Awkward frenemies with some questionable benefits, maybe.

I'm worried, though. He's hungry—hangry, even—but he'd become increasingly agitated as his phone kept ringing. Whoever was calling destroyed his inner calm, ruined his ability to function coherently. He'd gone from semi-playful and responsive to severely agitated. While he was outside, I'd finished preparing the plate of cheese and crackers for him and had washed some of the grapes. But now ... I don't know what to do.

Maybe he'll be back down. Without knowing for sure, I make my way back to the kitchen where I encounter Warren standing at the counter, eyeing the food Mason and I had abandoned. I shrug my shoulders, holding my hands up in a classic I-don't-know gesture. "Mason was getting food, then he got a phone call, and afterward he disappeared upstairs."

"The door slamming was him?" He snatches a grape from the plate and pops it into his mouth, followed by a piece of the cheddar.

"Oh, yes. Scared the shit out of me." I press my hand to my chest, realizing my heart is still racing. I gesture to the food between us on the counter. "I think he forgot he was hungry, though I don't see how. Something must have come up."

"Sounds about right." He nudges the plate in my direction. "Eat some of it. You look like you could use it."

I chew on my lip for a split second before I give him a smile, then stack a piece of cheese on a cracker. "Thanks. So ... hanging with the girlfriend tonight?"

"Nah. She has some sorority thing going on. I'm

trying to take Bear's advice." His cheeks tint pink. "Give her a little space a couple nights a week."

My brows raise. "Oh. Well, it can't hurt to try something different." I pause, wanting to ask a question, but a little nervous to trust anyone yet. My curiosity wins out. "Bear really is kinda like the dad around here, isn't he?"

Warren huffs out a laugh before he pops another grape into his mouth. "I don't know if that's how he wants to be seen, but he sort of falls into it naturally."

Tucking a strand of hair behind my ear, I let out a sigh, pointing to the cheese, crackers, and grapes. "I'm going to put a bit of this onto another plate and see if Mason is—" I pause, not wanting to sound like— *Shit*. Like I'm trying to step in where I don't belong ... but I want to. There's something about him that calls out to me. I wrinkle my nose, suddenly worried about what Warren's thinking, what he hears from the others in the house ... just everything.

"It's only food, Lennon. Honestly, Mason could use someone checking on him now and then. That guy—" Warren shakes his head, giving me a rueful smile. "I shouldn't say anything either. Sorry."

I shrug. "It's okay. I'd rather find out about him on my own terms, anyway, if that makes sense."

"Of course. Topic shift, then." He clears his throat before asking, "So, how are you doing here? Three days of classes down. Is KU everything you dreamed it would be?"

I freeze. "Um." My brows furrow, and I concentrate on getting out a small plate and filling it. Finally, when I look up, I realize his eyes have been on me this entire time, curious. "Warren, let's just say that coming to KU was unexpected, and I'm still grappling with both the idea of studying at a big-league university and life here in this house."

"I don't know about your classes, but as far as brotherhood stuff goes, I think you're doing fine. You're not even truly a grunt, but you're faring better than Arik and Quincy—those idiots are bumbling at every turn." He gives me a genuine smile. "But you, I feel like you're changing things up around here. It's good for all of us. When you're around, it forces all of us to be a little bit better than the degenerates that we can so quickly devolve into when a girl isn't present."

"Didn't stop Pierre from showing me his teeny weenie out at the pool, but point taken." I pick up the plate, winking at Warren as he bursts out laughing.

Yep, I like that guy.

Upstairs, I knock on Mason's door, but when I get no response, I let myself into my room. I suppose the worst-case scenario is that I eat the food I brought up for him myself. But with how hungry he seemed earlier, I'd rather he have it. I just need to figure out if he's in his room and ignoring me or if he's elsewhere.

Like a total creeper, I step out onto the balcony, plate in hand, and peek into Mason's room. It's a little before nine o'clock, and the entire suite is dark, but with the moonlight beginning to shine in, I can tell he's not in bed. In fact, there's no sign of anyone inside anywhere. I stand there for several seconds, staring at the doorknob and trying to convince myself that it'd be the world's worst idea to go into his room uninvited.

I take a moment to breathe, fixating on what the hell could have happened. It must have been something bad. Decision made, I turn the knob, pull open the door, and step inside. I flip a switch next to the door and a dim light comes on near the bed. It's wild in here, so much different than my room, obviously custom decorated for the dark prince, himself. The room is total doom and gloom, all blacks, dark grays, and deep, deep reds. It's rather stark, though, no real personal effects to be had. From somewhere above my head, there's a thump. And a crash. My eyes widen.

I have a feeling I know why there's nothing personal

about this space. *This* isn't where Mason spends the majority of his time. *Nope.* I knew there had to be somewhere else he would go to be alone. And from the sound of it, that place is the attic, which is mostly above my room. I whirl around, exiting fast via the shared balcony.

Yep. Back in my room, the sounds coming from above are infinitely louder. More chaotic sounding. If I'd been trying to go to sleep right now, the constant cacophony over my head would make it very, very difficult.

I abandon the plate of food on my dresser and ponder for several seconds whether I should go find Bear or Duke. Maybe they have experience in talking to Mason when he's upset. Or maybe they know what's up and would simply tell me he's letting off steam.

I pull my lower lip into my mouth, biting down as I tap out an urgent text message.

> Hey, I'm really trying not to be nosy.
> But Mason seems upset.
> There was a phone call.
> I don't know what he's doing in the attic.
> I'm hoping you're around.

Bear:
Oh, shit.

I'm stuck in a meeting on campus.

Duke:
I'll be back soon.
Had an errand to run.

An unsettled feeling swirls in my stomach. I don't think this can wait. I swallow down my nerves. I'm undeniably, inexplicably drawn to Mason. I see so clearly that he needs someone to understand him, and we have plenty in common. I'm probably an idiot to think I can fix what's wrong, but I have to try. I *want* to try, show him that he's not alone.

Mason is a raging enigma of toxicity. I recognize the damaged parts of him because they fit so perfectly with the broken pieces of me. That's a horrifying thought, but it doesn't seem to stop me from being drawn into everything that he is. I could search my heart and my mind for hours upon hours and not come up with a logical explanation for how I feel, but I don't have time for that.

Okay. I'm going up.

Duke:
Stella. Trust me.

MASON

Don't.

Bear:
Please, Little Gazelle.
Stay in your room.
We'll be back ASAP.

Crash! My heart misses a beat as my eyes flick upwards again.

Well, that may be, but ...
I'm not waiting around.
He could be hurting himself.

I won't knowingly leave him alone. If I can offer him even the smallest bit of comfort like he so unexpectedly provided for me last night, then I have to do that. I *want* to.

Taking in a few fortifying gulps of air, I hurry from my room, where I immediately see the light shining from the crack under the attic door, and I can't curb my curiosity. Mason disappears all the time, and I'm ninety-nine percent sure this is where he goes.

Steeling myself, I pull the door open and start up the steps as quietly as I can. The staircase is open to the attic, but everything here is unfinished, a direct contrast to the rest of the house. It's dark, and I wonder why that is—no good lighting, or because Mason prefers it that way? Hard to say, and this definitely isn't the time to ask.

As I approach the landing, my eyes clear floor level, and I can see the space where Mason spends most of his time. There are canvases leaning everywhere, of all different sizes. Some are hung haphazardly on the unfinished walls. There's also a gigantic pad of paper on an easel, where it looks like he sketches, or maybe that's the finished product, I can't tell. Mason's sketches include strokes and swirls of the darkest, most pitch-black charcoal. Some of it is frantic and messy, some is more controlled.

But *all* of it is gorgeous. My eyes widen trying to take everything in all at once.

"Motherfucker. Doesn't even know. Doesn't know what he's done," Mason hisses out, his body absolutely rigid as he crosses the floor again. He's stripped off his shirt, leaving him only in jeans. There are smudges of black as dark as sin all over him—a swipe over his pec, a mark running the length of his jaw, fingerprints on his washboard stomach, but most notably, his fingers are coated, as is the side edge of his left hand. I'm guessing he's a lefty.

Each weighted step he makes back across the room vibrates across the floorboards. As I watch, he rears back and chucks a piece of charcoal at the paper on the easel, which promptly breaks into several smaller pieces and lands on the floor. He covers his face with his hands before driving them up into his hair and clenching hard at the dark strands. "Fuck!"

Oh god. Maybe I should go. But obviously, some part of me disagrees because I find my mouth opening and his name falling from it. "Mason."

His head whips around, harsh, bitter eyes landing on me. "What. The *fuck*. Are you doing?" He glares at me, fury flowing freely from him. He stomps one foot in my direction like he's trying to scare an animal. "Get the fuck out of here! Who told you that you could fucking come up here?" His chest heaves with wrath, face turning red with temper.

I draw on every bit of strength I possess and slowly climb the remainder of the stairs, all while his jaw locks in place and his fists clench at his sides. He's seething mad, and every bit of it is aimed in my direction.

I straighten my spine and look him dead in the eye. I haven't forgotten for a single second that this is the same guy who on my first day here acted as if I'd come here to punish him. This is the same guy who choked me with his bare hands and coerced me into craziness in the backyard at the frat party. But he's *also* the guy who took care of the tequila shot for me. He beat up that Chris dude for touching me. And just last night, he came to my rescue, helping me in the aftermath of my nightmare. I haven't forgotten the scary stuff he's said and done—but I know there's some good in there. *Somewhere.* There has to be. I need to be here right now. For him. "I came up here to help you, if you'll let me."

He grits his teeth, shaking his head. "You can't—"

I throw up a hand. "I *know* you said no one can help, but ... I'm a good listener. And I'm already bound by the Bainbridge Hall keep-your-mouth-shut oath."

"This isn't a fucking joke." He's like a hurricane whipping, gale-force winds carrying his turbulent madness. It's palpable in the air, swirling around and around so viciously that I worry I might suffocate on his intense anger.

"No, you're right. It's not." My eyes wander the room. "Your artwork ... it's incredible. Beauty meeting savagery. Intense." I inhale slowly, taking in image after image of a woman with long hair and such sad eyes, I wish I could hug her—a woman who looks a bit like me, though I know it can't be. But now I sort of see why my presence here has fucked with Mason's head, even if I don't have full comprehension of why I affect him like I do.

My eyes flick to another sketch, and I swear, it's Mason himself, only a distorted, crazed version with hands hiding his face. The terror and sadness leaps from his work and punches me directly in the gut.

"Stop. Looking," he heaves out, crossing the room to me in three strides and getting in my face. His minty breath hits me like a slap. "No one is supposed to see any of this." He grips my upper arms, shaking me until my gaze locks on his pain-filled eyes. They bore into me, into my very soul. A shudder runs through my body as he backs me to the wall with one strong, dexterous hand gripping my throat. "Do you understand what I'm saying to you?"

I wet my lips. "I hear every word. But I've already seen it." My chin juts defiantly upward, elongating my throat for him. Mason doesn't know this yet, but I'm impossibly stubborn when I want to be. "I'm not leaving," I state as boldly as I can with my airway half-blocked by his hand. He and I? We're in the same damn boat and sinking fast, if only he'd recognize it. Fuck, I thought he had yesterday, which is why I came up here in the first place.

He cocks his head to the side, peering into my eyes as his grip tightens. His tongue slips out, slowly slicking over his lower lip. My eyes follow and my brain does an odd little flip, wanting to feel his perfectly plush lips on me again.

"You want to stay here."

"Yes." I struggle for air.

"With me."

"Y-yes."

"Because you want to help me."

I grit my teeth, and croak a final, "Yes."

His lips twist, eyes squinting. "Fine." He releases me and turns away, walking across the room to a table with a bunch of supplies. Glancing at me over his shoulder, a devilish smirk teases at his lips before he grits out. "Strip."

TWENTY

LENNON

I sag against the wall, catching my breath. My brow furrows. I couldn't have heard Mason right. "Sorry, what?"

"You heard me. Take everything off. You can leave it in a pile there on the couch." He comes back over to stand in front of me, a piece of charcoal in his hand. "I thought you wanted to fuckin' help, baby sis."

"I—"

He runs a hand through his hair, pushing it out of his eyes. "I wanna draw you."

I raise a brow. "Yeah ... okay. And that'll help?"

"Fuck yeah. It'll get me out of my fucking head for a while." Mason gives me a grim smile. "Get. Naked."

There's something in his tone that still worries the shit out of me, but whatever. He's already seen me naked. I reach for the hem of my tank top and peel it over my head while he goes back to the easel, prepping a fresh sheet of paper. I heave out a sigh and pop the button of my jean shorts and unzip the fly, then wiggle back and forth to push them over my hips. I step out of the shorts, pausing to worry my lip as I watch him dust off his hands.

Mason's eyes flick to mine. "Everything." He saunters over, standing in front of me as I reach behind my back to unclasp my bra. I tug it free, then hold it up by the strap and drop it to the floor. Inhaling deeply, I hook my thumbs in the sides of my underwear and ease them over my hips and ass, before letting them fall to my feet, too.

"Should I call you Jack and ask you to draw me like one of your French girls?"

He chuckles, but it's low and dark. Definitely not Jack-like at all. Crooking a finger at me, his brow lifts, waiting for me to obey.

My heart bangs around in my chest, but I come closer, patiently waiting for more instructions.

It's unnerving the way he's looking at me. Those hungry eyes of his are so full of anger and indignation that I've dared come up here in the first place that it feels as though rampaging butterflies have taken flight inside me. He circles around me, and all I feel is the heavy weight of his stare. He's behind me so long I shift around to peek over my shoulder. He gives a shake of his head. "Nope. Turn around." His hand settles on my hip, and I feel the charcoal drag over my back.

I suck in a surprised breath. "I thought you were going to draw me. What are you doing?" His breath is hot on my neck, his fingers biting into my hip where he's holding me steady.

"Letting you help me. I want to make a point first." He moves the charcoal in different ways, sometimes in sweeping motions, other times in brief staccato ones. If I'm not mistaken, some of what he's drawing has to be actual letters. Words.

I wet my lips, nervous as hell now. "Do what you need to do, Mason." I hope like fuck he can't hear my rough swallow and can't tell that I'm beginning to sweat bullets.

He's quiet, totally intent on what he's doing, so it catches me by surprise when a few minutes later, he rasps, "I need you to fuckin' understand me when I say this is my personal space. And unless I specifically tell you to come up here, you don't fuckin' dare."

"I get it."

"Do you? Turn around. I'll make sure you do."

An involuntary shudder rolls through my body at the cruel tone of his voice. When I do as he requests, this time he grips me near my rib cage as he's bent at the waist, going to town on me with the charcoal. I glance down at his dark, tousled hair, and let the idea that he comes up here to draw when he's upset—the fact that he always seems to be up here—wash over me. He's hurting. I saw it last night, and I can see it now, not only in his artwork but written all over his handsome features.

When his head tips up, I find he's the very embodiment of concentration. His teeth pull on his lip, his eyes glued to the marks he's making all over me.

My lungs constrict. My god, the charcoal is everywhere. If anyone were to look at me right now, I'm sure it'd be comical because my eyes have got to be as big as those huge round lollipops that you can get at carnivals —the kind that take an entire day to eat. And, oh fuck, my brain isn't even following any sort of logical thought because he's knelt on the floor and his face is down there, even with my pussy, as he draws all over my lower abdomen, then continues to my hips and thighs. *Jesus.* His warm breath tickles my skin, and there's an answering throb in my clit. I can feel myself getting wet. *Fuck, I must be deranged.*

"You okay up there?"

"Why do you ask?" I twitch, wondering what the fuck I've gotten myself into.

Mason glances up, one brow arched. "You're panting."

"I'm—"

"Panting. You're turned-on. Started the minute I got near your pussy."

I exhale hard, unsure if he's lying or not, but paranoid that he might be right. "Stop."

He chuckles. "You can deny it if you want, but the scent of your arousal is potent."

My mouth drops open, then snaps shut. I don't even know what to say to that, but my face burns.

He keeps right on marking me up. A few moments pass before he speaks again. "Trust me, Lennon, I know how you smell. It was all over my fingers last night. I was sad to wash my hands, but then I remembered my souvenir, and that's all it took to make me perk right up." He gives me a dirty wink. "Literally." He slides his palms up my outer thighs as he stands up.

I let out a nervous breath. "Are you done?"

"Oh, no, Lennon. I'm just getting started." As I watch, his free hand—smudged black from holding spare pieces of charcoal—cups my breast, and he lowers his head until he's able to sweep his flattened tongue over my nipple, which, to my embarrassment, is a hard, pebble-like bud. I shouldn't like this. I don't want to like this.

But I so fucking do. Greedy desire claws at me. I want to feel again what he made me feel last night. And I tell myself—if this is what Mason needs, then he can have it.

He laps at me, and I draw in a ragged breath at the onslaught of unanticipated pleasure. With each maddening stroke of his tongue, tension coils in my core. I bring my legs a fraction closer together in an attempt at relieving the building pressure. It doesn't work at all, and my face heats with the knowledge of how turned on I am.

Mason drops the charcoal on the floor, instead leaving fingerprints all over my breasts. "I want you to remember this. How I touch you. How much you fucking like it." He takes a moment to lave over the neglected nipple before his hands slide to my neck.

It's almost exactly how he'd touched me that very first day—only more intimately—leaving dirty streaks on my skin for everyone to see. And if it's at all possible, my nipples tighten further. My head buzzes with the energy he's created in this room; this dark, twisted way he wants to use me. My heart plays an irregular staccato beat, thrumming inside my chest like a psychotic drummer. My breath comes so fast, I for sure am panting a bit now, as he stares into my eyes with his dark ones.

"I want to know how wet you are."

I blink, squirming in his hold. "Mason …"

He huffs out a breath. "But I probably shouldn't touch you down there with my filthy hands." He squints carefully at me, then takes my hand and leads me over to a chair near a large canvas he's clearly been working at. "Leg up."

I'm so busy looking down at my breasts that are now covered in blotches of black, nipples protruding, needy and rosy pink from his mouth's attention. *Fuck me.* Scattered, I hurriedly murmur, "Sorry, what?"

"I said leg up. Hold onto the back of the chair if you need to." I hesitantly place my foot on the side of the seat, feeling totally exposed, and he grunts with satisfaction. "If I can't use my fingers, I'll use my mouth."

Shock waves vibrate through me, and a hard breath heaves from my lungs. My eyes dart over the features of his face, and I see no lies there. He's totally going to—

He slides his hands from my waist and over my hips as he gets down on his knees in front of me. A smirk teases at his lips as he breathes out, "Perfect." His left hand roams back, gripping my ass cheek, and the other—oh god—the other slips under my raised leg, hooking around and grasping the softly rounded part of my upper thigh. He adjusts me to his satisfaction, spreading my stance. A guttural sound emanates from his chest, and he dips down, his tongue flicking over my clit before he sucks eagerly. He's merciless. Ruthless with the way he strips all control from me with his mouth. I buck in place, pelvis tilting toward him. He looks up at me from under one raised brow, and my cheeks burst with color, a shot of embarrassment fueling their rapidly changing hue.

His grip on my ass and leg tightens, and he forcefully tilts my body to a better angle, allowing him better access. With wicked strokes of his tongue, he licks through my folds. He circles my slit, driving me a little out of my mind.

"Your pussy is dripping down your thighs for me. So fucking wet."

I can't. My eyes squeeze shut, which does nothing for my balance. I grip the back of the chair more tightly, hoping I don't fall over from the sheer pleasure of Mason's perfect lips on me.

"Look at me," Mason growls, squeezing handfuls of my flesh.

I exhale sharply at his words, my lower abdomen jerking. But I look. His face glistens with moisture, my juices coating his lips and chin. My mouth is so dry I can't speak. *Holy shit.*

"I want you to come all over my face. Give it to me."

I groan at his filthy words, and throw my head back,

breathing hard and trying like hell not to make too much noise.

"Uh-uh. Eyes right here. Look how dirty I've made you. You're so fuckin' hot. Now be a good girl and ride my face."

My head spins and spins, and I thread my fingers through his hair, pulling his mouth where I need him. A look of grim satisfaction steals over his features, and he renews his efforts, feasting on my engorged pussy. Every moan that leaves my lips results in a naughty twinkle in his dark eyes, and soon I find it impossible to hold back. "Mase ..." His name—albeit a shortened version of it—is wrenched from my mouth as my thighs begin to tremble. "I don't know if I can hold myself up." My hand clenches hard in his hair. It has to hurt, but he doesn't argue, just keeps right on driving me insane with his tongue.

He stops mid-lick to look up at me. With a nod of his head, he's barking out orders again. "Foot down. Hands on the seat of the chair. Ass in the air." He moves quickly, spinning me around when I don't move fast enough. My body humming, I bend forward, flattening my hands on the wooden seat. He applies some pressure to my back, making it dip, and positioning my ass to his liking.

"What—?"

But before I can get the question out, he's kneeling behind me, hands on both my ass cheeks. He spreads me, a groan rippling from his chest. A split second later, his mouth is on me, and I can say, in my limited experience, that I've never had someone go down on me from behind like this. It's a whole different story. His tongue moves from my clit to my entrance and back again, teasing the hell out of me, all while his hands reflexively grab at my ass. He's like a wild animal back there, devouring every bit of me. In no time flat, my legs are back to shaking, and I say the most ladylike thing as the orgasm crests, then breaks. "OhmygodohmyfuckMason-fuckingfuck."

TWENTY-ONE

MASON

Sweet Christ. The taste of Lennon in the throes of passion is unmatched. I bury my face in her cunt as she completely loses it, grinding against my face, whimpering and cursing my fucking name with that filthy-beautiful mouth of hers. Her legs quake so badly that I shift the positioning of my hands, hooking my thumbs at the juncture of her thighs to help hold her in place because with the way her legs are shaking, she's in danger of collapsing completely in ecstasy.

Easing back, I look over every square inch of her from her tiny puckered asshole to her dripping cunt. This pussy is the stuff dreams are made of. I knew it would be. The scent of her surrounds me like a sex cloud swirling around my head. It makes me weak with want.

My dick has been harder than steel since the moment

I began drawing on her silky skin, and my balls ache, heavy with the need to come. I want to watch her face as I fill her up. Make her take every fucking inch. Pound into her until she begs for mercy.

I dive in for more, lapping at all the sensitive, swollen skin of her pretty pussy as she comes back down from her high, a shaky, incoherent complication in my already mixed-up, messy life.

She's not supposed to be up here. Breathing hard, I look around, trying to see my sanctum through her eyes—the most private of spaces where I come to let out every one of my horrors, where I allow myself to be me. This is the one place I don't have to put on an act or pretend like everything is okay. It's where I allow myself the freedom to feel my pain and not worry about hurting anyone else with my thoughts or my aggressive expression of them. With most everyone in my daily life, I have to maintain a guarded stance, keep all my shit under lock and key. People don't get to know about the unfortunate circumstances of my formative years or the agony of life under the Mikaelson roof. They would run scared if they understood how fucked-up I am. Hell, if Bear and Duke's fathers weren't my old man's buddies, and we hadn't grown up knowing the ins and outs of each other's lives, I may never have told them a damn thing—and still, they don't know the entire story.

It's better this way. They don't know that I could have stopped what happened, that I'm responsible. When I let myself think about it, the darkness inside threatens to swallow me whole. And the terrible thing is, I don't even have the strength to fight it. Not right now. Not with Lennon having thrown my world off its axis.

My breath hitches in response to the direction my thoughts have taken, so I force myself to look at Lennon's delectable ass and pussy. She's still in a flat-out daze, holding onto the seat of the chair before her as if her life depended on it. And maybe it does. She should run. Run so very far away from me.

My mind bends, taking me places I don't want to go. I shake my head, freeing myself of awful thoughts and grip her by the hips, yanking her swiftly upright. She's curvy in all the right places, but still very lightweight, considering her height. I press my front to her back, letting her feel my erection lined up with the crack of her ass. Ducking my head down next to hers, I whisper, "I'm not done making my point."

I almost regret what I'm about to say and do to her. But I can't have her up here again. I purposely don't look at her as she turns her head to meet my gaze. "You don't want me up here. I get it. I promise. But I know you're upset about something. I thought we were taking your mind off it."

I let out a wretched groan. "There are consequences to doing shit you're not supposed to. I didn't fuckin' ask you to come up here to rescue me. Close your eyes for me. Keep them closed." I deftly pull out my phone and circle my artwork, capturing photos of all the beautiful ugliness I've drawn all over her body.

Satisfied, I whisper, "Okay, come this way with me." I walk with her over to the far side of the room, where I keep a full-length mirror. "So, go ahead. Get your fill of what I did. Tell me you still want to fuckin' help me." My words come out raw. Painful. The mirror is old and cracked, but it still does its job. The reflection makes Lennon jerk in my arms. "Fucking messed up, huh?" I whisper in her ear, letting her feel the hot fan of my breath over her cheek. I remain behind her and take each of her hands in one of mine, holding her arms out from her sides so she can get a really good look at my masterpiece.

In the mirror, her gaze sweeps down over every last chilling bit of the way I've marked her. Last night, she'd been vulnerable. It hadn't been her choice, rather something her nightmare had brought out in her. At this fucked-up moment in time, though, she's allowing this of me. She doesn't have to. I'm hardly holding her hands. She could turn around and hit me, even though Bear hasn't yet shown her how to throw a punch. She could scream or yell her defiance, but instead she just nods. She could go right now. She *should* get as far away from me as possible.

I study her reflection—especially the stormy look in her gorgeous eyes—and smile inwardly with approval of the fucking mess I've drawn on her. It's a swirling pattern that reminds me a little of Van Gogh's *Starry Night*, only there are words embedded within the design that came to mind as I thought about her and why she's here and who she is. "Siren. Devil. Tease. Tormentor." I take a deep breath and keep reading. "Bitch. Whore. Cunt."

She clears her throat before she asks, "Is this how you see me, Mason?"

"This is how you see *yourself*, because this is what people say about you." My jaw clenches, popping with tension.

Turning in my arms, her hands grab onto my hips, just above the waistband of my jeans. She presses her forehead to my chest for a brief moment before she looks up into my eyes and completely ignores what I said. "Who hurt you so badly that you lash out like this? Why do you push everyone away?"

"Why does everyone want to be in my fuckin' business?" *Get the fuck out of my head. Get out.*

Her brows draw together, and she gives me a troubled shake of her head, her hands drifting up to my pecs and stretching to reach around my neck. Her lush, fingerprint-covered tits brush my chest, and a moment later, I sweep her into my arms and her legs wrap around my waist. My hands slide over her round, toned ass, supporting her as I stalk over to the mattress I sleep on when I'm too bone-tired to make it back down the stairs.

I crash to my knees, hovering over her as I make quick work of the button and zipper on my jeans and shove them down, freeing my cock. It's fucking weeping for her, wanting to be inside her tight pussy. I kneel between her legs, eyes skimming over every swirl of the charcoal, every ugly word.

My breathing is heavy and labored as I stare down into her expectant blue eyes.

I point to her arm where I swear I felt something under her skin earlier. "Implant?"

Her eyes widen. She nods, her breath stuttering out.

"Good. Because I have no intention of pulling out." My jaw tightens, running my hand over all the awfulness. I want to rub it into her skin so she doesn't forget. "Gonna make this pussy come again."

Her hand tentatively touches the smears of charcoal on her stomach. "Are you happy with what I let you do to me?"

Agitation whips through me, and it's on a very, very

MASON

short leash that could snap at any moment. *I fucking hate her for trying to understand the fucked-up mess in my head.*

She shakes her head, reaching for me. "You shouldn't be alone up here all the time."

I nod, exhaling close to her ear, and fucking love the resulting shudder of need that runs through her. "That's where you're wrong, Lennon. Loneliness is a second skin to the soul that is forced to wear it. Damaged people damage people. The only time I'm truly at ease is when I'm alone."

"You're not alone right now and you seem just fucking fine." Her brows raise ever so slightly, pushing me for an answer.

I tilt my head, studying her curiously. She's like no other girl I've ever encountered. I ease into her dripping wet pussy inch by satisfying inch, watching her mouth go slack and her eyes roll back. She's incredibly tight. I groan aloud, "Fuck, Lennon, what are you doing to me?"

"Oh, Fuck. Mason. Fuck."

She feels like heaven.

I want to die.

TWENTY-TWO

DUKE

There have been no additional texts from Lennon, and it'd taken me a fucking hour to get to the point where I could exit gracefully without pissing off any of my father's cohorts. Ridiculous. Unfortunately, I'm willing to bet my headstrong stepsister did the exact opposite of what Bear and I both told her to do.

Wait for us.

She's seen some of Mason's bullshit already, but if he's really worked up, like it sounded like he might be from her urgent texts—and if he'd been up in the attic, well, that points directly to his state of mind—she shouldn't be anywhere near him if he's up there losing it. I grit my teeth. Nope. Bad fuckin' idea. I've always let him deal on his own with the devil that rides on his shoulder. Bear will occasionally step in if it gets bad. But fuck. Lennon? If he really goes off the deep end, there's no way she'll be able to handle it. Dude can be scary as fuck when he's well and truly caught in the nightmare in his head.

I race from the SUV I'd taken to campus and into the house, up the stairs, and throw open the door at the end of the hall, leading to the attic.

A groan. A whimper. The indistinct sound of movement. A swift intake of breath.

Oh, fuck. I'm too late.

Dual feelings of horrific worry and blinding fury clash together, then rush through my entire body, dulling my hearing and narrowing my vision. My heart leaps into a terrifying free fall off a cliff. What the fuck? What's he done to her?

I take the steps two at a time, reach the top, pivot, and stare. The sight that greets my eyes is nothing like I'd expected. Shock reverberates through me. I'd considered that maybe I'd encounter an argument. Mason hollering at her to get the fuck out of his space. Lennon sassing back that he's fucking crazy and needs an intervention. Not this. Never this. I see *red*.

Mason rasps, "That's it, Lennon. Take every fucking inch."

Over in the corner of the attic space, Mason's bare ass is hanging out of his jeans as he kneels over Lennon, balls deep inside her and thrusting. He's got her arms pinned over her head, and her slim legs are in a tangle around his waist. I draw in one ragged breath. Then another. They're both fucking filthy, Mason's charcoal everywhere. Clawed handprints on his back. Dirty smudges. Streaks of black. And Lennon—my god, she's covered, head to toe. That deranged fucking psycho drew all over her.

Wrath breaks free, and I'm across the room and on Mason in mere seconds, tearing him by the shoulders off her. "Fucking hell, Mason!" I roar, enraged. My heart pumps frantically in my chest, "What the ever-loving *fuck?*"

He stumbles backward and lands in a heap on the floor, jeans around his knees, breathing hard. Dick wet.

My gaze snaps to Lennon, my breath coming hard and fast. Violence builds behind my eyeballs, my brain rioting at what I'm seeing. She scrambles backward, trying to cover herself, but she's mostly unsuccessful because there's simply nothing to use but her own arms and hands. My eyes ping all over her, a sick feeling hitting me hard in the gut when I catch a couple of the words scrawled indecently across her skin.

In those few seconds while I'm preoccupied, Mason gets to his feet and tucks his cock back inside his jeans, giving the zipper a quick tug before he meets my blazing gaze, his jaw locked. "What the hell are you doing up here? Mind your own fucking business, *brother.*"

I drop my head back onto my shoulders, my mind in a frenzy. This *asshole.* Low and lethal, I grit out, "Touch her again, and I will hack your fucking hands *and* your dick from your body."

He shoots me one of those aggravating smirks—the kind I've wanted to slap from his face more than once—while gesturing to her. "Why don't you fucking ask her what she's doing up here." He looks pointedly at her. "I came up here to be alone. She knows that now. Didn't you figure it out, baby sis?"

Lennon glares at him, her forehead creasing savagely as she draws up her knees and presses her breasts to her thighs to hide them from view. "I texted Duke and Bear because I was concerned by what I was hearing up here." Her tongue darts out to dampen her lips. "And you're not being fair, Mason. You know I had good intentions." She looks at him with angry, distrusting eyes. "I was scared for you."

Mason stares back coldly, "Yeah, well, you found out the hard way it wasn't such a great idea to involve yourself. And it seems to me like you were only after another orgasm."

I'm catching a not-so-subtle undercurrent running between them. There's obviously shit where they are concerned that I've somehow missed. *Another* orgasm. My mind might explode.

She wrenches her gaze from his, but not before I see the hurt in her eyes. "Fuck off, Mase, you psychotic dick."

There's an anxious twitch of Mason's jaw, and his gaze bounces from her to one sick piece of art after another. As I quickly study them, it's unnerving how fucking hard it is to tell if the newer pieces are Lennon or his mother. And I can tell it's making him antsy as hell for both of us to be up here. No one comes anywhere near the attic but him. Yet here the three of us fucking are.

I close the distance between Mason and me. "Whatever is going on with you, leave her out of it."

He grits his teeth, shaking his head. "Oh, so now you're her champion? All I did was allow her to help calm me down when she begged me to let her. I started drawing. And that's what came out." He flings his head toward her naked, scribbled-on body. "I can't help that my hands were influenced by every goddamn thing you've said about her." His dark eyes taunt me. "This is partially on you. You'd think as her stepbrother, you'd be looking out for her."

He's asking for it. *So, fuck it.* I look around the room at the haunting artwork surrounding us. "What the fuck do you think I'm doing here but looking out for her? I'm sure as fuck not here for you, you fucking lunatic." I throw my arm out encompassing all the canvases of sad Lily Mikaelson, crazed Mason self-portraits, and now ... Lennon. I don't fucking like it. "I might be an asshole sometimes, but at least I can distinguish whether a person is dead or alive."

Bingo. I've hit a massive nerve.

Mason's chest heaves, and he slams his fist into my jaw. I see it coming and fucking let it happen, stumbling backward as the pain bursts through my head.

Once I've regained my balance, I focus a grim smile on him. The ache in my jaw fuels the fire raging at my center. "Motherfucker," I hiss before I leap, tackling Mason to the floor. I slug at him, punch after punch to the soundtrack of Lennon's shouts as she begs us to stop. We don't. We roll, grappling with each other for dominance. Mason gets in his fair share of hits, too, striking hard and fast when he gets the upper hand.

Grunting and sweating, I flip us again, straddling him. "Motherfucker," I pause, glowering at him. "Put your fucking boner away."

"You're the one who pulled it out, asshole," Mason huffs, struggling to get out from under me. "My dick was perfectly seated until you came along and whipped him out of his hidey hole." He smirks at how easily I allow him to catch me off guard with his words. "All because you couldn't handle the fact that I got that pussy before you did."

"Shut the fuck up," I grit, all my patience used up.

Lennon groans, and my eyes dart to her to find that she's covered her face with her hands. I leave my eyes on her for a few seconds too long, and Mason smacks his fist into my mouth. The taste of copper on my tongue is my reward for noticing her hair in wild disarray, and the shaking of her hands. My heart clenches viciously in my chest. I want to go to her. I grit my teeth in frustration, knowing I can't.

Mason heaves out a dark laugh as we roll again. "You want me to put it away ... get the fuck out of here, and I'll happily put it back in *her* box."

I sock him in the face from below, then block his heavy fists with my forearms before flipping us so I can pummel him some more, landing a couple of good ones to his chest and gut. "Enough of your comedy act, asshole."

He laughs. "Or stay. I don't give a flying fuck either way." He just barely has a chance to defend himself, catching my forearm in his grip. I snarl at him, and he has the audacity to grin. "Why don't you grab some popcorn while you're at it ... you know, make it a movie night."

"Mason, stop it." Lennon's face is bright red and her chest heaves. My eyes travel from there downward. Her pussy is right in my line of sight.

Asshole sees me look at her and shrugs, squinting at me a bit. "Oh, wait. What is it again? Oh, yeah. 'Stepbrother Watches His Frat Brother Bang His Sister While He Jerks Off in The Corner.' How's that for a Pornhub title? I mean, I'd watch it!" He wriggles his brows with another gritty laugh.

I don't mistake it for actual amusement, though. He's too busy trying to goad me for that. I bite out, "You are one miserable motherfucker, you know that, Mason?"

"It's okay to be jealous, stepbro. If her moans and the scratches on my back are any indication of her enjoyment level, I'm guessing she'd be down for finishing what we started. You can definitely watch." He glances up at Lennon with a shit-eating grin. "What do you say, baby sis, wanna give your brother a show?"

I growl, "I'm not her fuckin' brother."

At nearly the same time Lennon snaps, "Totally not my brother, asshole."

"Holy shit. What the fuck—?" Bear's muttered expletive from behind me has me taking my eyes off Mason for the split second it takes him to clock me in the chin.

I shake it off, seeing the fight with Mason for what it truly is—a method to divert attention from what he did to Lennon, who I haven't forgotten is still over on that mattress wearing only her charcoal-marred skin.

Bear scans the room, taking in the situation. The astonishment is clear on his face and his jaw sets hard before he barks, "You assholes get it out of your systems, because I swear to Christ if you're still going at it when I get back up here, I will knock you both the fuck out. No questions asked."

Out of the corner of my eye, I watch as his long strides eat up the distance between him and Lennon. He squats down in front of her blocking my view. A moment later, he picks her up, cradling her in his arms, and takes her right the fuck out of here.

Guilt eats at me as Mason and I go another round. We haven't spoken since I shut her up with my mouth. Removing her from this situation like Bear just did—it's what I should have done for her instead of getting into it with this dickhead.

But would she have even let me help her? The answer to that question makes my stomach turn in discomfort. I've given her no reason to trust me. None at all.

TWENTY-THREE

BEAR

I couldn't get back fast enough. Coach had kept us after to watch videos of play after play so we could talk strategy for the game. He said if we stayed late tonight he'd let us head home to rest directly after on-field practice tomorrow and Friday so we could mentally prepare for Saturday's game. I'd covertly checked my text messages every so often the entire time he kept us, but nothing else came in. Not from Lennon, not from Duke, and definitely not from Mason. It'd worried the shit out of me.

I look down at Lennon in my arms. Yeah. I'd been right to worry. I release an agonized breath as we descend the stairs from the mayhem. I don't have a fucking clue what she went through up there, but she clings to me, her fingers clutching tight to the front of my white T-shirt. Mason's human charcoal artwork has rubbed off all over my clothing, but I'm not worried about it. My concern lies solely with the naked, soiled girl in my arms.

We reach the bottom of the stairs, and I pull the attic door shut behind us, leaving the sounds of continued verbal and physical sparring behind. Fortunately, no one is around in the long corridor extending down this wing, and I'm able to let us into Lennon's bedroom without issue. I take her directly to the bathroom, where I set her on her feet in front of me. But she hangs on, not allowing me to step away from her.

Her breathing is a little erratic. The words she'd spoken to me upstairs—"Get me the fuck out of here right now"—were gritty. Mad, even. So I think she's probably okay. She's made of some pretty strong stuff.

My eyes flick to the mirror behind her, and my gut clenches. So many horrible words tucked into the beauty of what Mason had created using her skin as his canvas. I try to swallow past the thickness in my throat, but it's difficult when I imagine how this must have come about. I need the full story and fast.

From what I'd gathered from the argument I'd heard, Mason had his dick in Lennon when Duke walked in. My jaw clenches as my imagination runs wild, and I try to rein in my own fucking feelings about the situation. Lennon is free to do what she wants. Or who she wants, for that matter.

All I really should be concerned with is what I saw when I got up there. It'd been fucking ugly—insults flying every which way, fists pounding, mouths bloodied, faces swollen ... and one very naked girl posing as Mason's art.

Lennon leans against me, unmoving for another minute.

"I'm right here," I murmur into her hair. "Why don't I start the shower for you? You'll probably feel a whole lot better and think more clearly if we get you cleaned up."

She lets out an uneven, halting breath. "If you step away, you're going to see"—she tips her chin, looking up at me—"and I shouldn't be fucking embarrassed because this isn't about me. It's about Mason wanting to hurt me for going up there. That's on me, and I'm fine with it." She shrugs.

Her confidence and straightforward assessment of the situation astounds me.

I brush her hair from her face and cup her charcoal smudged cheeks. "You're rather impressive." I tip my forehead to hers before easing away to start the water.

"Really? I should have known better than to think offering to help Mason would go like I thought it would." She looks up, a grim smile on her lips as I return to her, then edges away and slips under the warm spray of water.

I have to force myself to tear my eyes away from her beautiful body. With a reluctant sigh, I turn and lean against the wall facing away from her.

From behind me, she quietly says, "I went up there to try to help. I don't know why he was flipping out, but he said he wanted to draw me. And when he told me to get undressed, I kinda knew that he was still upset." She lets out a ragged sigh. "I knew it could get bad, but I *see* him. I understand there's some sort of trauma he's sustained. But he seemed equally panicked to see me in the attic among all of his artwork." The moan that she lets loose as the water soothes her is enough to stir my dick to life.

Fucking hell. I'm not here to take advantage of this fucked-up situation. I grit out, "Yeah, that all makes sense. It wasn't your fault, but I'll be honest with you. That was the first I've been up there in probably two years. I'm not excusing his behavior, but Mason needs space to work through things sometimes."

She's quiet for several seconds, and I can practically see the wheels turning in her head, processing my thoughts. "There's so much," she whispers. "It's never coming off."

I peek over my shoulder to see black rivulets of water streaming from her body and rushing down the drain. She's right. It might take a whole lot more than standing under the water to do the job properly. Running a hand over my jaw, I exhale. "Have you ever looked carefully at Mason's hands? They're sort of stained at the tips from all the hours he spends up there drawing." I clear my throat, pushing off the wall. "I'll just, uh, wait for you in the other room."

"Bear. Wait." Her voice is a desperate plea.

I turn, raising a brow, and eye her warily, keeping my eyes focused on hers. "Yeah?"

"Um, I can't do this alone." Her eyes crash shut. "Please help me. My back is covered. I might have let him do this, but I don't have to allow it to sink into my skin."

I inhale raggedly, turning toward her. After only a moment of inner debate, I grasp my T-shirt at the back of the collar and whip it off over my head in one smooth movement, then go for my belt, which clanks as I undo it. I notice her eyes on me as I pop the button of my jeans and lower my zipper. She's gone for the soap, so now her skin is this foamy, bubbly gray mess. I bet it's slick to the touch. And like fucking satin.

My head begins to buzz. Maybe it's from a sudden lack of oxygen.

I have no idea how this is going to work, but I totally

have a semi just from being in the room with her while she's naked. Actually, that's a lie. It started when I held her. I kept telling myself it's a natural response. My jaw twitches, but I shove my pants down, anyway, and kick them to the side.

Getting into the shower with her, she glances down at my boxer briefs that are rapidly soaking through, her brow furrowing. I see the question in her eyes before she can ask. "I'm trying to be a gentleman."

She draws in a breath and nods. "Okay, then. I can handle the front, I think, but I need you to wash my back, please."

I bite down on my lip and hope like hell I can control myself. She hands me a bottle of shower gel.

Hesitantly, I watch as she uses her soapy hands directly on her skin. "Did you want me to use a washcloth or loofah or sponge or something?"

"Um. It'll just ruin them, I think." She pauses, glancing over her shoulder. "Don't you?"

"Fuck, I have no idea." My voice is way hoarser than I'd like, but I squirt a good amount of the soap into my palm and hand the bottle back to her. I inhale deeply as I rub my hands together, hoping the noise of the water pelting against the marble tiles is enough to cover my exaggerated exhale. "I'm going to start up here at your shoulders."

I smooth the soap over her skin, letting my head fall back to stare up at the ceiling. I can do this. I'm just giving her a hand with all the places she can't reach. I glance down, and my eyes track the gray-tinted water as it runs down her back and between her ass cheeks. *Oh, dear fucking god.*

Focusing on breathing carefully in through my nose, out through my mouth, I continue, moving my hands in a circular pattern, lathering the soap on her skin and removing the ugliness Mason has put there. Bitch. Tormentor. Devil.

Jesus.

Lennon's movements have slowed, her hands moving over her breasts. A little moan escapes her lips.

Fuck. I blow out a breath, turning my head to the side, trying to focus on anything else. Unfortunately, the item my eyes land on is the bright-pink object on the shelf of her shower. It stands out like a sore thumb. A vibrator. I'm being tested, I really am. My hands lower, cleaning the slope of her back. I close my eyes, my voice rough like gravel as I ask, "Do you want me to wash your ass?"

"Um." The word comes out breathy. "Y-yes."

Fuck me, I'm going to hell. "I need more of the soap, please."

She hands it back to me, and I squeeze some into my

hand, giving the bottle back before I bring my soap-covered hands down, moving in slow, soft circles. Every circle gets progressively larger, until my thumbs are meeting right at the crack of her ass. I swallow hard, looking down. Her cheeks are completely clean of any charcoal residue, but I can't bring myself to stop touching her.

Lennon draws in a breath, turning around to face me, and the look in her eyes—she's desperate. "Bear, I need ..."

My head bows, and I look up at her from under my wet lashes. "I'm trying to be the good guy. You're making it really fucking hard for me." The muscle at the back of my jaw twitches as I watch her. Her cheeks are bright pink, and if I'm not mistaken, it's no longer from embarrassment but from arousal. Hell, by all accounts, she just had Mason's dick inside her. And I suppose if Duke yanked him off her, maybe she's still ... all worked up. And now, here I am with my hands on all her wet, naked skin. I don't think I blame her one bit. My heart thrums a punishing beat in my chest.

Her eyes beg me. *Fuuuck.* I don't fucking care about anything leading up to this moment. I want her more than my next breath.

She scrapes her teeth over her full bottom lip, watching me, and when I don't move—other than my dick jerking as it strains behind the front of my sopping-wet boxer briefs—she reaches over to the vibrator, switches it on ... and brings it directly to her clit.

Heat washes through my body from head to toe as I can't unglue my gaze from the way her mouth falls open and her eyes drift shut. Her chest jerks with uneven breaths. As her legs begin to quake the slightest bit, she throws a hand out for balance, and it lands on my abs. I groan.

"Bear," she murmurs softly. I almost miss her saying my name between the spray of the water from the showerhead and the roar of blood rushing in my ears. A swift intake of breath precedes another desperate-sounding cry.

Fucking hell. My dick is tenting my underwear, and I'm so goddamn hard it makes it difficult to form any coherent thoughts. Reaching for her, I grasp her hips, telling myself over and over again that it's only to steady her, but that's a fuckin' lie. Now that I've touched her again, I crave the feel of all that soft skin at my fingertips.

"Bear," she chants again. Her hips rock, and she hasn't moved the vibrator from the exact spot she wants it. This is a girl who knows what works for her. My fingers dig into her skin. She opens her eyes, and the deep blue of them is almost overtaken by her dilated pupils. She's a ridiculous temptation.

I outright growl, sexual frustration swamping me. I wrench the vibrator from between her legs. She gasps, blinking up at me, but before she can say a word, I've spun her around. As soon as her hands hit the marble tiles, I yank her hips back, bending her at the waist.

I shove my boxer briefs down far enough to let my cock spring free. This is insanity, but I can't stop myself. Don't want to. And from the eager look on Lennon's face as she peeks at me over her shoulder, she doesn't want me to either. I notch my dick at the entrance to her incredibly wet pussy and slam it home.

"Oh, fuck." Her mumbled curse hisses out with the breath that heaves from her, back arching as she takes me fully inside her. And now that we're doing this, I allow myself to really look. My gaze skims over the curve of her hips, her slender waist, and if I tilt my head to the side, her breasts swing with every stroke I make inside her.

I thrust, the wet slap of my pelvis meeting her ass spurs me on. I grasp her hip with one hand, curling around her body. "God, Lennon, you feel so fucking good." My head grows hazy from every fucking sense being overwhelmed—the way the water splashes as we move together, the feel of her slick skin against mine, the warmth of her pussy, and—oh god—the sounds of our cries and moans intermingling.

It takes me a second to recognize that I still have her

vibrator in my other hand. I wet my lips, studying it. This little guy and I? We're on the same fuckin' team. I bring my hand between her legs, touching the buzzing vibrator to her clit, and her head immediately snaps backward. She lets out a throaty groan. The effects of using the toy are swift and unmistakable. Lennon's already ridiculously tight pussy squeezes around my dick in a rather violent manner. It catches her by surprise almost as much as it does me. And this girl—the orgasm just goes and goes. It must be a full thirty seconds before she finally sags a bit in my arms, her breath gusting from her.

"Holy fuck."

TWENTY-FOUR

LENNON

Bear switches off my little pink vibe and tosses it to the shower floor, belting my waist with one strong arm and bringing the other up to my breast. He growls again in my ear as he brushes his thumb back and forth over my nipple, "Did that feel good, Little Gazelle? Is that what you needed?"

It takes me a few seconds because my body continues to intermittently clench around his monster cock—which I'd thought was big when I felt it prodding between my legs the night of my sleepwalking incident but seems infinitely bigger now that it's buried deep inside me. "Yes." I shudder. I feel so good, I wish I could put into words that he's rocked my world.

"You're something else, you know that, Lennon?"

I crane my neck, finding his eyes. They burn with lust. "I've learned to take what I want."

"Good. I fuckin' like that. But I'm not nearly done with you." His hot breath cascades from his lips, one heady gust after another, raising goose bumps along my flesh. He subtly nudges his cock deeper, and I let out a strangled moan, nodding in agreement. Flames of desire lick my skin, making me needy for whatever he wants to do to me. My entire body is like melting wax, soft and pliant. He nudges his nose along the side of my neck, trailing his lips along the same path. His scruff tickling my skin makes me shudder with white-hot desire. He squeezes my breast, massaging it before moving to the other, toying with the taut peak. The toughened skin on his palm brushes over one nipple again and again, making my breath catch in my throat.

Bear uncurls himself from around my body, and I let out a whimper from the loss of his warm body at my back. But then he slowly slides his hand from the top of my ass, running it over every single vertebra until he reaches my neck where he skims his thumb over the sensitive skin. He rocks back, his cock withdrawing until just the tip is at my entrance before driving forward, plunging himself inside my greedy pussy. The knowledge that he's watching himself push his entire length into me, over and over, has a ripple of desire flowing through me.

He keeps up this drugging, addicting rhythm until tension has coiled so tightly in my lower abdomen that I'm frantic, needing release again.

"Please," I beg, fingers scrabbling for purchase on the tiled wall in front of me, though I find nothing to hold onto.

Bear's husky, deep voice hits me hard, like a punch to my lady bits. "What do you need?"

"I-I'm close."

He grunts and drags his fingertips from my back around to my waist. Each stroke of his fingers over my skin delivers blinding pleasure, but I want him to touch me. Need it.

I breathe a ragged sigh of relief as his fingers move swiftly past my belly and dive between my legs to brush over my clit. I gasp. "Yes. Right there. Fuck."

His breathing is more and more labored with each snap of his hips against my ass. The way his fingers stroke my clit, it's as if he's in a friendly competition with my vibrator to see how fast he can make me come. The honest truth is that it will take very little to send me over the edge. I'm steeped in pleasure, floating on the most beautiful cloud of lust.

"Fuck. Gonna come." Bear's big body stills behind

me, cock buried to the hilt. After a moment, I feel him jerk, then rock ever so slightly as he gasps out, "Lennon."

I imagine his cum shooting into my body, and I've never been so grateful for the implant I'd decided on years ago. Another harsh breath heaves from me as he provides just the right friction, then pinches my clit ever so slightly, setting off my orgasm. An avalanche of feeling cascades throughout my body.

A boneless, satisfied mess, all I can do for several minutes afterward is make sure oxygen reaches my lungs. I'm fairly certain if Bear were to remove his hold on me that I'd fall in a heap on the shower floor. I can't even think, I'm so caught up in the echoes of what we just did.

As the water coming out of the showerhead turns a lukewarm temperature, Bear pulls out and carefully releases his hold on me, making sure I'm steady on my feet. I turn around, a teasing smile on my face, expecting to find something similar on his. Instead, I'm greeted with a frown, his brows drawn sharply together in the middle of his forehead and his jaw working overtime about whatever is in his head.

"What's wrong?" I scan his face, looking for a clue, but find none. "Bear?" I reach out to touch my hand to his chest, but he backs away. Confused, I wait for him to say something ... anything to explain his swift change in attitude.

He shakes his head. "Sorry, I'd better check on Mason and Duke. Make sure they don't fucking kill each other. Clean up. I'll meet you back in your bedroom in fifteen."

I blink, hoping this is about them and not about me. It probably is. They're his friends, but who knows what they'll do when left to their own devices, especially when they've both shown their crazy tonight.

Bear quickly dries off, then wraps the towel around his waist. He picks up his clothing—including the soaked boxer briefs he'd had on in this very shower not fifteen minutes ago—and leaves without a word or a backward glance. *One-track mind, much?* The door to my room creaks open and clicks shut a second later.

A riot of emotion storms through me the entire time I finish up in the shower and pull on pajamas. I'm trying so hard not to let doubt creep in. Could that frown have been some form of regret? I sure as fuck hope not. Even so, my face burns at the idea of it.

He's going to be back any minute, and now that I'm beginning to process all that happened this evening, I don't know how to handle my own thoughts, much less someone else's. I have an agonizing sense of dread that what I've done today will have severe ramifications. The longer Bear is gone, the more I'm plagued by worry about what they're thinking, whether they're off on their own talking about it. *About me.* This is my fault. I let it happen. I *pushed* for some of it.

But dammit, I'll do what I want, especially with my body. I just hope my choices don't bite me in the ass later. If they do, though, at least it will have been me to make those decisions. I shouldn't have to defend my choices to anyone, but I will if it comes down to it.

The bottom line—if I really choose to think about it—is that I shouldn't trust any of these guys so freely or completely without knowing more about them. Not knowing what's coming my way, my best defense is to go on the offense, to show them—all of them—that they can't hurt me with their words or actions or judgment.

I fling the door open when Bear knocks and stand there, glowering at him, but not offering entrance. I brace myself for the onslaught of everything he might say to me, and attack first. "If you're going to tell me that what we did was a mistake or something like that, please go back to your room." I seem to have shocked him speechless, so I continue on. "I'm sure you're thinking that maybe I *am* some of those things that Mason drew all over me. And you know what he said? He told me that those words he wrote were the things I think about myself." I wet my lips before continuing. "Because other people have said them, too. Maybe he's right. Maybe I am trashy and manipulative and a *whore*." My voice catches, and I have to force myself to finish. "So, I guess he was right, and you can just let everyone know that it's true." I throw my arms out from my sides in frustration. I thought I was helping Mason. I'm attracted to him. And I'm comfortable enough with Bear because he seems like such a damn good guy that I trusted him to not judge me—and there's no doubt that there's an attraction there as well. Duke? Well, I continue to be amused that he's the only one of the three who has actually kissed me.

"Lennon?" Bear gets my attention, pulling me from where I'd wandered into the storm raging in my head. The bastard has the guts to sidestep me, entering my room, then backing up, hands laced on top of his head as he studies me. "The fuck, woman?"

My eyes track his movement into my room, and I'm ready to ask him what the hell he thinks he's doing when I notice an odd mixture of amusement and concern on his face. Perplexed, I grit out, "What's funny about this situation?"

"I think you've gotten all spun up in your head. I suppose I don't blame you based on recent events." He smiles at me through clenched teeth. "But we have a situation brewing that can't be set on the back burner."

MASON

My brow furrows, but curiosity wins out. "What's going on?"

"Um. So, Mason and Duke are still in the attic. They've stopped pushing each other's buttons like maniacs, and instead have opted to drink themselves silly, which ... I guess is cool if it means they've reached some sort of a truce. Apparently after we left, they fought for a bit longer, but then went right to 'Well, let's get drunk because everything fucking hurts.'"

My brows draw together, and I blow out a semi-relieved breath. "Okay. I'm confused. What does this have to do with me?"

Bear sucks in a breath, then scrubs his hands through his hair, eyeing me. "So ... Mason wants to stay upstairs, which is cool, but I think I got out of Duke that he'd rather sleep in his own bed."

I press my lips together, crossing my arms over my chest. I think I see what's coming, but I'd rather he spell it out for me. "And?"

"I was kind of hoping you'd stay with Duke for a while—make sure he drinks water and, if it's not too much trouble, patch him up. Help him apply some ice packs."

My eyes widen. "Oh my god, how banged up are they?"

"Not terrible"—he pauses to wince—"but bad

enough that I don't have enough hands to manage it very well. I could go get Tucker or Warren, if you aren't up for it."

"Shit." I chew on the inside of my lip before nodding. I will probably kick myself for agreeing to this later, but oh how the tables have turned. Now I'll be babysitting Duke instead of the other way around. "Yeah. Okay. Fine."

"You don't have to stay, Stella Bella," Duke slurs. "I know you fuckin' hate me. No need to torture yourself."

I glance down as my phone vibrates in my hand again and quickly read the text from Bear.

> How's he doing?
> Giving you any trouble?

I press my lips together, not quite sure of how to answer.

> He's still awake.
> Talkative.

MASON

> Thinks I hate him.

Stifling a yawn, I have to wonder how long it will be before Duke succumbs to the alcohol and passes the fuck out. This is the third time Duke's referred to me hating him, though I doubt he'll remember in the morning. He's smashed.

It'd been close to midnight when Bear and I finally got Duke down the stairs and settled in his room. Now, he's propped up in his mammoth-size bed among the pillows because he said he had the spins when he laid flat. I told him that if he planted one foot on the floor, or even flat on the mattress, that it'd stop that bizarre effect, but he won't listen to me.

I should know. I have experience with this. I wouldn't ever say that my mother is an alcoholic, but there'd been a good number of times in my youth where she'd tie one on and leave me to deal with the aftermath. So. I'm well versed in drunk people, even if that drunk person isn't usually me.

A one liner comes in from Bear, making my phone vibrate in my lap.

> Do you?

> Should I?

Do I hate him? I haven't ever understood why Duke chose to lash out at me from the moment we officially met. If there's any hate going on around here, I'm not the culprit. He's proven that he's perfectly capable of all sorts of asshole-ish behavior, though, that's for damn sure. I sigh, holding a bag of ice in a towel to the right half of his face. Mason either has a very heavy hand or was fueled by so much anger, his hits were ridiculously brutal. Duke's face is swollen badly, bruises already beginning to form. Finally, I murmur, "I don't hate you, but I'd like you more if you quit calling me Stella. Now, please drink more of this water before you pass out."

He eyes me through his drunken haze and takes the water bottle from me. He tips it up, gulping down almost the entire bottle in one go before handing it back to me. It's as I'm setting it on the nightstand that he lifts his arm again, closing his hand around my wrist—the one that's holding the ice to his face. "Why'd you let him do that?"

Even though it's obvious he's referring to tonight's earlier events, it feels like a lifetime has passed since then, and his question, seemingly coming out of nowhere, catches me off guard. My hand jerks, and my gut instinct is to pull away, but he's got me in a vice grip. Somehow, I doubt he's holding on this tight to keep the ice on his face. I'd purposely not brought up anything that went on upstairs for just this reason. I draw in a breath, finding his blue eyes pinned on mine in a way that belies the fact that he's drunk. I wet my lips, my gaze sliding over his features. He could easily grace the pages of a magazine. Too bad he's never been anything but cruel to me. The prettiest faces hide some of the ugliest souls.

"Stella ... talk to me," he grunts out. His tone carries a mild note of exasperation and something else I can't quite put my finger on.

"I don't have an answer for you. Nor do I believe I owe you one. Why'd you pull him off me like that? You could have skipped over this entire mess. Minded your own business. Don't pretend like you care about me."

Several seconds tick by, and I figure that's it. I've hit the nail on the head, and he doesn't feel the need to respond. He exhales audibly. "Because I was worried he would hurt you," he mumbles, his gaze fixating on my lips. "Because he has what I—" His eyes drift shut as the remainder of his words go unspoken.

I stare at him for several minutes after he falls asleep, torn as to whether I want him to finish what he was going to say or if it should remain buried.

Taking care not to wake him, I ease from the edge of the bed. After fetching another bottle of water to leave with him, I go back to my room, determined to get some sleep before I have to be up to get ready for class.

As I climb into bed, I hook my phone up to a charger, but realize there are a few texts from Bear that I'd missed.

> Mason is out cold.
> I'll see you in the morning.
> Text if anything comes up.
> Oh, and Lennon—
> I read you pretty well.
> I have no regrets.

TWENTY-FIVE

LENNON

Waking up the next morning, I scramble from my bed after having hit snooze twice. I needed a few more minutes, but now I'm running late. My head is blissfully quiet for all of three seconds before it begins to fill with reminders of the craziness from last night. Usually, I'm a huge proponent of the idea that things look better in the light of day. This time around, though, I'm not so sure, and I definitely have some anxiety surrounding how I'm going to handle looking any of the guys in the eye this morning.

I blow out a breath, step into the bathroom, and look into the mirror over the sink. How do I even look *myself* in the eye?

I hadn't given a second thought to what the aftermath would be. I'd felt things in the moment and went with it. It might be a flaw in my personality. A glitch in my brain. There's no taking any of it back, either.

I'd needed to be there for Mason in a way that I still don't quite understand. I'd reached for Bear to calm my body and my mind. And I even set aside all the bullshit between Duke and me to stay with him when it was asked of me.

Now I'll have to own up to everything I allowed to happen last night and figure out what it all means, and where we go from here. Not that it's all on me, but I'm the only person I can control in this shitstorm.

With a sigh, I open my closet and step inside, thumbing through the few garments I'd hung in there. I pull a sundress off the hanger and take it with me into my bedroom, laying it on the bed before crossing to the dresser. I rummage around until I find a decent pair of underwear and a strapless bra that should provide me with enough support under the bodice of the sundress. My eyes flick to the box of expensive clothing I've yet to look through. Duke would probably fall over if I showed up in something he purchased. I draw in a breath. Funny, though, Mason now has a second pair of my underwear because all my clothing was left in the attic last night. If this keeps up, I'll have to bust out that La

Perla bag and see what Duke picked out. But no. That'd only add to the pile of crap I'm going to be dealing with today. *Nope.* Not today, Satan.

I slip into the undergarments, then pull the sundress over my head, and after a quick glance in the mirror to slick some gloss over my lips and add a touch of mascara, I'm ready to go. Grabbing my backpack, I head downstairs toward the pandemonium.

As I've discovered is normal for this hour, there are a lot of voices coming from the direction of the kitchen and dining room, the clatter of silverware, and—oh, hell yes—the scent of bacon. My stomach rumbles.

"Guess I'm not the only one with a hangry stomach, huh?"

I jerk to a stop at the bottom of the staircase and inhale sharply, knowing exactly who has practically snuck up behind me. Was it really only last night that Mason and I were in the kitchen together, making that snack that he never ate? My brain twists, thinking about how everything had gone to hell the moment I went up to the attic.

I turn toward him, noting the split in his perfect damn lip, a cut on his brow held closed by a tiny bandage strip, and a swollen purple bruise on his left cheekbone. It takes everything I have not to reach out and smooth my finger over the injuries. I would imagine from the way they were pummeling each other and rolling around that there are more bumps and bruises hidden under his clothing. I'm definitely not going to ask, seeing as how he'd be the most likely to strip down and give me a private viewing. *Then again ...*

He seems unbothered by my perusal of him, and he stands there, lips twitching before he drops his gaze to my body. "Looks like you washed off my artwork before I could get a photo or two. Disappointing."

Eyeing the cocky amusement flowing from Mason despite his banged-up face, I figure the best way to fight fire is, indeed, with fire. I cant my hip to the side, giving him a bold once-over. "You'd already mostly messed it up while you were touching me with your dirty hands."

He smirks, his sinful gaze setting off little sparks over my skin. "Don't deny it. You liked my hands on you. And other things *in* you." He skims over my collarbone with the back of his knuckles. For a moment, he's lost in thought as he watches himself touch me. "Too bad we got interrupted the way we did."

I should have known better than to start something here in the foyer where just about anyone could listen in on what he's saying. And to my dismay, my nipples grow taut at his perusal, his words, and his touch. There's nothing I can do to stop the ache that begins to build in my lower abdomen. Was some of what happened yesterday with Mason just plain fucked? *Absolutely*. But it was so very Mason, and I won't fault him for dealing with his pain in whatever way he needed to. I was a little thrown by it, but I handled it, the way I always try to handle my shit. And am I thinking about how things would have gone between Mason and me if Duke hadn't interrupted? *Fuck yes*. Because I've never experienced anything so raw and wild before. He'd been a raging fire, and I'd been completely consumed by the wicked energy of it all. There'd been something so insanely hot about the way he'd touched me, smearing a portion of what he'd drawn and rubbing it into my skin. And his cock. Holy fuck. Long and thick. He'd filled me to perfection. Before he'd gotten yanked away, that is.

"You're thinking about it, aren't you?"

Stunned to realize I'd let my mind wander, I shake my head in confusion. "Sorry, what?"

"You're off in your head, fantasizing. Well, let me tell you, we'd have burned the entire house down with the heat between us." Those chocolate-brown eyes of his are drowning in unmistakable lust. "If Duke hadn't come along, I would have fucked you so good, you'd never have gone to Bear afterward."

Shit. My face blanches, blood draining from it. *Oh my god.* "How—?"

A small laugh escapes him. "Your eyes have just done one of those deer-in-the-headlights things. Never mind how I know. If I didn't already, now I definitely do."

Panic races through me. "I—" My mouth snaps shut. I have no idea what to say, haven't even wrapped my mind around how to explain to myself what I've done, much less ready to have a conversation about it.

"Don't worry. I won't tell Duke." He leans in, his lips grazing mine as he stares into my eyes at close range. "He'd go apeshit," he rasps.

Deflect. Oh god, distract him. I draw in a breath, willing my mind to work as fast as his does. "Are you sure your pissing match up there was about me at all? I mean, you left me naked on the floor without hardly a backward glance. Both of you."

Funny, but I hadn't pinpointed until this very moment what bothered me most about what'd happened. It wasn't that I let Mason use me like I had or that I felt embarrassed that my stepbrother had found us like that. It's that I became a superfluous part of the background the second Duke had shown up. I cross my arms over my chest.

He huffs out a laugh, ignoring my question completely while his eyes roam over me. "Kintsukuroi, if you thought that wasn't about you at least to some degree, you've got more issues than I thought."

"Kintsu-what? What are you talking about?" I exhale harshly. When he just smiles, his lip curling, I groan out, "Whatever. I don't know if I fully buy what you're trying to sell me, Mason." I shake my head. These two have a history of hatred, and I doubt what I'd witnessed had much of anything to do with me.

"Think what you want. Your perception of things doesn't change the truth, Lennon. And it doesn't change that you ran straight from me to Bear's arms when he offered them." He leans in close so his words brush over my lips. "Did he fuck you good, Lennon?" Blood rushes back to my face, my cheeks reddening. When I decline to answer, he chuckles, arching an infuriating brow at me. "Anything else we should talk about this morning?"

My gaze narrows. The only topic I want to discuss would be sure to set him off all over again—the drawings. I wasn't the subject of all those pieces of art. I want to know more about the woman who so clearly plagues him.

Without waiting for an answer, he turns his back on me and walks away.

I choose to let him get well ahead of me, hoping that the heat in my cheeks hasn't translated to a furious blush staining my face that the entire brotherhood will be able to read.

When I get into the kitchen, strangely, Mason is nowhere to be found, but I do spy Bear at the stovetop, transferring scrambled eggs from a skillet to a bowl. My heart sinks a little, knowing he must have opened his mouth and spilled to Mason after he helped me get Duke situated in his room. He might not have regrets, like he'd said in his text, but I'm feeling a good amount of worry over it. Mason drew all these awful words on my body, and it's hard not to feel like in a way I *earned* them. I let that tick around in my brain for a moment. No, fuck that. I'll be damned if I'm going to slut shame myself.

The second Bear turns around and sets the food on the kitchen island, four brothers—Tucker, Pierre, Kai, and Brendan—all grab at the spoon, and by the time they're done serving themselves, there's nothing but a bite of egg left in the bowl.

Great. Now there's not even any food, and I'm fucking starving. Disappointment floods through me as my gaze swings to an empty platter that obviously once had the bacon on it that I'd smelled all the way from the foyer.

Kai laughs when he sees me surveying dishes where the food once was before they came in like a four-man wrecking team and demolished it. "Baby doll, you need to move fast around here." He gestures in the direction of the same cabinet Brendan keeps his candy stash. "There are Pop-Tarts in the cabinet."

I roll my eyes at him, and make sure he sees it, too, but choose to say nothing. His attempt at making me feel somehow less than, make himself seem bigger and better—or whatever it was he was trying to do—didn't work. *I've done a great job at making myself feel like crap all on my own, thanks.* Besides, little does the jerk know, I happen to like Pop-Tarts. With a sigh, I pull open the fridge to get some juice.

"Hey, Little Gazelle. We'll be leaving soon." Bear's deep voice at my back sends my mind hurtling back to the shower last night, warm tingles shooting down my spine. Oh god, first Mason, now Bear. I swear, my face is going to be as red as a tomato if this keeps up. I don't know how to act around him. I really don't. Everything has changed now—including what little trust I had in him.

I pour some juice into a glass and carefully take a sip as I turn around. Briefly glancing at Bear, I tear my gaze away and look off to his side. "Okay. I'll be ready. No problem." I glance down at the plate he's offering me. A small heap of eggs. Two slices of bacon. I frown, hesitantly holding out my hand to take it from him.

He gestures to the plate, narrowing his eyes on me. "What's with the frown? Don't you like eggs and bacon? I was told you were hungry, so I made a plate for you because these heathens never leave anything behind. But I can make something else real quick, if you want."

Mason told him that I was hungry. And then disappeared? Recovering from the surprise that he'd done something nice for me—and still thrown off by the fact that Bear told Mason about us—I shake my head, mumbling, "No, this is great. Thanks."

Lowering his voice, he murmurs, "Did everything go okay with Duke? He didn't act like an ass, did he? Because I will kick *his,* if he did."

I swallow down my humiliation, figuring I can at least fill him in on Duke. "No. He was fine. Just kept drunkenly repeating himself. He had a lot of questions for me. But I highly doubt he remembers anything. He was out of it."

Bear nods, concern etching his rugged features. "Mason?"

I swallow, my eyes locking with his. There are way too many people around to say a damn word about any of it. My jaw works to the side and locks. "I spoke with him."

A flicker of surprise crosses his face, and his head tilts to the side. I'm certain he's picking up on my overwhelmed state of mind and maybe even the fact that I'm upset because a second later, he cups the back of my neck, his thumb grazing my jaw. His gruff voice hits me square in the chest. "We'll talk later, okay?"

I stiffen at first, but then have to bite my lip as warmth flows through me from head to toe at his touch. "We don't have to, really. I'm good." I pull away from him and head over to the kitchen table.

"Lennon?" I hear the confusion in his voice and feel his eyes burning into my back as I begin shoveling breakfast into my mouth. I hold up my hand and shake my head. I just can't. Not right now.

Just a few seconds later, Duke appears. "Leaving in two." I assume he's talking to me since I'm still eating my breakfast, so I nod, stab my last piece of egg, and pop it into my mouth. I covertly watch him while I chew. Oh yeah. He's moving stiffly, and his face looks painful. He's totally grumpy—hungover badly, I'm guessing.

Mason hadn't seemed nearly as affected by whatever they were drinking this morning. Everyone's different, though, and has different tolerances. And since they were in Mason's domain, I'd wager he'd been consuming something he drinks all the time ... and even if it were something Duke likes to partake in, too, maybe they consumed more than he's used to. I have a feeling Mason poaches his liver on a regular basis with whatever they drank.

I don't even know why I'm thinking about it, or why I care. Frustrated with myself—and fucking everything—I pick up my plate and fork and take them to the sink. Quickly rinsing and stowing them in the dishwasher, I then retrieve my bag from the floor.

"You might try squatting instead of bending over, Stella. No need to show the goods off to more brothers than you already have. Are you going for some sort of record?"

My mouth drops open as I smooth down the back of my dress, indignation spilling through my veins. *Fuck, does he know, too? How could he?* I whirl on Duke, my eyes wide. Little does he realize, after speaking with Mason, I've already reached my limit of what I'll take from cocky assholes today, so I let myself rip into him. "Oh, I'm sorry, did you see something you liked and you're too—"

He cuts off my question when he grabs my chin, taking my breath away as he tips my head back. "Nah, Stella Bella. If you think for one second I want sloppy seconds, trashy thirds, or filthy fourths, you're fucking deluding yourself."

Bear groans, "Jesus Christ, Duke, that was uncalled for."

"You bet your ass it was." I glare at Duke, wishing I could shoot flaming darts at him from my eyeballs. My face burns hot, humiliation pumping through me at an alarming rate. I wrench myself from his hold. I'm going to choose to think maybe he isn't aware of the rest of the mess I made last night and simply hit dangerously close to the truth. "What's crawled up your ass and died this morning? The next time you get drunk, and I'm asked to keep an eye on you, I'll go with my gut and let you choke on your own vomit." I'm so angry, I can't focus.

"Damn," one stupidly brave soul huffs out, which is followed by a whole lot of snickering, as well as whispered cautions to shut up. Fuck me, the entire brotherhood is watching us. Listening.

"Let's do this somewhere else," Bear grits, shaking his head, his jaw rigid.

I take off for the front door. "Fuck this."

"Stella, get your ass back here," Duke shouts from behind me.

I flip him off over my shoulder and keep going, charging out the front door and down the steps, the alarm system beeping behind me. "Fucking asshole," I groan out, securing my backpack over my shoulders just as the alarm blares to life. I give a little smirk. *Good.* I don't know for sure what happens when it goes off, but I have a suspicion that Tristan, at the very least, gets a call from the security company. I don't even fucking care.

There are some shouts from behind me, but I pay them no attention and continue down the driveway. *Fuck.* They have me so twisted up I can't think straight.

I NEED time alone to collect myself before I have to deal with Duke again. I'm not looking forward to seeing him. Not in the slightest. Not any of them, honestly. I'd been so livid when I left the house, and they weren't really keen on the fact that I'd started down the driveway on foot, especially after I set off the security alarm. Well, too fucking bad. That makes us all unhappy campers today.

I shouldn't have given in when they stopped the SUV beside me. I should have kept going. For all I cared, they could have followed me going three miles an hour the entire way to campus. In the end, though, Bear had pulled off and forced me to get into the SUV. He made sure I understood that in no uncertain terms was I going to be allowed to walk on my own to campus.

The stern but unfailingly kind look in his eyes is what finally did it; I'd cracked and given in. Even so, the entire way to campus, I'd refused to meet any of their gazes. I'd still been grumpy when Bear showed up to walk me from the science building to Cabot Hall for my history class, and I'm not any less so now.

I can hold a grudge with the best of them and so badly want to say fuck it and just take off, but I can't, so I dash down the lecture hall stairs after my history class lets out and flee to the bathroom at the end of the hall that I'd discovered the first day I had this class. I hightail it inside, knowing Duke will be waiting for me on the steps of the building in the next five minutes. His final class of the day is across the quad from mine, but he'd warned me earlier that he has a lab on Thursdays and has to get back to campus for it after he drops me off at home. I can't be late.

He can try to talk to me all he wants but fuck that and fuck him. I'd lost sleep thinking about how both he and Mason had ended up beaten and bruised—even if it'd been as a result of their own hands—because of something I started. I keep telling myself that if I'd just stayed put and left Mason to his tantrum, none of this would have ever happened. If it hadn't, I wouldn't be having daydreams of marking all my clothing with a scarlet S for *slut*.

I'm still sitting on the toilet when the lights go off and the odd sound of metal scraping on metal reaches my ears, then there's the distinct *click* of the door being locked.

"Hello, is someone there? Sorry, I'm still in here."

But no one answers, and I'm left in the dark with my panties around my knees.

TWENTY-SIX

DUKE

I RUN my hand through my hair, letting a frustrated gust of air leave my lungs. *Where the fucking hell is she?* My gaze sweeps from Cabot Hall, where I stand on the steps, and out across the quad, scanning the lush green grass and KU students hanging out in small groups, talking animatedly amongst themselves. She wouldn't have taken off. She knows better. At least I think she does. Lennon's angry with me for how I treated her this morning. I don't blame her. I was a dick. The things I made myself say to push her away ... fuck, I'm kinda mad at myself. Tired and hungover—and other things I'd rather not think about—do not mix. So, now I've pissed her off badly enough that I'm unsure she'll ever look me in the eye again.

An incoming text message grabs my attention, and I

pull out my phone, fully expecting to see a message from her.

Do you have her under control?

But it's not Lennon texting me, and there's only one "her" my father could be referring to. I grit my teeth. We knew, obviously, that they'd be alerted about the alarm going off. Whether she'd done it on purpose, I have no fucking clue. All day I've anticipated my father's call, and when it hadn't come, I'd hoped he'd brushed it off like it wasn't a big deal. Oops, there goes an over-anxious girl wanting to head to class or some shit like that. Yeah, I don't buy it either, but when my father hadn't immediately been up my ass about it, I'd been hopeful.

I'd also been wrong.

We're fine.
Just a misunderstanding.
Waiting for her to exit her class now.

If you can't handle her ...

If you didn't trust me,
you shouldn't have enrolled her at KU.
Shouldn't have left her with me.

MASON

> Gotta go.

See you at the game.

Yep, that's just like Tristan Valentine to not allow me the last word. And it might look like a friendly *See you soon!* to the untrained eye, but my father is a master at delivering subtle barbs. What he really meant was, *Congratulations, Duke. This is the fifth year you should have been playing ball, the fourth as a Kingston Lion. But instead, you let a girl derail your entire future. Bravo.*

And yeah. I did. I've been thinking plenty about it lately, but not in the way he has. The anniversary of Juliette's suicide snuck up fast. Next Monday commemorates the day my entire world turned into a nightmare of epic proportions.

When I'd looked at my phone this morning with my head pounding so hard I swore it was going to come off my neck, I'd gotten a reminder notice in my calendar app. It simply says Juliette. Four days. It's a sick little countdown I'd plugged in as a reminder to myself that first year after I lost her. Because yes. Four days from now will be the anniversary of my girlfriend's death. Though, why I thought I could ever—would ever—forget, I'll never know. More than likely, I'd plugged it in as a way to ram the knife into my chest and twist it every goddamn year.

I thought I'd handle it better by now, but it's just as fresh as the day I found out she was dead. And then, this morning, there was Lennon looking all kinds of beautiful. Lennon, who got to spend hours at that damn diner with Juliette. Lennon, who I need to push far away from me. She's constantly on my mind lately, and it's not fucking acceptable. It's not fair.

My mind twists and forces me back to Juliette, making my heart convulse in my chest. Juliette, my god, she'd been perfect in my eyes. Kingston, as her big brother, should have stood up for her, fuckin' helped her. But he was too wound up in himself and his own life to see the pain she was in. How the fuck had he missed it, living with her? How had he not seen it coming? How the fuck had *I* missed it?

To me, she'd been everything light and good. And then she was just gone. She's dead. She's never going to smile at me again, I'll never get to touch her. And all that's left is this hollow feeling in my gut and the need to make Kingston hurt as much as I do. His sister is *never* coming back. He shouldn't be fucking moving on with his life like he is.

I never have. I don't know if I can or will ever be able to. I know we were young, but I thought she was it for me. Closing my eyes, I make an attempt to shake it off and am surprised when I open my eyes not to see myself bleeding all over the steps of Cabot Hall. Because that's what it feels like every time I think of Juliette. It feels like I'm bleeding out. Like there's nothing left inside me that's worth a damn.

Lennon didn't deserve my wrath this morning. But lately, every time I look at her, I'm reminded of Juliette in her cute little diner uniform. She'd been so happy. So damn happy.

It makes no fucking sense.

My phone buzzes in my hand, jarring me from my anguished thoughts, and when I look down, I realize I've missed a phone call and no fewer than ten text messages from Lennon.

Duke.
Someone locked me in.
Help.
I'm in a bathroom on the second floor.
Duke.
Hello?
Are you there?
I'm freaking out.
Please help me.
Duke?

What the hell? I frown, turning and heading up the stairs and into the history building. I wasn't the one who dropped her off, so I don't have a fucking clue where her class is. I push through the crowd of students until I find a door marked Stairwell B, and while I'm running up the steps, I find her schedule on my phone. She should have been in room 248.

Bursting out of the stairwell, I race around, sidestepping other students and trying not to knock anyone over in my haste. I must look like a fucking psycho running around, dodging people. When I finally find the correct lecture hall, it stands empty. I glance around.

Bathroom, bathroom, bathroom ... where's the closest bathroom? "Lennon!" I shout, getting a lot of odd looks from people passing by. I stop a harried-looking professor, who must recognize me, even though I don't have a clue who she is. "Where's the closest women's bathroom?"

The woman points three doors down. "It's there, but you can't go in." She watches as I head toward the door, pushing it open. "You can't go in there."

I swivel my head toward her and glare. "If my stepsister is here somewhere, I will be going wherever she is." I suck in a breath before letting the bathroom door shut and shouting again. "Lennon!" But there's no answer. A sinking feeling in my stomach, I whirl back toward the woman, but she's disappeared.

Fumbling with my phone, I pull up Lennon's contact info and dial.

"Duke?" Her voice is shaky on the other end of the phone.

"I'm here. I'm looking for you."

"I-I'm in a little bathroom h-hidden away. L-l-left corner of the b-building."

My heart squeezes at the stutter in her voice and the ragged sound of her breathing. Locking my jaw, I take off like a shot, crossing the length of the building in five seconds flat and skidding to a stop. *There.* I hurry over and try to push it open but find immediate resistance. Sure enough, I glance up to find the damn thing is locked with a dead bolt at the top. I've seen these on public bathrooms. It's a way to keep people out when there are plumbing issues. I slap my hand to the door and heave into the phone, "Lennon, I'm here."

"C-can you open it?" Her voice sounds incredibly small.

Irritation fogs my mind. I want to fix this for her with a snap of my fingers. But I can't. "I'm going to have to find someone with a key, Stella."

From inside comes a distressed wail. "Nooo." Another slap to the door. "I-I don't like small spaces like this. Duke, please. I'm freaking o-out." She hiccups through a ragged breath.

Fuck. Her desperation is coming across loud and clear. I squeeze my eyes shut. "I'm going to try to find someone to help. I'm right here. You're gonna be fine. Hang in there."

Five minutes later, I have a janitor hot on my heels as we hurry back upstairs. Lennon has gone quiet on the other end of the phone.

The old guy flips through the keys. "Lemme just figure out..."

I shake my head and catch his eye. "You're going to hand those over, and I'll find it."

"Okay. But I have to stay right here until you give them back."

"I have no intention of keeping your keys. Though, you should figure out how the fuck she got locked in here in the first place." I begin trying one key after another, but there must be about thirty on the ring. My frustration rises within me the longer this takes, unsure what state I'll find Lennon in on the other side of the door.

Our call is still connected, though I had to put the phone in my pocket to have both hands free. "You still there, Stella?"

It's hard to tell, but it sounds like she's breathing

awfully erratically. Crying, I think. I bite down on my lip, abusing it, quite literally, and I'll continue to do so until I have her the fuck out of there.

Finally, one of the keys sinks into the lock and turns, sliding the dead bolt out of the way. *Thank fuck.* "Lennon, if you're on the other side of the door, step out of the way."

I give her a second to move while I hand the keys back to the old man. And then I'm done worrying about anything except the girl on the other side of the door. I push it open, my eyes finding her on the far side of the eight-by-ten-foot space. There are two skinny stalls on one side, a counter with two sinks taking up the other, and Lennon huddled on the floor under a paper towel dispenser with her hands over her face. Her chest rises and falls so quickly, my heart breaks a little for her. She wasn't kidding, she's freaking out. A moment later, her head lifts and when she sees me, she's off the floor and across the room in a flash, throwing herself against my chest.

I catch her in my arms, and immediately know how badly she was affected by this by the way her body shakes. "Baby, shhh. I'm here."

The moment I say it, I know I've fucked up. I don't know that she noticed, because she's practically burrowed herself into my skin, but I definitely called her *baby*, and it hits me hard. While mentally kicking myself, I hold her tightly because that seems to be what she needs from me. The sweet, fruity scent of her shampoo, the feel of her body against mine—it's enough to knock me for a loop.

When her breathing normalizes, and I think she can handle it, I ease her out of the bathroom, then tip her face up so I can have a good look at her. What I see is gut-wrenching. Her face is puffy from crying, and I cup her face in my hands, then gently sweep my thumbs under her eyes, collecting the moisture.

"Don't." She blinks rapidly, her eyelashes spiky with tears.

My brow furrows. "Don't what?"

She takes in a shuddering breath. "Don't be nice to me. It'll make it hurt worse when you go back to being my dickhead stepbrother." She wets her lips, and I have the errant thought that she's probably tasting the salt of her tears.

Why do I want to sweep my tongue over her lips and find out what they taste like?

My eyes home in on those pouty lips of hers. Ones I'd kissed in anger. It would be a huge mistake to repeat that. Ever. I release her face, bringing my hands down to her shoulders. "What can I do? Are you okay? Should we head home?"

She nods, motioning to the bathroom. "My bag is in there."

"I'll get it."

She sucks in a wet breath. "O-okay." I can tell she's trying so fucking hard to shake off what happened in there but is having trouble doing so.

With her bag in hand, I pick mine up off the floor and sling both over my shoulder. "Let's go."

"I can carry my bag." She holds her hand out.

I give a single shake of my head, letting my eyes fall shut as my jaw grinds. "Stella. Just let me carry your fucking backpack, okay?"

She takes a deep breath. "Fine."

"Focus on yourself. Breathe."

For a second, based on the indignant look on her face, I think she's going to argue, but then she thinks better of it. An internal laugh threatens to bubble up to the surface. How does one argue with breathing? I guide her to the stairwell, and we walk down and out of the building, no words exchanged at all.

Once we're heading for the parking lot, Lennon breaks the silence, looking at me from the corner of her eye as we walk. "Thank you for coming for me. I kinda thought maybe you wouldn't."

I frown. "I'm not inhuman, Lennon."

"How do I know that? Who's the real Duke? The

one who trash-talked me this morning in front of an entire brotherhood that I've been forced to live with and who implied I'm spreading my legs for all of you? Or the concerned guy who came to my rescue and held me until I calmed down?" She stops in her tracks, tugging on my arm so I'll face her. She cocks her head to the side, studying my face way too carefully for comfort. "Which is the real you, Duke? The bastard or the nice guy?"

With a curl of my lip, I do what I need to do to keep her far away from me. I know what I'm about to say will destroy any confidence she had living in the house with us. But maybe if I push her hard enough, she'll make my father bring her home. That's probably wishful thinking on my part, but it sure as fuck would make my life a whole lot easier in more ways than one.

I start walking ahead of her, tossing over my shoulder, "You probably shouldn't trust me. Fuck," I chuckle darkly, "you shouldn't trust any of us."

Everything was fine until she showed up and threw us into an unparalleled state of chaos—Mason sticking his dick in her, Bear swooping in like he's her fuckin' protector, and me letting her push all my fucking buttons and make me want to do all sorts of glorious, sinful things I shouldn't be thinking about at all. And of course there's my fucking father, trying to control what goes on here, even though he's the one who threw her at us in the first place.

I grit out the absolute truth. "We're all bastards. You'd do well to remember that tidbit, Stella." I turn around to catch her reaction, but she's gone.

TWENTY-SEVEN

MASON

With one glance at my phone screen, I know we've got trouble. My lips twitch a fraction as I consider the two texts Duke has sent. Lennon took off, and he needs help. How is this my problem? Duke is responsible for Lennon, seeing as how she's his stepsister, and it was his father who brought her here.

Guilt swarms into my head and won't fucking go away.

Maybe I'm the tiniest bit responsible for her upset earlier. Fuck, okay, maybe a lot. Though no one knows that except her and me. I caught up with her on the way downstairs first thing this morning. She'd looked so fucking good in that dress ... and it'd irritated the fuck out of me that we hadn't gotten to finish what we'd started. *Lennon.* She's something else. Curves in all the right places, long legs that'd wrapped around me so fucking tight.

I don't know what had possessed me, but I'd teased her a bit. And once I got going I couldn't stop, I'd outright jabbed, remembering how I'd smelled her shower gel on Bear. The realization that I knew what they'd done had massively upset her, though she'd tried to hide it—and she doesn't even know that I'd simply made a good fucking guess.

And now she believes Bear ran his mouth, even though that wasn't the case at all. He wouldn't do that. There'd been no reason for me to explain that I hadn't actually known, even if I *had* hinted at that fact. She'd been too flustered to notice.

Pressing my lips together, I notice I've missed a portion of the conversation with Bear and Duke. I take a quick second to read it in its entirety.

Duke:
Lennon took off.
I need help.
The plan was to take her home and come back
to campus.
I don't have time to go looking for her.
I have a lab in 15.
And she's pissed at me.

Bear:
WTH?
Coach will shit if I miss class.

I sigh. Well, looks like this has just become my problem.

I'll give a look for her.
I just have studio art.
Prof hardly knows who attends.
Any clue where she'd be?

Duke:
Fucked if I know.
I'll explain everything later.
Well, I'll try.
I don't know WTH happened.
She got locked in a bathroom.

Bear:
Uh, what?

Duke:
Had a panic attack.
Long, weird story.
Then I pissed her off (again).

Turned around, and she was gone.

I'll see what I can do.

What the actual fuck? I pick up my backpack and sling it over my shoulder, walking back out of the art class I'd walked into not fifteen minutes ago. Like I predicted, no one even notices me leave. Artists. So fucking focused on their own shit, they don't see the world around them. The honest truth is that I do my best work at home anyway; I'm not comfortable enough here to create anything meaningful.

I blow out a breath, pushing one of the back doors of Brandywine Hall open and exit into the garden at the back where the hawthorn trees are. I do like to sit out here sometimes and sketch. Chewing on my lip, I walk along the pebbled path for a bit, then sink onto the bench for a moment to think.

I haven't known Lennon long, but if I've learned anything about her at all, then I believe she'd have sought out a quiet location to calm down. Somewhere she could be alone with her thoughts.

I highly doubt she's back at the house. She doesn't have the code to get back inside yet, so we'd know it if she opened the door and set the alarm off. I suppose she could hang out on the back patio until someone got home. But, nah. I doubt she wants to be anywhere near any of us. Duke admitted he pissed her off, so who the hell knows what actually went down.

I stand with a sigh, running a hand through my hair, and push it back out of my eyes. May as well start walking around. I wonder if any of the guys back at the house would know how to put a tracking device on her damn phone, because that would make a scenario like this a hell of a lot easier.

I stop off at the library, but there's nothing but nerds studying in there. I try the coffee shop on campus, but it's full of people and way too noisy. I find the same is true of the two eating facilities. I let my eyes wander as I walk, checking hidden spots on campus I've visited myself.

This is fucking stupid. She could be any-freaking-where. And if she sees me coming, who knows what her reaction will be.

Fuck.

And then, like a miracle, I spot her across the street from campus grounds. *Oh, don't fucking tell me.* But yep, in she goes, hesitating only a moment at the entrance to Kingston University Cemetery before following the footpath inside. I've gotta hand it to her, it's one of the nicer places to be laid to rest in this area of the state.

I should know. It's where my mother is buried.

And it's quiet, I'll give Lennon that. The dead don't speak.

I huff out a gasping breath. Dreams are the exception—or more specifically, nightmares. In my worst ones, my mother is talking to me, but I have no idea what she's saying. Crying. Begging me, I think. Shaking off my morbid train of thought, I hurry after Lennon, determined to see if there's someone specific she's visiting or if she's simply taking a quiet walk where no one would think to look for her.

Pulling out my phone, I shoot a quick text to the group chat.

> Finally found her.
> Don't know how long it'll take to bring her home.

Duke:
Okay. Lemme know if you need help.

Bear:
Maybe you should give her some space.

Duke:
Me?

Bear:
Fuck yes, you.

> That's my plan, Teddy Bear.
> I'm just watching her right now.
> But I want to know what's in her head.
> Don't worry, I've got this.
> See you fuckers when I see you.

I cross the road and follow behind Lennon, moving at a slow pace. This is no meandering walk. It would seem she has a destination in mind because she makes a beeline, cutting a diagonal line off the established path, weaving through the gravestones.

My forehead creases hard right down the center as my brows snap together. It seems like she's heading directly for the Hawthorne family plots. What the fuck? I continue to watch her from a distance. Nope, I'm not wrong.

Lennon comes to a stop at Juliette's gravestone and kneels down in the grass next to her.

Juliette died the year before Tristan and Nikki got married. As far as I'm aware, Lennon and Duke met at some point after Tristan and Nikki were dating, if not engaged. I don't quite remember. So, it makes no sense to me why Lennon would know Juliette at all. There must be some other connection because holy shit, she's talking quietly, using her hands to gesture as if she's having a full-on conversation with her.

I move closer. I need to know what the hell the connection is, even if it makes me feel like an absolute creeper. Coming as close as I can, I stop, leaning against a tree, and strain to hear.

"Such a prick." She rubs her hands over her face. "I used to think he was a nice guy, picking you up at Stella's after work. And now …"

She says something else I can't quite hear, and I curse inwardly, realizing I've missed something. *Stella's.* Wait, is that the name of that little dump of a diner across town? Stella is Duke's nickname for Lennon—and I think he means it as an insult. The synapses in my brain must not be firing because that makes no sense to me. Is Lennon saying she and Juliette both worked there?

What the hell would Juliette fucking Hawthorne be doing working in a dive like that? My brows knit together, my confusion reaching epic proportions. If she's saying she saw Duke pick her up, then he knew about it. Interesting bit of information to have. Not sure what good it'll do me, but I'll tuck it away to ask about later.

As Lennon finishes, her voice lowers to a whisper, and the only word I can confidently make out is "slut."

A visible shudder rolls through her entire body. She sniffles and swipes her fingers under her eyes. Shaking her head, she lies down in the grass and curls up on her side.

Seeing her like this, so clearly in distress—I don't want to feel a fucking thing, but it does something to me. A gaping, sucking chasm opens in my chest. I don't know how long she intends to stay, but it'd take a nuclear bomb going off to get me to leave her like this.

Quietly, I open my backpack and pull out a sketchpad and a charcoal pencil. The pencils aren't my favorite to use, as they're a little waxy in texture, and it affects how I get my ideas on the paper, but they're more practical to carry with me. My preference is compressed charcoal sticks—soft, like the ones I'd used to draw on Lennon's skin. I dampen my lips thinking about how gorgeous she'd looked with my work on her. I pull out my phone and scroll to the photos I'd quickly snapped. So. Fucking. Hot.

Blood flows south, and I groan, having to readjust myself before I lean back against the tree. Breathing slowly, I attempt to ignore my still-hard cock and begin to sketch out an image that comes to mind. I never draw directly from life, it's always a memory or something in my head—in this case, it's a sad, lonely girl kneeling among flowers, hands covering most of her face. Tears snake around her fingers to drip down over her hands. It's almost like she's trying to keep the tears inside, but they're overflowing—and she can't do anything to stop them.

I pause a moment to rub my hand over my tightening chest. The girl's hair is swept into a messy bun on the top of her head, a pencil jammed through it to hold everything in place.

If I hadn't known I was drawing Lennon, I do now. A shuddering sigh escapes me. Once I have the basic sketch down, I go back in, adding detail, fine-tuning the shape of her hands, and adding depth and dimension to it.

While I work, my tongue plays with the split in my lip. Fucking Duke. I'd laid into him good. After we'd gotten out our aggression, I'd offered him a drink. And that turned into many more. I smirk, not knowing if Duke remembers our entire conversation. He was wasted by the end of it.

"What the fuck were you thinking, drawing all over her? Sticking your dick where it didn't belong."

"Did it occur to you that she was a willing participant? You know, you could have just watched if you wanted—or joined in for all I care. After all, it wouldn't be the first time, would it, Duke?"

"You're fucking crazy."

"No, you're the one who acted like a complete psycho tonight, dickhead."

I grit my teeth and go back to work, every few minutes looking up to make sure Lennon is where I left her before going back to the version of her on my sketchpad. She's coming along nicely.

It must be an hour or more that I sit there under the tree before a shadow falls over me.

"What are you doing here, Mason?" The unsteady softness of Lennon's voice catches me by surprise.

I draw in a breath as my head and my heart war over how to handle her. Do I concede that she's suffered through enough at our hands in the last twenty-four hours? My hands specifically. Or do I continue to punish her for something that gutted me? Her in that space. My space. Where I go to deal with the chaos in my head.

She hadn't so much as flinched. She'd looked and looked until I thought I'd go out of my goddamn mind. Nothing on those canvases made her turn and run. And some of it ... it's pure, undiluted rage in its rawest form. I know it's awful to look at, and even worse to consider what type of person would be messed up enough to create anything like that.

It's me.

With her eyes watching my every move, I carefully close the sketchpad and set it aside with the pencil.

"I like it here. It's quiet. Why are *you* here?" She doesn't need to know I followed her in. Probably better if she has no idea.

The emotions she'd been sorting through by talking to Juliette are still evident on her face—pink cheeks, red nose, tired eyes. She steps close enough for me to reach her, and I follow my instincts. My hand darts out to grasp hers, and I tug. Caught off balance, she stumbles and falls right onto my lap, just like I'd hoped she would.

"Mason," she hisses out, her voice full of exasperation. "What are you doing? Stop." She begins to extricate herself from the slightly awkward position.

I let a low groan rumble from my chest. "Fuck. I lied."

She pauses in her struggle. "About?"

I think the only way for her to listen to me at all is to — "I knew you were upset, and I followed you in here." She blinks. I blink back. "I watched over you to make sure you were okay. Sat here and sketched for well over an hour, hoping the sleep did you some good. Please stay. I just want to talk to you." Bringing my legs up behind her, my thighs nudge her, and she falls forward, her hands bracing against my chest.

Air gusts from between perfectly pink lips. She leans away from me, her eyes traveling my face, and I know she must be looking for any hint of a lie in my words. But there isn't one. She wets her lips and gives her head a little shake. "Why should I listen to a word you say?"

I study her, unsure if I should allow her to know that I see her, that I know she's a little damaged just like me. I reach up and cup her flushed cheek. "Because broken mirrors still cast reflections, and when I look at you, I see myself, Lennon."

Her surprised exhale is audible, and she pulls back slightly, staring at me for a few seconds. I read the hesitation all over her features. Moving slowly, I put my arms around her body and pull her closer so I can rest my forehead on her shoulder. "Just a few minutes, then if you want to go, I won't stop you."

Her chest rises and falls several times before she murmurs, "I'll stay on one condition. We can talk about whatever you want, but I get to ask you a question, and you can't fly into a sociopathic rage about it."

"Tall order." I lift my head and tilt it to the side, studying the minute changes in her as she ever so gradually gives in—she's breathing easier, and her entire body is more relaxed. I show her a hint of a smile. "Deal." I lift my hand to brush a few loose tendrils of hair back from her face.

I let my eyes travel over her and rest my hands on her waist. "Bear didn't tell me a damn thing. He's my friend, and I shouldn't have let you think that."

Her lips part, brows pinching. "But—"

"Your soap or whatever. I smelled it on him. When he was upstairs with me. Put two and two together, and got one, if you catch my drift." I pause. Her blue eyes register confusion as her forehead sets in a deep scowl. "Are you upset that I let you think that?"

"A little ... I mean, you let me treat him like crap earlier."

"Yeah. Kinda why I'm telling you. I felt bad about it. He's my friend."

She purses her lips. "Well, what about Duke? Did you tell him? Because that bullshit this morning was—"

"Nope. Pure coincidence as far as I know. I don't know what to tell you there. And he and I have our own shit, which is a story for another day."

She looks past me for a few moments, like she's trying to decide whether to say something else. "Are you mad that Bear and I ..." She frowns. "I mean, the two of us, we aren't together, but I wondered"—she swallows hard—"like, a lot about what you were thinking this morning after you told me you knew. The things you put on my skin. I know that what I did could come across a certain way." A shudder runs through her. "But I like sex, I like how it pulls me from my head."

I halt her with a raised hand as I work my jaw to the side. "I think you did what felt right to you, and that'll always be okay with me." I shrug. "I was angry about Duke's interruption, and really fucking pissed that we didn't get to finish what we'd started. I also know what I drew on you was a lot to take. But ... did anything happen up there that you regret? Did I *make* you—"

Lennon looks into my eyes, the blue depths calling to me. "No. I don't want you or anyone else asking about that again. I went up there and I made a choice to allow you to touch me the way you did. And when you laid me down, I wasn't thinking of anything but making both of us feel good." She leans in and touches her soft lips to mine. As she eases back, she sweeps the pad of her thumb gently over the split in my lip. "Does it hurt?"

"No. I'm fine." And I might die if I don't kiss her again. I need my lips on hers, need to know how she tastes. I catch the back of her neck and tug her to me, bent on proving just how fine I am. I crush my mouth to hers, and when her lips part on a gasp, I breathe her in. She's fucking intoxicating. Her hands find my shoulders and hang on tight as I draw her closer, until our bodies are firmly pressed together. There's not a sliver of space between us. My heart rockets around in my chest as I swipe my tongue across her bottom lip. It results in sparks of fire shooting down my spine, and my dick hardening at an incredible rate.

She sighs into my mouth, and that's all it takes. I

ravenously stroke my tongue into hers, wanting to know this part of her, too. And fuck, her kiss is just as addicting as the rest of her mind and body is for me. Lush lips, wicked tongue, and a hint of tease as we crash together over and over again. This girl, she kisses with her entire body, moaning as she grinds against my dick, hands roaming to my neck and into the hair at the back of my head. Her breasts are pressed tightly to me, and I can't fucking help myself—I run one hand along the side of her thigh and under her dress, not stopping until I have a handful of her taut ass cheek.

I groan, coaxing her to ride the ridge of my dick. I'm consumed by her. Every cell in my body is in tune with hers, all my sharp edges fitting so perfectly with her jagged pieces.

"Mase," she gasps out my name, her body rocking faster and faster. I grip her ass more tightly. I want my dick inside her so fucking bad, it's all I can think about. She pulls away, her face glowing pink as she stares into my eyes, and then suddenly her gaze shifts, taking in our surroundings. "We can't do this here."

But the entire time she's saying she can't, her body continues to move over mine, dragging her clit up and down my cock. My hand slides from her ass, fingertips seeking out her panty-covered pussy. I brush them over the damp fabric between her legs. My eyes connect with hers as I withdraw my hand, fixing her dress for her. "You're probably right."

She heaves out a breath, lightly smacking me. "You know I am."

So fucking pretty all flushed like this. My brain is so full of her, it's as much a surprise to me as it is to her when I whisper, "Lennon, why do you think Duke calls you Stella?"

TWENTY-EIGHT

LENNON

I freeze, my eyes widening. "Oh, um—" Why is Mason asking me about Duke's nasty nickname for me?

He gives me a subtle smile. "You don't have to lie or make shit up. Or be embarrassed. I'm fairly certain I know the truth. But I want to hear it from your lips. I want to know what *you* think."

My brows dart together, and my fingers reflexively clutch at the front of his shirt, digging into the skin below. Is this some sort of insane trick question? Finally, I blurt out, "Stella's—it's where I was working to save money for school. So he calls me Stella." Is that really what he was after? "It's a little run-down diner that does, in fact, have the best burgers anywhere near Kingston University. It's definitely a dig at the fact that I had to work there." I look past him for a moment, unsure how much more to share. "I don't even know why I'm telling you this, but—"

He slides his hands up the sides of my thighs, dragging the fabric of my dress out of the way. His hands on my bare skin makes me tremble. His voice is husky when he asks, "But what, Kintsukuroi?"

That brings my gaze flying back to him. I squint. "I'm going to look that up because I know you won't tell me." *Kint-soo-ko-roy. Who the hell knows how it's spelled, though.*

He smirks. "You'd be right. Now, what were you saying?"

I drag in a ragged breath. "I used to look at all the university students who came in and think, *That's what I'm killing myself for.* To be able to go to school and then eventually be able to support myself—be able to hang out on a Friday night and have burgers and fries with my friends instead of being the one doing the serving. It's something I wasn't sure I'd ever earn enough to swing." She heaves out a sigh. "I guess it was for nothing, with Tristan putting me through school, no matter how dickish he is about it."

"No. I highly doubt you learned nothing from that experience. We always learn from the shit we go through. How long did you work there?"

He catches me by surprise with that little wisdom

bomb. And he's right. I learned plenty, I suppose, about people. About how the world works. "From when I was fifteen to the day before Tristan brought me here and told me I was done at the diner."

"I have my own thoughts about Tristan telling you that you can't work, but I don't want to get off track." He gestures to the headstone I had been napping next to. "So, how do you know Juliette?"

Eyes widening, I shift, glancing back over my shoulder. "I, um—" I inhale sharply. "She didn't want anyone to know, but I guess that hasn't mattered in a very long time. Her dad is a dick. Very controlling. I worked with her there while she was trying to save up. We were in similar situations, just at complete opposite ends of the social spectrum."

"So, tell me—if Duke's girlfriend also worked at Stella's, why would he turn that into something of a dig when it comes to you?"

I frown, looking into his deep, dark eyes. "What are you getting at?"

"It's something to think about, that's all. Maybe something you might eventually want to ask him." His lips twist. "I don't think he means what you think he does, and that's all I'm fucking saying about it." He lets out a long sigh, eyeing me warily. "Your turn."

I exhale hard, frowning. I don't know what Mason is

getting at, but I'm too focused on what I want to ask him to put any more thought into it at the moment. My heart pounds hard, and I toy with the material of his shirt, twisting it with my fingers. "Remember what you promised?"

His fingers dig into my hips like he's trying to hold onto his sanity by holding onto me. I have to assume he knows what I'm going to ask, but you never know. *Is he nervous?*

He clears his throat roughly. "Yeah. Go ahead. I promise not to flip the fuck out. Can't guarantee much more than that, though."

I catch the corner of my lip between my teeth and chew on it, trying to figure out the best way to ask. In the end, there's just no easier way to do it except to forge straight forward. "The woman in the images, the one you— Well, I assume you mistook me for her out on the balcony. Who is she?"

He drags in an unsteady breath, his eyes darting to mine for a split second before his head drops. "Why do you want to know?"

"Mason." I duck my head a bit trying to get him to meet my gaze, but it doesn't do much good. This guy is shutting down faster than Blockbuster. "I think at this point I kinda deserve some answers, don't you?"

"Fair enough." His hands grasp my waist, and, to my

surprise, he lifts me from his lap. He sets me on my feet at his side. He stands, then stoops to grab his things, slipping the sketchbook and pencil I'd seen him with earlier into the bag, then takes off toward the path that winds through the graveyard.

Perplexed, I have no choice but to follow his quick strides that are eating up the ground at an astounding rate. I finally catch him a few moments later and walk at his side for a little bit, occasionally sneaking peeks over at him. The smooth cut of his jaw is rigid, but a slight twitch of the muscle at the back betrays his upset at the question I asked. I have no idea of what else he could have possibly thought I'd ask him, but here we are. After a short walk, we reach another pretty spot in the cemetery. "She's there." He points at a headstone.

Lily Mikaelson. I knew. But I wasn't ready for the punch in the gut when I verify by the date of her birth that this is likely Mason's mother or the absolute anguish when I read that the date of death was thirteen years ago. Mason would have been around eight years old. Somewhere in the back of my head, I knew the person visiting him in his dreams and in all his waking nightmares—the person who torments him so—I knew it was his mother.

He gets my attention, pointing at the headstone. "You've seen. Now can we get the fuck outta here?"

I have to give him credit where it's due. He hasn't

flown into a mad frenzy. He's almost eerily calm. In a way, it's worse because I don't know what is ticking around in that dark heart of his.

"Yes. I just needed to know." I reach out to touch his arm, but he pulls it away.

Mason tilts his head to the side, staring coldly at me. "Did you, though?" He turns on his heel and begins to walk away, stalking through the cemetery, back the way we came.

Everything in me wants to soothe his pain. I hurry to catch up and grab his bicep with both hands, pulling hard on it. He stops, pivoting, his jaw clenching hard. "What, Lennon? You saw her. You got your fucking answer." The lost look on his face spears me right in the heart.

"Don't do this. I thought—" My eyes crash shut. *I thought we understood each other.*

"You thought wrong," he grinds out, looking away.

I don't accept what he's saying. I know he knew what I was about to say about us. "Whatever. Next time keep the poetic reflection-in-the-broken-mirror bullshit to yourself if you don't really mean it, asshole."

He draws in a steady inhale through his nostrils. Like I'm testing his patience or something. "Let's just fucking go," he grits out. "I'm sure Duke is chomping at the bit to get at you after you took off like you did."

Holy shit, the entire locked-bathroom-door horror comes rushing back to me. "Maybe if he'd quit saying dickish things, I wouldn't feel the need to be alone to collect my thoughts. He was being perfectly nice. He helped me, was totally there for me when I freaked out, and then—"

"And then what?" Mason slides his gaze my way, his curiosity apparently piqued enough that he'll act like a human again.

"He threw up a wall, just like you are now. Said something about all of you being bastards, and I shouldn't trust any of you." I give him an unapologetically smart smile and begin the walk back to the house on my own, throwing my middle finger into the air.

"He's right, you know," Mason shouts as his footsteps sound a few feet behind me. "We are bastards. Don't you fucking forget it."

"Where the fuck have you two been?" Duke stands on the front steps, his piercing blue eyes blazing.

Ugh, just what I need is an overprotective stepbrother waiting to chew me out. I shrug, rolling my eyes at his overbearing tone. "What have you been doing, watching for us out the front window like we're past curfew or something? It's freaking four in the afternoon."

Mason smirks, laughing a bit. I swear, his mood shifts give me the worst case of whiplash. He runs his hand over his jaw, eyeing Duke from under his hooded stare. "I told you I had her. It's not a big fucking deal. Calm your tits, Duke. She's fine."

I move to go inside, but Duke shakes his head, grabbing hold of my arm. "Nope, we still need to talk about why you took off the way you did, especially after someone locked you in the bathroom, and we have no fucking idea how it happened." His grip tightens on me until I wince in pain. I try to pull away, but he doesn't budge.

"Let go of my arm, you fucking heathen," I demand through clenched teeth. *What the hell is his problem?*

"Stella," he heaves out, "what if—?" Duke doesn't finish his sentence, instead, looking away as he releases my arm, his jaw locked up tight. His hands fist at his sides.

Cocking my head to the side, I study his body language. I do kind of wonder now about the nickname, but I'm really not up to asking him at the moment. I'm not opposed to jabbing at him a bit, though. "What are you saying? Were you *worried* about me, stepbrother?" My brows flick up on my forehead challenging him.

He exhales hard, crossing his arms over his chest as he brings his gaze back to mine. "I'm responsible for you, and I didn't like seeing you like that. Who the fuck knows why that happened in the first place or who fucking did it. Were you a target or an unintended victim? There I am worrying over all those details, and then you were *gone.*"

My brows furrow as I watch the ever-changing emotion on his face. One minute he's snarling about where we've been, and the next ... *Shit.* I might have hit the nail on the head. He *was* worried about me, despite it being his asshole words that sent me running. I press my lips together, then murmur, "Look, I was pretty flustered after my panic attack and needed a bit of time to myself. I went to—" My eyes flick to Mason's, and, as I suspected, he gives me a slight shake of his head. *Yeah.* I'm well aware it's bad timing to bring up Juliette. "Never mind where I went." I jerk my thumb toward Mason. "Creeper, here, followed me, and apparently watched while I took a nap. Really. That's it. I woke up, spotted him, so we talked for a few minutes, then we came home."

Mason's lips twitch. "Creeper. Really? You weren't saying that when we were locking lips, Kintsukuroi." He shoots me a sly wink before raising his brows at Duke, then turning and walking back into the house, his stride full of swagger.

Shit. My eyes flick to Duke's.

In an instant, he's pivoted and grasped me by the neck, pulling me swiftly to him, our bodies coming together with a soft thud. I don't know what to do with my hands, so I leave them at my sides. His eyes bore into mine, searching. "So, is this a thing now? You and him?"

I can't catch my breath. Something about being close to him makes my heart beat so fucking fast. His citrus-scented cologne invades my senses, swirling around inside my head until I can't even think. Hesitantly, I shake my head. "I don't know what it is." I blink up at him. "And I don't owe you an explanation."

His fingers thread through the hair at the back of my head, holding me firmly in place. We stare at each other for several moments, then his other hand cups my jaw before he slides a firmly, almost punishing thumb over my lower lip. "Did he suck on this?" Continuing a path around to my upper lip, he applies enough pressure that if I had lipstick on, it would be smearing everywhere. "Or did you put these around his dick?"

My heart is pounding so damn hard in my chest, I hardly can make sense of his words. "What?"

"You going to be his little slut now?"

MASON

I blink hard, coming to my senses. My eyes narrow on his cruel blue ones. "Fuck you," I spit, bringing my arms up and clawing at his sides until he releases me with a grunt. I take a half step back, which gives me enough room to bring my hand up, and smack his cheek. The violent crack echoes in the air around us. My face burns. "Fuck. You."

TWENTY-NINE

BEAR

THIS HOUSE lately has had me in a constant state of *what the fuck*. I walk in the door a little after five to dead quiet. It's Thursday, and I'd expect there would be brothers roaming the kitchen, foraging for food. There are two types of bastards here: those who graze on anything they can put their hands on because they're too hungry to wait and those who will wait around forever until I show up to ask if I'm making anything for dinner.

I don't mind cooking; I actually find it relaxing when it's just for me. Cooking for a small army, though? It's exhausting, especially coming off a hard practice. I shrug. At least it would appear I'm off the hook for tonight.

Heading up the stairs to drop off my bag in my room, I allow my mind to wander to the upcoming weekend. The first game of the season is Saturday evening. My head is a bit foggy with everything I need to make happen this year. This is my final chance to prove myself, so I hope nothing gets in the way, most especially my father.

Interesting that I haven't heard a fucking peep out of him, especially with this weekend's game fast approaching. That can only mean he's busy working on something else that'll be a pain in my ass.

I wish I could just do my damn thing, but no. There's always some sort of obstacle, something that my father feels I owe him for being born a Pierce. I hate to tell him, but I'd rather be anyone else's son. Well, that's a lie. Probably not Murdock's or Tristan's either. I know it sounds like a poor-little-rich-boy scenario, but I'd seriously give it all up just to be me, no last name attached. I'm convinced it would be an easier road to travel.

I frown. Neither Mason or Lennon are in their bedrooms, as their doors stand open, but I definitely hear music upstairs in the attic. That accounts for Mason's whereabouts, at the very least. Leaving him be, I slip into my room for a minute to set my bag on the bench at the end of my bed, then pull out some sweaty clothes and toss them into the laundry. I stretch my arms over my head for a moment, glancing around, then figure I'll go take another look downstairs. I especially want to talk to Lennon if she's hiding somewhere because the way she was acting this morning was so damn strange. And then the whole ordeal with her getting stuck in the bathroom? I don't know what to make of that, but I guess I'm putting on my fuckin' Dad-of-the-house hat again. I need to know she's okay.

Downstairs, I pass through the kitchen and duck my head into the dining room. Still no one.

Finally, I spy Brendan, Tucker, Pierre, and Arik out on the back patio playing a card game and drinking beer. I open the door and step outside with them. Tucker tips his chin in greeting. "Hey." The other three hold up their hands in greeting but continue to study their playing cards. Spades if I had to guess. It doesn't take that much fucking concentration. Something's obviously happened that I don't know about.

With that in mind, I grit out, "Is something going on I should be aware of?" My entire body bristles at the strange atmosphere out here.

Tucker presses his lips together. "Duke's been a dick all afternoon. Mason and Lennon showed up around four. Seemed like it made things worse. Everyone kinda fucked off, at Duke's request. Kai and Quincy went to the store, Warren is between Maria's legs again"—he smirks with a shake of his head—"and where the other three are, I don't know. Something obviously got fucked up. Mason was pretty laid back about it, but Lennon and Duke both slammed the door on the way in."

Figures shit would hit the fan while I'm at practice. "Okay. Thanks for the intel."

Back inside the house, I decide to look for Lennon. Duke was probably up in his room since the door was closed, but hers was open, so ... she's gotta be here somewhere. I wander from room to room, poking my head everywhere I can think of that she might be on the main floor before I head downstairs. Sure enough, there's some soft music coming from the direction of the gym, so I follow it.

Lennon is a fucking sight to behold. Her little pair of stretchy black exercise shorts and black-and-white sports bra has me halting where I am to drink her in. I have no idea if she knew I'd come looking for her, but I think maybe she's trying to kill me. If that's the case, I'm ready to go to heaven. My mind flips back through what'd happened between us last night, and it's a kaleidoscope of bubbles, soft skin, moans, spraying water, and the wet slap of our bodies as we became one. I remember the way my big hands had looked hanging onto her hips ... and how fucking much I'd enjoyed watching my cock disappear into her tight little pussy. I groan, my dick immediately tenting my shorts at the memory. I have zero ability to stop the flow of blood downward. Not when Lennon is in front of me looking like a sexy yoga goddess.

I draw in an unsteady breath as I watch her hold different poses. She does it like she was born to, all graceful limbs and smooth transitions. I catch a peek at her face in the mirror and for as much as she seems calm—almost tranquil—she's also a little flushed.

That'd probably have something to do with the door-slamming incident earlier, if I had to make a guess. I move closer, finally choosing to take a seat on a weight bench to watch. *What I wouldn't give to peel those shorts down and stuff her full of my—*

"Bear?"

Fuck. I have pussy on the brain. "Yeah." I clear my throat, and it sounds rough as hell to my ears. "Sorry. I wanted to see what you were up to, but then when I found you, I didn't want to interrupt."

She nods, switching to another pose and holding while breathing carefully.

"Can I ask you a question or is it going to bug you?"

Her pink tongue darts out to wet her lips before she glances at me from the corner of her eye. She lets out a deep breath. "You can talk. I was just"—she pulls out of the pose, shrugging—"trying to forget about the absolute crapfest that my life has become in the last week." She turns fully toward me, lifting her arms to deal with her hair that's trying to escape the mess on top of her head. As she stretches upward, her breasts jut from her chest inside the sports bra. I bite back a groan as she yanks the pencil from the bun, letting her blonde hair fall around her shoulders for a moment—and absolutely killing me in the process—before she scoops it back up and knots it on top of her head again.

Fuck me. No, I mean it. Lennon, fuck me. Now.

"You know, we can hit Target and pick up hair ties for you. Or whatever those things are called. Seems like you missed them in your dash to pack. Tristan didn't exactly give you much time."

She smiles. "That'd be great. But no rush. It's not like I'm training for a marathon or whatever." She draws in a deep breath and drops back to the mat into what I know is called child's pose. Coach makes us do yoga sometimes. It's a fuckin' riot, all these bulky football players contorting themselves into knots, but it does help with our flexibility. I eye her muscular ass and wonder if this is the only exercise she does or if she's simply genetically gifted. Whatever she's doing is working, that's for fucking sure. She tips her face toward mine. "So, what did you want to ask me about?"

I huff out a breath. "Um. Yeah. So, I wanted to get your take on the whole locked-in-the-bathroom situation. Namely, do you think it was done on purpose or was it a simple janitorial error?"

She pops into a plank pose, holding it with a stunning degree of strength. Her arms aren't shaking a bit. "I couldn't tell you. No one knocked first or called out to see if the bathroom was occupied. Scared the shit out of me, though. I'm really bad with small spaces. Even closets wig me out." She shakes her head for a second before she peeks over at me. "I don't really labor over what clothing to wear, ever." She wrinkles her nose at me. "Not the typical girl in that way, taking her time, thumbing through her choices. I don't even like looking into small spaces, so my closet door is always shut unless I need something out of it."

"You afraid there's a monster in there?"

"No. More like I'm afraid of the monster who would shut me in."

My brow furrows. "I'm not going to pry, but that's fucking disturbing."

"Yeah. It is, so let's not talk about it." She gives me a tight smile, moving into a cobra pose, stretching her back. *Fuck. Those tits are killing me.* "Actually, I wanted to say something to you about this morning."

"What about?" I drag my eyeballs to meet her gaze as she peeks over at me.

"I recognize I was a little hostile and gave you the

brush-off when all you were trying to do was be kind to me. I think you deserve to know why." If possible, she stretches further into the pose.

My brows raise at her words while my brain tries to keep track of what we're discussing. "I definitely noticed, but figured you were in a bad mood or something. I wouldn't have blamed you after dealing with Duke and Mason."

"No. I—" She clamps her lips shut, her blue eyes staring into mine before she shifts back into child's pose, then a few moments later into downward dog, that delectable ass of hers pushing into the air. *So fucking tempting.*

But not liking the downward turn to her expression, I get up from the weight bench and move closer, kneeling on the mat beside her, hands resting on my thighs. "You can tell me anything, Lennon. Promise." I angle my head to the side, trying not to focus on the glory that I know is under that scrap of material between her legs. I swear, I'm about to have to put my fist in my mouth to have something to gnaw on because I want to eat her up. Every delicious bit of her.

Slowly, she nods, breathing steadily, then lets out a sigh, peering at me from under her arm. "Right before I got to the kitchen this morning, Mason caught up to me and, well … you don't need to know about the entire conversation, but what kinda set me off was that he knew about the two of us." I can barely see it from here, but she's biting at the corner of her lip.

I frown, not understanding what she means at first, but then my brows shoot up. "Oh. You mean— But how could he know anything about that? He was with Duke while we ..."

"Well, that's what I thought." Her face screws up for a second. "I'm trying to remember his exact words to me. It was something like, 'If Duke hadn't shown up, I would've fucked you so good, you'd never have gone to Bear.'"

"The fuck?" I growl internally, just barely holding it in.

She bites down on her lip. "I assumed he meant you had told him everything."

"I didn't, I fuckin' swear on my life, Lennon."

At my adamant tone, she drops out of the pose she was holding. Her face is beautifully flushed, and despite the topic of our conversation, I'm rock hard.

"No. I know you didn't. While he and I were hanging out this afternoon—in the cemetery of all places—after the locked-bathroom disaster, he let me know that you hadn't."

I tilt my head, considering her words. "Crisis of conscience, I guess. He doesn't have them often, but when he does, it's ... well, it's something he feels pretty strongly about."

"Well, that should cement in your mind that your friendship is solid. He definitely didn't like that he'd let me believe that about you. It had nothing to do with you. That was about me."

I nod, scrubbing my hands over my head. "So, he knows, then?"

"Yep."

"Is it a secret, Lennon?"

She blinks rapidly. "No. It's not. Not at all. But ... I have to tell you, that thing with Mason upstairs. That wasn't a one and done either. I—" She takes a deep breath and looks me dead in the eye. "I own what I'm doing, and although some may judge me for it, I won't apologize for going after what I want—with any of you."

My teeth scrape over my lip as I consider her words and the bold confidence emanating from her. I lunge, taking us both tumbling to the mat, and brace myself over her body. Her eyes go wide, and become even wider when I rear up, tugging my shirt over my head and tossing it aside before coming back down. I pin her hands on the mat, and she sucks in a surprised breath, her chest stuttering beneath me. Last night, I hadn't kissed her. Well, the back of her neck, maybe, but I want nothing more than to feel those full lips moving against mine. I inhale, realizing that the scent of her shower gel still lingers on her from last night. It mingles with every single cell inside my body, and into my very soul. It makes my heart thud and my dick swell.

She smells delicious, but I bet she tastes even better. I want to slide my tongue over every part of her, know all her secrets. On a groan, I dip my head down, burying my face in the crook of her neck, letting my lips kiss and nip at the spot where her pulse thrums madly for me. I slide my flattened tongue over as much of her skin as I can get to. She lets out a whimper that turns me right the fuck on.

I lift my head, staring into her eyes as I lower my mouth to hers, so achingly slowly, I wonder if our lips will ever touch. But fuck. They do, and my eyes close as I savor the soft feel of them and how she doesn't hesitate to invite me inside. I plunge my tongue into her mouth, sliding and curling it with hers. We're an out-of-control wildfire, threatening to burn an entire forest. Unstoppable. Untamable.

She's just as ravenous as I am, licking my lower lip and sucking it into her mouth. When she lets it pop free, I groan out, "Ah, fuuuck." She's totally going to kill me with how uninhibited she is.

A wicked little smile twists her lips as her body strains upward and brushes my chest. "Please."

I let a low rasp of a chuckle exit my lips as I release her hands so that I can move down her body. Letting my mouth do the walking, I trail over her skin, grazing her collarbone before skipping over her bra top in favor of her stomach. I teasingly lick just at the hem of her shorts, making her belly twitch and dip in anticipation.

I look up at her from under hooded eyes. Desire flows through my veins and crackles along my spine in a way I've never felt before. I hook my fingers into the waistband and pause. But then Lennon's hands are in my hair, and she's pushing me downward. She knows what she wants. She takes it. And I fucking love it.

Without further ado, I pull the stretchy shorts from Lennon's body only to find she's not wearing panties underneath. I groan out a stuttered, "F-fuuuuck," before peeling them all the way down her long fucking legs and tossing them aside. I stop, my chest clenching. She's drawn her legs together and bent them at the knee, her feet planted on the mat. Her brow lifts, and the corners of her mouth curve. The tease in her expression is evident, but I don't see it coming when she slides her feet apart and drops her legs open, giving me the view of a lifetime.

"What do you need, Lennon?"

Her cheeks flush, but she opens her mouth, and the

most amazing fucking thing falls out. "I want your mouth on me. I want you to lick me until I come."

Something inside me snaps, and I dive between her legs, putting my face on level with her pussy. Gripping her by the back of her thighs, I push her as wide open as she'll go, which is crazy because this girl is flexible. My heart knocks around in my chest, ears buzzing as I get a good look at her. I can't help myself, I want to draw out the moment, so I turn my head, nipping at her inner thigh before gliding my tongue over her skin in a lazy pattern, coming close to where she wants me, but never quite there.

She shudders with need, her breath coming shallow and fast. "Bear, you're a fucking tease," she gasps, her tongue darting out to wet parched lips.

I watch the changes in her expression with every inch closer I get to her pussy. I think she's going to lose it if I don't go there, and soon. But that's half the fun of it—knowing I can make her absolutely lose it.

Lennon. This girl has come into our lives and thrown everything off-kilter. And I don't even fucking care. I really don't. I inhale deeply, the scent of her arousal making me moan in need. My brain spins, knowing what it's like to have my dick buried deep inside her, but now I need to know how she tastes. I simply can't wait any longer. I attack her sweet pussy with everything I have, licking and sucking at her most sensitive skin, then dipping my tongue inside her. "Fuck, you're wet," I groan, lapping at her like I'm a starving man and she's the first food I've had in weeks.

There's a soft click from the direction of the doorway, but I don't fucking care. I couldn't stop now if we had an audience of a million people, not if the room was burning around us. I wouldn't stop for anything.

THIRTY

LENNON

My body jerks at the onslaught of Bear's wicked tongue and lips and—fuck, yes—all that scruff making contact with my pussy. He has a firm hold on my thighs, fingers depressing into the skin. I'm at his mercy, and fuck, he's relentless with that tongue sliding all over my sex. "Oh, god. Bear. Fuck. Fuuuck," I cry out, like he's just ripped the words from my throat. He laps at me, and the pressure from his talented tongue is just perfect. I can't help myself, I grip his hair and let my hips move like they want to, rubbing my pussy all over his mouth.

I'm already a writhing, gasping mess, and I swear, I'd be levitating if I weren't clutching at his hair. "Please, please, please." With my head thrashing against the mat, my hair pulls from the bun I'd sloppily tossed it into.

"I bet he likes you begging." The voice comes from

off to the right, and it's definitely not Bear's deep, gruff one.

My entire body jolts before freezing, and I gasp as my eyes fly open to find Mason standing off to Bear's side, taking in the view. His dark, desire-filled eyes roam over me, and I don't know what to think about the lightning that races down my spine or the trembling in my legs as he studies me in this completely vulnerable position.

"The fuck, Mason," Bear growls, shooting an *Are you fucking kidding me?* eye roll in his direction. To my consternation, Bear's friend standing right there watching every stroke of his tongue hardly slows him at all, and he continues devouring me like he's trying to win a cake-eating contest.

I have no idea what I'm supposed to do in this situation, but then words are muttered against my clit that change everything. "Join in or get the fuck out. So long as it's okay with Lennon, anyway. Whatever she says goes."

Mason smirks, cocking his head to the side, "Funny, this is the second similar conversation I've had recently."

I don't have time to wonder what he means by that because Bear releases one of my thighs and slowly strokes his finger from the top of my opening downward before slipping the thick digit inside me. His gaze connects steadily with mine as my breath heaves from me. I'm overwhelmed by how good it feels when he curls it just right, sending me reeling. His deep voice snaps me back to him while he slowly drags that finger in and out. In and out. *"Your* choice, Lennon. Do you want him to stay or fuck off?"

My eyes flick from Bear's golden gaze between my legs to Mason's. Butterflies erupt in my stomach and flit around like mad creatures, wickedly fanning the flames inside me. Knowing they are both waiting for my response, both looking at me, both ... wanting me? *Oh, fuck.* I'm thrown into an even more heightened state of arousal—I know this because I've just gone from wet to wetter. My face flames with heat and a desire so profound, I hardly know what to do with myself. *What would it be like to have them both touch me?*

I don't even have a clue what my answer is until I open my mouth and the truth falls out. "I want you both." My voice hitches a tiny bit on the last word, and my chest jerks at my admission.

It's actually Mason whose brows draw together, checking in with me. "You sure, Kintsukuroi?" And just like that, he's the guy I'd spent time with in the cemetery before he went all cold on me again. He drops to his knees, and glances at Bear. I doubt he thought I'd agree to let him stay after I'd stormed away from him earlier and especially after he'd shot off at the mouth about being a bastard like Duke said. But I've come to realize that Mason's moods shift and change quickly, depending on his surroundings or what people say to him ... and I get that. I can wig out quickly, too, sometimes. I hold out my hand to him.

He takes it, letting me tug him closer, then leans down, ghosting his lips over mine. Easing back, he surveys my trembling body as he whips his shirt over his head. And a moment after that, my bra's been hiked up and off, and Mason has taken one of my nipples into his mouth, moaning around it while he holds the other in his hand, lightly massaging. His hair falls over his brow, tickling my skin. At the same time, Bear removes his finger from inside me, sending his tongue deep instead. I buck against his face, my own flaming red at my reaction.

My body gives an all-out shudder at the sensation of having two sets of mouths and hands on me. It's like nothing I could have ever imagined before. One second, I'm enjoying the sensual slide of Mason's tongue circling the taut peak of my breast, pinching the other hard enough to make me gasp, and the next, Bear's pushed my legs up farther, and turned his head to run his tongue side to side, up and down my slit.

Letting them see me like this—touch me like this—I'm so very vulnerable ... but there's also a certain power in it. They're on their knees. Worshiping *me*.

Being with two guys like this is all different and new and kind of scary, but every bit of it has me on a collision course with the orgasm hovering on the horizon. The impending explosion shimmers at the outer corners of my being, sneaking ever closer with every beat of my frantic fucking heart.

I strain toward Bear, my pussy riding his face, and he groans out, "Good fucking girl, Lennon," before sucking my clit into his mouth again, flicking it with his tongue.

Mason catches my jaw with his hand, before whispering against my lips, "We're gonna make you have the best orgasm of your life. Now, say please again."

I inhale a ragged breath. "Please. Pleeease."

He draws my nipple into his mouth, and between his ministrations and Bear's, it's all over. Coiled tension snaps in my lower abdomen. My body convulses with pleasure as brilliant lights shoot from behind my eyelids as they crash closed.

"Bear!" My heart slams around in my chest as I scream again. "Mason! Oh, fuck!" I'm floating on a cloud of bliss as the guys continue to touch me, hands and lips moving over me, creating new fires that lick over my skin, making me want so much more.

A swift intake of breath from the doorway makes my heart leap into my throat. For a second time, my eyes pop open to find an additional person in the room with us. My body is still riding the high of my orgasm, and I don't quite know what to do with Duke's eyes on me. "Duke?" I rasp, unable to do much more than acknowledge his presence.

Bear and Mason both quickly shift to kneeling, and I scramble to sit up, trying as best I can to cover myself. I give a furtive glance around, but I don't know where my bra and shorts ended up.

Seeing my discomfort, Bear crawls forward, snatching my shorts from the end of the mat and hands them to me.

I slip them on while Mason chuckles, eyeing the storm cloud that is Duke. "Man, you sure are good at coitus interruptus. It's fuckin' uncanny."

I steal a peek at my stepbrother. His eyes are a confusing mixture of disdain and heat. I don't know for sure what to make of it ... but I have an idea. I swallow roughly, covering my breasts with my forearm as best I can.

Duke shakes his head. "You just can't help yourself, can you, Stella?"

"Don't do that, Duke." Bear grimaces, standing up and propping his hands on his hips. He doesn't give a shit that he's fully hard and Duke totally notices. "She's not doing anything wrong."

Mason snags my bra from beside him and hands it to me. "Here."

"Thanks." I glance quickly from Bear to Mason. "Sorry, guys. Apparently, Duke can't handle this." I pull the top over my head, slipping the band over my breasts, then stand up. I walk slowly toward Duke. "You know," I whisper, "the entire stop-touching-my-stepsister thing would be so much easier to buy"—I stop right in front of him, gazing into his eyes—"if you didn't have a raging hard-on in your pants." I palm his dick, give it a good squeeze, and walk out.

THIRTY-ONE

DUKE

By the time Friday night rolls around, I'm still in a fuckin' awful state of mind. I've kept mostly to myself, letting Bear and Mason tote Lennon around to her classes and generally staying away from everyone.

Seated with an entire galvanized bucket full of cold beer at poolside, I slowly move my legs in the water, watching the ripples created from my movement. I chuckle softly to myself, staring into space. The ripple effect Lennon has had on our lives is unreal. Every single thing she does and says has an effect on us, from the sway of her female hips to her sassy mouth. That girl ... I said from the moment she moved in that she could bring down this entire brotherhood, destroy us. And after just one week, it's already begun—fuck. I was totally on the money with my assessment of what it'd mean to have my stepsister under this roof.

Dragging in a breath, I sip at my drink and allow my mind to continue to roam. I wish I could say I didn't care if Bear and Mason kept tabs on Lennon or not, but I do. Not only because of the agreement I made with my father, but if I dig really deep, I'd have to admit that the incident the previous day made me really fucking nervous—the lock-in incident, that is, not the three-way action I'd walked in on. That was something else entirely.

Lennon. She's rather quickly put an invisible leash on both Bear and Mason. Bear doesn't surprise me all that much. He was immediately protective of her, even when it wasn't necessarily apparent. He's had his eyes on her from the beginning. Of course, we'll see how long that lasts when she finds out the sort of things he's involved in.

But frankly, Mason surprises the hell out of me where she's concerned, especially with how things began with the two of them—all the choking and rage and confusion. It's strange the way they see inside their troubled minds, yet accept each other with all their damaged pieces, sharp edges and all. Do I think them getting friendly is the end of the tempestuous moments? *Nope.* I fully expect thunderstorms to brew and hurricanes to roar.

Goddammit, I want to feel the whip of her wind and the torrential rain that she brings down, need to feel her fury unleashed. I want it directed right at me. My brain goes fuzzy with the idea of having Lennon's sole focus, no matter what that looks like. *Fuck.* I want her hand on my dick again. I give myself a mental shake. No. I'm not ready to admit any of this shit. Not prepared to explore where she resides in the deepest recesses of my mind and definitely nowhere close to verbalizing it to anyone else.

I finish up my beer, chuck the bottle into the recycling bin, and grab another, knowing full well that if I allow myself to think about how Lennon had looked and sounded lying naked on those mats, I need to be on my way to buzzed. Tipping the bottle to my lips, I let my internal mental slideshow rip. Flushed skin, parted lips, throaty cries, undulating hips. Screaming out names that weren't mine. I inhale sharply through my nose before giving in to the jealousy and chugging.

I look around, noting that not a soul has ventured out here with me despite the fact that it's September in Georgia and there's no fucking better way to spend a Friday evening than in the pool with a drink in hand. I've intimidated the fuck out of everyone, scared them into giving me a wide-as-hell berth.

I suppose this is both the best and worst part of

being Duke Valentine. It's really fucking nice that people stay the fuck out of my way with one pointed *What are you fucking looking at?* stare. It's also a little lonely. Oh, well. What the fuck do I care? I'm sure rumors are swirling about what's caused our pack to break up and for me to be the lone wolf. When those rumors get back to me, I'll decide whether or not I give a flying fuck.

Finishing my beer, I toss the bottle, then go for another. I glance at my phone as I twist off the top and flick it into the trash. Brothers should be making their way down here in the next ten minutes or so. Since we'll be busy with Bear's game tomorrow and who knows what else this weekend, I'd called a brotherhood meeting tonight to discuss upcoming plans.

They're going to fucking riot, I'm ninety-nine percent sure—mostly in a good way, if I had to bet on it. The only one I see dissenting could be Warren, and that's because his woman doesn't like this sort of shit. Last year, she'd been invited to the event we'd thrown. It was a mud wrestling competition, and I swear, I thought she was going to talk his ear off with what she thought about it. Personally, if I were him, I'd have shut her up by tossing her into the mud pit with one of the girls and see what she did with it, but hey, that's just me. If I'd been running that particular event, I'd have suggested it to him to shut her up.

It's not more than a minute later that Arik and Quincy come through the back doors with girls on their arms—two for each of them. The six stop dead in their tracks, noting the unamused glint in my eye. *Nope.* My brow arches as I jut my chin at the guys. "The brotherhood is meeting out here tonight. You weren't invited. We don't have grunts at meetings until they prove themselves." My lips twitch. "So, I suppose the question is how badly do you want to stay?" My gaze cuts to the patio door when the noise level goes up, distracting me. "One sec."

More people spill outside, including Bear, Mason, and Lennon. She was included tonight only because I don't trust her not to take off again or get herself into some sort of trouble.

I shake my head, my jaw already working. Bear's got his big hand on her shoulder, and Mason leans close on the other side to whisper in her ear. My eyes flick to her face as she listens to him. Whatever he said, she thinks is funny because she gives him a quick grin before she goes back to sucking on another one of those fucking lollipops she likes. A zip of annoyance rolls down my spine.

I stiffen as my eyes scan over the small crowd. It's not my fucking imagination; every dude in the vicinity is now imagining what it'd be like to have her lips wrapped around his cock because of the way she's sucking on that candy. I scrub my hand through my hair. Not my concern if she wants to open herself up to that.

I stand up, draining most of the beer I just opened. "Everyone, gather around, so Arik and Quincy can decide whether or not they want to prove they're willing to do what it takes to attend tonight's meeting." The two grunts look warily at each other. My lips twist in amusement. I've been so fucking caught up in Lennon, I haven't really laid into these two properly this week. It's time.

Bear and Mason leave Lennon as she sits down on one of the patio chairs and come over to stand with me. At least during brotherhood events, they understand we need to be a united front. I drag in a ragged breath, meeting Bear's gaze out of the corner of my eye. His brow furrows, but he gives me a reassuring nod.

My eyes shift to Mason who gives me a half smile, but also one of his signature naughty winks. It strangely feels like an olive branch.

I let my breath hiss from between my lips. My eyes connect with each of theirs in turn. *If either of them so much as says a word about Lennon grabbing my dick yesterday ...* And then my gaze darts to Lennon, and my chest jerks hard before I tear my eyes away from her.

I've got to fuckin' get my head in the game. I clap my

hands together, catching the eyes of the girls on Quincy and Arik's arms. "Ladies." Their eyes widen, but these four ... they're curious. It's obvious they're all freshman sorority girls looking to climb the social ladder here at KU. And they're totally not staying here at Bainbridge Hall tonight. *Nope.* Not a fucking chance. "Yep. All four of you. Could you come here for a minute, please? I need your help with something."

Giggling, they let go of Quincy and Arik, probably assuming they're heading for greener pastures. I beckon them closer, ducking my head and softly whispering what they're going to have to do to stay in my good graces. Once I've finished relaying my instructions, I have them turn around, facing the brotherhood. A couple lounge in chairs and some had come down in bathing suits and have gone for a dip in the pool, while the remainder sit on the edge, feet dangling into the cool water. Everyone is looking on expectantly, waiting for whatever bomb I'm going to drop on the grunts.

I crook my finger, beckoning to Arik and Quincy. "Come here, please. Stand across from these gorgeous young ladies." I wet my lips, situating myself between two of them, casually wrapping my arms around their shoulders. "Ladies, are you ready?"

All at once, as seductively as possible, they reach up

under their dresses and slip their underwear over their hips and down their legs.

"Oh, fuck yes. Best meeting ever," Tucker hoots. "I fuckin' love it."

He might not love it so much in a few minutes. I smirk with the knowledge of what these two idiots will have to agree to in order to hang with the big boys.

Mason raises a brow, watching as, one by one, each girl holds up her panties. "Well, fuck." He rubs his hand over his jaw, nodding his approval.

Bear catches my eye, his gaze narrowing. I totally read it as *What the hell are you doing?* I shrug, my lips twitching in amusement.

I feel Lennon's eyes on me. I see the wheels turning in her head as she tries to get inside my head and see where I'm going with this. She licks her lollipop again, and my dick positively jumps in my shorts. *Fuck.*

"Arik, Quincy? Take two each. But be wise in your choices." There's a hot pink thong, a pair of purple lace boy shorts, a black-and-white polka-dot bikini pair, and another thong, only this one is black and just the tiniest scrap of fabric. My brows raise at that last one. *Fucking hell, those are skimpy.* And fucking perfect for what's next. "Go on. Choose."

The grunts step forward tentatively, possibly beginning to suspect that their hopes for how this evening would turn out were way off base. Arik glances around, searching for help. Quincy's face is flushed, his pale skin doing him no favors. I'm beginning to wonder if the poor kid is a virgin.

"Take the thongs!" Kai shouts, laughing.

Brendan points at the lace pair. "Dude, no, the purple ones!"

All at once, Quincy and Arik lunge, grabbing up their choices.

I take a moment to meet each of the girls' eyes. "Thank you for your time and your panties, ladies. Now"—I give the two girls I've been standing between a gentle nudge—"please exit around the side of the house. Your presence is no longer required."

"But—"

"Really?"

"Yeah. You heard him." Bear intimidates without hardly meaning to, stepping toward these girls, who shift away from him. "See you some other time."

When they hesitate in their exit, Mason steps forward, aiming the full force of his cold stare on them. "If you don't leave right fucking now, you aren't welcome here ever again. Get the fuck out."

I blink, then laugh at the way they burst into action, scampering across the yard, every single one of them sans panties. If we didn't have business to attend to, maybe

I'd have taken one of them on, let them try to convince my dick that Lennon is nothing special. I grit my teeth together, and without meaning to, I let my eyes find her again. She slowly slips the lollipop into her mouth, twirling the stick between her fingers and thumb so the candy spins in her mouth. She doesn't look away.

"Duke?" Bear touches the middle of my back with the palm of his hand, stealing my attention. "What are these fine young men doing with their newly acquired panties?"

"Well, first. Quincy? Arik? You two fuckers understand now that Friday nights aren't for bringing a gaggle of girls around just to fuckin' show off your new status here at Bainbridge Hall? You're grunts. You haven't shown us much of anything yet."

Quincy nods his head. "Yes, sir."

Arik is a little less cooperative, a sly look stealing over his face, dark eyes narrowing on me. "Yeah. Okay. Understood."

I nod, pausing a moment to let our expectations sink in. "Okay. So, if you'd like to join us tonight, I'll allow it."

Mason leans forward to get my attention, his brow furrowing.

I shake my head. I know what I'm doing. "You have two pairs of panties. If you'd like to be part of this meeting tonight, you'll go into the pool house, strip, and decide which pair of panties you want to wear tonight. Bring the other pair back out with you."

The look on their faces is priceless.

"What the fuck are you two waiting for?" Bear raises his brows.

Mason chimes in with "Either do it or go to your room and start packing, as you've proven you can't hang."

"Lennon?" I get her attention. "Can you remind the guys of the rules they're supposed to have learned?"

She tilts her head, studying me for a quick second before nodding. "Yep. Obey, demonstrate loyalty, and keep your fucking mouths shut."

"See? Lennon's got it. The two of you'll get a chance to show us what you're made of tonight. Unless, of course, you're pussies. If that's the case, get the fuck out of my face."

I inhale. Exhale. Jut my chin in their direction. Faces pale, they turn tail, hurrying to the pool house.

I shrug. "They have to learn. Feel free to get drinks or whatever. We'll wait for them, assuming they follow through."

"I need something strong for this, I think." Mason jerks his head toward the house. "I'm going for the vodka. Anyone else want some?"

Raising a hand, I nod. "Yes, please."

Bear shakes his head, grunting, "Game tomorrow."

I watch Mason take off, stopping to ask if Lennon needs anything before he heads inside. I tear my eyes away to find Bear looking at me strangely.

"You okay?" He scrubs his hands over the scruff lining his jaw, golden eyes glittering with concern. "I know yesterday was—"

"Not the time or the place. Fuck off," I growl, my jaw setting hard. I don't know which he was going to bring up, the threesome I walked in on or Lennon calling out my hard dick in front of the other two. Either way, he can fuck right off.

Bear lifts his hands, stepping away from me. Under his breath, he mutters, "Right. Got it."

Mason hands me a tumbler half full of vodka. His gaze shifts from Bear's crossed arms to my stony expression and rolls his eyes before mumbling, "It's the good stuff. Your favorite."

Mason knows my alcohol preferences well, but I don't care what it is at the moment. I take a large swallow of it as Arik and Quincy emerge from the pool house a few seconds later. This might be the most heinous thing that's ever happened here. *Jesus.* I almost regret making them do this because these two? They make the worst decisions ever.

"Oh fuck, my eyeballs," Pierre groans. Kai and Brendan both cover their faces, shaking their heads.

Warren rolls his eyes skyward. "Oh my fucking god. Why'd he go with the lace pair?" Indeed, poor Quincy chose poorly, his dick fully visible through the pretty purple lace flower pattern.

"Never mind that, Arik's junk is hanging out of that thong. I need to bleach my brain. I can't unsee this," Tucker moans, shaking his head.

Indeed, Arik chose the larger of the two thongs, but it's still not doing the best job of hiding things.

Mason huffs out a disturbed laugh. "I do not want them near me. Arik's pubes are everywhere. Time to manscape, my dude."

A huge gusting sigh from Bear is his only response.

"Come here," I grit out. The two idiots walk toward me. Arik can't seem to decide whether he needs to put his hands over his dick or his ass, and neither one knows which way to turn, as the path to me is between those in the pool and the loungers. Internally, I'm dying laughing, but I keep a straight face. "Got the second pair?"

They both nod, holding them up.

I glance down, unable to stop the ridiculous laughter that spills from me. "Well, it looks like you know how to obey. And you're showing a degree of loyalty by trusting us enough to go along with this. But how about for that third bit—you know, the keeping your mouth shut part?" I pause for effect before I growl out, "Stuff the panties in. Now. Then go stand over there and await further instructions." I point to a spot near the shallow end of the pool as they grimace, shoving the pretty little panties into their mouths.

"Good. Back to business. We're hosting a ... gathering ... here next Saturday. Arik, Quincy, I'm sure you've heard rumors of what goes on at our annual event, but you won't fully understand until you've participated. No one discusses anything after the fact. What happens at Bainbridge Hall stays here. Mouths shut. Everyone knows this, including the members of other frats who are invited. And yes, we have banned entire fraternities from events before for leaking information. We're serious when we say we like people who can keep their fucking mouths shut.

"So. With that said, we're going to be hosting an auction of sorts. It'll be held in the ballroom. I've been coordinating with my father and Bear's to get the best caterers in the area in, a stage set up, and invitations sent out. It's a masked event. They'll be provided for you. Everyone will be expected to dress nicely."

My gaze lands on Lennon again. I wonder if she's opened that damn box yet. There's a dress in there that would be perfect. Her lollipop is tucked into her mouth, but she's interested in what I'm saying. Well, she won't like this last piece of information.

I check in with Mason and Bear. "What am I forgetting?"

Mason slides his gaze to mine, shaking his head with a laugh. He knows damn well I didn't forget. It's the entire point of the event. "More info on the auction. What are we auctioning, Duke?"

I smirk. "Right. We've invited about twenty women to join us."

Brendan's eyes light up. "You mean …?"

Bear nods, shrugging. "Yes. A bunch of sorority girls have agreed to auction themselves off for charity."

"Fuck. Yes." Tucker nods his head enthusiastically. "I like this."

Lennon raises her hand, a bit of a confused frown on her face. "I'm a proponent of doing whatever feels right to you, but do these girls get something out of it?"

I'm about to answer when Bear takes the bullet for me instead. "We could tell you that they're excited to do it for the local women's shelter we will donate the proceeds to, but that's not it. Notoriety. Being invited to Bainbridge is one thing, but getting auctioned off? People will know they were here—but not any real details—and it'll boost their social standing on campus."

She rolls her eyes and nods once, shrugging. "Whatever floats their boat, I guess." She puts the lollipop right back into her mouth.

Warren's lips press together before he raises his hand to ask a question. "Anyone of note coming?"

"Hawthorne Hall. They're here every year." I haven't quite decided how I want to approach any of that yet. But I do know it'll rile me if Kingston brings his female initiate. These days—the ones approaching the date of Juliette's death—are fucking difficult for me. Three more days. My calendar had alerted me this morning. So, the more I think about Kingston? The more I know I'll hit him where it hurts. In a blinding flash, it comes to me —I'm certain I saw his weakness at that party last weekend. Maybe it's a good thing if the girl shows up after all.

Kai raises a hand, "What about Lennon? Will she be participating in the auction?"

"Yeah, you know ... supporting the brotherhood?" Brendan pushes himself up out of the pool to sit on the edge. "Earning her place here. I agree."

Pierre snickers behind his hand.

And the grunts, though they stand by in panties, have the balls—we can see 'em—to nod vigorously.

"Yeah, no. Those girls can do whatever they like, and I don't have a word to say about it, but I, personally, am not interested." Lennon shakes her head.

Warren glances her way, then back at me. "I think we

keep Lennon out of it, honestly. It'll only cause problems here in the house."

"What the fuck? I'd buy her. It's for charity. Come on, sweet cheeks." Tucker swivels his head in Lennon's direction. "I'd pay a pretty penny to have those lips wrapped around my cock."

Lennon arches a sassy brow and flips him off. "You wish."

"Fuckin' case in point, dickhead." Mason's jaw clenches, and I notice Bear's entire body stiffening.

Honestly, I'm no better. It hadn't occurred to me that anyone would suggest Lennon be involved. Maybe it should have, based on what they've heard coming out of my own damn mouth.

Fuck.

THIRTY-TWO

LENNON

I wake up with visions of Quincy and Arik, who I've begun to think of as a unit in my head—Q&A, haha—wearing those awful teeny tiny panties last night. Shuddering, I sit up and swing my legs over the edge of the bed. Tucker may have been right about one thing. Brain bleach might be necessary to rid me of the image in my head.

Fucking Tucker, though. He'd given me a look from across the patio that had me feeling completely slimy. No one else saw him, but it'd left me with zero doubt that if he were in charge here, he'd have demanded I be in the auction. And he'd probably have rigged it to ensure he'd be the highest bidder. I wouldn't have had a choice in any of it.

Not that I think I had a choice tonight, either, but in

reverse, if that makes sense. If I'd said *yes, I'll do it*, I think at the very least, Bear would have put a stop to it. Probably Mason, too. And even though Duke wouldn't even look me in the eye after their poolside meeting, I actually think he would have put his foot down as well. He might say shit that makes me want to punch him in the face, but I'm ninety-nine percent sure it's a cover. A front.

My mind rolls back to my locked-in misadventure two days ago. When Duke opened that door and I'd jumped into his arms ... he'd held me so tightly and whispered soft words of reassurance. It sure as hell hadn't felt like he hated me. I haven't said a damn thing to him, but he slipped up that day.

He called me baby. And it'd made me *melt*.

Too bad it hadn't taken him long to revert to asshole-stepbrother mode. Bleary-eyed, I glance at my phone. It's ten. I haven't slept that well in a long time.

After brushing my teeth and showering, I pull on a pair of shorts and a tank top, and sweep my long hair off my neck, securing it on top of my head.

A knock sounds on my door, and my brow furrows. I hurriedly adjust the pen in my hair and head out of the bathroom toward the bedroom door.

"Lennon?" It's Bear. My face flushes. The things that guy can do with his tongue ...

"Coming."

He opens the door before I can get to it and pokes his head in. "Hey. Morning. I wasn't sure if you were up or not, so I thought I'd check before I left for campus."

My brow furrows. He's acting weird. "I'm up. What's going on?"

He slips into the room and stands stock-still with both hands behind his back. "Are you coming to the game later?"

"Oh. I assumed I was, but maybe that was dumb of me. Am I not supposed to be there? Just tell me."

A smile breaks out on his face, and he closes the distance between us. "I was hoping you would come, yeah. I should have said something sooner." He stares down at me, taking a good ten seconds to study every feature. It makes my heart flutter in my chest. He reaches up, taking a tendril of hair and tucking it behind my ear. From there, his fingers glide along my jaw before he catches my chin and tips my face to his. "Lennon, it would make me very happy if you came to watch me play today."

I draw in a breath, staring into his eyes before I place my hands flat on his abs, and rock up onto my tiptoes. He still has to lean down and duck his head to reach me, but his lips caress mine for a moment before his tongue flicks out. With a desperate gasp, I open for him, accepting the stroke of his tongue into my mouth as easily as I breathe air. He brings his other arm around my back, lifting me almost off my toes, and crushing me to him. A throaty growl rumbles from him that has my fresh underwear quickly dampening. There's something about his size, his heat. The knowledge that he'd protect me from anything or anyone. It sends something primal coursing through me. He deepens the kiss, his big hand sliding down to my ass, where he grabs hold and brings my lower body fully against his. His cock nudges my belly, stoking a fire there, embers of need and desire spark and flare to life.

He tastes like cinnamon, like my favorite flavor of lollipop. I pull away smiling, and then my brows dart together as he brings something out from behind my back. "What's this?"

A hint of color touches his cheeks, which I can't say I've ever seen before on his usually confident face. He pulls back, letting the shirt unfold until I see that it's a Kingston University Lions football T-shirt. "I thought maybe you'd like a little school spirit to wear to the game."

I grin, looking over the bold face of the lion mascot. "I'd love to."

"It's one of mine. I shrunk it by accident and haven't worn it since. I really want you to wear it. Is that weird?"

"No. But you promise you wore it?"

He nods. "Yeah, of course. Probably three years ago, back when I was a freshman and doing laundry on my own for the first time ever." He huffs out a laugh. "I've learned since then that one-hundred percent cotton means it's gonna shrink and to get a bigger size."

I hold it up in front of me. It's huge.

"It's still going to be really big on you."

"I'll knot it. It'll be fine. In fact—" I set the T-shirt on the bed and peel my tank top off.

"Ah, fuck." Bear blows out a hard breath as I grin and pull the worn shirt over my head. It hangs down below my shorts. A gruff noise escapes him, an animalistic grunt of approval. He rubs his hands over his face, shooting me a wolfish look. "I'm going through my drawers tomorrow and finding everything that's too small so I can see you in all of it. Because ... fuck, Lennon, I'll be thinking of you exactly like this every goddamn time I see you in one of my shirts."

"I will happily wear anything you give me."

He tips his head to the side. "Not to bring down the mood, but"—his eyes slide to the box still sitting next to the dresser—"is there really that big of a difference?"

I inhale sharply, staring at the box of clothing Duke had bought for me. Chewing on my lip for a few seconds, I take the time to consider his question. "There was when I thought it was other girls' leftovers that he was giving to me in front of everyone with the implication that he was doing me some big favor." I scrape my teeth over my bottom lip, hoping Bear gets what I'm saying. "It just— It hit wrong. I do know now that some of my assumptions were incorrect."

Bear nods. "I'd probably like seeing you in all that stuff, too."

"I'll think about it. Promise. For now"—I scoop the bottom of the shirt up until it's at my waist and gather it at the side, knotting it off—"how's that?"

"Perfect." Bear's hand finds my hip and tugs me close. "Mason and Duke are taking you to the game with them. Do me a favor and stay with them so I don't worry about you while I'm playing."

"Will do. Is there assigned seating, or is it a free for all?"

He grits his teeth a bit. "You guys can sit wherever, and there are seats reserved for you down on the fifty yard line, but you might be expected to visit the VIP box where the OG Bastards will be. Duke and Mason should go with you, though. Don't go up there on your own."

"Okay. So ... Tristan and your dad?" My interest piques, especially since he doesn't seem to be super excited about me meeting his father.

"Yeah. Derek Pierce. He doesn't miss a fucking

game. Just look for the huge guy who can't stop talking about the score of the game and the point spread. But honestly, steer clear if you can."

I don't miss for a second the way his body has gone rigid like his father isn't someone he likes discussing. "You two have issues."

Bear gives a tight nod. "Don't worry about it. There are also one or two former KU players from Bainbridge Hall who like to sit up there, along with their wives and girlfriends. You'll see. Honestly, sit where you're most comfortable. I just want to know you're there." He leans in and brushes my lips with his. "I'll be looking for you."

THIRTY-THREE

LENNON

Holy shit, this whole college football thing has been overwhelming, and not at all what I was expecting. I've only attended one or two high school football games. You know, the kind with the rickety bleachers and the concession stand in a truck off to the side—the sort of game where there weren't very many spectators on the home side and even fewer on the visitors'. Half the high school team hadn't even gone through puberty, so there was quite the range of sizes of players. I wondered at how some of the younger guys didn't get crushed.

But this—this is no high school game. This is D1 collegiate football, played in a whole-ass stadium like I've seen on TV. It's enormous. Then again, I suppose Kingston University has the money to not only support their football program, but also draw in the best players.

And Bear? He's good. I can tell, and I don't even know exactly what he's supposed to be doing.

I patiently watch the field, waiting for Bear to slip on his helmet and head out there again. I've never been much of a football fan, but this is a lot different than watching on TV. We're at the fifty-yard line in some of the best seats in the house. Every grunted tackle, all the plays being called, the whistles of the refs, it all feeds into my experience.

I'm seated between Duke and Mason and am astounded by how many people know them. They're like KU royalty, I see that now. The rest of the brotherhood are slightly lesser in status, but still, the swarm of people who'd greeted us in the parking lot had been insane.

Me? I'm the curiosity. Some of them genuinely want to meet me, and of course, Duke has introduced me as Tristan's stepdaughter, so that gives me an immediate in with these people whether I wanted one or not. I've definitely attracted attention, most of it unwanted, never mind that it's also unwarranted. Hoards of guys have popped over supposedly to say hello but mostly to give me leering once-overs—and I don't think I'm imagining that there are a whole lot of hateful glances coming from the female football fans.

Apparently, I'm in the unique position of having been given something these girls want, even if it was thrust upon me. I've got to let the bad attitudes roll off my back. I was the one forced into living with these guys. I didn't ask for this, and I wish I could stand up and shout it, but— Yeah. That'd be a bad idea. Speaking of, I glance up and over my shoulder to the seats further up in the stands. Exclusive seats—the spot where Derek and Tristan are seated and being waited on hand and foot by a catering staff.

Every once in a while, I feel their eyes on us down here, like we're being observed—or maybe it's only me being paranoid.

Mason has shifted his body so that he's taken command of the armrest between us. He's been mindlessly drawing on my thigh with his fingertip for the last few minutes. I don't mind it at all, but Duke seems to. He's given one furtive, irritated glance after another in Mason's direction, but I hate to tell him ... I don't think Mason realizes he's doing it. He seems to be somewhere in his head. His eyes track the plays on the field, but he's not reacting to any of it.

A few minutes later, he shifts slightly, catching my eye before he glances at Duke, then back at the field. "So ... got any plans for Monday, Duke?"

Duke's jaw goes rigid, and he exhales sharply through his nose. "The fuck's wrong with you?" he grits out. "You and Bear both need a class on how to not be such dickheads. Not everything needs discussing all the damn time." His gaze lands on Mason's hand, which has stopped drawing patterns on my leg and simply rests there now, his warm fingers lightly squeezing. Duke shakes his head, pulling out his phone, and focuses on it, even though I could swear he's not actually seeing much at all.

I feel the anger, the agitation simmering in him. It's gonna be ugly when it finally blows for real. That little outburst was simply a little steam escaping before the pot of rage boils over.

I must have missed whatever he's referring to with Bear, but ... I sneak a peek at Mason, who's now working his jaw back and forth. Whatever Mason brought up seems big. And the weird thing is, it obviously has something to do with the anniversary of Juliette's death coming at us like a runaway freight train. But shit, why does it feel even bigger than that?

We'll be lucky if we make it through Monday without Duke taking Mason's head off if Mason doesn't stop antagonizing him. I press my lips together. And here I am, wedged between them.

Maybe I can talk to Bear about it. Just then, the big guy—who looks enormous and terrifying in uniform with all the padding—turns around, lifting his arm to us. He's done that every so often. Almost like he's making sure I'm still here. I raise mine back, giving him a little wave with a smile, as Duke is too busy frowning at his phone and Mason is off in his twisted-up head again and back to drawing on my thigh with his finger. I wonder if the action calms him, if it's the drawing or the contact with my skin that he wants, but I suppose it doesn't really matter. He's not hurting anything, even if he is annoying Duke.

"Ah, shit." Duke lets the expletive loose before tucking his phone back into his pocket and getting Mason's attention over my head. "My father wants us to come up before the game's over."

Mason glances at me before his eyes connect with Duke's. "Well, personally, I think that's a shit idea, but I don't think we can get away with blowing them off. Game's going well, it's the fourth quarter …" He turns ever so slightly. "Yeah. We're going to have to pay our respects, so to speak."

"Oh. Can I stay here?" I bite my lip, my head swiveling back and forth between them. I gesture to where the offensive line is getting up from the bench to head onto the field. "I don't want to miss anything."

Duke expels a harsh breath. "'Fraid not, Stella. We've been summoned. All three of us. And if I'm not mistaken, it's you they actually want to see."

Oh, god. I should have known. All at once, my heart

begins breakdancing in my chest, my lungs squeeze painfully. I take a couple of deep, fortifying breaths. I don't want to be anywhere near Tristan. And Bear's dad? I'm curious about him—and their relationship—but the more I hear about him, the less I want to meet him. If I'm not mistaken, from the way Bear was talking about him, he's more interested in the game than his son. And there're definitely things Bear simply didn't want to discuss earlier. I'm teetering on the edge of a freak-out at the thought of going up there.

"Come on. If we go now, we won't miss much." Mason rests his hand on my upper back as I sit forward. "We'll be with you. It'll be okay."

Duke snorts. "Easy for you to say. Your shit dad won't be there." It's the sort of statement that doesn't require a response because from the look on Mason's face he agrees with the assessment.

Duke leads the way from our seats to the stairs, while Mason and I follow. We push through doors at the top of the stadium, and my confusion must be apparent on my face because Duke murmurs, "Can't access their box from outside. Have to enter from inside. They have an entire hospitality room to themselves."

"Oh. Okay." I shrug, taking in the huge hallway lined with concession stands of different types of food. The smell of hot dogs, burgers, and fries waft up my nose. We ate when we got here earlier, but I can always eat.

Mason draws me close to his side, seeing the direction my eyes have wandered. "There's food in the VIP area if you're hungry. In fact, I'm certain Tristan would be so fuckin' happy to have you sample it and tell him how delicious it is." He gives me a conspiratorial wink. "The guy goes overboard on the catering every time."

I try to smile, but the mention of my stepfather doesn't do much for my appetite. Mason ignores the irritated look Duke throws him over his shoulder at the mention of his father. I shrug. "Honestly, I'd like to get back to our seats as soon as we can. I liked the view down at field level."

"I bet you did. Football players in tight pants. Can't go wrong if you're into that sort of thing." He's put on this funny-guy act, but I see right through it when he takes my hand in his, squeezing gently. I look up at him to gauge what he's thinking, but he's staring straight ahead toward frosted double doors.

Duke has a card that he swipes to let us into a spacious room. Upon entering, I'm surprised by the sheer size and grandeur of the space. It's like some sort of weird trick of the eye. I wouldn't have thought this room was as big as it is. But *man*. They are living the high life up here. Delicious-smelling food, their own open bar, and a waitstaff ready to meet their every need.

And it's for that reason my eyes are wide like saucers when I turn around and come face to face with Tristan.

"Good to see you're taking in a game, Lennon." His blue eyes, so like his son's, are trained on me, studying me like I'm an ugly, wriggling bug under a microscope. His piercing gaze dips down to my T-shirt. "You've even got a bit of school spirit, huh?"

I tamp down every feeling I have about my stepfather because at the moment, all eyes are on us—and I know there'd be nothing worse than if I made a scene in front of all of these *important* people. *Insert eye roll here.* But yeah. He'd take offense to it in a big way, one that I'd be sure to regret later.

When he and my mother were married, they had a huge—*expensive*—outdoor wedding at a beautiful venue. For some reason, I thought once we got past the ceremony I'd be able to slip away unnoticed to sit in the shade of a tree a short distance from their reception.

Boy, was I ever wrong. Afterward, Tristan had let me know exactly how much of an affront that was, what a disappointment I'd been, and how humiliated my mother had felt when I hadn't been there to meet his *very important* friends.

The funny thing is, Mom had been fine—totally in

her element—mingling with all the people she'd always imagined she should be rubbing elbows with. She's been living out her dream from the moment they got engaged.

Mom honestly hadn't given a shit where I'd been. I'd asked her about it later. I still have a hard time looking at Tristan without remembering how he'd shouted at me. His fury had been unrivaled. Duke had witnessed his father's tirade from a distance, and I remember the embarrassment I'd felt, having his eyes on me while his father laid into me. I still have no idea if he'd heard what his father was saying.

Before I get a chance to respond to Tristan, his son puts a careful hand to my back, surprising me in much the same way he had when he made the same protective gesture at the frat party. I glance at him out of the corner of my eye, but he's too busy staring daggers at his father to notice he's caught me off guard.

Tristan does, indeed notice Duke's gesture of reassurance and Mason holding my hand. His jaw works to the side, as if he can't quite figure us out.

Bolstered by the show of unity among the three of us, even if I wasn't expecting it, I finally nod, meeting Tristan's eyes. "Yes. Bear gave me the shirt to wear this morning."

I hardly breathe the entire time he slowly assesses me. "We'll have to get you a proper jersey. A new one. They make a woman's cut that looks way better on the female form." He reaches out, tugging on the knot at my waist. "This doesn't quite suit you."

I suck in a breath, flinching, but I don't know if he saw it, because his eyes are still trained on the knot at my hip. My heart rate accelerates. I couldn't care less about the cut of a jersey, and I can't stop the smart comment that flies from my mouth. "This T-shirt suits me because it's *Bear's*. I'm sure he'll get me a jersey if he wants me to wear one."

Before Tristan can respond to my direct snub, a huge guy with broad shoulders and a massive chest joins us, and my eyes widen. This can only be one person.

"Did I hear you say you're wearing something of my son's?"

Duke's hand flexes on my back momentarily, almost as if he's warning me of something. Same with Mason, who gives my hand a squeeze. The crazy thing is, I think I understand them perfectly well. They want me to be alert, to stay on my toes with this one. And I have a feeling if Bear were here, he'd not only share the opinion but might also stand between us, physically shielding me.

I draw in a breath as Derek's dark eyes wander over me. It's uncomfortable. Like the exact opposite of how I feel when Bear looks at me, even though it's obvious the physical apple didn't fall far from the gigantic-man tree.

He glances at Tristan. "Well, isn't this something? I'm finally getting a chance to meet your lovely stepdaughter." His eyes shift back to me, and he holds out an enormous, thick hand. "Derek Pierce. Bear's father. I missed meeting you at the wedding. And every opportunity since, it would seem." His eyes narrow, his head cocking to the side.

Crap. He would bring that up. Tristan's eyes are on me, too, and he gives a definitive jerk of his head toward his friend's outstretched hand, like if I don't shake it, I'll regret it. Not that I'd be rude to someone I've never met before who is explicitly offering me his hand, but I suppose this is simply another instance of Tristan thinking the worst of me, like he always does. I don't know what it is about me that he dislikes. Maybe I'm not close enough to a carbon copy of my mother. I have no freaking idea. I've always been my own person. I've had to be.

I tentatively hold out my hand, and like I assumed it might, his hand swallows mine whole. Not only that, but he shakes it for way too long by about five seconds. *I counted.* And maybe because I'm so overwhelmed by meeting this imposing man, I realize that I haven't said a word, and hurriedly blurt out, "Lennon. Lennon Bell. And yes, Bear gave me the shirt."

He releases my hand, squinting at me. He chuckles, looking me over again. "Yeah. You're his type."

I blink.

And he laughs, his eyes dropping to my hand in Mason's. He leans in and whispers, "Don't worry, honey. It's all good. We aren't stupid or naive. A girl living in a house with ten guys? I'd expect plenty of shenanigans. Just don't get knocked up."

My mouth drops open, and my face flushes at his words, but apparently, he doesn't think a damn thing about it, as he's already slapping Tristan on the back and walking away, their heads tipped together in quiet conversation.

"What did he fuckin' say?" Duke grits.

I swallow down my disgust, deciding it's far better to keep it to myself than cause an uproar in the middle of this semi-prestigious event with a bunch of people I don't know. Besides, I don't have any idea what Tristan's reaction would be to his friend's dirty thoughts. I turn toward Duke, putting my hand on his chest because I know it'll distract him and quietly murmur, "Let's not worry about it right now. I really want to watch Bear." I look up into his eyes as I scrape my teeth slowly over my lower lip. "Please?"

Up close, I can see the way his jaw pops and twitches with the knowledge that I'm not going to tell him right this instant, but as I suspected, he's very aware of where we are right now, what's acceptable and what's not. He bristles before he finally relents. "Fine. But you'll tell me later."

I exhale raggedly and meet his bold blue gaze with a nod, patting his chest. "Yeah. Okay."

Mason comes in close to both of us. "Come on. Let's watch the game." He tugs on my hand, and I don't miss the subtle nonverbal communication between him and Duke, messages passing between them with the flick of an eye and a jerk of the head. Neither one is happy with how this is going.

The next several minutes go by in a blur as Mason and Duke take me out to the VIP seating area. Trying to ignore all the talk around me, I go right back to watching the game. Funny how these rich, supposedly important people have the best seats in the house, yet they are being wasted on them. The majority aren't even watching the game. Kinda dumb. Then again, I actually preferred our seats right down on the field. It's a completely different experience up here. I'm not a fan, especially since I find all the non-football-related chatter to be distracting.

While our defense is on the field, Duke gets up from the seat beside me, mumbling something about needing to talk to someone. Mason gives me a furtive smile.

"Sorry this went a little sideways. I think they have some of that cider you liked at the bar. You want one?"

My eyes flick to his. I'm only nineteen, and he knows it. "If you're sure it's okay."

Mason nods. "I'm sure. They'll give me whatever, and no one's paying attention. We don't have to worry too much up here. Besides, it's like slightly spiked apple juice." He chuckles. "I'll fight anyone who says otherwise. Be right back with it." He shoots me a smooth wink as he stands, then walks away to fetch the drinks, leaving me on my own.

My attention returns to the action where Bear comes off the field after a phenomenal play—or, I mean I think it was, anyway. It seems like we scored again, and everyone is cheering all around the stadium. The sound of the clapping and hollering is almost deafening. Bear looks into the stands where we were seated earlier, but, of course, we aren't there anymore. I get up from my seat and wave, hoping he sees me. Sure enough, his gaze tracks upward until he spots me. Then, he stiffens.

Confused, I slowly lower my hand just as Derek Pierce's arm drapes over my shoulders, his meaty paw grasping my bicep. Every cell in my body folds in on itself. The look on Bear's face is murderous, and I actually feel Derek's chuckle, rather than hear it. "My boy doesn't much like to share. Just so you know."

What. The. Fuck. I'm so thrown by his words, that I almost fire back with "Sure didn't seem that way the other night," but I don't. And *ew*. Why the fuck would he bring up sharing in reference to his son when he's the one with his arm around me. I shudder and shrug free of him, ducking under his arm. I back away. "I need to use the restroom. I'll be back." Perverted. Old. Man. *Fuck*. The look on Bear's face. I hate that this could potentially distract him.

I dart back into the VIP hospitality room, then out the door, hurrying away so I can wrap my head around the many things Bear's father had the balls to say to me.

My breath heaves, and my chest catches like I'm going to cry, only I won't because that's fucking stupid. He doesn't know me well enough to deserve my tears. I turn a corner, blindly walking along corridor after corridor, going wherever my feet take me and not especially caring where I end up. Anywhere but in the vicinity of that awful man.

A vibration in my pocket has me pausing, and I duck around a corner where it's quiet and I won't be standing in anyone's way.

Mason:
Hey. Where'd you go?
I have your drink.

Duke:
Stella?
What happened?

I chew on my lip as I stand motionless, staring at the phone screen, unsure how to answer. Had I imagined what he'd said? Taken something the wrong way? *Fuck.* I really don't think so. I tap out a few quick texts, fully realizing that I haven't answered either of their questions. But how do you say "Your friend's father said a bunch of gross stuff to me, but I'm not entirely certain I understood him correctly, and I was way too embarrassed to stand there with him after that, but even more so, I didn't want to give him a chance to say another word." Yeah. How the fuck does one relay that long, run-on thought in a text?

Um. Bear's father ...
I just need a minute.
Can I meet you back in our original seats?

I take a couple of deep, calming breaths. It'll be fine. I'll meet them down there like I said, and we can hash it out later, though how I'll ever explain any of it to Bear, I have no fucking clue.

I pivot on my heel, ready to head back to the main

hallway when I hear something behind me, then hands latch onto my arms as some sort of fabric comes down over my head. A bag. A sack. Fuck, I don't know, and before I can scream, a hand slams down over my mouth. In the next instant, I'm being dragged backward, my feet scrabbling for purchase, but finding mostly air. The hands on my arms clench down in a steel vice grip, and panic rises within me. Because if there's anything worse than being stuck in a small space, it's having something over my head so I can't see or breathe freely.

It does me no good to pay attention to where they're taking me because I'd lost all track of where I was while I was wandering around. A moment later, one of them lets go for a split second, and I try like hell to get free of the other guy—because these are definitely dudes—but he clamps down on my arm in a punishing enough grip to bruise. My heart slams behind my rib cage as the other guy returns, grunting a bit as I catch him—maybe in the abdomen?—with my elbow. They proceed to drag me backward as I kick and twist.

The acoustics change, and every sound made now has a slight echo to it. *Where the fuck am I?* They pull me along roughly, eerily silent the entire time. All I'm able to focus on is the rustling of the bag over my head, and the scuff of feet against the floor. And of course, my muffled cries of terror.

And then I'm lifted and forced into a narrow space, my body bent in half with my knees to my chin. I'm shoved up against the backside of whatever the hell this is. A box? A coffin? I'm held inside, the area nowhere near large enough for me to even crouch.

In one swift motion, the hands holding me shove hard and miraculously release me. My heart gives a lurch. *Will I be able to escape?* When I reach out, my hand meets wood. I understand, finally, and dread sweeps through me, head to toe.

Oh my fuck, I'm inside a tiny fucking space with a bag over my head. I scream through the rough material, my hands fumbling with what feels like burlap or something, but it's somehow tied around my neck, and I can't get it off. "Help me! Someone, please help!" I shout, pounding on the door.

I stop, listening, but I hear no one. It's the middle of the fourth quarter. Everyone is watching the game. There is no one to save me.

Wait. My phone. Gasping for air, I pat myself down while I become more and more lightheaded. *Fuck. Where is it?* Did one of those slimy assholes take it? Did I drop it? My hands shake. I'm becoming disoriented, my body flailing and smacking into the solid wooden walls of this prison I've found myself in as I attempt to find a way out of this mess.

And even though I can't see a damn thing, I can feel the walls surrounding me and they feel closer and closer. They're caving in on me. My heart is going to explode from my chest. *I'm never getting out of here. This is how I die.* Cold sweat coats my skin as I struggle, pulling at the bag all while banging my elbows into the sides of whatever this living nightmare is I'm trapped in. Anxiety and panic rip through me, and without thinking about what I'm doing, I throw myself every which way, trying to find an escape until stars shimmer at the edges of my vision before a black cloud rushes in, taking me with it.

THIRTY-FOUR

BEAR

I come off the field with the rest of the team, victorious, only to find Mason and Duke waiting right at the tunnel for me. Their expressions are grim and don't leave much room for interpretation. Something's wrong. Tell me it isn't something my fucker of a father did or said.

I'd wanted to leap up there and rip his arm from around Lennon when I saw the two of them together up in the VIP box. The look on her face when he put his arm around her—it was fairly obvious that she didn't like it. Not one fucking bit.

My teeth clench tightly together until I'm certain they're going to crack from the pressure. Mason and Duke should have known to keep her the fuck away from him. He's lecherous on his best days, a downright perv on his worst. Horrible that I know that shit about my own father. *Fuck.* But what were they supposed to do? When we're summoned, we're expected to show up. It's more trouble in the long run if we don't. None of us like the way our fathers breathe down our necks—Mason's old man even manages to do it from prison. And my guess is that they didn't have a choice. Especially with Tristan being up Duke's ass about how he's handling Lennon.

My lungs constrict in my chest, preparing for the worst, because very seldom have I ever seen panic like this on Mason's or Duke's face. I quickly jog up to them, adrenaline surging through my body in preparation for whatever lies ahead. My gaze darts between the two of them. "What's going on? Where the fuck is Lennon? Why isn't she with you?"

Duke's hands dive into his hair as he shakes his head while Mason tugs hard on the back of his neck, his jaw clenched.

Mason is the first to speak. He blows out a hard breath as he flings his hand in the direction of the VIP seats. "We were upstairs with Tristan and Derek because Tristan requested we come. We were watching the game, and everything seemed fine, so I got up to get her a drink and *poof,* she was gone. I don't even know how she got past us."

Lennon is ... *missing?*

I blink sweat out of my eyes, then swipe my forearm over my brow. She ran. And now I have to consider very seriously that there might be a connection to my old man talking to her and her taking off like that, but I need all the facts first. "Duke?" My breath gusts from me.

He shakes his head. "Tristan waylaid me inside, he wanted to talk about the auction. My back was turned, so I didn't see her leave either. I didn't even know she was gone"—he gives a jerk of his thumb toward Mason—"until he pulled me away."

There's no telling where she could be. The stadium is a huge place. Concern flares within me, glowing bright. *Fuck.* "You guys start turning this fucking place upside down. You hear me? I'll get out of my gear and join you as quick as I can. If we don't find her in the next twenty minutes, we call for help."

Duke nods. "I'm going to call her again." He dials and puts the phone up to his ear as we run full tilt together through the tunnel. As we get inside the building, the two of them split up while I head into the locker room.

It's chaos in here, as usual. Sweaty bodies, shouts of glee, celebrating our victory. Lots of fist bumping and ass smacking. I can't think about fucking any of it right now. *Could she have run? Little Gazelle, don't do this to me. Fuck. What the hell is going on?*

I'm in the process of tearing out of my gear, stashing assorted pads in my locker when I hear a very distinct "What the *fuck*" from behind me. It's Jimenez, one of our huge defensive tackles. "Oh my fuck. There's a body in my locker."

His words shake me to my very core. I don't waste more than a half second before I pivot, eyes widening. My heart lodges in my throat. Horror fills me. A girl's body, head covered by a rustic-looking sack, threatens to fall out of the locker Jimenez opened.

As if in slow motion, my eyes land first on a pair of legs, long and smooth, which hang out of a little pair of cutoff shorts. Her feet are bare, and fuck—she's wearing a Kingston University Lions football shirt with a knot tied at the waist. That wouldn't necessarily mean jack shit, except it's the old version that not many of these fuckers would have—it's only the players who have been around as long as I have that would have them. And it's the very same one I'd given to Lennon this morning.

It's Lennon. This poor girl with the bag over her head is Lennon. My brain is near exploding with the knowledge that someone stuffed her in a motherfucking locker. My mind goes blank for a moment, unable to process. *Who the fuck would do this? How did no one see it happen?*

My eyes focus on the knot of fabric, trying not to completely spin out as anguish roars through my veins. "Nooo!" I dash forward, catching her as she begins to tumble from the locker. "Fuck. Fuck! *Lennon.*" With her limp body in my arms, I turn, shock slamming into me.

"I swear I didn't do that." Jimenez sucks in an astonished breath with his hands up, palms out in front of him. His head shakes rapidly back and forth, his eyes wide and panicked. "I-I didn't put her in there. I swear. What is this, some sick fucking joke? She was in my locker like that when I opened it. I don't know this chick. Like what the fuck? Why was she in my locker?" He's beginning to irritate the shit out of me. "Is this her phone?"

"I'm sure she doesn't know, and yes, that's probably her fucking phone. Put it down." My gaze sweeps the room, finding everyone's eyes on us, and anger bubbles up inside me. I shout, "Get the fuck out! Every single one of you!" My chest heaving, I lay Lennon's limp body on the floor. My head threatens to spiral into this terror, but I can't afford to let myself flip out. Hurriedly, I feel for her pulse, fingers probing along her throat. My eyes slam shut as soon as I feel it strong and steady, if a little fast for my liking. I take a deep breath before my eyes pop back open again.

I tear at the strings on the bag, my fingers feeling like they're made of noodles. Whoever did this. They're dead. The twine is wrapped around her neck and tied off to keep the fucking thing on her head. Her pretty blonde hair is sticking out from the bottom. *Fuck.*

In my peripheral vision, I notice our quarterback, Bradley Gaines, who apparently didn't piss off when I told him to. "Here, man. Use these." He hands me a pair of scissors. Without a word, I snatch them from him and snip the ties, then toss them to my feet as I fumble to loosen the bag. Gaines steps in to help me, and together, we pull the bag off.

"Damn. Is she breathing?"

I straddle her body, leaning in to slip my hand under her neck and elongate her airway. I pause, my face close to hers, listening for breath sounds. "Yeah. Yeah, she is."

"What the hell, man? Who would do something like this?"

"I don't know." My jaw locks tight. Frustrated, I mutter, "Go out and see if you can flag down Duke and Mason for me."

Nodding, he gives me a little salute. "You got it, man." He takes off like a shot.

Protective rage wants to burst free, but I know that's

not what Lennon needs right now. I have to get myself under control. *But fuck.* I'm on the verge of losing it. I want to scream my fury and find the sick fuck who did this to her.

I also need her to be okay, to look into my eyes and tell me she's all right. I need her smiles and sass. I need her witty comebacks and confidence. It hits me like a bolt of lightning. I need *her*.

Picking her up, I gather her to me in a cradle hold and ease myself down onto the floor. My lips find her temple, gently pressing there as I rock with her in my arms. "Little Gazelle, wake up. You're gonna be okay." My heart tugs hard. "Lennon," I whisper, "please open your eyes, baby."

THIRTY-FIVE

DUKE

I'VE RUN ALL over this stadium, checking everywhere I can think of and acting like a complete beast to everyone I encounter. It's a lot of ground to cover, and with every second that passes, the level of paranoia racing through my mind rises. She could be anywhere, with anyone.

Fuck this. I need to find Bear and Mason so we can come up with a better plan because we're wasting time.

> I think we need to reconvene.
> Come up with another plan.

Mason:
> Haven't heard from or seen Bear.
> Heading back to locker room area.

I quickly shoot him a response.

> Good idea. OMW.

It doesn't escape me that Bear isn't responding. My gaze scans over the screen, letting the five unanswered calls to Lennon's number sink in. Something is definitely not right. She said she'd meet us back at the original goddamn seats we were in, but she'd never materialized. I should have known there was a problem right then, especially after what she said about Bear's dad in that text. Who knows what the fuck Derek said to her. Goddammit, we hadn't prepared her well enough—at all, really—for what she might encounter in that VIP suite. I have no real excuse except that my head has been a jumbled mess, the state of my emotional well-being seriously cracked and ready to break this week. My fault. My own fucking fault.

I head in the direction of the locker rooms so we can sync up, like Mason had suggested, but— Pinpricks of dread jab along my spine at the sight before me. *What the fuck is this?* The entire football team has spilled out of the locker room, grumbling and confused. My brows draw sharply together.

Gaines, the team's quarterback comes flying at me. "Bear needs you. He's in there with her."

Her. *Lennon.*

At first, a sweeping sense of relief rushes through me. We've found her. Bear has her. But that feeling is immediately obliterated by the questions that surge to the forefront of my mind as I begin to move, pushing and elbowing my way through the mass of bodies. Why was she in the locker room of all places? If she were fine, why would Bear have kicked everyone out? A sense of foreboding makes my stomach churn. I can only think of awful twisted reasonings. And why my mind immediately jumps to worst-case scenarios, I have no idea.

I push the door open. "Bear!"

"Over here," comes his grunted reply, and I don't know what to expect based on the carefully contained anger I hear in his voice.

Darting swiftly down the hall to the main area of the locker room, I come around the corner and my eyes widen at the scene in front of me. Bear's half out of his game gear and has Lennon securely in his arms, but it's very clear that she's passed the fuck out. Completely unconscious. My gaze darts to the floor beside him where some sort of sack is lying, then to the locker that's open beside them. With my stomach lurching violently and my eyes glued to the locker, I grit out, "She was in there?"

Just then, Mason races into the room, but stops dead

when he sees us, or more to the point, Lennon. "Whoa. What—?" He doesn't even get the question out as he looks to me for answers with wild, disturbed eyes before they drop back to Lennon. I shake my head, looking to Bear to fill us in.

He takes a couple of deep breaths, glancing to the side like it pains him to do so. "Jimenez's locker. She was trapped inside there." He juts his chin toward the bag that I'd noticed on the floor. "That was tied over her head so she couldn't get it off." His chest heaves, and his jaw works to the side as he meets our eyes with his stony stare. "The other day, we discussed her reaction to being locked in the bathroom, and she specifically mentioned that among other small spaces, she can't stand closets. I don't know what the fuck is up with that—she gave no details—but I got the sense something may have happened to her when she was younger. She didn't want to talk about it."

I exhale in a steady stream as I rub my hand over my jaw. "And what's a locker but a teeny motherfucking closet." I blink, trying to figure out how this happened. Was it a random attack? Because it sure as fuck doesn't feel like it.

Mason pushes past me and crouches beside Bear and Lennon. "Kintsukoroi, don't do this to me." His voice is gritty and rough. He's barely hanging on. He pats her cheek—not too hard—trying to bring her around, but the girl is out cold.

I can't imagine what that was like for her. "She must have been terrified," I mumble. Swallowing, I fight to contain emotions that threaten to spill out that I can't show. My heart squeezes dangerously hard in my chest, and I raise my hand to that exact spot and claw at myself as I watch their efforts to rouse her.

Mason's hands shake as he hesitantly smooths his fingers over the skin of her upper arm. It's odd to see Mason react this way, usually he's all piss and fire when he's angry or upset. But with Lennon, he's different. He pulls his hands away and scrubs them through his hair instead. He heaves out, "She's all banged up."

With no warning, he shoots up from his crouched position and whirls around to punch the wall behind him with bone-chilling speed and intensity. I suck in a breath. *Okay, I was wrong. The rage I expected is still there, like I'd assumed it would be; it simply took a second for it to come out.* Now that he's started this cycle, I know for a fact he'll have trouble stopping himself. He and I are exact opposites in that way. He has zero control when it comes to shit like this. And me? I almost have too fucking much.

He swings and swings, busting the shit out of his knuckles with each hit into the wall. His breath gasps from him. Fury coats his features. The emotion is so raw, it hurts me to watch him like this. I exchange a quick glance with Bear, his expression totally readable: *This one's on you.*

Fuck. Bear's got his hands full already with Lennon. I step in and just miss getting nailed by Mason's elbow as his frantic pounding of the wall continues. "Mason. Fuck. Stop." I press my lips together, watching for an opportune moment, and finally see it when he takes a second to breathe. I duck in, grasping him by the hinge of his arm, and wrap my other arm around his back. I yank him away from where he'd been beating on the wall before spinning him around and slamming his back against it, caging him. I use most of my body weight pressed against him to hold him in place but have also managed to catch one wrist and have that pinned next to his head.

As expected, he struggles, bucking his body against mine in a way I'm positive he thinks will get me to back up. *Not this time.* "Lemme go. Get the fuck off me, Duke." His body smacks against the wall with each attempt at escape, his dark eyes boring into mine with frightful ferocity.

Leaning in, I forcefully grip him by the jaw, steering his face so we're nose to nose, prepared to do whatever it takes to get him to stop. Our chests rise and fall as one, and his eyes positively burn into mine. Whether it's temper, madness, or something else entirely, I couldn't say. "No, Mason. I'll let you go when you're calm. She doesn't need to wake up to this."

He swings at me with his free hand and catches me in the side of the head. My head rings with the pain of it.

"Fuck. I'm trying to help you, you fuckin' maniac. She needs *you* right now, not your rage."

"Mason!" Bear shouts. "Put your crazy away. I think she's coming around."

I remain pushed up against his body for several measured, agonizing breaths. He finally stops, exhaling hard through his nose. He relaxes in my hold, wetting his lower lip before he nods. "I'm good."

"Yeah?" My brows hike high on my forehead because I don't know if I can trust him to tell me the truth.

He grimaces and nods, though I know it probably irks him to do so.

I release him and back up, watching him carefully for any sign he's going to turn around and whale on the wall again. I glance at his hands. They took a vicious, ugly beating during his tirade, that's for fucking sure.

He pushes away from the wall, returning to Lennon and Bear, where he drops into the seat adjacent to Jimenez's locker space, his forearms propped on his thighs with his busted-up knuckles dangling between his legs, blood dripping. He'll regret that later when it hurts to draw for the next week, but at least he got it out.

A moment later, Lennon's lashes flutter, and never have I felt such intense gratitude in my life. Breath gusts from my lungs and I drop my head back on my shoulders, staring at the ceiling for a quick second. *Thank fuck.*

"Lennon. It's okay. You're safe," Bear murmurs near her ear. "We've got you. I promise."

"Bear? Where am I?" Her voice is shaky as she cautiously takes in her surroundings.

"Locker room," he grunts. "Mason and Duke are here, too. We don't know how you got here. Do you remember anything?"

She looks up at me and slowly shakes her head at first, her brow knitting together in confusion. But only a moment later, she freezes, like maybe it's all coming back to her. "I-I was wandering around, needed some time alone. Some guys grabbed me." Her breath stutters from her as she tries to sit up. "They didn't say a damn thing, just threw that sack over my head and manhandled me in here. I didn't know where I was or what was going to happen to me." She stares at me, dazed. "I thought I was going to die in there." Her gaze flicks to the locker, her skin taking on an ashen tone, before moving to each one of us in turn. "I really did."

MASON

Wrath rips its way through my veins. "Motherfucker," I hiss under my breath, clenching my fists. If I ever get my hands on who did it, it'll be all over. I'll make sure of it. No one messes with us and doesn't regret it.

Back at the house, Lennon had to make no fewer than ten promises to us that she really is going to be fucking okay—*her words*—before we allowed her to leave our sight and go to her room. She'd sworn she only needed to sleep it off, and everything would look better in the morning.

Personally, I think she's going to see the bruises on her skin and feel the stiffness that comes from being forcefully shoved into a locker, and possibly freak out, but I hadn't wanted to argue with her. She doesn't want to appear weak. I get it.

If only she knew we don't think being frightened or upset about what happened is a sign of weakness. Those sorts of feelings keep a person on their toes. And she might need that awareness if shit continues like it has.

I rest my elbow on the couch arm, tumbler of amber-colored liquid in hand, swirling it around and staring at the movement. I don't know if I buy that it's that simple to compartmentalize what happened today. It's possible she's good at it, but I don't know. I have a feeling the enormity of what happened hasn't quite hit her yet. She can push us away and say she's fine, but— I shake my head, taking a swallow of my drink. I kinda doubt it. I grimace to myself, hating that I'm probably right, but also not quite sure what to do about the strong-willed girl upstairs.

Bear sits on the couch beside me, legs extended in front of him and resting on the coffee table in front of us, a tumbler of whiskey in his hand that has yet to touch his lips. "Look, until Lennon tells us what the fuck she meant by the text about my father, I don't know if we have any clue that this is connected."

"I don't think it fits, no matter what he said to her. Some goons stuff her in a locker? And someone locks her in a bathroom?" Mason shakes his head, a glass of his favorite vodka in his bandaged hand. I eye it, trying not to think about the fact that three years ago, I drowned myself in a bottle of that stuff I'd been sharing with him.

Bear lifts his forefinger from where it's wrapped around the glass, pointing at nothing in particular. "That's assuming those two events had anything to do with each other."

My head rears back, and I grumble, "How could they not?"

"Just playing devil's advocate." He turns his head to me with a shrug.

I study both of them before shaking my head and tipping my drink to my lips again. I let the whiskey slide down my throat, warming me from the inside before I respond. "So, there's no way to snap our fingers and figure out what the hell is going on. Our time is better spent making a plan to keep her safe. Because we've obviously had a huge fail there, both between classes and taking her to an event." If they think I don't see that I was a common denominator in both instances, they're crazy. I blow out a hard breath. "So ... we'll take extra precautions wherever we go. But whoever is escorting her between classes meets her at the classroom door. And we're there before class ends."

Bear scrubs his hand through his hair. "I'm good with that. I'll talk to my professors and see where I can duck out a few minutes early. We coordinate it right, and it shouldn't be that big a deal, maybe a couple times a week for each of us."

"Mine are mostly studio art classes. I'll just walk the fuck out." Mason throws me a cheeky wink. "Don't care. No one will notice."

I'm glad he's able to flip the switch on his moods so

fucking fast, but I'm not. It wasn't that long ago that I had his raging self pinned up against the wall because he was so fuckin' out of control.

Something jiggles free in my head, and for a few seconds I pause until it fully sinks in. I clear my throat. "I have one more thing to bring up. Something that kinda hit me just now." I bring the tumbler of whiskey up to my mouth but lower it to the arm of the couch without taking a sip. "How do we know—" I pause, my jaw setting hard, then harder still while Bear and Mason stare at me, waiting for me to spit out the unfortunate thought in my head.

"Just say it. Whatever it is, so we have all the cards on the damn table." The expression on Bear's face says it all. He's waiting for the other shoe to drop.

So, instead, I heave my concern at them. "My father told me to watch specifically for anything that Lennon says or does that seems off or strange." I hesitate, unsure if I should continue or not.

"What are you getting at?" Mason looks at me, asking point blank.

"This is all really fucking weird, right? What if—" I hesitate, pursing my lips and staring into my whiskey glass. "What if the sleepwalking and nightmares my father and her mother were concerned about were her reaction to someone messing with her? And it's continued here? Do you think it's possible she's not told us about other things happening?"

There's a long silence where Bear and Mason both take large swallows of their drinks.

Bear scowls. "Are you saying maybe she's been attacked like this before but didn't tell Tristan, so he assumes she's crazy?"

"I think it fits what's happening, don't you?" I bite down on my lip, shaking my head.

Mason expels a hard breath, throwing his hand out. "I can tell you right now, having witnessed one of those nightmares, there is more going on with this girl than any of us knows or can even fathom."

THIRTY-SIX

LENNON

The guys hadn't wanted to let me be, but—fuck, after a day like today, I need time to process and regroup before everyone starts asking a whole lot of questions I don't have answers to. I've already gone over what I can remember about the attack. The only thing I haven't spilled to them is the icky feeling Derek Pierce had given me and the gross things he'd inferred—all of which I'm sure he'd blow off if asked about them. In my experience, dirty old men always seem to find a way to not be held accountable for their wrongdoings.

In any case, I don't see how any of that is related to me finding myself stuffed in a locker, so I jam my feelings about everything that went down today into the back corner of my mind where I don't have to think about it at all.

MASON

If only it were that easy. My head spins and spins with the position I'd found myself in and why someone would do that to me. I'm terrified to find out who is responsible, because I haven't a clue what I'd done to anyone to merit half the crap I've been through this week.

I groan, rolling over in the bed again, my legs getting tangled in the sheets. My body is sore from being yanked around and crammed inside that locker, and I'm fairly certain there will be a good amount of bruising that marks my skin by morning. The guys estimated I was trapped in there for at least thirty minutes. I couldn't even say how long I thrashed around before the panic got the better of me. My breathing had been so labored inside that bag, I don't know whether it was lack of oxygen or my anxiety that made me pass out. Maybe it's for the best that I lost consciousness because what I remember about it is awful. The anxiety had flowed freely through my body, no help in sight.

I shudder and throw back the sheet before pushing myself to a seated position on the side of the bed. I rub my hands over my face. *God.* I wish there were a way to erase everything from my brain. I need to do something to get my mind off it. With a glance at my phone on the charging stand, I see it's close to midnight. I have no idea if everyone else is in bed or not, but the fact remains—I can't lie here all night and fret over what might have happened. It'd reminded me of my childhood and other things I'd rather forget—things I've fought hard to overcome.

But no, whoever is doing this to me is bringing all of that roaring back to the forefront of my mind. I hate them. I don't deserve this.

With a sigh, I slip from my bed and walk on quiet feet over to my door. I open it, listening. Silence permeates the house. I bite my lip. Maybe if I look at some of Mason's art, it'll occupy my mind. Maybe if I go to the place he finds solace, I'll find my own. I'm desperate for it.

Turning to the right, I close my door behind me, then make my way to the attic door. I don't think he's up there; I've come to recognize the subtle sounds from above that are him, versus standard house noises. I open the heavy door and ease up the stairs, cringing a bit as a few creak and groan. At the top, I'm pleased to find I have the place entirely to myself, just like I'd thought. Slowly, I turn, looking for a light switch. I don't see one in an obvious spot, but the moon is shining brightly in the night sky, providing a small amount of light through some of the windows. Barefoot, I tread cautiously, then spend several minutes looking at each piece of work.

They're downright angst-filled, sadness seeping from

them. And in some cases, they're a bit morbid. It's gut-wrenching to see Mason's pain so clearly on display. But damn. If this helps him get out the dark feelings, then I'm all for it. It strikes me like a bolt of lightning while I'm standing there in front of one particular sketch—the one I'd noticed the other night that I believe is a self-portrait—that Mason bearing witness to my nightmarish behavior is very much like me looking at his art. The outward expression of our pain is a window into the harsh reality of the darkness that lives inside us. I just wish he didn't feel the need to hide it, but I do understand. It's very personal. I probably shouldn't even be here, but being with Mason's things gives me peace. I can't explain it. But I need this tonight more than anything.

Soon, I find myself in front of a drawing that was obviously torn from a small sketchpad. I tilt my head to the side. *Is this ... is it me?*

Suddenly, I suck in a breath. It is. It's what Mason was drawing the day he found me in the cemetery. And it's beautiful. He'd perfectly captured the pain I was feeling. I haven't visited Juliette often because it tears my heart out every time. Being on the grass above while she's buried deep in the earth—I'll never get over it. With the anniversary of her death coming up fast, and her resting place so close now that I'm at KU, I dunno. I'd needed her that day, likely because of her connection to Duke. I'd needed to talk to someone who would understand my confusion. The problem is she won't ever respond. Can't ever answer my questions. I still have so goddamn many. My heart sinks in my chest, throbbing painfully. Finally, I wrench myself away from the sketch. It's making me sad. But it did distract me from the other concerns plaguing me, if only for a while.

I look around for at least another twenty minutes, paying respect to as much of his artwork as I can. The sketches of his mother gut me, knowing that she's gone. Judging by the sheer quantity of similar images, he was obviously terribly affected by her passing. I can't forget that he dreams of her, too. Becomes confused when he wakes. It's like his mind has bent, unable to accept that she's truly gone. Every bit of it makes my heart ache for him.

There's no denying Mason's talent, no matter how twisted-up he is in the head. It's a somewhat terrifying place to be, but it suits me just fine.

Yawning, I wander over to the spare mattress he keeps up here—the same one he'd laid me down on—and curl up on my side. Despite the fact that there are no pillows or blankets, I feel much better up here than I did in my own bed. I close my eyes, hoping the solace I've found stays with me until morning.

MASON

I AM NOT OKAY. Something is wrong. My head is stuffed full of cotton, my brain unable to register my surroundings. Dazed, I struggle to move, but can't. My skin is sticky with sweat. I try to swallow, but my throat is thick, and I can't even open my mouth to speak, much less scream. My heart pounds and pounds, a vicious, thumping rhythm. Eventually, I take comfort in it, I focus on each individual thud inside my chest and the way it sends blood pounding into my head, so loud I can't hear.

I'm not alone.

There are other people here. Deep voices. Laughter. The smell of tequila travels up my nose and makes me want to retch. And it's dark, so dark I can't see who or what or where I am. I try to lift my head, but I only succeed in turning it. I'm a rag doll, unable to control my limbs. I wait for whatever is coming, worry moving through me like a flash flood, threatening to carry me away.

My mind twists, and I'm suddenly at Stella's. I frown.

Juliette. Relief sweeps through me until she looks

into my eyes. Hers are wide and frightened. She's shaking. I don't understand.

Don't understand.
Don't understand.
Don't understand.

THIRTY-SEVEN

MASON

I DRAG my ass up the stairs well after everyone else has gone to bed. For some reason, it seemed like a good night to sit outside and contemplate my life's decisions. It's the stress of the day. Shit like this always stirs me up.

Rubbing my hand over my jaw, I take in a deep, fortifying breath, stopping at the end of the hall to consider whether to sleep in my bedroom or to head up to the attic for a bit. The vodka I drank hasn't done much more than create a warmth in my belly. I'm tired but wide awake, if that makes any fucking sense at all.

A heartrending cry makes my decision for me. My brain does a little flip, though, realizing that it hadn't come from Lennon's room. She's in the attic. *My* fucking attic.

I throw open the door and race up the stairs with

what feels like claws tearing at my chest. As I burst from the stairwell, my eyes scan the space, my blood pressure already rising. I expect to see her standing, a look of horror on her face, before one of my sketches, but that's not what I find at all.

Lennon must have come up here to sleep. Right now, I don't have time to ask myself why, but I sure as hell will later. I'm across the space in three strides, diving to my knees. She's on her back, arms extended out from her sides, and she's kicking, thrashing, really, as if she's trying to get free of something.

Her breath heaves from her, one after another, her face contorting in agony and fear. She mumbles for a moment then vocalizes several things in a rush of confusion. "Why are you so scared? Who is he? Wait. Who is he, Juliette? Wait!"

She's very clearly asleep, but … Juliette? What? *Jesus.* I don't know what the fuck to do. Wake her? Hold her? My mind scrambles. I've never had anyone wake me from my nightmares. Not once. But maybe that's because I never had anyone care enough about me to try to help. Instead, I live in misery, never knowing when the next one will strike and turn me upside down. My heart clenches as her chest fills with air right before she expels a primal, raw scream.

Oh, fuck. I have to do something. I kneel at her side,

bending so I can place a hand on her cheek. "Kintsukuroi, wake up, baby. Please wake up."

She moans, then abruptly swings her head back and forth. Tears stream from the corners of her eyes.

No care for my own well-being at all, I brace myself over her. If she lashes out, so be it. "It's me. It's me, Lennon," I whisper with my lips grazing the skin near her ear. "You're having a nightmare."

"Mm," she mumbles.

I pull back, assessing whether she's coming out of it or not. Her lashes flutter a few times. "Kintsukuroi." I suck in a breath. "Come on, baby." *I know this shit is awful. You don't want to be trapped in this. It's no better than being physically stuck in a locker. Worse, maybe, because sometimes with the way our minds work it can feel like it goes on forever.*

"Mason?" She blinks in the dark. Her soft voice sounding in this space that is mine throws my world into chaos. She shouldn't be here. It messes with my head so fucking bad to see her here.

I stare into alarmed blue eyes. I nod, brushing the backs of my knuckles over her cheeks. "Yeah, it's me. You're okay." My breath hitches, my hands fisting at my sides. "But what the fuck are you doing up here?" The muscle at the back of my jaw twitches as I struggle to hold myself together.

She wets her lips, looking around, surprise etching her features, but I see it the second she realizes where she is. "S-sorry. I—" She presses her lips together and stares into my eyes, as if she's willing me to understand without having to say it.

My eyes crash shut for a moment, trying to calm the torment creeping in. "You know how I feel about it. You know. I thought you understood." When I open my eyes, my gaze pierces hers, and I struggle to get ahold of the frustration that whips through me so I can accept the apology in hers.

"I'm sorry. I don't know what else to say except I like it up here. It calms me down. To be close to you." Her brows knit together, and she swipes her fingers under her eyes, cringing when she finds liquid emotion there. "But ... I guess my nightmares follow me everywhere. I wasn't even safe here, where I thought I might be." She bites down hard on her full lip, so hard I imagine the skin around her teeth would be white from the pressure if I could see the color in the dark.

I stare stonily at her for several seconds before scrubbing my hands over my face. My damaged heart skips over beats. I'm unsure if I want to share this with her, or if I even should, but I rasp, "Lennon, I have nightmares, too, and sometimes they're so fucking real, I feel as though they'll drag me away into the darkest shadows. I can't conceptualize the difference between reality and dreams. Kinda like that night with you on the balcony."

"Mason." My name on her lips guts me. *I can't.* But she reaches for me anyway.

Why does she fucking want my scarred heart? I'm no good for her, but I can't help myself. Her pull is too great, the desire in her eyes too much for me to ignore. I yank my shirt over my head, then lock my gaze on her glittering blues. I go for the fly of my jeans, unfastening them and pushing them down over my hips, leaving me bare, my cock thickening with every passing moment. "Kintsukuroi." My breath is shallow and fast. "You don't know what you're asking for when you reach for me."

"I do, Mason." She grabs the hem of her T-shirt and tugs it over her head, exposing the smooth skin of her abdomen and her full breasts before she tosses it aside. "I want everything that is *you*. All your rage and confusion. All this talent. All the damaged parts of you. You aren't *you* without them." She hesitates, her eyes a little glossy. "And especially right now ... I need you."

As I stare down at her, my jaw working to the side, she hooks her thumbs into the waistband of her panties, lifts her hips, and pushes them down, kicking them free.

She lies there, watching me, skin glowing in the moonlight and a sad smile on her lips. "Please, Mason. Let me lose myself in *you*. I need our connection, need you to make it all go away. I know you understand me in a way no one else possibly can. We're alike, you and I. That's why you haven't kicked me out of here, even though it makes you uncomfortable as hell. So, go ahead. Punish me for being here again." The challenge in her eyes is bold and sure. But does she really understand?

My jaw tight, I nudge my way between her legs, spreading them wide. I skim a palm over the top of her smooth thigh. "If we take this further, I will wreck you." My head dips, lips gliding over her lower abdomen. "If I let you in, let you see me fully, I will ruin you."

Her pussy is wet, and I don't know how she's gotten into that state so damn quickly, but even in the dark, I can see her arousal. I dip down, a hand on either side at the juncture of her hips. Her scent is intoxicating. I nudge her opening with my nose and nip at her with my lips before I give in, needing the taste of her, too. I spear my tongue inside her cunt as deep as I can get it. The gasped moan that escapes her makes me do it again and again. Her hips buck toward my mouth as her pussy clenches around my tongue, and I can hardly wait to fill her up and feel those muscles spasm around my cock.

I give her a devilish lick all the way to her clit, where I circle and tease before sucking hard. "Y-yes!" She'd been watching me, but now her head falls back to the mattress. Her hips rock, and from the sound of the whimpers escaping her mouth, she's close already.

Without warning her, I plunge two fingers inside her heat. The air whooshes from her lungs, and she brings her gaze back to me, her mouth dropping open with the surprise of it. She heaves out a breath, coming up on her elbows, and I drag my fingers slowly in and out, curling them just so. "That's it. Watch the way I'm going to dismantle you, piece by broken piece."

Her breath catches, and I don't know if she objected to the words or not, but her body agrees with me, the orgasm hitting her out of nowhere. The look on her face is priceless. A thing of beauty.

She rides my fingers and my mouth, not shy at all about the moaning she's doing. When it's over, she drops to her back, breathing hard, but then she eyes me from where she's lying. "I don't care if you take me apart, because you'll put me back together again like the pottery you nicknamed me after." At my arched brow, she nods. "I know what it means, Mason. But I don't care what you put me back together with—it doesn't have to be gold or beautiful—so long as it's you who's doing it."

"You finally looked it up," I grit out. It's not a question, and she doesn't bother responding. She shudders as I run my fingers through her wet folds and collect the moisture there before bringing it to my cock. I stroke my hard-on with her eyes on me, glued to every smooth glide of my fist, every slight twist of my wrist when I get to the head. I crawl over her, clasping her hands in mine over her head. I dip my head, taking one of her nipples into my mouth, slowly circling the pebbled skin before I take it between my teeth, biting hard enough that she gasps before sucking in air.

"Oh god."

I nod, shifting to the other breast, only this time, I suck hard on her nipple until her pelvis bucks beneath me. She throws her slim leg around my back in an attempt to bring me closer, so I give her what she wants, still tormenting her nipple, but now letting her feel the underside of my cock. She tips her pelvis, getting just the right friction, and before long, her body is twisting, and she's crying out beneath me.

I release her breast with a wet pop. My gaze roams over her, then I ease back, releasing her hands for a better look. One nipple has a bite mark around it that I think might be visible in the morning. The other I've sucked so hard it's red and wet from my mouth. It makes my balls ache, looking at her laid out like this.

"Do it. You know you want to." She slides a hand down her stomach, fingers briefly brushing over her clit before they scissor and stroke the sensitive skin on either side of her slit. Her back arches, and her breath stutters. Eyes locked on me, I can't stop myself from watching her fingers move, how she touches herself, so bold and sassy, just like she is outside of the bedroom. This is the real her. There are no lies here. Slowly, she dips those same fingers inside herself, pumping them in and out. "Mase," she gasps out.

I groan, taking my cock in hand and stroking it firmly. She removes her fingers, and I line the head up with her opening, grasping the backs of her legs, then slide into her. My head riots, my vision going dark around the edges. Her pussy. It's so fucking tight, squeezing every last bit of my dick until I'm fully seated inside her. It's exactly like I remembered from the five seconds I was inside her before. Only this time, I'm fucking finishing.

Her mouth has dropped open, passion etching every feature.

I ease back, watching how her eyes practically roll back in her head, then push into her again. I grunt with the pleasure of it. It's too good. Too right. *Fuck.*

Touching my thumb to her clit, I rub in feverish strokes and circles, not willing to stop until she comes undone again. She watches me as I slide smoothly in and out of her. My head goes hazy as she widens her legs, and before I know what she's doing, she's slipped her hand between them, fingers brushing the underside of my dick where I'm entering her.

Her breath goes ragged, and I don't have a fucking clue what she's enjoying most—my thumb on her clit, my cock in her pussy, or her fingers down there, feeling me fuck her. Maybe it's the entire damn thing combined. A moment later, she grabs at her breast, pulling at the nipple. She bites down on her lip before she cries out, her hips undulating, and fucked if my balls don't draw up, completely ready to come.

No. *Not yet.*

I stretch out over her, thinking a change in angle is what I need, but instead, I groan, the contact of skin on skin almost too much for me to take. I pause for a moment, looking into her dazed eyes. I could fucking drown in the blue depths of them. My heart pounds and pounds, wondering how I thought this would end well. She's doing something to me. My chest clenches hard, and I try to breathe through it, but I don't know how to stop the feeling creeping inside me.

Lennon catches the corner of her lip with her teeth, sliding her arms around my neck at the same time her legs lock me in at the waist. "You feel so good inside me, Mase."

I wet my lips and begin driving into her in a steady,

drugging rhythm that has both of us under some sort of fucking spell in no time.

Her fingers thread into my hair, tugging a bit. "Kiss me. Why won't you kiss me?"

I stare down into her eyes. Because I fucking know what will happen.

But I do it anyway. I crush my lips to hers, a great sigh releasing from me as I stroke into her mouth. With every twist and curl of her tongue, she pulls me deeper and deeper, coaxing me into a playful duel that turns hot and sexy in no time flat.

I'm on fire, explosions going off at every nerve ending of my body. I'm burning up from the inside out for this girl. Her wicked, devilish kisses have pushed me straight over the edge.

I gather her closer, licking into her mouth with wild abandon, as I thrust my cock into her body. With both of us gasping for air, I stop to nip at her lips, and stare directly into her eyes. I feel more connected to her than I have to anyone in my life. When I'm with her, all the things that hurt me, they fade to the background. I don't feel them—the sorrow, the pain, the loneliness. All I know is her, and how she makes me feel alive again.

I'm weak for her.

It's a problem.

THIRTY-EIGHT

LENNON

Mason pulls out of me without a word, but before I have a chance to even process the loss of fullness, he has me flipped over and on all fours. I feel the nudge of his cock between the lips of my pussy as he pushes his long, hard length back into my slick heat. I don't understand the abrupt change in position, but I tilt my hips, bowing my back to give him a better angle of entry. His dick hits me just right, and I moan long and low. The way he's leisurely thrusting into me is good—but he needs more. And so do I.

"Go ahead. Fuck me." I toss my hair over my shoulder as I angle my head back. Those dark sinful eyes of his spark with untold lust, his fingers automatically digging into my hips where he's holding me.

He doesn't hesitate, he rears back and slams

himself into me. I let out a throaty yelp. "Keep going." And after I give him that permission, he goes to town, snapping his hips against my ass with every pistoned thrust. It feels so good. It reminds me that I survived today. I'm alive. There's something different inside him that has reached out and tethered me to his damaged heart and his cracked soul. His crazy calms me because it shows me that for everything I've been through, there's someone else out there who might have a fucking clue.

Mason draws me up against his body, my back pressed tightly to his front. His dick is now at the perfect angle, dragging over my G-spot with every movement. He strokes his fingers over my clit, sending me half out of my mind with desire. He sucks on the side of my neck, his tongue flicking over the delicate skin. "Yessss," I moan. "Yes, Mase."

He must take that as a plea for more because he doesn't hold back, he thrusts over and over inside me while molding my body to his, one rough hand roaming over every inch of my torso as the other continues to work my clit with a vengeance. Tension coils in my belly, making it apparent that the orgasm building is going to be the likes of which I've never felt before.

A few moments later, both of us sneak right up to the edge of the chasm and begin the free-falling descent over the edge. "Fuck, Kin, *fuuuck,*" Mason rasps in my ear.

I feel him jerk to a stop, but then on an agonized moan, he nudges deeper and deeper inside of me. I can imagine his cum shooting out of him, decorating my insides. Unable to control the words that tumble from my lips, I moan out, "Don't stop, don't stop."

He continues to stroke his thick cock inside me, and he rubs my clit with renewed vigor. It's not a minute later that the orgasm crashes through my system. "Mase!" My first shout echoes through the rafters, then I can't seem to stop the tirade of curses that spill from me. "Oh, fuck. Oh, hell. Oh fuck, *yes.*" My pussy clenches down hard on his cock as it pulses with my release.

I'm on some sort of post-orgasmic cloud, dull throbs intermittently reminding me of what Mason and I just did. We breathe together for several seconds until he slowly pulls out, and we drop to the mattress. I can't resist curling up beside him and resting my head on his bicep. We're quiet. Too quiet. I can tell he's not sleeping. Does he know I'm still awake? From here, I have the perfect view of so many sketches of his mother, and my mind is going a mile a minute. Finally, I gather all my courage and ask, "Mase, will you tell me about her?"

His eyes follow the direction mine have taken to the portrait sketches hanging on the wall. I don't dare look at him. I'm nervous to rock the boat when I feel so damn good I could cry. Slowly, he shakes his head. "No. That's all you get of me, Lennon. I don't own enough of myself to share it with anyone else." At this angle, the twitching of his jaw is very apparent. I think he's done, but then he continues. "I don't want to infect you with the darkness that lives inside me."

Disappointment and devastation are twin emotions riding on my shoulders. I hear him. I understand to a certain degree how he might think the way he does, but I don't have to like it. I murmur, "You don't know what I can handle, Mason. But I do." I untangle myself from him, pushing to a seated position so I can look into his eyes.

He reaches for me, but I pull away, scrambling from the mattress and stopping only to pick up my shirt and underwear. I clutch them to me and begin to back away, very aware that his dark eyes are on me while his cum is sliding down my inner thighs. "I thought we really had something."

"Lennon, it's not that I don't like you ... I just can't. Not with you."

My face feels hot, but the rest of me is cold all over. I'm more frustrated than I've ever been. "I'm trying to tell you I can handle every twisted up, shattered fragment of you. What do I have to do to make you understand?"

He leaps from the mattress, stalking toward me. My eyes widen at the sudden fury on his handsome face.

Switch. Fucking. Flipped.

He stands before me, his face mere inches from mine, as his chest rises and falls with rapid breaths. Suddenly, his hand is around my neck, and he tugs me forward, bringing his forehead to mine. His fingers dig into the delicate curve of my neck so hard they'll leave me with more bruises. A blend of lust and madness fills his wild eyes, a crazed desperation that warns me: *Run*. But I won't. I told him I wanted all his broken pieces, and now he's trying to scare me away.

"You don't get it," he growls. "Loving me is a curse, Kintsukuroi." His grip tightens, crushing my windpipe, but I do all I can to keep fighting the desperate battle that's waging in his head. He makes me retreat until my back hits the metal railing that runs the length of the staircase. My body curves into his chest. Fear spikes in the base of my throat, shallowing my breathing.

"Stop. Pushing. Me. Away," I choke out with a stuttered protest.

"I can't do that." His words pierce through me with sharp precision. "I fuckin' killed her." Rage courses through him, rattling the hand that's clutched around my neck. "Me, Lennon. I pushed my mother off a balcony."

My eyes widen as shock reverberates through my core, chilling every inch of my skin. I pull at his choke hold, but it does no good. He's out of his mind. "Mase. You're hurting me. Mase." There is no sign of the beautifully broken man I've come to understand, instead his demons have come out to play.

"You shouldn't have clawed your way into my heart, Kintsukuroi." His dark eyes bore into mine as he gasps out, "Now you'll be next."

TO BE CONTINUED ...

ALSO BY LEILA JAMES

ROSEHAVEN ACADEMY

SHADOW RIVER ELITE

KINGSTON UNIVERSITY

ACKNOWLEDGMENTS

Krista Dapkey, leave it to your favorite PITA to finally start writing you some bad boys, only to churn them out real slow and turtle-like.

Michelle Lancaster, this image. I knew I wanted it the moment I saw it. And the funny part is that I honestly could have chosen any of his and they'd have been just as good. What an amazing shoot!

Lori Jackson, love, love, love the new backgrounds and the color changes for this trilogy. It still looks like Kingston University, just with a twist.

Shauna Mairéad, I'm glad you love Mason despite his crazy-ass antics. He's your spirit animal, for sure. Thank you for the all day long back and forth agonizing over our books. And talking about kids. And the weird shit Mr. Shauna and Mr. Leila do. But for real, people are going to LOVE *Destructive Truths.* You're freaking amazing, woman.

Savannah Medina, thank you for being my rock, my support system, and my cheerleader. Also, thank you for adding weird emoji bursts in messenger every time we type a character name. Thank you for being the go-with-the-flow to my Type A. You keep me sane.

Alpha Readers, we made it, ya big PITAs. Thank you for taking time to read and for all of your thoughts and suggestions. They are valued and appreciated.

To my ARC and Street Teams, YES! Thank you, as always, for your excitement and willingness to help me promote my book babies. I have the best team around, hands down.

To my family, I keep warning you, but you don't stay away. I hope you aren't ready to keel over after this one. Love you!

ABOUT THE AUTHOR

Leila James has one goal: keeping you up past your bedtime turning the pages of her books. She writes emotional, angsty, and dark new adult romances with lots of unique characters and plot twists.

Leila's family will tell you she's as big a reader as she is a writer. And ... she's completely obsessed with both. She resides in Virginia with her husband and two children.

KINGSTON
UNIVERSITY

Printed in Great Britain
by Amazon